SIDROC
THE DANE

Also by Octavia Randolph

The Circle of Ceridwen

Ceridwen of Kilton

The Claiming

The Hall of Tyr

Tindr

Silver Hammer, Golden Cross

Wildswept

For Me Fate Wove This

Light, Descending

The Tale of Melkorka: A Novella

Ride: A Novella

The Circle of Ceridwen Saga Story

Sidroc the Dane

Octavia Randolph

Pyewacket Press

Sidroc the Dane: A Circle of Ceridwen Saga Story
by Octavia Randolph

Pyewacket Press

ISBN 978-1-942044-23-9 (Hardback)
ISBN 978-1-942044-09-3 (Paperback)

Book design by DesignForBooks.com

Cover photo: Shutterstock © luxorphoto, background photo and photo rendering by Michael Rohani. Maps by Michael Rohani.

The Circle of Ceridwen Saga employs British spellings, alternate spellings, archaic words, and oftentimes unusual verb to subject placement. This is intentional. A Glossary of Terms will be found at the end of the novel.

LIST OF CHARACTERS

Hrald, a farmer on the West Coast of Dane-mark, father to Sidroc

Gillaug, a freedwoman; serving-woman to Hrald

Jorild, a freedwoman; serving-woman to Hrald

Stenhild, a woman of Gotland

Oddi, a former thrall, now a freedman

Yrling, younger brother to Hrald, uncle to Sidroc

Ingirith, wife to Hrald

Sidroc, son of Hrald

Toki, cousin to Sidroc, nephew to Yrling

Signe, sister to Hrald, mother to Toki

Ful, husband to Signe, father to Toki

Jari, a young adventurer

Asberg, a young adventurer

Merewala, Lord of Four Stones in Lindisse

Ælfwyn of Cirenceaster, a young woman of Wessex

Ceridwen, a young woman of Mercia

SIDROC
THE DANE
THE YEAR 847
Norse
Svear
Gotland
Paviken
Danes
Jutland
Ribe
Ful's farm
Laaland
Danevirke
Haithabu
Four Stones
Wessex
Prus
R. Vistula
Pomerani
Polanie
Frankland

SIDROC THE DANE

NORTHUMBRIA
Jorvic
Four Stones
Abbey of Beardan
R. Trent
LINDISSE
R. Dee
Ceridwen's Village
EAST ANGLICA
WELSH KINGDOMS
MERCIA
Cirenceaster
WESSEX
Kilton
Witanceaster
Frankland

CONTENTS

SIDROC THE DANE

To know the man, look to the boy.
To know the boy, look to the father.

PREFACE

Sidroc the Dane was Fated to become one of the greatest Jarls in Angle-land. This is his story.

He was a son of Dane-mark, in the 9th century the most powerful of the Nordic lands. Its Kings were the mightiest, and its young men thirstiest for adventure. All the Norse were an active folk. The Svear to the East wandered deep into the heartlands of the Slavs. The men of Norway struck West to Eire and beyond.

Yet the men of Dane-mark had the boldest plans. The great island of Angle-land lay across the North Sea to the West, with rich yet disordered kingdoms ready to plunder. From the middle of the 9th century it was the favoured target of the Danes. Sidroc was one such adventurer.

Not all struck out for riches with spear and sword. Twenty years earlier, on a farm on the large Danish peninsula of Jutland, lived a young man named Hrald . . .

Chapter the First

JORILD

Dane-Mark

The Year 847

HRALD had been gone nearly a year when he returned to the farm he owned with his mother.

He walked a day overland, from the great trading post of Haithabu where the merchant knorr dropped him, and its cargo. His clothes were those he had left in, a brown-dyed tunic of mixed linen and wool which reached his hips, over dark woollen leggings loose enough for working ease. Thin straps of leather lent protection while hiking, wrapping his lower legs to the knees. His brown boots were low and of cow-hide, almost entirely worn. The mantle on his back was a length of hemmed and heavy blue wool, held by a bronze pin. He had no cap.

His route on foot took him across the narrowest part of the vast Jutland peninsula. At first he walked directly along the Danevirke, the earthen and timber wall that shut out the Frankish Saxons on the other side. From there he headed North, up the coast.

After another two-day walk he turned his back on the sea, and the barrier islands blocking the way to open water. The fishing was ever good in their shoals; before his father's death the old man had taken their small boat once a week up the narrow river on which the farm lay, returning at dusk with a wet basketful of shimmering haddock or herring. Now Hrald traced that path, walking on the grassy bank, his leathern pack pulling at his shoulders, until he came in sight first of the boat hove-to on the sandy bank, and then the farm. It was a small holding, just inland enough to be out of sight and smell of the North Sea brine.

The first thing he noticed was the rye field. It had not been planted. Spring had been fully come for more than a month; the rye should be high and green, reaching toward the bright Sun which struck his already sun-browned face. Likewise the barley; the furrows showed only Winter-shrivelled stalks left behind from an imperfect harvesting. Beyond the barley, fenced behind their low wooden palings, thirty black and cream-coloured sheep should be grazing; even more, for lambing time was well over. It was empty.

He gained the pounded earthen track, leading to a woven withy fence enclosing house and out buildings. The farm housed his mother, Ashild, and his little brother, Yrling. Five others lived there as well, both free and thralls. No one moved between house and barn, stood at dye-pot or cooking cauldron in the kitchen yard, or called out in greeting. Yrling's darting form and ringing laughter was not seen, nor heard.

He was running now, forgetting his tiredness, his thirst, his eagerness to show his mother he still lived.

"Oddi," he called, as he neared the closed gate. Oddi was chief hand about the farm, a thrall freed at the death of Hrald's father three years ago, by the dead man's will.

He had reached the gate, plucked at the hoop fastening it closed. The lifeless work yard struck him with a dull and unreasoning fear. The geese, always so noisy, should be honking in alarm at any who entered; there were none. When a lone brown hen strutted into view he almost jerked to attention.

He left the gate open behind him, standing just inside its confines. Two women came around from behind the timber-framed house, passing so close to its corner that the shoulder of one brushed the low thatching of the roof.

He had never before seen them. They stopped and regarded him, one young, one older.

"Where is my mother?" were the first words that dropped from his lips.

The elder of the two answered with a question of her own. "Are you then Hrald?" Her hands had risen towards him, almost in entreaty.

"She is buried in the field," she went on, without waiting for his answer. "She caught cold at Jul, and was so sore-pressed to breathe it was a mercy when she died."

He blinked at her, but could find nothing to say.

He turned his head to the family burying ground, on the other side of the rye field. Hrald had stood by his father's grave the morning he left, and spoken a few words over the low mound which marked where his body rested. Now his mother must be lying next him. Indeed, he could make out the contour of a second mound, upon which new grass sprung.

He forced his eyes away. The woman came closer, the younger one at her side. They were both thin and worn, and he saw tears welling in the eyes of the elder. "I am Oddi's sister," she told him, "and am sorry to tell you this."

The hands she had lifted to him were gaunt and thin-skinned, the veins standing out upon the backs of them. "My name is Gillaug. I am from above Ribe; when your mother took ill he asked me to come and care for her."

"Where is Oddi," he managed. He did not quite recognise his own voice; he had spoken to no one for days.

"Oddi is now at Signe's house."

Signe was Hrald's older sister, wed and living up the coast, a day's walk away.

A new thought struck him.

"Where is my brother?" he asked, his voice rising as the hand of fear clutched at it.

"The boy is well, and living with Signe. It was deemed best he go live there, young as he is."

He found himself nodding, his chin just moving enough to show he heard, and understood. Signe and her husband Ful had two small daughters; Yrling would not be alone.

"Where . . . where are our serving women, our thralls?" he asked next. They had had two freewomen, and two male thralls, when he had left.

"The women, off to other households; one wed. The thralls were taken in taxes, with most of your beasts. The other animals we had to eat, to live."

Besides the two thralls, able-bodied both, when he had left they had the sheep, three milk cows, an ox, a pig who had just farrowed, and many geese and fowl.

"Taken in taxes," he echoed. His belt was filled with silver.

"Já," Gillaug said. "We could not find the silver to pay; Oddi dug everywhere, looking for where your mother had hidden it. The King's men came twice, and were rough with my brother the second time."

Hrald knew that King Horik still ruled; he had heard that when he landed at Haithabu. There was trouble in the King's own hall, and he had levied higher taxes; the trading folk were still grumbling about it.

He fought from turning his head to the grain-house. The woman said that Oddi had not found their silver; he must believe her. And they all had suffered real want from lack of finding it.

He took a long moment now, his eyes slowly moving from house to barn, from smoke-house to grain-house. They returned to her lined face.

"Are you freed, or thralls," he asked.

"We are both freed," she told him. "My niece from when she was a child."

He could not then understand what kept them here. "Why did you serve my mother," he asked.

"For the sake of Oddi, who honoured her name, and that of your dead father. After her death he asked us to stay on, against the day that you returned, that you might find the place in some order."

She began to weep now, tears rooted in hardship, and relief both, he thought. "My niece never left your mother's side, nursed her as a daughter would," she was saying. The young woman's eyes had also filled, but she swept the tears aside with her reddened knuckles. She had as yet said nothing.

"What is your name," he asked her.

"Jorild," she answered.

In the hours that followed Hrald had them kill two of the remaining fowl, that they might all eat; he had next to nothing in his food-bag. There was dried barley enough to boil, and the root cellar yielded a shrunken cabbage to his shovel. He had gone into the nearly empty grain-house, having to duck his head as he did, to see the floor boards undisturbed. He need not pry them up now; he would look at the pot buried underneath later. For today this was all he could do; this, and walk at dusk to the rye field to stand beside the mounded graves of his parents.

His mother Ashild was almost a score of years younger than his father; it made the loss the crueller.

"Do not tarry on Gotland," Ashild had told him, at their last parting, though her face was smiling. "No dice, and no wine; keep your wits about you." Hrald had heard these warnings in the days leading up to his departure, and had again nodded his head.

He had been to Haithabu the week prior, his first trip there since his father's death. The sheep they raised had done well, and he had twelve good fleeces to take for barter. There were nearer trading posts on their own coast, but he thought he could get a better price for them at a place as rich as Haithabu; the fleeces he chose were all white, the wool long, dense, and clean, the kind most desired for dying. He had taken the single ox, loaded the small cart, and hauled them overland to the long river where sat Haithabu.

It was the largest trading-town in all the lands where Norse was spoken, and a thousand people lived there in Summer's height. King Horik's men guarded its boundaries, kept order within, and collected fees from all who set up stalls to sell goods there. Traders came from the best merchant-towns of Frankland, carrying wares from even further West, and came too from the southern and eastern reaches of the Baltic, bringing goods from deep in the lands of the Rus up the river-routes. Hrald had been only twice before, with his father Hroft, and knew himself lucky to be able to carry his fleece to such a trading centre.

The roadways of Haithabu were paved with wooden planking, and all the larger walkways were also so laid. No mud mired the many wheels of the waggons and carts that rumbled along the rows of workshops and ware-houses; and up the side-roads, each plot where lived the artisans and merchants was edged with trenching to carry off rain and waste-water.

Hrald had his pick there of what to barter, though certain things would be beyond his ability to make pay; the tiny handful of black pepper-corns offered in exchange, for instance, that a merchant brought from Serkland could only be sold to a King's household. Sword blades from Frankland, huge bones of whales from Norway, wax tapers destined for the high tables of war-chiefs, wools and linens of fine weave and vivid hue, bronze and soapstone pots; all lay before him.

Walking along the river port where ships tied up, or up and down the planked roads, Hrald was at times jostled by the sheer mass of folk about him, bargaining for these and much else. Goods in chests, casks, baskets and huge jars were hauled down gang-planks from landed ships, and carried up those of ships departing. From their decks men called out orders to others, in Norse, and in many tongues Hrald could not understand. Men and women, singly and in clusters, went from stall to stall or workshop to workshop, buying with silver or bartering for goods they had brought. Comb-makers sat at work-benches, joining together with minute rivets of bronze the two slices of red deer antler that held a third piece into which they would saw finely-spaced teeth. Amber-workers stood at lathes turning golden chunks into finished gaming-pieces, or drilling holes into roughly shaped amber beads, ready for polishing. Workers in leather cut, pierced, and stamped fanciful designs into belts, packs, harnesses and small draw-string-mouthed purses; and shoe makers folded and sewed boots and shoes. Hrald lingered at a display of fine-grained whetstones, shaped from the hardest slate, before being distracted by a stall whose tables were laden with glass beakers. This was Rhenish glass from Frankland, and with their pointed ends, looked like cups of ox horn, but were clear enough to see through. Some had ripples of yellow-coloured glass seemingly interwoven into the pale green glass at their lip, or swirled around their narrow bases. Hrald had never held anything so delicate in his hand, and did not hazard picking one up now. As glad as he would have been to carry one back for his mother as a special gift, he knew only local chieftains would open their purses to such a luxurious item.

At the heart of the selling area he neared goods of greater and greater worth. Swarthy-skinned men in loose and flowing robes stood at tables upon which bolts of precious silk shimmered, or opened chests holding aromatic spices and resins. Others presented great handled jugs of

Frankish wine, tasting cups at the ready. Silver-smiths and gold-smiths smiled, waving their hands over necklaces, bracelets, brooches, and mantle pins; and merchants in gathered, baggy leggings opened tiny caskets holding red carnelians and garnets from the Black Sea.

Hrald moved back, to the fringes of this central area. He found himself stopping before the stall of a man who had poured a domed pile of glittering salt on a fabric square spread on the table before him. Next to it was a small cask of wood, no larger than that which holds whale or seal oil. The crimped dullness of its lead lining proclaimed it protected more salt. Behind the man stood a much larger cask, an upright barrel, sealed with a wooden lid, from which an edge of sheet lead lining extended; even more salt. A lad of perhaps fifteen years sat on a stool near the large cask, shaping with a knife wooden plugs for a series of tiny crockery jars. Over all of this was an oiled fabric awning stained deep red, warding off any errant damp.

The man grinned at Hrald, and beckoned him closer with the small horn spoon he held in his fist. He dipped the bowl of the spoon into the salt, let it sprinkle down, a cascade of pure white, with flakes as large as that of new snow on a Winter's day.

"From Anglia," he told Hrald.

Anglia, Hrald thought. That huge island due West across the North Sea, beyond which was nothing. Angles had named it; they and the Saxons had settled and possessed it. His father had told him many good things came from there. Their salt was certainly clean.

"No larger flakes to be found on Midgard," the salt-seller went on. He took a pinch from the pile, gesturing that Hrald should open his palm. "And look." Hrald brought the thing dropped there to his eye. It was a single crystal of salt, square at its bottom, rising to a sharp point. Hrald had never seen anything like it; it was broad enough at its base to span the nail of his little finger, he gauged.

"Taste," ordered the man.

Hrald flicked it onto his tongue. It had enough structure that the sharp edges did not soften at once, and he gave it a crunch with his teeth. The flavour was free of mineral sourness, intensely salty, and pure. He had never seen, nor tasted, any close to it. At the farm they traded for two grades of salt, one coarse and oftentimes ill-flavoured, for brining and pickling, and another smaller quantity of whiter, purer salt for use in baking, at table, and in finished cooking. This so far outstripped the best his father had ever been able to obtain that he knew at once he wanted it.

The salt-seller, a man of forty or more years, read the interest in the young man before him. The youth was tall and rangy, and perhaps younger than his height proclaimed. He was decently dressed, with a more than serviceable knife at his hip. His long and uncombed hair, brown in colour, suggested he had been on the road a day or two to reach the trading town. When he had called the youth over he had been walking with a rolled fleece on his shoulder, which he had set down at one end of the table, carefully, so as not to scatter any of the salt-seller's small and costly wares.

Hrald stood staring at the pile of salt, the pleasing sharpness of its tang still making his mouth water. He had never before bargained alone for anything of value, and wondered if he could procure the entire small cask sitting upon the table. He would take it from farm to farm, scooping out cups-full in return for fatted geese, smoked haunches of pig, and even silver-hack and coin. He had but one of his twelve fleeces with him; the others, ox, and cart were in the keeping of the watch-pen, where men armed with spears guarded the property given over to them. He unrolled the fleece now, showing it to the salt-seller.

It was indeed a good fleece. The salt-seller knew exactly where to take such fleece, his next stop of Aros. But wool was bulky.

"I deal only in silver," he told Hrald.

He watched the young man's face change, subtly, but noticeable to a trained eye.

"I have no silver," Hrald admitted. He had but a few bits of hack-silver – broken bits of jewellery – in the purse at his belt, no more.

The salt-seller shrugged his shoulders.

"My wool is the best in Jutland," Hrald now proclaimed, opening his hand to it. He had heard his own father say such things to traders.

The older man considered. One could not always trade for silver, and he wanted this young man's custom. He had a great deal of salt to sell.

"That is a fine fleece," he agreed. He would see if he could get its bearer to name a price. He did so through his silence.

"I can offer six of them, for your small cask of salt," Hrald finally said.

"Six only. That is a pity. The price to carry away this full cask would be six-and-ten."

"Six-and-ten? I have only twelve," Hrald found himself saying.

The salt-seller nodded readily enough. "Let us go look at them," he offered. He gestured to his son to come and take his place at the table's edge.

That is how Hrald came into possession of such good salt from Angle-land. He did not like trading every fleece for it, and the fact that he had made him determined to get the best possible price for every precious crystal. All the long walk home he considered its worth. By the time he arrived at the farm gate he knew what to do.

"I will take it to Gotland," he told his mother.

Ashild had just finished tasting a giant grain of the stuff, Hrald placing a single crystal in her palm as the salt-seller had done to him. That mouth now opened in surprise.

"Gotland!"

It was a whole sea away. One must either take ship here and round the long horn of Jutland, or walk overland to the deep inlet on which Haithabu sat, which her boy had just retraced. Then awaited the voyage South and for many days East, out into the Baltic and its dangers.

"There is no richer land," her son was saying, "and the further I carry it from Angle-land the more precious it becomes."

This was true of course; any coveted goods grew in value with distance from its source.

Ashild said little; they were sitting in the kitchen yard, Hrald's packs still resting on a work table. He had unhitched the ox and led it to pasture, but after this needful task had wasted no time in sharing his discovery with his mother. She disappeared into the spring-house, half-buried in the ground to keep its contents cool, and came back with a crock of butter. She brought a loaf, baked this morning, and tore it in two. Together mother and son dipped wooden spreaders into the golden butter and smeared the bread. Then they each took pinches of the huge flakes of salt and dropped them on the glistening butter. The yeasted, crusty loaf, the sweet and grassy butter, the sharp and clear bite of the pure salt over both; all blended in every bite. Hrald was hungry, and Ashild had had little herself for hours. The savour of what they took into their mouths was unequalled; the quality of the salt beyond dispute.

Hrald had been speaking about how he would go about this. He would return to Haithabu with its harbour filled with trading ships, find a captain to take him for a little silver. The wooden cask of salt had the advantage of being small; he and it would not take up much room on the broad deck of any knorr plying its trade along Baltic coasts. He was ever a steady lad, but now his voice rose in excitement as he detailed his plan to her. When they began to eat the salted bread and butter they both were quiet.

She finished her bit, pushed the rest to her son. He had twenty Summers and had known no adventures. If Hroft still lived he would tell the boy to go. Something bright within her breast opened, thinking of Hroft; their son Hrald was much like him. The same fylgja, their guardian spirit, spoke to them. Hroft would send the boy off, she knew. She and Oddi, and the thralls, along with her two serving women, could well keep the farm for the month or so such a trip would take. But one thing she must ask.

"And Ingirith?"

This was the maid Hrald was promised to; they were to wed after harvest. Her father Oke had been friend to Hrald's father, and the two had always planned to join their young this way. That Hroft had died before Hrald and Ingirith could join hands had not deranged the plan.

"I will be back well before harvest, if I leave soon," Hrald countered. Oke's farmstead was North, almost at the smaller trading post of Ribe, and he did not want to take the time to walk there to tell his intended of his plan; better to surprise her with unexpected silver. Ingirith was a maid who liked silver.

Gillaug and Jorild had boiled the hens up with a couple handfuls of barley, the shredded cabbage, and some spring onions. Hrald sat at the same scarred work table at which he and his mother had sampled the Anglian salt. It felt a lifetime ago, and in the most important way it was; his mother no longer lived. The Sun was lowering when Gillaug carried the pottery bowl to him. He was hungered, and felt almost ashamed of it. He recalled the times his mother had urged him to eat, laughing about his growing height, and lifted the horn spoon to his mouth.

Gillaug and Jorild sat together at the smaller work-table. Hrald could not help notice how they fell to, holding the bowls close to their mouths. They must have been living on eggs and the slightest amount of grain; that and whatever they had found in the root-cellar, and what they could gather of pot-herbs for greens.

When he was done Jorild came over to him. The dusk had deepened into a deep bluish haze. They had had only well water to drink, and she had a jug of it in her hands. She refilled his cup, and made a gesture to ask if he wished for more in his food bowl.

He shook his head. He thought then to tell her it had been good; he always told his mother and the serving women so; it was bad manners not to comment on any food others had prepared for you. She ducked her head, her knees bending slightly in a rapid curtsy.

She had said nothing to him save her name, upon his arrival. Her aunt was now moving about the wash-tub, busy. He felt the need to hear another's voice.

"I thank you for caring for my mother," he found himself saying. He recalled Gillaug's words, assuring him that Jorild had acted as a daughter would to the dying woman.

She bobbed her head again, biting her lower lip. Her eyes were downcast, looking into the emptied bowl he had eaten from, now held in her hands.

"She called for you," she finally said. "As she grew worse, she called on your name."

Jorild raised her eyes to Hrald, saw the pain on his brow.

"I am sorry she could not know you lived, and are well," she ended.

A lump had formed in Hrald's throat. He could do no more than nod.

He gave her no sign of dismissal, and in fact lifted his face to her as she stood before him.

She would perhaps ask him what they all had wondered over the long months of his absence. The worst he might do was scowl and drive her away; he did not seem a man who would use the back of his hand on her.

"Something . . . something delayed you," she offered.

"I was stranded, on the Pomeranie coast, over Winter," he answered.

Her face told that she had not heard of that place. She nodded, just the same. "Not Gotland," she said. "Oddi told us you went as far as Gotland."

"I did, but on the way back the knorr I was on began taking on water, and badly. We made for the Baltic coast, but ran aground on a sand bar when we were close to landing. The hull stove in." His voice sounded thin and tight as he told her this; he and the rest of the men aboard had in fact to swim for their lives to the deserted shore.

"We made our way to an inland village, had to spend the Winter there."

She was taking this in, nodding in understanding. Such things happened to many sea-faring men. She remembered Ashild's mourning for her son, her laboured rasping out of Hrald's name near the end. She would hazard saying something about the woman, for his sake.

"Your mother . . . she would be happy now, knowing you return."

His eyes shifted, moving around the empty and unnaturally still work-yard.

"Já," he agreed, in quiet answer.

She seemed ready to move away, and lifted the bowl in her hands slightly.

"Gillaug said she caught cold," he said now, to keep her from leaving.

"Já," she returned. She paused a long moment before she went on. "It was hard for her to breathe; she feared she was drowning as she lay there."

His eyes closed in a grimace, hearing this.

"We propped her up with many cushions, to try and give her some ease."

"How was she buried?" he asked now.

Her eyes widened at this, and he thought she had taken fright at his question. She might fear he suspected the mistress of the house had been laid out with less than all that was hers, and that she, Jorild, or her aunt, might have held back something.

"With all of her brooches and beads, her weaving shuttles and sword, and her linen smoothing board of whalebone," she numbered. This last was her prized possession; any woman would covet it. "My Uncle Oddi was there; Oddi saw all, and will tell you."

Hrald lifted his hand in assurance that he believed her, waving away her fear.

"Then Oddi had to sell the beasts," he began, uncertain of events.

"Já, já," Jorild confirmed. "But first the King's men took many away, and the thralls. After the Winter's Nights festival, King Horik almost doubled the levy. Oddi worried; he wanted the taxes paid from the farm itself, fearful that if any of your kin stepped forward to pay, it might be lost to them; they might lay claim to the farm."

It was like Oddi to believe, and hope, that he still lived, and like him too to be a good steward in Hrald's absence.

"When there was not enough to feed the three of us, Oddi left for Signe's. He had already taken your brother there. He told us he would come for us by Mid-Summer, if you did not return."

Hrald did not need to be told that the two women could not last the Winter alone, not with unplanted fields and a dearth of animals.

He must get them all food, and now spoke aloud his thoughts.

"I will go tomorrow, take the handcart to the next farm, buy grain and fowl, smoked pig, whatever I can." He looked out above the shaggy roofs of the outbuildings surrounding them. "Then I must set out for my sister Signe's, see my little brother, let them know I am alive." He thought of both Signe and Yrling, and the doubled loss they thought they had sustained. "See Oddi," he went on. "I will need Oddi back, to build up the farm." His eyes lowered again to the empty work-yards, and the glowing coals of the cooking ring fire.

He was looking at Jorild now. She had been standing before him the whole time, but he finally took her in. Like her aunt she was tall and thin. He thought he recalled her eyes were a greenish blue; he had looked at her when he had asked her name earlier. The face was plain, but her features regular, her skin unblemished, and she had lost no tooth. He could not guess her age; she might be of twenty years, or five and twenty. The light was dimmer now, making her brown hair seem darker than it was; it was not overly long, held off her face by the short kerchief tied at the nape of her neck. The oval fasteners at the straps of her over-gown were merely of animal bone, but she or someone else had taken time to incise a flowing pattern in their ashy whiteness.

"Can you stay," he asked her. "I have need of you." He and Oddi would have their hands full, and he did not know how long it would take to find and buy a worthy thrall.

She thought of the woman Ashild, calling for her son, and of how she must have loved this man.

"Of my aunt I am not sure. But I can stay," she said.

Chapter the Second

GOTLAND

THAT night Hrald once again lay in his alcove in his parent's house. It is my house now, he reminded himself, feeling the bitter price of his gain. He thought of his eagerness to see his mother, knowing that once her tears of relief had dried he could tell her of his adventure. That story ran through his head now as he lay, exhausted yet unable to sleep. He would have told of the shipwreck, which had begun in mild alarm, grown to real fear, and ended in the cold swim, his silver twice-strapped about his body; the long months staying at the cattle farm of the Pomeranie family who took them in; the sail, in stages, and on three ships, back to Jutland, once trading season came round; but most of all, his time on Gotland.

It was Gotland that had gotten him into trouble. He had stayed far longer there than he had planned, unable to tear himself away. He thought of his first glimpse of it after the long voyage, a dark and low smudge against a sky of startling clarity. It was an island, and he wondered if all such were blessed with some special attraction, simply due to their difficulty of access. Dane-mark itself was nothing but scores of islands, great and small, most of them so close to one another to be only a few oar strokes away. Gotland was set apart, a green gem in the vastness of the blue Baltic.

The knorr he had taken passage on landed him at the largest trading post on Gotland, Paviken, on the western coast. It was well-sheltered, set in a lagoon of still water, but its size surprised him. It was so much smaller than Haithabu, and smaller even than the Summer trading-town of Ribe back home in Jutland. Yet its prosperity was everywhere evident. Coming in to land they passed a bustling boat-works, where ships were not only being repaired, but built from keel up. Hrald could see the stack of thick and seasoned oak which would be shaped to serve as keelsons, as well as the thin pine planking waiting to be riveted together as new hulls. There were three long and solid wooden landing piers awaiting them, and the timber buildings fronting the trading road were substantial, not the mere Summer-huts of most trading towns in Dane-mark. Plenty of folk crowded that road, clustered about the rolled-up awnings of stalls, for it was mid-day, and the weather fair. Two men unloading their own ship had paused to catch the thrown line from the knorr that carried Hrald, and as they hauled her in they called laughingly out to the ship captain at the steering oar. Their Norse was so distinct as to leave Hrald wondering what they really said.

He sold his salt that very day, cask and all, and for a sum that he wagered was worth the shorn and cleaned fleece of every ewe back at the farm, and a bushel of oats as well. The trader who bought it carried it directly aboard his stout ship, and left Hrald with a full ingot of silver, a handful of tiny coins stamped with the profiles of men's faces, and an assemblage of broken silver jewellery. Hrald had taken the precaution of bringing a second, larger, purse with him, one his father used to carry when he sold cattle or a quantity of sheep, and the worn pouch was now packed, as was that smaller he wore at his belt each day.

"That salt will go right round the island, across the Baltic, and to a trading post of the Prus," guessed the captain of the knorr which had brought him. Hrald was sitting with him on a bench at a brew-house, ale cups in their hands, watching the salt buyer's ship cast off.

Hrald had come so far it was hard to countenance sailing further, and he narrowed his eyes at the oars now dipping into the water.

"Did I do right to sell it so quickly," he asked the man, uncertain now of the sale.

The captain laughed, and tipped his head at Hrald's waist. "Your belt will tell you that," he answered, looking to the lumps of silver-filled purses resting there. "And the first offer is oftentimes the best. He was ready to buy, eager to set sail with one more prize on his deck. If you had turned him down, you could sit here for days, and end at last selling for less."

Hrald was glad to hear this, and showed it on his face. Over their time sailing here the older man had taken a liking to the youth, and wanted him to prosper.

"I will not leave for three days, if you mean to sail back with me. Mind the silver you have earned," the captain went on, standing and stretching. "Do not spend it all here on Gotland," he ended with a grin.

Other than buying needed food and drink Hrald intended to spend none of it. He finished his ale and looked about him. The Sun had passed its highest point and begun its westward journey towards the sea he had just crossed. Hrald thought he would walk about and see the place more fully. He had sold the Anglian salt from the deck of the knorr; had not even the effort of carrying it onto land, for the merchant who bought it had strode down the planking to meet the newly landed ship and inquire what it carried. Hrald knew Gotland had no King, nor even any great chieftains, but he was still surprised when no man of authority stepped forward to demand a tariff from his sale. Trade was free here; no wonder so many merchants favoured the place. He had already seen one with bushels of rare miniver skins, the furs snow-white and of a plushness to make a King open his purse. For its small size, Paviken attracted only the best of goods.

He could return to the knorr and sleep on the deck when it grew dark. For now he would fully stretch his long legs. And he could use a wash. He did not see a wash house, but had already seen a number of women kneeling by a stream that ran into the lagoon, swirling their laundry through the current, then folding and laying it on the flat rocks to beat the water out with wooden washing bats. The flowing stream water would be fresh; he could splash his face and wash his feet.

He went a little upstream from the women, took off his tunic and pulled handfuls of the cold water over face and chest. He had a single piece of linen towelling in his leathern pack, now as soiled as his clothing was, and dried himself with that.

He turned back to the stream, thinking to drink from it, when he heard a woman's voice.

"I have a wash-tub at my farm," she said.

He pivoted, still crouching, to see her. She was young, with light brown, almost reddish hair. She was well formed in her person, and with a measure of comeliness to her face. She had a child too young to speak with her, who held a tiny handful of her mother's green skirts bunched in one hand, and had her other thumb in her mouth. The woman had a pack, half-full of something, hanging from one shoulder. Her eyes were steadily trained on Hrald.

Hrald returned her look. The tone of her voice had been nearly flat, almost as if she were sharing a fact with him. She spoke in the same strangely inflected Norse that he had heard from the mouths of others here, but he could understand her. She was not smiling as she regarded him, but there was no hardness in her eyes. She was dressed as any country-woman of the Danes might be, a long-sleeved shift of undyed linen under a sleeveless over-gown of light wool, with broad straps of the same over her shoulders. The paired brooches pinning her gown in front were bronze, and not simple embossed ovals of the stuff as wore the women of Dane-mark. Hers were shaped like the heads of cats; he had seen similar brooches on other women in town. They brought to mind the Goddess Freya, who sometimes went about the heavens in a cart pulled by two tom-cats.

He did not know what to say. She spoke, for him.

"If you follow the main road, you will come to a grove of spruces. Turn left there, follow the cart track. The croft with the birches is mine."

Hrald found himself nodding. The woman picked up the child and set her on her hip and left, walking the way she had told him. He watched her go. He paused, trying to sense his hamingja, his luck-spirit, to see if this was a good move. After a moment he rose to his feet and put on his tunic.

His mind was turning on the way there, turning and coming to no conclusion. He was aware of the quickness of his breath, even though he had not hastened his steps. The thought that she was one of a family of brigands luring him to robbery and mayhap death rose in his tumbling thoughts, and was just as swiftly discarded. She lived on the outskirts of the trading town. Paviken might have no chieftain to exact taxes, but it had laws, and violence of any kind in a trading place was always harshly punished.

He saw the clump of birches and the low fence just beyond it, enclosing a small timber house, larger barn, and two or three outbuildings. As he lifted the wooden hoop that latched the gate he saw the woman. She was standing off to one side, in what must be her kitchen yard. He almost thought she was standing waiting for him. Her little girl was sitting on a low stool, pressing a purple plum to her mouth.

He neared. The woman had moved to the cooking ring fire, which she must have just poked into life, the fresh lengths of wood catching over the smouldering coals. The iron cauldron of water hanging above would not take long to warm, and with a poker she swung it over the growing fire.

Without a word she turned to a big tinned washing tub propped up against the wall of one of her outbuildings. Hrald made a move to help her with it, but she had righted it before he could reach her. She truly did mean what she had said on the stream bank.

She vanished into the house, came back with what looked like alcove curtains and a length of hempen rope. There was a wrought iron hook sunk in the wall of the outbuilding, and she tied the line from it to the cross piece of a tall post driven into the hard ground. She slung the curtains over the line, screening the tinned tub from the back of her house.

The water was simmering now, the air above the black cauldron moving in its heat. She dipped a handled pot into the cauldron and began moving the water, pot by pot into the tub. When it was at a hand span's depth she stopped, went to her well, and carried back a wooden pail of well water, which she set by the side the of the tub. The last thing she brought was a small round crock, one which might hold soft tallow-and-ash soap. Then she looked at Hrald.

"You can wash now," she said.

He almost might have laughed, if her face were not so grave. Her voice was strained as if she could scarcely speak. They had exchanged no word since his arrival, and he had yet to say anything at all to her. There was no reason for laughter, he knew, save to break the tension he felt, and which he thought she also must be feeling.

"Thank you," he said.

Her lips were tightly pressed, but began to bow in the smallest of smiles. Then she turned and left him, stopping to take her little daughter by the hand.

He dragged the bench by the fire-pit nearer to the tub, and stripped off his clothes and set them aside on it, with his leathern travel pack. His belt and knife and purses he carried with him, dropping them on the other side of the tub, where his right hand would be near.

The water was hot enough that he pulled back his foot when he touched it, and he splashed some of the well water in to temper it. Then he squatted down on his haunches in the water.

With him in it, it rose up another hand span's worth. His knees were tucked up almost under his chin, but the water was hot and it was the first real bath he had had in many a day. He dug his fingers into the soap and made use of it, scrubbing himself well, the ash both gritty and slippery in his hands, the tallow smoothing. There was an herbal scent to it, thyme, he thought, looking at the green flecks dotting it. His mother also pounded herbs into the soap she made, masking the tallow smell.

He had finished cleaning himself and just sat, enjoying the warmth a moment longer. Soon his folded legs would begin to complain.

Suddenly the woman came around the corner of the curtain, a linen towel in her hands. He was of course naked, sitting in her low wash tub, and at this point growing ready to stand.

Their eyes met; hers were brown, the shade of sandy soil. She lowered them, and kept them cast modestly down. She began to gather up his clothing from the bench.

"I will wash these," she offered.

He considered. The day was far gone; it was not likely they would dry in the remaining Sun. They would need to hang overnight by the fire. It was nothing short of an invitation to stay the night.

"I thank you," was how he met this offer.

He had a single change of clothes with him, meant for the return trip, and he put these on. She gestured him to sit at the table near the back door of her house, and he did, a jug of home brewed ale of surprising savour before him. She busied herself, first washing his clothes in the water he had bathed in, then coming and going from house and outbuildings, carrying out bread, and pots of cheese and butter from the spring house.

As he sat there her cow came round the edge of the barn from the field it had been grazing in, and he stood and followed it into the dimness of the barn. The basin was clean and waiting, and he sat on her milking stool and drew forth squirt after squirt of warm milk. When he came out with the basin in his hands and the woman saw him, her own hands rose, a small gesture at her breast of surprise. She smiled at him then. He had already seen her reach down into the half-buried spring house, and he went to it and poured the milk into the crock waiting there.

They ate in near silence, the woman feeding bits of bread and cheese to her daughter. The bread was two or three days old, and hard; but broken and toasted over the fire and spread with sweet butter or the tangy cheese it filled, and satisfied. The plums from her tree were sweet and bursting with juice. They finished with more of her ale. Night-birds were beginning to call, and insects chattered from the tall grasses where the cow had been feeding. A low sliver of Moon began its ascent, golden as it crested the tree-line, paling as it rose higher, and seemingly, much further away.

The girl had climbed into her mother's lap and was now sleeping against her breast, and the woman rose and carried her into the house.

When she came back she sat down, and Hrald spoke to her.

"Where is your husband," he asked.

"Away. And for a long while," was how she answered.

Hrald thought of this. It was not likely he had gone off fishing; they were too far from the coast, and there were no fish-drying racks.

"He went off trading?"

"Já," she answered.

"When?"

"More than a year ago." She held his eyes a moment, then looked over the dimming fields.

There was silence between them.

She tidied up, banked the fire, shooed a few lingering hens into the fowl house. She came back to the table, standing before him as she had at the stream. He rose and followed her inside, and to her sleeping alcove.

Hrald had once before known the touch of a woman's skin, but it had been even longer ago than this one had waited for her husband. Two years past at a Mid-Summer's fire he had found himself in a field at his sister Signe's farm. He was almost a stranger there, and the woman who had taken his hand and led him to the ploughed furrow someone he would never see again. She was, like this woman, older than he. She had also been drunk; he was as well, having spent much of the day downing ale and then by the heat of the fire, mead.

It was the first Mid-Summer after his father's death, and in his young grief he had felt reckless and driven to extremes. His father's old friend Oke had travelled down to Hroft's funeral feast a few months earlier, and had reminded Hrald's mother that Ingirith and Hrald would be man and wife. Hrald felt all was happening too fast; his father's sudden death, his being thrust into being the man of the house at seventeen, the marriage to a maid he did not know. The fire, and the drinking, and what came after was a way to forget all this.

He was not drunk this time, and neither was she he lay beside. If anything he felt a kind of heightened awareness, made more acute by her silence, and her choosing of him in the bright light of day.

He awoke first in the morning. Dawn was just lightening the sky when he swung his legs out of her bed; he could see the crack of light framing her closed window shutter. He dressed and went outside. He stood looking around at the small work yard. The tub in which he had bathed and his clothes had been washed still held water; she had forgotten to tip and drain it, and he did so now, sloshing the water out upon the hard ground and slanting the tub up against the wall. The cow would be happy to be milked again, and was there inside the barn waiting for him. When he finished with her he freed the fowl from their little house, and they came clucking and strutting out into the early light. Firewood was stacked under the deep eave of the house, with kindling sticks next it. There were few of these latter, an armful at most. He went back to the barn, found the axe, and began splitting wood on the oak stump at the edge of the work yard.

The woman came out at this, wearing her shift and clutching a shawl about her arms. When she saw what he was doing for her, she began to cry.

Her name was Stenhild, she told Hrald, as they ate together, her girl on her lap. At one point the child reached the bread she was holding out to Hrald, as if to share it with him, and he laughed; his brother Yrling had done the same as a babe. Stenhild stopped in her own eating and looked at him, and he feared she might begin to weep again. She did not, just smiled herself, and guided the girl's hand back to the pink little mouth.

The morning was again dry, and they ate outside. Hrald looked about the place. Small as it was, he could not imagine how she kept the farm alone. He noticed for the first time the diminished rows of vegetables; less than half of the fenced plot showed leafy growth. But then, he thought, she was feeding only herself and her child; she would not need much. The barley would grow, undemanding after the first few weedings, and harvest was hot and hard work, but for a field as small as hers would not last more than a few days. She had a hand quern for grinding, as would all women, and the bread she baked from its flour was good. He saw no pig; there was not perhaps enough waste food and cabbage scraps to fatten one, and slaughtering a full grown beast was man's work. The cow and hens would keep her in milk and eggs, with boiled and roasted fowl from unwanted cocks, and hens who no longer laid. Fish could be had at Paviken, fresh from the fishing boats that landed each day, and she must trade something for them when she could. But he saw no sheep; how she kept herself in wool he could not guess.

Hrald meant to leave then, after their meal, make his way back to Paviken, wander the stalls, which would be opening now, as he had meant to do yesterday. But he did not. He watched Stenhild lift his clean and dried clothes from the line which had screened his bath, smooth and fold them and lay them next his pack on the bench he had dragged there. She was biting her lip as she did so.

He stood and walked into her barn. At the worktable by the door he scanned the tools, arrayed in order on the dusty table. He chose a few.

He went to the fowl house, took the door from its hinges, planed it down on one side so it would close again; it had bound badly when he opened it that morning. He re-hung it, tightening the iron handle, which had grown loose and rattled in the hand. He shovelled out the leavings in the cow stall, carried them to the manure heap out back, and spent an hour turning it so that the strawy mixture could decay the faster. Then he went back to the oak stump and chopped a vast pile of kindling, stacking it neatly against the side of the house, and carrying armfuls of it into the house to the fire-pit there, ready for cold-weather fires.

That night had a sweetness to it the first had lacked. They had spent only a full day in the other's company, but they had spoken together, and worked alongside each other. They knew the other's name, and some of their story. After she led him to her alcove she kissed him, held him, and welcomed him the more, and when he pulled away from her did not turn her face from him in seeming shame as she had the first night.

He felt his own awkwardness still, wondering what more he might do; his hands on her naked breasts and running over the gentle roundness of her hips excited him so he feared he might not control his own body. When she quickly shifted to place herself beneath him, he was relieved. He fell into sleep with her hand on his chest, something he had never known before.

The next morning he took his leave, shouldering his pack and leaving her at her croft gate. He turned back to smile, and to wave. She had lifted her child in her arms, and the girl was waving after him, cooing as she did so. Stenhild's eyes were wide, as if she forced them from tears.

At Paviken he neared the brew-house he had sat in with the knorr captain. No fewer than eight ships were tied at the three wooden piers, several in the act of lading or unlading over their narrow gangplanks, and the brew-house was already busy. Hrald saw his captain, lifting a cup as he talked with another man. He saw the man's knorr too, quiet and waiting until they left tomorrow; new cargo was already on board.

He lifted his eyes to the expanse of the Baltic. Nothing could be seen on the horizon; he might be at the furthest reaches of Midgard. The sky was deepening to its richest blue, the few clouds swimming in it small, dense, and white as washed wool from his best ewes. The air was dry and crisp, and he had still the taste of the sweet plums he had broken his fast with in his mouth.

He looked again at the number of ships, number of captains. He need not leave tomorrow. There were ships and captains in plenty to take him back to Dane-mark, and would be for another month or so.

He turned and walked back to Stenhild's farm.

The Moon went from crescent, to full, to crescent. Then to dark. It was too late in the season to plant other than just more pot-herbs, but they did so, knowing she could dry what she could not eat before frost. He tied up her grape vines, and pruned the three plums, now that they were done fruiting. He walked to Paviken and took in all the merchant's goods, and carried back a doubled handful of choice glass beads for Stenhild. She strung them on waxed linen thread with the nearest he had seen to delight on her face.

After a week, fearing he might be growing restless, she encouraged him to explore some of the island, to walk the coast North or South, visit the smaller trading posts he would come across. He would see something of the rauks, those limestone towers rising from the shingle beaches. Some he had glimpsed on the knorr's approach by sea, and she told him that at their bases lay stone flowers, and sea-shells of white stone. Just as night-wandering trolls had been caught by the rising Sun and frozen into the twisted forms of the mighty rauks, these small plants and animals had somehow also suffered the same Fate.

He did this, heading first North to stand beneath limestone cliffs looming above the rich blues and greens of the Baltic. These sharp cliffs looked mountains to his widened eyes, accustomed as they were to the flatness of sandy Jutland. He scaled one of them, to stand staring down and across the Baltic Sea from its vast height. They were different waters from that which he had ever looked upon at home, and the difference between his own North Sea surprised him; it was another hue, another and seemingly milder temperament. He went on, dropping down to water's edge again. The stark and narrow beaches were of bleached limestone pebble, blinding in the clarity of the light, and he found himself squinting as his eyes scanned from shimmering sea waters to the brilliant white sharp-edged stones he trod. He came upon group after group of rauks, thrusting up from the shingle or arrayed on slopes. If they were truly once trolls, these must have been returning to their forest caves after night-bathing when the rising Sun caught and froze them. He spent a night in the shadow of one, finding it useful as a break against the ever-blowing winds. As his fire flickered and died he half wondered if at night the rauks once again became living beings, freed by the darkness from their stony prison. Awakening in the dark, he put out his hand to reassure himself it was still cold stone he slept under. He managed a laugh at himself and wrapped himself back in his blanket.

Next day he turned South, then overland through dense pine and spruce forests dotted with lakes to the eastern coast. Oak, ash, and elm trees grew to mighty height in grassy glades, spreading leafy arms which had never known the trimming hook of any man. Wild horses, quick and hardy, moved through the trees; he spied them from the tracks he walked, nibbling at the edges of the glades, their furred ears moving as he neared. The red deer hinds he spotted were as large as the harts on Jutland; the hares too of unusual size. He saw more birds on land and water than he had ever before seen; it made sense, being an island landing place it would serve as refuge for many.

Along the coasts his footsteps slowed as he came upon the huge burial mounds of great chieftains, long dead, their burnt bones deeply covered by hills of carefully placed round stones. He gave these mounds a respectful nod, skirting them carefully. In other places he stood staring at towering standing stones, looming over even his height. These worked slabs of limestone were covered over with paintings of warring men and bucking ships, with runes inscribed around the edges, telling the tale of the men and women who remembered those now lost.

He dropped down further South, crossing over barren expanses of limestone alvar, with nothing taller growing from its sere whiteness than creeping lichens of gold, green, and grey. He made his way back to Paviken and Stenhild after six nights. She ran to him when he appeared at her gate, and he was happy to catch her up in his arms and laugh.

The days spent with her passed. Twice a week she gathered a basket of ripe plums and walked to the trading road with them. The air was dry enough, the Sun hot enough to dry many of the rest for her Winter's use. But that Sun was setting noticeably earlier, even in these northern climes. Every fair mid-day held true warmth, almost that of a Summer's day; but the nights were cooler as well as longer. And he had walked to Paviken often enough to see that fewer ships were docking; trading season was coming to a close.

He watched her as she moved around the small house one night. Her girl was already abed, and they themselves had finished their meal indoors; a light but chill rain had begun to fall. The dark, the rain, the coming cold – it all put him in mind of what he need tell her.

"Stenhild, I must leave. My mother will be worried."

His voice was quiet, but firm, one of sudden decision which even he heard in it. He had tarried for weeks, and felt like a man who awakens long after he had intended to arise. He feared too, of leaving her with a babe to come, and had been relieved a few days ago to find out he was not.

She stopped in her plate-clearing and came to him. She carried a kind of stillness with her.

"Já," she breathed, in quiet assent. "Your mother. And . . . your wife."

"I have no wife, not yet; I will wed after harvest. But I told my mother I would be no more than a month, if the Gods favoured me. And they have, in both my trading, and in you. Instead of heading back, I have spent that month here with you. The ship that takes me back could make many stops. It might be another two weeks or more before I reach Haithabu. Then I have a three-day walk to reach the farm. I must leave, and tomorrow."

He had been plotting this all out in his head in the moments before he opened his mouth, and was surprised at the flat reasonableness of it all.

She stood there, nodding her head, breathing out a low sound of assent. He was looking at her, but she would not lift her eyes to his.

"What will you do," he asked her. She could not go on like this, her stores dwindling, her buildings needing work, with no man to do it. "You must wed again."

"Já," she conceded. "I must wed. If he does not come back by next Summer, I will wed."

Hrald could say nothing to this faint hope. Her husband was dead; dead, or taken by slavers. There were plenty of his Danish brethren plying the waters, snatching what they could.

She looked at him now, a young man tall and lanky, a man who one might notice because of his height, and for nothing more. His dark brown hair fell about his face to near his shoulders, and his darker beard was growing in; it had been closely trimmed to his face when he first crossed her gate. His hands were large and strong but far from clumsy; they had chopped the kindling she laid this fire with, milked the cow, rested gently on her naked waist.

His eyes were that light brown shade that had flecks of blue in them, and they were fastened on her now.

I would wed you, Hrald of Dane-mark, her heart was saying. I would wed you.

Chapter the Third

INGIRITH

THE woman Gillaug had boiled eggs and filled a water skin for Hrald; there was little more he could carry away with him on his way to the neighbouring farm to buy more. Kol was an old farmer who lived there with a widowed daughter, and Hrald trusted that they would have something to spare. The trackways were dry; there had been no rain. Even pushing the hand-wain he should make good time. It was just after cock-crow, the Sun not yet showing its face above the dark edge of pines.

As he was readying himself Jorild came to him.

If she had been still a thrall she would not speak until spoken to, but her aunt had told him she had been a freedwoman since childhood. Even so she waited, watching him tighten the wooden wheel of the wain by pounding a splint into a crack near the hole of the axle.

"I will be back before dusk," he told her.

She bobbed her head at this, then spoke.

"I could carry something, in baskets, and on my back," she offered. "I am strong."

He looked at her. The walk would not take more than half the morning. If she wore a withy basket on her back, filled with a half-measure of grain, and could carry something too, that would be so much the better.

Jorild kept a good pace just behind him; he needed the width of the narrow track to guide the barrow so the single wheel missed the deeper ruts. It was all of wood, and heavy, and Hrald was glad when Kol's farm came into view. Dogs rushed out, barking, and Kol came out of his barn, blinking in astonishment at Hrald, alive and before him.

When they returned to his farm Hrald pushed sacks of barley, rye and oats, and smaller sacks of new carrots, greens, and fresh peas. He had a bag of dried beans, and a lidded basket into which three squawking hens had been deposited. They could spare as well a few loaves of bread, and as it was Spring, several small crocks of both butter and cheese. A crock of ale brewed by Kol's daughter was set over the wheel, to balance its weight. As Kol pushed it across the wooden bed of the barrow Hrald wondered if Gillaug or Jorild brewed; his father had been good at it, but then his mother took over after his death.

Jorild had indeed a half-measure of oats in the basket on her back, but the handbaskets she had carried remained empty. They were now topping the hand-wain Hrald pushed, as she needed both hands free. Each held a slender line of hempen rope trailing from her fist, the other end looped into the nose-ring of a spotted piglet, for Hrald had also persuaded the old man to part with two of his big sow's litter.

Hrald took from the silver he still bore at his belt for all this, that which he had earned from the salt in far-off Gotland. Counting part of it out to meet Kol's price was the last thing he had imagined doing with it. He had pictured setting both purses, still mostly filled, before his mother, and seeing her delight at such a sum. Now this silver was no different from that which had always sat in the dark ground under the grain-house floorboards. Reflecting on this as he made his way home, Hrald thought of the woman behind him, of how she and her aunt had suffered fear and want for lack of Oddi's finding that silver.

By the time they crossed the gate his arms and back were aching. But they had enough; it was a start. Tomorrow or the next day he would head for Signe's. She and her husband owned an oxcart, and he would return with far more than this, and sheep too, and Oddi to help.

His sister's farm was a full day's walk away, North up the coast. Hrald had not slept well, and was tired, his arms and legs still feeling the effects of wrestling with the heavy hand-wain. He ended up spending the night on the side of the trackway he followed. He went on at first light, walking faster now, until he reached Signe's place.

It was Yrling saw him first. Hrald had made his way past the sheep and cattle in the front pasture lands and had neared the woven fence surrounding house and outbuildings. The boy was walking from the fowl house, a wooden bowl in one hand and something small in another; yet another egg, Hrald thought, as he raised his arm in greeting to his little brother. The small mouth opened; the hand, too, and Hrald saw the egg drop to the packed ground. Another figure came in view, that of a man, and Hrald saw Ful, Signe's husband, take the bowl from Yrling and cuff the boy across the head in return.

Hrald called out then. Ful turned to see him, but did not move. Yrling was already running to his older brother.

The boy still had his arms flung about his waist when Signe hurried out, her young daughters at her side, one holding her spindle in her hand. Then Oddi was there, hurrying across the far field, to stand and grin, nodding at him, from a distance.

His sister cried over him, and Yrling would not let him out of his sight, even after Ful had told the boy to go back to his chores. The boy looked well-fed, but Hrald had not liked seeing Ful slap him due to a broken egg. But Signe's elder girl led him away by the hand kindly enough; that was something.

It did not take Hrald long to understand that Ful was not pleased by his return. He knew it would be a surprise, even a shock, to judge by the reactions he had already received, but he did not expect displeasure. Ful's greeting words of welcome had been half-hearted. He had listened dismissively to Hrald's tale, and had chided him at certain points. Hrald made no mention of what had detained him on Gotland, only that having sold the Anglian salt so quickly he determined to wander the island a while, having come so far. At least this was one point Ful could agree with.

"You'll not go so far again, once you are wed to Ingirith," was his remark, sealed with a rueful grunt.

"Ingirith," repeated Signe with a small gasp. "She does not know you live."

"I will go now, tomorrow, to see her," Hrald assured her. It was less than a day away, far less if Ful would let him ride his horse.

First he need ask them for their help. Hrald's father had always taught that it was unseemly to bargain with kin; one deserved their support as readily as that help was extended to them. Hroft had not liked Ful ten years ago when he wed Signe, and never did like him. Hrald knew this. As he detailed what he needed to begin to set his farm to rights he watched the grimace on his brother-in-law's face deepen.

"I have silver," Hrald felt forced to say. He did not believe that he would have to buy stock and grain from his own kin, as he had from Kol. Even though Signe made a semblance of protest, it was only then that Ful nodded in agreement.

It angered Hrald; what he asked for was in effect a loan, to be repaid in kind as soon as the farm was producing.

"I will give you silver now," he amended, feeling some little heat, but keeping his words as cool as he could. "And you will hold it, and return it to me when I repay what you have lent me, less one tenth."

"Já, that is just," his sister was saying.

Ful could never have held the farm without the silver and goods that Signe had brought with her when they wed, and she had more than once reminded him of this over the years. Ful was not successful in stifling his scowl, but was forced to nod. Signe clucked in approval and poured them all more ale; they were sitting outside under the deep eaves of the house, facing the paddock with its single horse.

"Good," Hrald summed. "With what you can lend me, Oddi and I will be able to make a start." He watched Ful's face darken the more, but went on. "And his female kin are there, his sister and niece; they will stay on with me."

They knew of course of Gillaug and Jorild's coming, but it was of Oddi that Ful wished to speak.

"It will be hard enough to spare what you ask of me, without losing Oddi," he told Hrald.

Hrald set his cup down so hard upon the table that a few drops of ale splashed out upon the darkened surface.

"Oddi was my father's thrall," he said, with no attempt to hide the edge in his voice. By law Oddi owed his allegiance to him, Hrald, the son of the man who had freed him, and Ful knew this. Hrald could not believe that Ful would dispute his claim to the man, and felt certain that given a choice Oddi would readily return to him.

His brother-in-law had two male thralls of his own, and two serving women, just as Hrald and his mother once had; workers enough, Hrald reckoned.

"King Horik's demand for double taxes makes for a lean year for us," Ful said, as if in defence.

How can you whine to me of this, Hrald thought. It was the same demand, and the penalty in the lateness of Hrald's farm to meet it, that had ended in the confiscation of his thralls and beasts. Hrald had heard upon landing in Haithabu it had been imposed on all, rich and poor, but was to be a one-time burden.

Ful did not press the matter further, and they turned their talk to other things. Hrald recalled what Jorild had told him of Oddi's fears that kin of his would lay claim to the farm in the face of his apparent loss at sea. Oddi was a man of some forty years, and had wisdom. This turned in Hrald's mind as he sat there opposite his brother-in-law.

All in all it was not the reception Hrald had expected, but then nothing had been. After Ful left the table Signe reached her hand to Hrald and closed it over his own a moment. She had not been with their mother at her death; Ashild had been perilously ill by the time Oddi left to fetch her, reluctant to leave lest the King's men return in his absence. Signe arrived to find the woman cold and Oddi digging her barrow.

Hrald left for Ingirith's family farm the next morning, and on Ful's horse. Yrling begged to join him, and Hrald could not refuse. The boy's unabashed affection for him gave Hrald some of the pleasure he missed from his lost mother's joy. They skirted a bracken marsh and long stretches of birch woods, and reached there before noon.

As Fate would have it, Ingirith was the first person he saw. She was on her knees in the bean patch, pulling up weeds with her two sisters, and had stood up to drape a handful of fallen tendrils back upon their spindly wooden support. She then placed the palms of her hands on the small of her back and stretched the roundness from her spine.

"Ingirith," he called. He knew her from the back; her yellow hair had always been longer than her sisters'.

She whirled about, the other girls popping up as well from where they crouched amongst the vines.

Yrling was on the saddle before him, and Hrald had one arm about him, the other holding the reins. He could not wave, but he did smile. Even staring at him as she was she was pretty, and he felt a sudden gladness in seeing her.

Ingirith squinted at the figures on horseback; the Sun was behind them. Hrald kept coming towards her. After a few more paces she let out a cry.

She did not run to him. He did not expect that. Living as far away as she did, they had seen the other only a few times, mostly at the Summer Thing, the gathering where disputes were heard and justice meted out. Folk came to trade sheep and cattle as well, and young people traded sidelong glances as their parents made inquiry as to their respective character, work habits, and likely fortune.

Ingirith's parents were now making their way from the work yard and house, her father Oke calling out in welcome. Ingirith had two little brothers, and they ran out as well. Hrald passed Yrling down to Oke, and swung down himself. All were gathered around him now. Yrling stuck close to his leg, surrounded as he was by strangers.

Hrald had told his tale enough times that it had begun to take on a sense of distance to him, as if he were repeating a minor episode of a little-known Saga. The fact that he was the key character in the story only made it the odder to relate. It was also growing shorter, the quicker to tell of it. Oke had many questions about the fabled island of Gotland. Hrald looked at Ingirith, watching him closely, her pretty brow furrowed, the tip of her pink tongue showing as she listened. He recalled Stenhild, and his month with her. He remembered the scent of her skin and her hand resting on his bare chest. He closed his eyes a moment, then told Oke of the wild horses he had seen.

Hrald and Yrling must stay the night, it was only fitting given the importance of his return. Oke's surprise at seeing him again was no greater than his eldest daughter's, but his pleasure at it much the greater. Though Hroft had been years older than Oke, their friendship was a true one, and their desire to join their children stemmed from Ingirith's birth, the year after Hrald's.

For Ingirith's part, her shock at seeing Hrald alive was followed by cool and baffling confusion. You cannot be back, her heart drummed. You cannot still live. On the heels of her shock and confusion rolled a wave of resentment, flushing all other feelings from her breast.

Her parents had always told her what a good match Hrald would be. But it was their match, not hers, just as she knew Hroft and Ashild had determined that Hrald would take her to wife. Ingirith had never been to their farm, and regretted from the start that it was so far down the southern coast of Jutland as to make a trip to Ribe almost impossible.

Ribe was the trading post North of her parent's farm, a Summer post only, but one at which great quantities of cattle, sheep, and pigs were sold, and all Summer long, not just for the few days of the Thing. A few families lived there year round, one who did brewing and baking both, always needed in such places. Ribe was one of the trading posts ruled by King Horik, which meant that choice goods flowed in from Norway, Frankland, and the rest of Danemark, as well as points both further West and East. Her father had been down to Haithabu, and she knew Ribe to be smaller than it, but Ribe was big enough and rich enough for her.

And Ribe had an iron-smith, a master tool maker. And that smith had a son.

Last month Oke had yoked the two oxen and headed to Ribe for a new scythe, and pair of shears. The trip out and back could be made in a long day, and after the earliest of the morning chores were complete he and his three daughters headed there. It was a treat to do so, and each girl had a small sum of silver in a tiny drawstring pouch to spend while there; Oke could afford to indulge them to that extent.

He did not let the girls out of his sight in the trading town. It was still early in the season and not as many stalls were open as they would be at Summer's height, but there were goods enough on display to catch the eye, and enough men strange to Jutland and its ways to make Oke wary for his daughters' sakes. Thus they all were in tow as he made his way to the iron-worker of his choice.

His forge, as all the fire-workers' were, was set aside and back from the crowded side lanes of leather cutters and comb makers. On one side was the workshop of a bronze-worker, already bent over one of his crucibles, pouring metal into clay moulds to form brooches. There was nothing to see, but on the other side of the tool-smith was a glass worker, who squatted down by the heat of his own fire, rolling and shaping molten lumps into multi-hued glass beads. Ingirith's two sisters were allowed by their father to stay there and watch the man. Ingirith herself disdained necklaces of glass, no matter how gaily coloured; she had always fancied those of golden amber and hoped one day soon to own one, and even a necklace of silver beads or braided chain as well. So she stayed at her father's side as he dealt with the iron-smith working in his open-fronted shed.

He had two other men and a boy working with him, his sons, she imagined; their backs were mostly to her so she could not see a likeness. She watched the boy work the bellows, seeing the reddish sparks fly up at the air hole at the back of the forging oven. The day was a chilly one, and the warmth coming from the fire enough to draw her nearer. Then one of the men turned, long tongs in his left hand, a white-hot piece of metal caught in its grip. He took up a hammer and began pounding and shaping the glowing thing on an iron anvil.

His eyes were trained on his work, and his brow glistened with small drops of sweat. He was young, two or three years more than she herself. His hair was a shade or two darker than her own. When he raised his eyes from his work she saw they were blue, like her own. He looked at her, and smiled.

Ingirith thought him the handsomest man she had ever seen. And he was a tool-smith. No other workers in metals save silver – and gold-smiths earned as much, she knew, none but the makers of knives and swords.

She dropped her eyes for a moment as she had been taught, and then raised them back to him. She had been promised to a man she barely knew. If Hrald had not tried to make a trading trip to Gotland they would have now been wed for more than six months. It had angered her when she heard he had left, word of which had not come from his mother until it became clear that their hand-fast must be delayed.

She was in no eagerness to wed Hrald, and her anger was rooted not in the delay but the fact that as a man he had the freedom to go off without telling her. As weeks turned to months and no news of his arrival reached her, her parents began to console her over his loss. When word of his mother's death came, it seemed a final note to a song she had wearied of hearing. She was free.

Ingirith smiled back at the young smith. She felt herself straightening up as she looked on him, glad she had chosen her deep blue over-gown to bring out the blueness of her eyes. She had her best linen head wrap knotted at the nape of her neck. It was small enough to show off her spilling yellow hair, hair as straight and pale as ripened wheat. Her mother owned a single pair of silver brooches, and as Ingirith was the eldest daughter, and her mother had ever indulged her, had allowed her to wear these today at her shoulders instead of her workaday bronze brooches. She was thus arrayed more closely to the prosperous women who were selling goods at Ribe than the farm girl she was.

She could hear her father speaking with the master smith, and the man assuring him that the tools he sought would be ready next month. Oke would not need the scythe until the first harvest, anyway. That would mean another trip back here, she quickly realised.

Her father was set on her going to Hrald, and she knew he had held out hope over the long Winter that news would come of his return, or he himself appear on their threshold. Thus she did not feel she could, on the long ride back to the farm, ask him to inquire about the tool-smith's good-looking son. But the farther they travelled the more her thoughts stayed fixed on Ribe.

Why should she not wed a man who worked the Summer months in such a grand place? She imagined travelling each Spring from wherever the smith's Winter home was, and the setting up of their Summer quarters in a snug hut on one of Ribe's side lanes. She pictured keeping house there for her handsome husband, pictured the silver brooches he would give her, far larger and more beautiful than those her mother had lent her. She imagined the expectant waiting for ships on the horizon, and traders arriving in waggons. She saw herself walking the planked streets of the busy trading post, a pert basket hanging over her wrist, respected, envied, and rich. It was a far better life than that on a farm, with its endless hard work. This played in her thoughts as the steady hoof-fall of the oxen took her further from that dream.

Ingirith's younger sisters spent the silver their father had given them, one on a cluster of glass beads, the other on a square of Frankish linen with fine cut-work. But Ingirith herself arrived home with hers still clutched in her hand. She had seen what she had wanted, and it could not be bought with a few pieces of silver.

"You will make your hand-fast soon," Oke said at table that night, after all had been cleared away. He was grinning at Hrald and Ingirith as he said it. "We will keep it at harvest-tide, just as it was meant to be last year."

Late Summer was the best time for the clasping of hands. Not only did it almost ensure plenty for the wedding feast, but it gave the best start to the babe who might be conceived soon after. The new mother had the richness of all Summer's bounty to feed her in the early months, and babes born in late Spring were the heartier for it.

Both of the young people knew this. Ingirith looked down, and if Hrald's face had not been browned from the Sun the slight flush on his cheek would have been discerned by any looking at him.

"The bridal-ale here, then you make your way home to Hrald's," her father was going on. Ingirith raised her eyes and saw both parents smiling at her.

"It is quite a good farm," he assured his daughter. He had travelled there once or twice and had direct knowledge of it, and it was fitting to praise it within the hearing of he who now had possession of it.

"You will be sole mistress, Ingirith," her father pointed out. "With respects to your dead mother," he added, with a nod to Hrald.

Ingirith's eyelids dropped over her blue eyes as she lowered her chin. She had not looked forward to having an old woman, strange to her, telling her how things should be done once she got to Hrald's farm. She would be free of that, but now saw she would be alone in all the many things that needed to be done. With Hrald's mother dead, there would be no one to guide her, no one to consult, and no one to work alongside her. She would have to make do with the freedwomen Hrald had mentioned, no one else. And they were likely slatterns.

As if her mother read her thought she spoke now. "She will have help," she posed to her future son-in-law.

"Já, já" Hrald answered. "Oddi's kinswomen are there; they kept the place together, and for months. They will be great help to Ingirith," he promised.

Ingirith's parents looked at each other, and both rose. "Stay at the table a while," Oke invited, scraping the bench he shared with his wife out of the way. "We have work outside which must be done."

With no more pretense than that the prospective couple were left alone, and together. Ingirith sat almost opposite Hrald across the table. He knew he should rise and come sit at her side, and he did.

He lowered himself on the bench next her. It was close to the table and his legs had not enough real room, but she made no sign of rising so he could pull it out further. Sitting down, there was not quite the same difference in their height as standing. When they stood together the top of her head just grazed his shoulder-line. She often seemed to keep her eyes there, at his shoulders, and not raise them to his face.

Now she drew herself up, clasping her hands in her lap but lifting her chin. It was the blue over-gown she wore now, her best, and her mother had urged her to wear it at table that night to welcome her returned intended. As her fingers folded against its wool all she could think was it was this gown she had worn on the day she had met the tool-smith's son.

She had begun to think of it like that the very same day of the trip to Ribe; she had met the man, when in fact they had exchanged no more than a smile. He would know her father's name; his father would have told him that when the son had inquired about her, and Ingirith felt sure after that shared smile that he had.

There was a long silence after Hrald sat down next her, and she was still looking ahead into the dusk of the house, and not at him.

"You do not seem happy to see me," Hrald hazarded at last.

"You have been gone a long time," was all she answered.

"Já," he agreed, in a quiet voice. "Já."

A new silence began, one even more awkward than the first.

"As your father said, you will be mistress at the farm," he tried.

She still did not turn to look at him.

"I have silver," he began again, to offer further assurance. It was the same statement he had made to his brother-in-law the day prior, and once again it was not something he had thought he would have need to say. "That which I won by trading the Anglian salt, and that which was my mother's."

He should say something of a more personal nature, and went on, in a low voice.

"I will work hard at the farm, and do right by you."

She nodded. It took effort to be rude to one so earnest, and she knew she was being rude. If her mother saw her she would give her a shake by the shoulders for it.

She gave a quick nod of her head, but her thoughts were saying, I do not want life on your farm. I do not want the roughened hands and aching back my mother suffers, and that even I suffer now, young as I am. I want to live at Ribe, and wed the smith who makes the tools that men like my father pay good silver for. You cannot give me that, Hrald.

At this last thought she turned her face to his, and looked fully at him. She could not hold his gaze for more than an instant; she squeezed her eyes shut. The smiling face of the handsome yellow-haired tool-smith rose in her mind, and the way his blue eyes had met her own. She had imagined a new life for herself founded on that one look, a life she could not have.

Hrald did not know what to do with her silence. It made him feel even more unwelcome than had Ful's chiding. He thought she would want to speak with him about their life together. That is why Oke and her mother had left them alone, he knew; so they might touch hands, sit close to the other, and murmur hopes about their shared future. Nothing about her suggested she wanted him to move closer, or take her hand. Perhaps she could not yet picture her life at the farm.

His thoughts went to his little brother, already asleep in the curtained alcove in which Hrald himself would soon lay his head.

"Yrling will come back home with me, and we will raise him together," he told her.

This forced her mouth to open. It was bad enough that she must go so far away to be his wife, and work as hard as she knew she must work. She would not raise his brother as well.

"He is better off with your married sister," she countered. "He has lived with her for months, and has already found a home there. He should be with his female kin."

You are soon to be his kin, Hrald was thinking, but did not say. "We will speak of it later," he ended. He knew his return was a surprise. He would not press such things now.

Hrald and Yrling rode off after dawn next day, back to the farm of Signe and Ful. As he was loading seed-corn onto the bed of Ful's ox-cart Yrling was begging to be allowed to go home with him. The cart was so chock-full that Hrald would have to walk alongside it, but one small boy would make no difference to the ox team; he could ride atop. Oddi would follow in a week or so, herding the nine sheep Ful allowed Hrald; Ful insisted Oddi stay for shearing-time.

Hrald had thought he would of course bring Yrling home, just as he would bring Oddi back to the farm. But his sister Signe did not agree.

"He is my brother too, and here he has the girls. He is making a home here," she told Hrald. They had sent the boy off as they began speaking of him like this. Hrald knew that before Yrling came here to live, he scarcely knew his older sister. Yrling had been the child of Ashild's old age, and Signe had been wed and out of the house before he was born.

Signe's words echoed what Ingirith had said about the matter. His sister seemed to want Yrling. At last he agreed. Perhaps both women were right, and all was unsettled at the farm just now. But he wished that the maid he would marry had been more welcoming to the boy.

Chapter the Fourth

THE BRIDE

HRALD returned home and told Gillaug and Jorild that Oddi would soon join them, and with sheep. Right now they had seed-corn, and that wanted for grinding and boiling. Before he could address himself to this he need return Ful's ox and cart, and set out next day to do so. When Yrling saw him again so soon the boy was certain he had changed his mind and come for him. Telling him he must stay was the hardest part of the wearying trip.

Once home he got to work, hacking away with a mattock at the weedy growth crowding the fields. Gillaug and Jorild had already opened fresh rows in the vegetable bed and sprinkled in the bean seeds. A rooster had been left to them, and with the three hens from Kol there would presently be chicks. There was no waste with which to feed the two piglets, but Jorild tended them with care, driving them to the wood edging two sides of the farm where mast trees grew. The dark soil held grubs which yielded to their ploughing snouts.

Even with so much to do Hrald found his thoughts wandering. At night he lay in his alcove in a house far quieter than he had ever known it. Gillaug and Jorild were there, sleeping in the alcoves at the other end of the house in which the two serving women had once slept, but they were nearly silent. It made his thoughts in the night the louder. In another two months or so he would be expected to return to Oke's farm and wed Ingirith. There would be a bridal feast, and then he would bring her back here to begin their lives as man and wife.

He thought of the hearty laughter of his dead father, and the teasing smiles of Ashild, his lost mother. Their union had been a good one, Hrald thought. He wondered if he would know the same with Ingirith.

During the month he had spent with Stenhild on Gotland he had never thought of himself as her husband. He always knew he would soon leave for home. Without having to be told he knew they should not be seen together, to spare her awkwardness lest her husband one day reappear. They walked on different days into Paviken. When the day came she decided to again wed all she need do was appear with the man before two or three witnesses and they proclaim themselves wed; she had friends in Paviken and on other farms who would witness for her. When a man had set to sea and not returned for a year, no woman could be expected to wait longer. Life was too difficult to go on alone.

But now he thought that during that month he had in fact been almost as much husband to Stenhild as any man could be. They had arisen together, and worked alongside the other. She had cooked and brought his food, washed his clothing, and crouched with him in his weeding. He had dug and spaded her vegetable plot, looked to those things needing attention by mending and making new, chopped kindling he piled to the eave-line. They had sat by fire's glow, she with her child on her lap, and spoken in low tones, one to the other. And at nightfall he lay in her alcove, awaiting her as she did the final cleaning up and banked the fire.

It was after their third night together that she asked him to do this, to go ahead, and into the sleeping alcove first. When she parted the heavy woollen curtain and saw him, a brief smile bowed her firmly pressed lips. Later he thought he understood why; for well over a year she had parted that curtain to an empty bed, and climbed in alone.

This was perhaps the most meaningful part of being wed, Hrald thought. There was the pleasure of her body, and her willingness to give it. It would be a lie to say it had not been a large part of what kept him there with her, when there was so much more of the island to explore. But it was the rhythm of their life together that was even more lulling. He was not alone, and he was not lonely. She cared for his clothing, and his body, and wanted to be near him, had invited him to come. She made him feel a man, and worthy of such care.

There was never any question in his mind of his returning to Dane-mark; his mother was there, and their farm, both of which needed him. And he was promised to a maid his father had always wanted him to wed. His parents had worked thriftily and hard and he felt bound to the soil they had tilled. But as he walked across the gang-plank to the ship which would begin to carry him back to this he felt a pang of regret, and one of loss.

By the time he wed Ingirith it would be a full year since he had lain with a woman. Ingirith was pretty, far prettier than Stenhild had been. He should be glad to know that she would be at his side. But he felt no gladness thinking on her, and imagining her body and her touch did not thrill him as it had before he had left for Gotland. It was her manner to him, he knew. She was not a shy and overly-retiring maid, or one fearful of men; he had seen her talk and jest with strange young men around night fires at the Thing until her mother called her to their tent. It felt to Hrald that Ingirith was not welcoming to him.

His parents had found joy in the other, but any man who was wed could take a second wife, and even a third or more. He must be able to afford to keep them all, and equally; and so only prosperous farmers could have more than one wife, though chieftains sometimes had five or more. His father had never taken a second wife, though Hrald knew of several men who did. He recalled his father laughing and saying that one was sometimes more than enough, and his mother saucing back at him.

Even when Hroft had died, Ashild had not seemed lonely. She had wept, openly and often, at his death, but had told Hrald in the months and years that followed that she felt his presence still.

Now with mother and father gone, Hrald felt himself lonely. He had much on his plate, but he knew other young men had more; he must make of it what he could. Losing his stock and thralls was a blow unlooked-for, but it must be met. He had silver; that gave some comfort. And he knew he could work hard. He only wished he could place more trust in she who was to be his wife.

The next day Hrald was washing his face and hands at a basin of warm water Gillaug had poured out for him on a work table in the kitchen yard. He freed his wet hair from his face with a shake of his head, then straightened up. Across the rye field he saw Jorild. She stood at the base of the mound under which his mother Ashild lay.

She was not there long; her Aunt Gillaug was busy with the evening meal. After they had eaten their browis of boiled barley, peas, and pot herbs the women busied themselves with cleaning up. Hrald walked out to the edge of the rye field.

Neither of his parent's mounds were big, and those of his father's dead kin were lower, worn with age, some showing sunken spots with the passing of time. The grass over all grew thick and green, and on his mother's it was the brighter, the new roots free and untangled. There on that freshest mound were laid a few stalks of yellow and blue wildflowers.

It was Jorild set them there, he knew. His mother was a good woman, and even in her last illness that goodness must have been apparent. Gillaug said Jorild had nursed her as a daughter would. Ashild must have returned that affection.

His head dropped, thinking on this. The Sun was lowering in the paling sky, and now passed behind a cloud, casting a deep shadow from kitchen yard to where he stood. He turned back and saw Jorild, standing over a wash tub, looking at him.

She had already told him of his mother's last days; it had been painful to hear. And he had thanked her for her care. Yet he wished there were more; more to say, more to hear.

Earlier that day he had watched Jorild wash his clothes in the same tub, saw her wring the water from them and hang them to dry in the warming Sun. It had occurred to him then that she herself had but one shift and over-gown; she had worn the same day after day. Arising early he had seen these garments hanging some mornings by the fire. She must have wrapped herself in a blanket to make her way back to her alcove the night before.

He gestured to her now, and she left the tub and followed him inside the house and to the alcove in which his parents had slept. His mother had gowns, and shifts too, lying folded and rolled where she had left them in the low wooden chest beneath the box bed. He pulled that chest out.

"Take what you will, and for your aunt as well," he told Jorild.

He thought Ingirith would want none of this; the clothes were worn but decent, well-sewn by his mother, but not the bright colours Ingirith favoured.

Jorild's pale lips parted. He gestured her to the chest. "Take these things," he offered.

She thought she would take one each only, for herself and for her aunt. Her hand lifted, then paused over the folded gowns.

Hrald's own hand reached out and touched hers, poised in the air. Jorild let out a breath.

He lifted his hand from where it lay, gently resting on her own, and again used it to gesture to the fabric. She drew out two gowns and two shifts, and bowed her head in thanks.

Sleep did not come to Hrald that night. He lay in his alcove, thinking on Jorild. At last, scarce knowing what he was doing but feeling compelled to do so, he pulled on his leggings and stepped out. He walked in the gloom of the quiet house to her curtain.

He stood there a moment, the heavy wool looking black in the little light.

"Jorild," he finally breathed out.

She parted the curtain. She too was awake, and wearing one of the shifts he had just given. Enough light fell on her face that he could read her expression – mild, and neither expectant nor surprised. She put her feet on the wooden planking of the floor and followed him back to his own alcove.

Jorild was not a maid. There had been a son of her former master who had had her first; then after, a boy, also freed, whom she had liked. There had been no pleasure for her in her first few couplings, with her master's son. But the boy she had cared for, and she had thought he wanted her as well.

This night she said nothing through it all, and Hrald too was silent. There was meaning enough in her touch. During the caresses he gave her, only one thing did he utter, and twice: her name. He liked the name, and breathed out, as he spoke it, was close to sounding like his own.

By the time Oddi arrived with the sheep nine days had passed, the nights of which Jorild had spent in Hrald's sleeping alcove. Each night Hrald had appeared at her curtain to lead her back to his own. He did not think Gillaug knew this; Jorild was careful to return to her own bed before dawn, save one morning when they heard her aunt up and stirring. Jorild then waited until they heard the door to the kitchen yard open and shut before venturing out from Hrald's alcove to her own, to dress.

The day Oddi came all this changed. Oddi had eight ewes and a ram with him, enough to begin to build a flock. He had also a young hound pup, a handsome little fellow with wiry brown and grey fur, which he had picked up at a farm he had stopped at on his way; it was unwanted from the litter and about to be drowned. Oddi thus entered the farm in a swirl of bleating activity, the hound pup yipping and jumping on all who neared it, its tail whipping in happy frenzy against their legs. For the first time since his return the farm began to sound normal to Hrald's ears.

He was glad to see Oddi, and Oddi was unabashed in his pleasure at being back at the place he had spent nearly all of his life; he had been bought by Hroft as a boy of twelve or so. But his coming marked the end of Hrald's bringing Jorild to his bed.

He did not say anything to her throughout that day, but after they had all supped they were alone a moment. Their eyes met, and she could read in them that the interlude was at an end. She held his eyes a moment, and slowly nodded.

Hrald could not lie with Jorild now that her uncle was back. It was true that until his freeing Oddi had been a thrall, and true as well that Jorild had been born a thrall. They were both freed now. It placed them in a status below that of even the humblest freeman; one that would continue throughout their lives. If a freed woman bore the child of a thrall she would be tipped back into thralldom again. No one would look askance at a farmer lying with his serving woman, freed or thrall. He might have his wife's displeasure to contend with, no more; and children born from such couplings were seen as useful increase to the farm.

But Jorild was different. She had come, a stranger to Hrald and his people, and served his dying mother well. She had stayed on at his request. In all she did she was more than able, a tireless worker. And she was kind.

And Oddi too was different. He had always been part of Hrald's life, and Hrald trusted and needed him. His father had taught Hrald a lot, but Oddi knew how to do many things. Hrald liked Oddi. And Jorild was his niece. Somehow Hrald now saw that to use her in this way was to abuse them both.

He had not even known Oddi had folk of his own, and his lack of knowledge about the man's life struck him, thinking over this when he and Jorild had walked together to Kol's farm. Thralls did not talk about themselves, not to their masters anyway.

For now he must set his mind on the farm. Signe had insisted that the sheep Oddi had brought be sent unshorn, so her brother would have the wool of them, so they began with shearing. They had no oxen to furrow the soil with, but it was not the first time that men had harnessed themselves with straps of leather to an ard and pulled it along the rows. It was Jorild who steadied the ard handle, keeping it set in as straight a furrow as she could as the two men strained before her, pulling the blade through the damp and waiting ground. It took all her strength to do so, and her arms trembled at the end of every day so spent.

Meanwhile Gillaug cleaned the shorn fleece, cutting out the soiled parts near the tail, picking out sticks and leaves from the underbelly of the long strands. She washed the oily masses of wool in hot water, plucking out the lumps of valued wool-wax with a wooden paddle as they rose to the cooling surface. The good soapstone pot used for cooking held heat better, but the bigger iron cauldron was the right size for this task, and she had a hot fire going beneath it. The kitchen yard stank of the waxy stuff, but there was little better for soothing chapped skin. And too, wool-wax pounded with the yellow buds of the broom plant was the best remedy to staunch a flow of blood on a sheep if the shears slipped and cut the skin. Gillaug was careful to skim every gobbet she could.

Once cleansed and laid out in the Sun to dry, the wool looked like the treasured stuff it was. She and Jorild together combed and teased it into fluffy masses of roving, ready to be spun by their hand spindles. The ewes were of cream, grey, and black, and the ram white, so they would have wool to dye, as well as that naturally dark.

The rye, oats, and barley got planted. The rain was kind and fell gently, and just enough. The sprouting beans showed green stalks and bright leaves and then pale flowers. Bees came, crowding their way in, to ensure those flowers would herald beans. Onions and cabbages and carrots too found footing in the vegetable rows. All demanded weeding, and all worked at it. Hrald went back to Haithabu and brought back a milk cow. Everything they ate was better with the sweet butter Gillaug and Jorild rolled from the churn, and Hrald turned the foaming milk into soft cheese to set in the spring house. Chicks now surrounded the clucking hens, and they had as well eggs. Oddi and Gillaug brewed ale, the savour of which was often pleasing. The pup, who Hrald had named Hlaupari – Runner, for he loved to run – was already showing signs of growing into a good watch dog. They had lost no fowl or gosling to a fox since he had come to the farm.

Summer reached its peak. Hrald fell exhausted into his alcove every night. And harvest-tide began to near, when he must go and wed his bride.

Hrald had no choice but to walk to Oke's farm. He went the shortest way he could, and overland at times, to arrive there next morning after spending the night in a birch wood. He trusted that Ingirith's father would realise he would have to lend the couple an ox-cart to take his daughter and her household goods to her new home. Oxen could be bought all Summer long at Haithabu, but would be cheapest just before the trading season closed, at the end of harvest-tide, and Hrald needed to watch every piece of silver, having spent so much already.

With his parents dead, Hrald went to his wedding feast alone; Oddi could not be spared to join him, though Hrald would have been glad for his company. But when he arrived at Oke's farm he was told his sister Signe had sent word she would come for the feast on the morrow. The distance was slight enough for that.

The wedding ale would not be a large one; Hrald had so little family, but the farm was still abuzz with preparation, for the bride's parents had kin throughout the area who would make the journey. Ingirith looked happy; there would be a party, and one in her honour.

That first night Hrald sat alone with her parents after they had eaten. He must present his bride-price, and they their daughter's dowry. The price agreed long ago by both fathers had been ten ewes and five bushels of oats. Oke had made it known to Hrald on his earlier visit that he realised Hrald could not provide such goods from a greatly diminished store. Silver to an equal amount would do, though Oke regretted the loss of Hroft's good sheep nearly as much as Hrald did.

For their part, Ingirith would come to her new home with her loom and weaving tools, a large chest full of linen, new bedding and pillows, and a sum of silver. Given the state of Hrald's flocks, she would also carry two sacks of new wool with her, ready for carding. The linens and bedding were those the maid had been working on for years, with her mother's help, and formed an important part of the valuables she came to her husband with. In Ingirith's case they amounted to three linen bed sheets, spun, woven and sewn by she herself; six linen towels, three great and three small; four woollen blankets of cream and charcoal-grey; and four sets of thick woollen alcove curtains, boldly woven in varying stripes of cream, red, yellow, and blue.

Ingirith's mother and father detailed all this to Hrald, her mother numbering all on her fingers. He had been told much the same a few months ago, but nodded gravely when it seemed warranted. He had the silver ready for them in a little pottery jar, the better to sink it under their floorboards for safekeeping. It was an added touch he imagined his mother suggesting he do.

That night he climbed into the alcove he had been given and shut his eyes, hard. Across the cold fire-pit area he heard Ingirith's sisters, chattering away in their excitement for the coming day, but he could not discern her voice amongst theirs. Perhaps she lay silent in her alcove, as he did. He thought of his father and mother and that they were not here to witness that which they had planned so long to happen.

The day of his hand-fasting was a jumble of noise, strange faces, and lifted cups. He dressed himself that morning in his new clothes, leggings of dark brown wool, and a linen tunic of green. This was fabric woven by his mother and their former serving women, and laid by for future use. He pulled them on, aware that Jorild had cut and sewn them for him, and for this day, and that she had with Gillaug dyed the tunic with the bark from crab-apple trees.

Ingirith wore a gown of rosy hue. It surprised him as he knew she favoured blue, but she looked pretty indeed to his eyes. What Hrald did not know was how she had rejected her mother's suggestion that she wear her deep blue gown for her wedding day. That Ingirith would not do, but she did not share the reason with her mother. Her mother had forced her to wear it at table the day Hrald first showed up. The blue gown was that she had been wearing on the trip to Ribe, when she had seen the man she wanted. She thought of it as part and parcel of that day alone. She would not sully it and her memory by wearing it to wed another.

The day was dry and fair and made for good travelling for the guests. They poured in, on foot, in waggons drawn by ox teams, and for those who were rich enough, wains drawn by horses. Signe and Ful and their daughters were amongst them. When Yrling ran to his older brother, Hrald scooped him up in his arms and lifted him in the air.

There was a fine old birch, with black-flecked bark of pure white, that stood not far from the burying ground of Oke's ancestors. This had been deemed a good place for the hand-fast; the birch lent beauty, and the dead would be honoured by the nearness of the festivities. A few benches had been brought near. A white he-goat with curling horns was tethered nearby, which Hrald would Offer to the God Freyr to ensure the fecundity of the union; Freyr and his sister Freyja were Lord and Lady of all increase in man and beasts.

The folk had gathered there, in a circle about the tree, Hrald and Ingirith standing almost opposite each other across its breadth. It was, like all the few weddings Hrald had seen, the work of a few moments, but there was a simple magnitude in those moments. He stood in that circle next Signe and Yrling, glad to have at least some kin to support him, looking across at Ingirith in her rose-hued gown, standing between her father and mother. At a nod from her parents Hrald and his bride stepped into the centre and stood before the birch tree. Hrald held in his hand an emblem of his life's work, that by which he now vowed to support his wife. It was a small hand-sickle Hrald grasped, for he would make his way by farming, as had his people before him. Most brides would hold spindle or shuttle, emblem of the daily task of spinning and weaving, as token of their willingness to clothe and care for their husband and coming children. Hrald saw that Ingirith had chosen neither of these tools, but instead held a dull-edged iron weaving sword, used to beat the wool woof up against the warp. A sword, Hrald thought a moment.

Now he must speak his promises to her, and in a voice loud enough for all to hear. He tried to smile at her, but feared he was only making a face. She too was unsmiling, and must feel, as he did, all eyes upon them both as they stood there.

He cleared his tightened throat. "I, Hrald, son of Hroft, take you Ingirith as my wife. I will provide for you and do you no harm."

He could not think of more to say. Walking here he had thought he should thank her parents for entrusting her to him, or invoke his own dead mother and father with gratitude for making the match for him. Say these things he could not. As the silence grew he looked down.

Ingirith was speaking now, but in a tone so low that even those nearest took a step forward to hear her. "I Ingirith, daughter of Oke, take Hrald as my husband."

She paused long enough that her next words were hurried out. "And I will provide for him."

Now they must exchange the tools of their livelihoods, in accord with the promises made. He passed the wooden handle of the sickle to her, and took the weaving sword in his hand. They held these tools a moment before returning them. Ingirith's mother stepped forward, holding a length of gaily patterned tablet-woven ribband. Man and wife must join hands, and have those hands made fast by the binding of the ribband. Hrald held out his hand, and Ingirith took it. Her mother wrapped the ribband twice around their joined hands.

Hrald knew he should look in Ingirith's eyes to seal their vows, and he looked at her as he gave her hand a squeeze. She glanced up at him.

It was enough. Her mother's hands met in a single clap of joy, and all around gave a cheer. Ingirith's mother unwrapped the ribband, and held it out to her daughter with a smile. It was always given into the woman's keeping, this symbol of the bond between them.

Now Hrald must send the goat to Freyr. Hrald had not made public sacrifice before, and hoped he could do so swiftly and skillfully. The fowl he had occasion to Offer on his family's farm during Blót, the month of sacrifice, had been done alongside his father's greater offer of a piglet. Only since his father's death had he dispatched that piglet himself, and then only twice. The goat was full grown, vigorous, and in the prime of life.

It had been pulling up the grass where it was tied the while, and only when they turned to surround it did the goat grow restive. The axe was sitting there, ready to be taken up in Hrald's hands. He looked at Ingirith before he picked it up. Her eyes were fastened on the goat. As he neared, it began to shy, pulling on the rope that held it, and then to drop its head defensively. One of Ingirith's uncles helpfully caught up the back legs of the beast, giving Hrald clear aim with the butt end of the axe head.

"To Freyr," he cried. He was grateful to hit it squarely, the dull crack of the skull sounding over it. The goat toppled. Hrald dropped on his knees to open its throat with his knife, that the waiting soil receive its share of animal life-force.

He stood to further cheers. He went to Ingirith and lifted her hand in his, above their heads. She still held her weaving-sword in her other.

Women were moving amongst the laughing crowd, passing out cups and filling them with ale. Soon they would all walk back to the tables set up outside the house and begin the feast. Just now they seemed alone, the guests turning to each other or to the family of the bride. Hrald turned to her.

He had just made Offering that they might know abundance in their shared life, in goods and in children. He was grateful she was so pretty, and came with useful goods and some silver. He knew he was nearly a stranger to her, and she would be going far from her home to live with him. She was younger than he and likely frightened.

"You are very pretty," he thought to tell her. It was true and no lie, she had full measure of beauty.

She gave a slight movement of her shoulders.

"I hope you will be happy with me," he offered.

She nodded, then turned to a sister who had come up to kiss her.

The feast was notable for its richness. Ingirith was their eldest and first to wed, and Oke's pride rested on making good show. He had raised up a large flock of fattened fowl, which knew the further luxury of being roasted and not boiled. The crackling skins had been stuffed with whole sage leaves and butter, and each guest had half a bird to himself. There were egg puddings, crusted and golden, dotted with pine-nuts, and loaves of newly-ground wheaten bread, instead of that of everyday rye and oats.

Hrald sat next to Ingirith and ate with her from a single plate. Mead had been dipped out, and his cup filled and refilled. He began to feel more ease. Ingirith too seemed to know ease. She smiled and chatted with those who stopped to speak to her, turning on the bench to do so. Even the back of her neck was lovely, Hrald thought, seeing the hollow there where her yellow hair was gathered under the knot of her head wrap.

They would spend their first night in her parents' house; it was too long a journey back to his farm to do otherwise. By the time they were led to the alcove they would share Hrald felt warmed through by food and drink. The wedding-ale would continue outside without them, and they were sent off with hooting shouts to their rest.

It was her parents who led them thus. Oke clapped Hrald on the shoulder, and whispered something about the goat and the many kids it had sired; Hrald could not catch all but understood from Oke's wink he should laugh. Her mother gave Ingirith a kiss on the forehead as they left her.

It was dim in the house but there was still light in the sky, so even with the curtains drawn it was not dark inside the alcove. Hrald stood on the platform, turned away from Ingirith to give her privacy as she undressed. The noise from the guests ebbed and flowed as folk neared the house and then retreated. He heard the front door open and the excited tittering of Ingirith's sisters before hearing them being sharply called away.

He heard the rustle of bed linens. Without turning to her he sat down on the edge of the box bed and began to undress. Once naked he slipped in beside her as smoothly as he could. She still wore her long-sleeved shift. Her gown of rosy hue hung on one of the wall pegs, but she had not undressed.

He put his arm around her, tried to pull her close. Her own arms were running straight down her body, as if to keep her shift in place. He pressed his thigh against her and felt her hand was closed in a fist.

He let her go. Her eyes were not shut, but they were not looking at him. They were focussed up into the dusk of the timber roof.

"Ingirith," he said.

She did not answer him.

"Ingirith."

"What do you want," she finally said.

The mead he had drunk should have made him laugh at that, but he did not. The warmth of that potent drink drained away from him at her words.

He found himself breathing out a deep breath, a sigh. One of the guests, a drunken man, began singing outside the door of the house to them.

"You are tired," Hrald told her. "Let us sleep now." He turned his back on her, as he thought she wanted.

It was not easy to emerge from the alcove next morning to greet the family, and those guests who had remained. Hrald dressed and left first. The grins and smiles he met with made his face warm, which all who looked upon him took for signs of a long and happy night. They were hardly more restrained when Ingirith appeared, in a gown of yellow. What surprised him was the good natured coolness with which she returned the gibes.

Oke and Hrald loaded up the oxcart, and made their farewells to Ingirith's family. If all went well they would see each other next Summer at the Thing. At the last moment Ingirith promised to journey up over the Winter's Nights festivals. All Hrald could do was agree, weather allowing.

Then they were off. Their first stop would be to Signe and Ful's farm. Their wedding gift was waiting for them there, and Hrald had not spent any time with Yrling, and wished to have a few moments alone with the boy.

The cart was not so full that Ingirith could not ride upon it. Hrald walked at the beast's head, to save its strength, but also to feel the solidness of the ground under his feet.

They had not gone more than an hour when they met another oxcart, loaded with bushels of newly flailed grain, heading in the opposite direction. It was driven by a man and two boys, who yielded the track to them. After Hrald thanked them Ingirith called out.

"Do you head to Ribe?" she asked, in so pointed a manner that the man paused.

"Já, to Ribe," he answered. "All good things are there," he ended, with a grin.

Hrald watched his new wife duck her head in agreement; all good things are there.

Signe's gift turned out to be a generous one. She had made the couple four pillows of tightly-woven linen, fully stuffed with washed fowl feathers. Any gift meant for the sleeping alcove of a newly-wed couple occasioned smiles, and this was no different. But Hrald did not expect what his brother-in-law Ful said to him, when he stood alone with Hrald as he checked the ox's harness shaft. The man had turned and was looking at Ingirith as she stood with Signe.

"She is well worth flattening on those cushions," he said, tapping Hrald on his chest with the back of his hand.

It was all Hrald could do not to step back from the man's touch. As it was he turned his face so quickly away from Ful that he laughed.

The parting with Yrling was hardest. If things had gone well last night he would have brought up his plan of taking the boy home with them. But seeing how Ingirith had shooed Yrling away when he had gotten too close to her with muddied hands kept him silent. Perhaps when they passed this way again in Winter Yrling could return then. As it was he spent a few minutes with him, rolling an old iron cask hoop on the hard ground, chasing it with sticks to keep it rolling. Hrald had done the same as a boy and for the first time in a long time found himself laughing with his little brother. Then they were off.

The oxcart moved more slowly than a young and long-legged man like Hrald could walk, and they would spend that night on the road. As they made their camp he took heart that this would be the true start of their marriage. He let the ox browse in the tall grass at the side of the track, and unloaded much of what the cart carried. The space freed would make a more than adequate bed. The cushions Signe had just given seemed providential, though he had to force his thoughts from what Ful had said.

Ingirith heated water for washing, and after they had eaten they both used it, Hrald vanishing amongst the trees to allow her to do so in private. When he returned she was under the bedding she had brought. He washed himself and climbed in after her. She again wore her linen shift.

Married folk slept naked; only children and the ill wore clothing while in bed. Ingirith was neither child nor sick; she was his wife. But she lay there, as rigid and unyielding as last night.

He moved closer to her. There was still light in the sky, but they had spent hours on the road, he walking, she being jostled as she sat. He had wanted to stop and rest in good time. The place he had chosen was dry, with wild grasses on one side and pines on the other. That smell of pine resin he had ever liked was in the warm air. A few night birds were beginning to sing, calling out to their mates. It was otherwise quiet, and they were alone.

He bent over her, and kissed her brow. He thought she closed her eyes at this, but his own face was too close to be sure. He let his lips touch her forehead again, then drift to her cheek. He rested them on her lips. They did not respond, and he knew she held her breath.

"Ingirith," he whispered. "You are my wife . . . "

Hrald had never lain with a maid, and never with a woman who was unwilling. Ingirith was both.

Now she turned her chin away. He felt shamed by her refusal, and unwilling to go further in the face of her coldness.

He could not ask her why she wed him. Few young had any say in the matter. Their folk chose for them, and they must trust their judgment had been good. Right now Hrald would have given a lot to speak to his dead father on the matter.

He had been propped on his elbow at her side. Now he let himself fall upon his back. A star was beginning to twinkle in the deepening heavens, one impossibly distant from his own unhappiness. He stared at it until his eyes burned.

On the morrow they would reach the farm. The thought of entering his alcove with her still a maid clenched the pit of his stomach. It was the bed in which Jorild, thin and plain, had been so generous in her giving to him.

Ingirith was his wife; he must end this nonsense. His embrace had been welcomed by other women; she would learn to welcome it as well. He would not force her body; he could not see himself doing that, but she must see reason, and now.

"Should I take you back to your family's farm?' he asked her, still looking up at the sky.

Oke would be a laughing-stock and she the object of ridicule. A repudiated bride was next to unmarriageable; at best she would end up some old man's second or third wife.

He let his question sink in.

At last he felt her turn to him, one hand drawing her shift a little up her body.

He did not try to pull it off, just moved himself so he was over her, Ful's words sounding in his ears.

Chapter the Fifth

THE BABE

IT was not a scream Hrald heard, but a sharp cry. This was followed by a stream of female oaths, piercing and deliberate.

He came around the edge of the shed he had been hauling things from and into the kitchen yard. The fire frame and cauldron had been moved inside the house now Winter was here, but the work tables were still often in use. Near one stood Ingirith, less than an arms-length from Jorild. She was leaning towards her, almost on tip-toe, her arms rammed down the sides of her body, trembling in her anger. A wooden hauling bucket sat near her, its sides showing wet where the water had sloshed out when she set it down in haste. Jorild too was standing, shrinking back, face pale, her hands gathered in her curled-up apron.

"Slattern!" Ingirith repeated, hissing out the word. "We have barely enough to eat, and you get yourself with a brat!" She lurched at Jorild, and with an opened hand reached up and slapped the woman's face.

On the packed ground to one side of Jorild, someone had been sick. Hrald saw it now, saw beyond it. A woman with child often retched up her food.

Ingirith was moving in again, and Jorild making no attempt to avoid the coming blow.

Hrald strode forward. "Do not touch her," he ordered.

Ingirith jerked her head at him, her face distorted by the scowl upon it. She stared at her husband.

"It is your brat, is it?" she shrieked in demand. "Yours!"

Her eyes shifted, as if she were doing some reckoning in her head. She glared back at Hrald. "When all the time you were readying to wed me!"

Hrald looked at them both, Ingirith staring at him, Jorild barely able to raise her eyes. It was cold, and Jorild, shivering. The gown she wore was loose enough not to show any thickening of her body. But he realised now she must be four months along; it was the month of Blót.

He kept his voice as steady as he could, firm and steady. "Ingirith. Go to the house. Go."

She waited a moment longer, looking from him to Jorild, but did turn and leave.

Gillaug had run to her niece's side. She had known for some weeks that Jorild was with child, and knew too Hrald was the father; Jorild did not lie when asked. Gillaug had told her brother Oddi, who had taken in the news with a solemn nod; such things happened. Standing at Jorild's elbow now, Gillaug saw that Master himself did not know; it showed on his face.

Hrald came up to them. He wanted to put his hand on Jorild's arm. He did not. He could not even ask if it were true, and did not need to. Jorild lifted her eyes and looked at him. Hers were glittering with tears as she nodded her head once at him.

He heard himself breathe out a long breath. So be it, he thought, though his head was spinning.

"You will not be harmed," was what he told her.

Inside the house Ingirith was not raging. She was sitting slumped at the table, sobbing, her head in her arms.

"Ingirith," he said. "It is true. The child is mine."

She did not lift her eyes, and she did not stop crying.

"Send . . . her . . . away," she implored, her words little more than halting gasps. "Please. If you value me, send her away."

She did not sound like Ingirith. She was begging him, and Hrald bethought him that she had likely never done so to anyone before this moment. She turned her tear-streaked face to him, waiting for his answer.

He tried to think. Jorild had done nothing wrong. He had come to her alcove, and likely as not she felt she could not refuse him that first night, or any other. And her manner to him had been more than yielding, it had been willing, and even warm. To cast her away would be a grave injustice.

"I . . . I cannot," was all he could tell her. "It is my child, my doing."

His tumbling brain grasped at anything else he could tell her.

"I was with her for a few days only, after I came back." He did not know what more to say, but went on. "I was gone nearly a year. My mother had died. My stock was gone . . . "

"And you knew you were coming to wed me," she reminded, as she wept.

"Já," he admitted. There was little more he could say to that; he always knew he was soon to wed.

It was common enough for a man to have children with his serving women or thralls; what was hard was his doing so just before his hand-fast. He understood that.

She stared at him, her disbelief clear upon her face. He had made his choice. He would not send the woman away. To Ingirith it was declaration that her husband placed a former thrall-woman over his rightful wife. The insult was deepened by how plain the woman was. He had demeaned her own beauty in lying with Jorild.

"It is a shock, I know this," he offered.

His voice conveyed it had been mutual. He came to her now and placed his hand over hers. Their wedded life had not begun with any delight, but perhaps now they might go on together and begin anew.

"You did not know?" she asked. Her voice was calmer and held the surprise she felt.

He shook his head slowly. "I did not," he told her.

He had not known. That was something, Ingirith felt. She had discovered it before he had.

What he also did not know was that she herself was carrying his child. She could tell him now, fling it out at him, but decided to wait. She felt a stinging anger arise, that this ugly freedwoman would bear his child before she, his lawful wife, would. And the babes would be but three or four months apart. It was a doubled affront, one that made her want to shriek.

She pulled her hand out from under his.

"Where?" she demanded, wishing now to shame him. "Where did you take her?" She pointed at their alcove, curtains drawn. "In the bed which is ours? Or out in the hay-loft, as would be fitting?"

"Stop it," he ordered.

When he had heard her angry cries he had been gathering his kit to go down to the boat. He would oar her down the swollen stream and out into the North Sea channel. The fish he netted there once a week were a useful supplement to their food stores, and soon the seas would be too rough to go. It made him think of one thing Ingirith had said to Jorild.

"And we have plenty to eat." He looked at the back she had turned to him. He did not know what more he could say. "I am going now, to fish," he ended.

Out in the work yard Jorild had taken the abandoned bucket of water and spilled it over the mess she had made.

Once in the boat Hrald did not think of what he had just learned about Jorild, or even how Ingirith had reacted. He was thinking of the first day they spent as man and wife here on the farm. After he had moved her things in, he told Ingirith to bring the silver her parents had given her, and took her to the grain-house. There he showed her the spot where the family silver was secreted, showed her how to lift one short floorboard at the wall to make it easy to lift the other two.

"This is ours," he said, feeling some pleasure in being able to say so. "The silver my parents left, and that which I earned in Gotland."

He opened the several small jars for her, detailing what was in each, numbering the coins, showing her the hack-silver chunks of broken jewellery, and simple silver rod.

"Put your silver here," he said, replacing the crockery jars and making room for the pouch she carried. "It is the safest place on the farm; even King Horick's men did not find it."

But instead of dropping it in, she held it more closely to herself.

"This is the safest place for it," he repeated.

She dropped it in at last, and he replaced the boards, scuffing the grain dust over where he had been kneeling.

The next week he had need to lift the three floor boards again. Ingirith's pouch was not there. He opened every jar, making sure nothing else had been removed. All was accounted for.

"Your silver," he asked her. He did not need to say more than that.

"I have hid it myself," she answered. Where, she would not tell him.

Things did not improve as Winter deepened. Shut up as they often were inside the house, the enmity Ingirith bore for Jorild seethed in her breast. At last Hrald determined that new sleeping quarters be made for Jorild, and he and Oddi turned a little-used cattle shed into a small house for her and her aunt. They re-thatched the gaps in the roof and made tight the door, as well as the shutter at the single window. They dug a fire-pit in the middle of the place, and planked the soil around it, giving dry footing even in Winter rains. And they built two simple beds for the women.

Ingirith resented every hour Hrald spent doing so, and every scrap of linen that went to bedding and towelling for the women. But she dare not complain aloud. At least she was out of the house. And there was a rueful fitness, too, in the fact that she who would bear her husband's bastard should live in a cattle shed.

Ingirith's anger at Hrald was such that it kept her from telling that she too was with child. Her body betrayed the news the same way Jorild's had. Ingirith was standing at the soapstone cooking pot one dark morning, ladling a porridge of oats and dried peas into bowls. They were inside the house, the cooking frame having been moved there for cold weather. Of a sudden Ingirith began to heave, and dropping the ladle back into the pot, made for the door. Her belly was still empty and she retched up bile onto the damp ground. She wiped her mouth with her hand and straightened up. There was Jorild, walking from the well, carrying the bucket of water she had just drawn up. She paused when she saw Ingirith, then with her free hand pulled her mantle closer about her enlarged figure. Ingirith turned from her to see her husband in the door, come after her. He took in what had happened.

"You . . . " he began. There was almost wonder in his saying of it.

She drew herself up. The fact that Jorild knew as well made it all the more bitter.

"Já," she snapped. "Me. Your wife." She gave a short laugh.

"How long have you known," he asked.

It gave her satisfaction to tell the truth. "Many weeks."

"And you did not tell me." His voice did not mask his hurt.

He wanted to feel joy in this. He knew that he should. But no part of Ingirith gave him joy. He knew that she did not care for him on the day they wed, but hoped that this was something she would learn. But now he knew she did not like him, either, and perhaps loathed him. Her coolness to him had rapidly become coldness. Finding that

Jorild would bear his child had sealed her dislike of them both. Now she too would do the same, have his child. It was something he had done which had led to sorrow for both women. And it could not be undone, not unless the mother wished to rid herself of the coming babe. Then there were herbs that could be eaten, and brews drunk. Jorild had not done so, but she might think she did not have the right.

Ingirith just stared at him. She had been raised being told she would be Hrald's wife, and had accepted it. Then when he had vanished, and been absent so long, she thought herself free of her father's promise. Her eye had fallen on a handsome young smith, fallen, and then been filled by him and the dream she built around him.

This had been dashed by Hrald's appearance, and she could not summon her former acquiescence. She was right to be sulky, she had thought, and right to make him earn her affection. But when he threatened her with returning her to her father she had begun to hate him.

She knew she was pretty and deserved more. She should not be here, on yet another farm, but back at Ribe, or wherever that handsome tool-smith lived. Then to learn Hrald had taken that ugly thrall to bed . . .

Her face softened, looking at him, and she took his hand and placed it on her belly. She then said that which she thought would give him most hurt.

"Take care I do not drown the thing at birth," she told him.

Spring came. Jorild had grown large, and Ingirith too was showing that her own child would be born in Summer. Neither woman could work as they once did, and it was lambing time as well. Hrald and Oddi were busy too with planting.

When Jorild felt the first birthing pangs, Gillaug found Hrald out ploughing and told him. His neighbour Kol's widowed daughter was sent for; Oddi went to fetch her. Capable as Gillaug was, it took more than one woman to welcome a child to Midgard. There were spells that must be chanted, invocations uttered, thank-offerings promised. These things were secret to child-bearing women, but men knew of them, and that they must be observed. And Hrald would want the neighbouring woman afterwards, to witness for him.

Ingirith would do nothing for the woman, not even heat water or gather linens, and Hrald felt this a lack of some kind of common decency. As it was he listened to Jorild's groans coming from the shed, and finally went into the depths of the barn to muck out the cow stall. He could not continue his ploughing, and so put himself far from her cries; Oddi had taken the oxen he bought last year to bring aid for Jorild.

The babe took a long time coming, but all said first-born children often did. Being alone with Ingirith in the house was the worst part. She moved and acted to him as if he were not there, and with Gillaug busy had to put the meal on the table herself, banging the bowls and cups down as if she were a child.

Hrald spent a restless night lying next to the sleeping Ingirith. He rose at first light and went out into the kitchen yard. As he stood there, squinting in the gloom at the cow shed, its door opened, showing a figure outlined by the glow of the fire within. He moved forward. It was Gillaug.

"You have a son, Master," Gillaug said, a smile cracking her lined face. She gestured him in.

He had not been inside the shed since he and Oddi had finished outfitting it for the two women. Now he saw Kol's daughter sitting on a stool by one of the beds he had built, a bed which held the long form of Jorild. She was sitting up, but her eyes were closed. The babe was lying against his mother's breast, covered by a light blanket, so that only the dark little head could be seen.

He came closer, and Kol's daughter moved to let him near.

"Let me see him," Hrald asked. The lowness of his tone did not hide his wonder.

Jorild's eyelids fluttered open when he spoke. Gillaug lifted the infant up, Jorild's hand holding on to one tiny foot. She was smiling as she held it.

He sat down on the stool near the bed. "Give him to me," he said now.

Gillaug wrapped a piece of towelling around the babe, and handed him to his father.

Jorild had closed her eyes, the hand that had held the little foot falling back empty to her breast.

"Jorild," Hrald summoned. "Look at me."

He set the babe on his knee. "This is my son, freeborn, who I acknowledge as my own."

He raised his eyes to Kol's daughter, and to Gillaug, and they nodded. Having spoken these words before them, Hrald accepted his son, with witnesses to attest to the fact. This boy would be his heir. He looked last at Jorild.

The babe began to mewl, the red face scrunching, mouth seeking. Jorild slowly lifted her hands to him, and Gillaug placed the child back upon her breast.

Later that day Hrald returned to the shed. The babe had been washed and swaddled, and was sleeping next his mother.

"What will you name him," Jorild asked Hrald. For months she had hardly spoken to him, saying only what was strictly needed, and in the fewest possible words. Her voice now was that he remembered from their nights together, soft and warm in his ear.

It was a father's right to name his son, and often the name chosen was of the new father's own sire. But somehow Hroft did not fit this child, or his circumstances. He had no name ready.

"What would you name him," he posed to Jorild.

She looked down at the babe tucked up under her arm. He would be tall, they both were; and he would be dark. He had been born in sorrow, but Jorild did not think of the getting of him in sorrow.

"There was a great Jarl who lived long ago, who I heard tell of," she began. "His name was Sidroc."

Sidroc, thought Hrald. A fine name, and a strong one.

"Sidroc," he repeated.

Chapter the Sixth

ANOTHER

INGIRITH'S child was born at the time of the Thing, thus she and Hrald could not go. She had rashly told her parents they would visit over Winter, a promise she did not keep, and now she could not travel to the Summer gathering at which they, and all she knew, would be.

Kol's daughter was again fetched, and Ingirith grudgingly let Gillaug help her, but Jorild was as ever banned from the house. What Ingirith did not know was it was Jorild at the cooking ring in the kitchen yard, making broth and hotting water, and even carrying it within the house to set it on the large table, to save her aunt the steps. Jorild's own babe, Sidroc, was tied up on her back as she did this, and never out of sight or touch.

It was a girl Ingirith bore. When Jorild's child had been born and lived, and been not only perfect but a boy, Ingirith began to pray to Frigg, that her child be the same. She even wrung the neck of a hen in Offering, asking that her child be worthy. When it was born and found to be a girl she wished to scream.

Hrald welcomed her nonetheless, setting the child upon his knee and proclaiming it his. Ingirith saw the dark head of her daughter and grimaced in disgust. She wanted a babe with hair as fair as her own, as fair as the toolsmith's in Ribe.

She named the girl Ulfhildr. Wolf-battle, thought her father. Her mother gave her a bloody name, but the babe herself was mild and sweet-natured. Sidroc too was good-natured, quiet, watching all about him. When he began to crawl Ingirith tried to bar him from her threshold, extending the same ban from the house that lay upon his mother. Hrald put swift end to that.

"He is my son, and heir, and will come and go from my house as he will," he decreed.

Ingirith bit her tongue; there was nothing she could say to that. But there was plenty she could say to Jorild.

"Wean him quick," Ingirith told her one day when she came upon suckling child and mother. The leaves had all fallen from the trees, but by the kitchen fire it was still warm enough to sit outside. Jorild made bold to speak for her son.

"Mistress. He is too young to wean."

The quietness of her statement gave Ingirith pause. She did not want to be known as a woman who had caused a babe's death. She said nothing in return.

When a few weeks later she saw Jorild feeding the boy scraps of milk-soaked bread, she spoke again.

"Wean him, so you can go," she told Jorild.

"We will go," Jorild said. She had thought this day not too far in coming, but hoped it would not be in Winter.

"You will go," Ingirith corrected. "The boy stays here, with his father."

Ingirith spoke without thinking; now she grasped what she had just said. Her husband had time and again placed this ugly woman and her get before her – a boy that in her eyes was little more than a slave. Hrald would be forced to agree to the child staying, but the thrall-woman going. They had both injured her, and now she saw she could punish both.

"The boy stays," she repeated. "That is the law."

It was the law, and the boy's mother knew it. A freeman had rights over that of the mother, if she were a freedwoman, or a thrall. Hrald could keep his son, and Jorild felt that surely he would want to.

If she took Sidroc with her he would be raised amongst those once thralls, as she herself was. She could give him nothing but a life in a dirt-floored hut. If he stayed with his father he would be seen by all as free. His father had a farm with livestock and her Uncle Oddi to help run it, and Hrald had silver too.

Jorild must leave, and her aunt would not stay without her. They need not go back to the holding she and Gillaug had been released from. Gillaug had a married daughter further North, with a croft large enough to take them in. Skilled hands such as theirs were always welcome.

They would wait until the boy was a year old. It pained Hrald, but they could not go on as they had. Ingirith was hard, with no tenderness in her, and Jorild's presence was making her worse.

Hrald said his goodbyes to the two women at the door of the shed they had lived in. Everything was swept and tidy; Hrald did not know an earthen floor about a fire-pit could be so clean. Oddi had harnessed the oxen and would take them in the farm cart.

Hrald had a sum of silver in a tiny leathern pouch, which he pressed in Gillaug's hand; he could not bring himself to give it into the hand of the mother of his son, as if she had been a whore. Sidroc was hanging from her skirts as Hrald spoke.

"Jorild. I am sorry to have brought this upon you. Thank you for giving me a son. Even though you go, he will always be yours, and ours.

"I will raise him as my father raised me. There is no taint upon him, nor will there ever be. He is my full son in every way."

Her eyes were reddened and beyond tears; she had spent all night weeping. She picked up her boy and passed him into his father's arms. Then she turned, and with Gillaug climbed into the oxcart with Oddi.

As they rolled away Sidroc began to reach his arm after her, then to cry. Jorild did not turn in her seat to see him; to do so was beyond her strength. Her boy pressed one hand against his father's chest, straining after her.

Ingirith had come out, and stood at the threshold of the house. Ulfhildr was in her arms, and seeing and hearing Sidroc cry, began herself to wail.

Chapter the Seventh

ALWAYS BE REACHING

WITH Jorild gone, things seemed at first to go better for Ingirith. She did not pet or spoil the boy, but when Spring came around again and a travelling trader commented that she had a fine son, Ingirith did not scowl, but rather looked upon Sidroc and nodded. If she must go to the trouble of raising the boy she might as well take credit for producing him.

Ingirith was a thrifty house-keeper and brooked no idleness in the two serving women and male thrall who now lived at the farm. She made no attempt to hide her dislike of Oddi, and Hrald was at pains to keep them apart, at last ordering Ingirith to leave the man entirely to Hrald's direction. She was civil to Hrald before these dependents, but alone they spoke as little to each other as they did when they worked alongside the others.

As soon as her daughter Ulfhildr was weaned Ingirith wanted another child. If there had been amity between man and wife Hrald would have looked forward to his nights with her. But Ingirith had never lost her coldness to him. He knew she was pretty, a woman other men might envy sleeping next to, but lying with her brought release for his body and nothing more. He felt her stillness and lack of response was a rebuff not only of his attempted caresses, but of he himself. When she told him she was again with child it was hard to take pleasure in the news; she paid little mind to their daughter and almost ignored Sidroc.

Hrald did not know his wife's ardent thoughts were focussed on another: the Goddess Frigg. Frigg was wife to All-Father Odin, and patroness of married women, and child-birth. Ingirith wanted a son. In secret she made Offering to the Goddess, wringing the necks of cocks, pouring milk at the roots of a chosen birch. But just as she had once turned her face away from her young husband, the Goddess Frigg turned her face from Ingirith, spurning her offerings, ignoring her pleas for a son.

Her second child was again a girl. The babe was perfect in body, crying lustily on its way into Midgard. Ingirith looked down on the little stranger lying on her breast and wept. Even the Goddess thwarted her.

"I do not know what you want," Hrald told her not long after this. Indeed, she could not seem to find contentment in anything.

She again turned her face away. I want the life at Ribe I lost when you returned, she was thinking. Life with the tool-smith, a snug house in the town, a basket over my wrist and silver brooches at my shoulders.

As time had passed this had become far more than a mere possibility to Ingirith; the love of the handsome smith, the small house, the smart brooches, all were assured, all within her grasp if Hrald had not appeared. It was as if he had snatched them from her. She did not forget this, and she could not forgive him.

One Summer when they travelled back to Oke's farm to see her folk they stopped as well at that of Signe and Ful. Signe had given birth to a child at the same time Sidroc had been born, a boy they had named Toki. When Ingirith saw him running about – yellow-haired and blue-eyed, laughing – she blanched, making her pale skin the whiter. This is what her son should look like.

It was the second time they had made the journey to Ingirith's parents, which meant the older couple had before seen and accepted Sidroc as Hrald's son. Now the boy was of speaking age, watching all, interested in everything. Hrald knew Sidroc was not the beautiful child Toki was, but was proud of him nonetheless. Oke made show of carrying the boy on his shoulders, an act which made Ingirith bite her lip and turn away.

During their stay her father asked them if they would like to make the trip up to Ribe; he recalled how much his eldest daughter liked going there. Her refusal was so swift and definite to be noted by all. She feared seeing the handsome tool-smith again; feared seeing a young woman, less pretty than she, with a babe tied on her back walk smiling to the forge bringing her husband his mid-day meal. In the end Hrald travelled up with his father-in-law and young Sidroc. Hrald wanted to see Ribe, and he did not want to leave the boy in the keeping of his wife as he did so. And Ingirith had her hands full, Ulfhildr scampering about, the younger girl still in arms.

The wheel of the year kept turning. The farm did as well as could be expected of a small holding. The land was low lying, and in Spring, rising tides and heavy rains would swell the river, flooding the margins of the fields. Hrald and Oddi deepened the drainage trenches, and the sodden soil warmed and dried in the lengthening days. Winters brought more wet, and snow, but Hrald rarely feared hunger from black-rot on his rye, or animals failing to thrive. Crops and beasts did well enough. It was house and kitchen yard that troubled him.

Ingirith was hard on all the children, even her own. Her irritation was greatest with Sidroc, and betrayed itself in every way. She would force the comb through his tangled hair, pulling on it and making him flinch. She was little gentler with her daughters. Hrald saw this, and felt his helplessness in the face of it; they were all small, and he and Oddi and the thrall out in the fields most of each day. If his mother Ashild were still alive they would have found a friend in her, and not just had him to defend them. He did not believe her parents had treated her thus; he had seen enough of them by now to judge. Perhaps she did not recall her own girlhood.

One day when Sidroc had been harshly punished by her for some minor offence, Hrald went to the boy, who he found behind the grain-house. Sidroc was kneeling on the ground, his arms around the hunting hound. The boy's face was buried in the dog's neck.

"Mother does not like me," the boy told his father when he looked up.

The hound Hlaupari had raised his head at Sidroc's words, and was looking up at Hrald as well. Sidroc had trained the hound to come to his whistle, and the dog was often at his side.

Hrald looked down at his son. Ingirith had given birth a third time a few months earlier, to another girl. She did not try to hide her ire at this, and had turned on Hrald the night of the birth and bitterly accused him of depriving her of a son of her own.

Now he looked at Sidroc and felt moved to tell him the truth, young as he was.

"Sidroc," he began. He squatted down to be nearer to the boy's level. "She is not your mother."

He paused a moment, saw his son's eyes fixed upon him.

"The woman who was your mother – she cared for you," Hrald found himself saying. "She was a freedwoman. She was here at the farm when I came back from Gotland.

"She was a good woman, hardworking. And most of all she was kind. She could not stay long after your birth, but . . . "

Hrald's hand had gone to rest upon the hound's head as he told his son this. He did not forget that the beast had been saved from death by Oddi, the uncle of Sidroc's mother. Even in his own mind he did not quite think of Oddi as his son's kin, though he knew he was. He rubbed and pulled at Hlaupari's furry ear now.

Sidroc knew six Summers at this point, and did not ask his father any question about what he had just been told. There was much he did not understand, but he knew what he had just heard to be important, to both his father, and to he himself. And he knew it was something not to be spoken about, save to his father alone; his father's tone conveyed that.

After this Ingirith's scolding and frequent cuffing were easier for Sidroc to take. If his father were near he would stop her, but sometimes he was far afield and Sidroc would have to bear it.

What his father had told him made a difference to the boy. Without his father having said so, he knew that he did not deserve the treatment he met at Ingirith's hands. He felt that there was something more outside of his life, something good that had happened before which had changed things and made him who and what he was. And he felt too there might be something to come in his future which might do the same.

Sidroc did not forget that Gotland was a part of what his father had said. His father had told him of this distant island, and that he had spent happy and adventuresome days walking its coasts and forests, and spent a night sleeping at the feet of frozen trolls. When his father spoke of this place his face and voice were different, recalling his time there. In Sidroc's mind his true mother was a part of that difference, too.

The farm did well. All upon it worked hard, and King Horik's men, when they arrived each harvest-tide, demanded only the normal taxes each year. The stream down which Hrald took his small boat flooded in heavy rains, ruining parts of the rippling fields of rye, oats, and barley, but there was never hunger. Hrald fished as he could, guiding the boat down to the North Sea, and there dropping his nets for herring, haddock, cod, and salmon. When the leaves were falling from the trees he took to the woodlands, bow in his hand, quiver at his hip, to stalk the red deer that leapt there, and the big and strutting wood grouse. Now that Sidroc was old enough he sometimes went with his father, both to fish, and to hunt.

One day in mid-Summer Hrald was surprised to see a group of men appear at his gate, several of them bearing spears. Calling out to him was Ful, his sister Signe's husband. Their farm had not done as well, and he had joined up with a few other farmers and gone raiding at the start of Summer. Now he was back, and stopping on his way home.

"To Angle-land," Ful said in satisfaction, lifting the cup of ale a serving woman had brought them.

"Angle-land," repeated Hrald. This was where the large white crystals of salt were from, that which had taken him to Gotland to trade.

They sat with three other men, Ful's confederates in his venture, all younger than he. Off to one side, shackled together at the wrist with iron chains, sat five men and boys of Angle-land, their yield in their raiding. To Hrald's knowledge Ful had never gone slaving before, but had surely met with success now.

Ful saw Hrald eying the men. "Do you need a thrall?" he asked. "I can part with the young one, and for a good price."

The youth Ful spoke of had no more than thirteen or fourteen Summers, Hrald thought. The way he sat close to an older man made him think they were father and son. Now Ful offered him the son.

As they sat thus, looking on the slaves, Sidroc came up to his father.

"He has grown," Ful observed. "The son of a thrall-woman, no? Too bad I have only men to offer you now." He laughed at his own words.

"Sidroc is free-born; his mother was a freedwoman," Hrald corrected, not masking the edge in his voice. Ful knew this, and for years.

Sidroc had hung back slightly, but now stepped forward. He narrowed his eyes at Ful in a way that told his father that he too did not like the man. Ful had his cup of ale to his face and did not see.

Hrald looked back at the new thralls. They had been allowed to haul water from the well, and had drunk deeply of it, washing their faces afterwards. Their clothes were tattered, and of course they bore no knives at this point; anything of value they had owned had been taken by Ful and his fellow venturers. They may have had small crofts of their own back home, or been part of some war-chief's holdings. The slaves were by now careful not to look directly at their captors; a bold gaze invited a punishing blow. Coming from Angle-land they had been at sea and on the road for more than two weeks, mayhap more, and had learnt this. And some may have been slaves at home.

Hrald could use another hand, especially with the animals, and the boy looked handy. Despite the hardship of travel they were a good-looking lot, all fair-haired, all well-formed. The boy's father was broad of shoulder, showing that son might grow strong as well. Hrald now saw the older man's arm was wrapped with a scrap of fabric at the forearm above the wrist; he must have been injured when captured. The boy Ful was offering him was about the same age as Yrling, his brother.

Hrald shook his head. He would not separate father and son. And he knew he could not afford both.

"How is my brother," Hrald asked instead.

"Yrling," said Ful. "Too clever by half, but strong as an ox. He is doing his share of work in my absence, I wager. It is Toki who needs birching every week. I missed in naming him; he should be Loki."

Loki, the trickster God, who was always getting himself and the other residents of heavenly Asgard in trouble. Hrald knew Ful had a quick hand for punishment, and was glad Yrling was getting little or none of it.

Ingirith had come out. She had of a sudden nine more mouths to feed for the night, and she resented every one of them.

Ingirith did not like Ful, who she had caught on more than one occasion in the past leering at her. She could guess that now Ful was trying to sell at least one thrall to Hrald. She took in the yellow-haired slaves, saw one was a boy. She watched Hrald consider him. She had produced no son in her marriage, no boy to work alongside his father, or to inherit the farm with her when he died. There was only Sidroc, and her three useless girls. Hrald had named Sidroc his heir, and until she gave him a son so it would remain. Mayhap then he would see reason and send the dark and clumsy thing to its ugly mother.

A few days later, before the Sun had crowned the line of birch trees rimming the farm, Hrald took his son and his fishing gear and headed to the boat. He was teaching the boy to handle boat and net, and their times spent thus were a pleasure to them both. It was early enough that a scrim of mist shrouded the grasses they trod to where the small craft lay waiting, and their shoes were made wet by the dew. The odour of the fresh water, a bright and green scent, rose to their noses as they pushed her down the mud of the bank and through the reeds.

The boat was large enough for two sets of oars, but Sidroc could not yet span the distance between them with any strength, so he took a single oar and used it to help guide the prow as his father oared them down stream and to the North Sea. It was a broad channel they came to, for a barrier island sat between them and true open water, but the fishing was oftentimes good none the less, as schools of smaller fish were chased by whales to shelter in the lee.

Once out into the channel the current could be swift, and this morning there was a head wind to contend with as well. This gave a fair amount of chop to the water, which Sidroc liked as it brought to mind what riding a bucking horse must be like. His father was now busy over the deep basket, drawing forth the carefully-gathered fishing net which they would drop. Sidroc took up the other end, the body of the net draped at his feet. As they began to lower it a knotted loop caught on his oar-lock, and the boy leaned over to free it. The boat then lurched in such a way that he was pitched, still holding to the net-edge, over the side.

Hrald's back had been slightly turned away from his son as they began to feed out the net. He felt the swell of the sea against the boat hull, and saw the shifting body of his son as he was cast overboard. He saw too one of Sidroc's feet entangle in the net as he fell. Then he was struck by the splash, cold and salty, as his son hit.

Hrald lurched forward, rocking the little craft hard to port as he gathered up handfuls of the fishnet. He knew he was yelling, but could hear only Sidroc's sputtering cries. The boy was caught in the net, thrashing as he reached one free arm out of the water. The smooth steatite ovals that served as net weights were heavy, and pulling him down.

The broad net had never seemed larger than it had that moment. Hrald yanked in lengths of it, as his son's desperate actions pulled more of the webbing in after him. With one great heave Hrald drew Sidroc close enough to reach the small extended hand and grasp it. With the boat's gunwale perilously close to the water Hrald was able to haul his son back in.

Sidroc was gasping, but the force with which he clung to his father told Hrald he had not swallowed enough water to begin to drown. He choked some up, Hrald keeping an arm about his waist in support. He was still entwined in the net, and only when Sidroc's breathing began to steady did Hrald start to free it. The boy was shivering, his teeth chattering in his head. Hrald pulled off his tunic and wrapped Sidroc in it, and swept the dark hair from his son's wet face. He held him close against his chest.

The net, of which Hrald always took great care, lay in a confused mass around them. He did not know if it were rent, and did not care if it were. He would look at it later. Now they must get back to shore. He waited until Sidroc let go of him, then began to ball up the fishnet. There was something dark caught inside.

"Here are your shoes," he said, and smiled at Sidroc. "But next time remember that we need no bait to net herring."

The boy was able to grin at that, and nodded.

"And you still have your knife," his father noted, seeing it at his son's waist. Last Summer Hrald had given

Sidroc his first small blade, and had been teaching the boy to handle it. Sometimes they whittled figures of horses or birds for the girls, as play-things, and Sidroc had already carved a comb for himself. His father looked at the soaked belt and sheath that bore it. "We will oil the leather tonight, to get the salt out of it," he told him. Any trifling reassurance of routine after such a scare was welcome.

Hrald oared for their inlet. They were back at the farm much earlier than expected, and with no fish to show for it. None of this mattered. They walked to the kitchen yard, where one of the serving-women ladled up hot broth for Sidroc. Hrald sat across from him, just looking at his son.

"I will teach you to swim," his father told him, when he had drained the bowl.

It was true that part of the fright for both of them was Sidroc's being caught in the net, but he did not want this to mark the boy with fear of water ever after.

"Now?" Sidroc asked. He had chores to do, now they were back.

"Já, now. We will go to the lake. Oddi and the others do not expect us until later anyway."

The lake was a small one, but far enough away to make the walk there rare. Going was a treat, and Sidroc had never been there alone with his father. And Hrald felt nothing more important. So they set out.

As the morning lengthened they felt the height of Summer's heat, a warmth gratefully received by both as they walked along the trackways they followed. Lindens grew there, the fragrance of their pale flowers heavy and sweet. It hung in the air as the view opened up before them. The lake was ringed by slender birches, and bushy stands of young beeches. The water was almost still, the dark-leaved beeches casting green ripples over it. It could not have been more unlike the churn and blow of the sea channel. The banks were firm, with a few places gone to sedge. They stripped off their clothing and waded in.

Hrald had learnt how to swim in this very lake, and now taught Sidroc as Hroft had taught him. Even when the water was up to Hrald's waist it was still warm, and with that softness to it that lake-water always bears. The bottom yielded underfoot, as if almost sand.

"Watch me," Hrald said, and cast himself, belly-down, full-length into the water. The long arms reached out, grabbing handfuls of water as the long legs thrashed up and down. But he stayed up on the lake's surface, moving steadily before his son's eyes.

Before Hrald could stand and come back to Sidroc, the boy had cast himself in. His eyes opened wide as he sunk, arms flailing. Hrald swooped in with one kick and caught the boy up around his middle, and threw him into shallow waters. His father was laughing, which Sidroc always liked to hear, and always wished he heard more of.

"You must move your legs, too, and at the same time," his father advised. He had Sidroc lay full length in the water, and pull water with both arms, and kick his legs as he held him up.

"You do well," Hrald told him, as Sidroc began to move along the bright surface. The boy was thin, and so tall that he looked older than his seven years. His father showed him again how to stretch out his arms, cup the water, and pull it back towards him. "Always be reaching."

Always be reaching, Sidroc repeated to himself, as they waded back to shore. He had kept reaching his hand up earlier that day, and his father had caught it and saved him. Always be reaching.

They sat on the shore, the Sun falling on their backs and shoulders, warming their bodies and the air around them. Whirring insects, large and small, dropped from that warm air to hover over the surface of the water. Hrald remembered his times sitting here with Hroft, and the filmy wings of insects just like these dipping and darting before their eyes. As they watched them Hrald began to speak.

"There is something that we share, Sidroc, something in our blood-bond."

He was aware that his boy's eyes, which had been trained on the tiny bodies flitting above the water, were now turned to him.

"It is our fylgja. Our guardian-spirit. She comes from my father to me, and from me to you."

"She?"

"Fylgyur are always female. Every family has one, passed along, shared within it."

"What does she do?"

His father made a soft laugh. "Nothing. It is up to us to listen to her, listen for her.

"If we do so she can guide us, help us make the right decision."

"What does she look like," Sidroc wanted to know.

His father considered.

"Think of the most beautiful woman you can imagine. She looks like that."

He told his son this, even though he sometimes wondered if his fylgja was not almost a child-spirit; there was a kind of innocence about her. But Sidroc could discover that part later. Right now it might be more useful to imagine her womanly, and wiser than he.

"Do the girls have one," he asked now, thinking of his little sisters.

"Já, já. All do. But some do not listen. Some never feel their presence."

"How . . . how do I feel her?"

"You will sense her. Here." Hrald tapped his own chest, which made Sidroc lift his hand to his own. "If there is a decision that must be made, make yourself still, here. Listen for an answer. Often it will come. You will know if it is right. Sometimes you will even feel your fylgja move within you, as if she is nodding her head, Já, or shaking it, telling you not to do that."

Sidroc was sitting at his side, blinking up at him, but also nodding his head, absorbing, not questioning. The stillness of the place, the beauty of it, the swim together after the fright of the morning, all lent quiet force to that which they shared now.

Hrald thought of what more he could say. The times he had sensed his fylgja moving within him had led to the best outcomes in his life. But sometimes she had had no part in the path he must walk. Hrald had not asked his fylgja if he should wed Ingirith. That decision had been made for him. And there were many forces that intervened in men's lives, for good or ill. Magic and sorcery could bend anything. And the Gods could cause great mischief if they chose.

They walked back to the farm. The hound Hlaupari barked his welcome, and ran to Sidroc as he always did. Äse, Sidroc's youngest sister, was tottering around the base of the fowl-house. Ulfhildr and Thyrvi, the middle girl, came out from the dim interior, a shallow basket clutched to each small chest.

Sidroc grinned at his sisters. "I can swim," he announced.

As the older girls were clamouring over this achievement, Ingirith came out from the house. She had the forked beating-stick that she used to clout the grit from the bedding in her hand, a tool which the three older children had also felt. Both Sidroc and Ulfhildr fell silent for a moment, wondering if she would use it on them. The hound slunk away. Sidroc stepped closer to his father, almost without knowing it. But she looked at the group and pressed her lips tighter together, and went to where the feather cushions from her bed were sunning. From the way she beat the pillows that her sister-in-law Signe had presented her, one might think she meant to burst their linen tickings.

Hrald watched her. He could not tell her that Sidroc, caught in a fishing net, had nearly drowned this morning. She cared nothing for Sidroc, and disdained, if not hated, him. The distress he had felt would move her not, and she would be happy to be rid of his son. Looking at her, slapping the dust from their wedding gift, he felt his loneliness as a man more sharply than he ever had.

"Do not ever use that on the children again," he found himself saying to her.

It was so unexpected, and his voice so grave, that her hand froze in mid-stroke. She turned her head to look at her husband, and then whacked the beating-stick down into the pillow in a single stroke of fury.

Grain harvest came, the fields bleaching from green to gold. Every morning Hrald squeezed a maturing kernel, feeling its progress from soft and milky to hard and ripe. Each small plot of oats, rye and barley was now ready to be scythed, gathered, threshed; and the rye and oats winnowed as well. Hrald and Oddi and the thrall worked almost from dawn to dusk of each hot and dry day. Sidroc worked at the threshing, beating the dried stalks of rye and oats with a grain-bat to free the seed heads, and he and Ulfhildr at winnowing, tossing the freed heads in the cross-breeze of the barn. This was dusty but light work for the youngsters, as the crisp chaff blew away, and the dense nugget of grain dropped to the tarpaulin spread on the floor.

Ingirith and the two serving women worked at the digging and storing of the first root vegetables. Turnips, parsnips, onions, carrots, beets, and many-fingered cream-coloured skirrets yielded to their prising tools. These were laid in the deep root cellars, their thatched roofs just set above the surface of the soil, where they would stay cool yet free of damaging frost. The last bean stalks were stripped and the pods cracked open to dry the plump beans within. The cabbages, left alone along their rows in the plot, grew huge, immense furling spheres of swirling green and white.

One day when the laying-in of the grain harvest was almost complete Hrald left Oddi to walk to the kitchen yard. The jug of water he had taken to the grain-house had been emptied into their thirsty throats, and he went himself to refill it at the well, glad to clear the dust from his eyes and nose. It was late in the afternoon and he would not be surprised to see Ingirith there, ready to begin the making of their evening meal. But as he rounded the corner he heard a stifled cry, followed by a stream of shrill invective.

There was Ingirith, pinching Sidroc's ear at the lobe with one hand, as she thrashed him with the forked beating-stick across his back and legs. The boy had pulled so in his attempt to flee that she had ripped his ear, and a trickle of blood flowed from it and down his neck. He was now pushing her away as best he could, his head bent at a painful angle as she gripped his earlobe. A large pottery bowl lay in pieces on the ground.

Hrald yelled out as he lunged, dropping the jug in the dust. His hand was on his wife's shoulder an instant later, whirling her about as he broke her grip on Sidroc. He snatched the birch beating fork from her right hand and snapped it in two, throwing it at her feet.

"Your filthy get from that ugly bitch," she shrieked. "As clumsy and as stupid as you!"

Hrald could take no more. He reached out and slapped Ingirith across the face, and hard. She staggered back, almost falling, both hands going to her cheek.

Sidroc was holding his own hand to his bleeding ear, and crying. Hrald now saw the two serving women, hustling away and out of sight. From the open door of the house Ulfhildr, in tears, peered out, her two younger sisters clinging to her.

"We will part, Ingirith," Hrald was saying. His own anger made his voice hoarse. "We will sunder this marriage."

Oddi had appeared, drawn by the noise, yet had stayed well back, as was fitting. Hrald saw him, and moved his head in his direction. "Oddi is witness to what I tell you.

"I will do now what I wish I had done the second night of our union, send you back to your father. You will take your wedding-goods and go. Begin now to pack up your things. You will leave tomorrow, with the oxcart to carry you. I will give you half the silver we have earned. But you will go."

Her head was ringing from the blow, but his words were clear enough, though she could not believe them. The laws of Dane-mark made it simple for any union to be dissolved, and many unhappy couples parted. Ingirith did not like Hrald and despised Sidroc, but she had never told her husband she wanted the marriage dissolved. It felt a shock, akin to the repudiation she feared on the road here, eight years ago. That a maid as pretty and desirable as she should be rejected by her new husband would have been a shame beyond recovery. It was even worse now; she had seven and twenty years and could not hope to attract a fitting man. The Goddess ignored her, and she hated herself for having brought forth only daughters. Who would want her, with three girls? She was proving she could not get a boy.

She had nothing to hold him by, no son she could threaten to take from his father. "I will take the girls," she spat back.

Hrald cared for them, and the loss of them would pain him, but he told her the truth. "They are better off with their grandmother, who is a good woman."

She howled. "You – you have wrought some spell-work on me, so that I could not bear a boy. Some dark Gandr-work to keep that thrall's son your heir!"

The accusation caught Hrald up. Sorcery was practised by women, almost never by men. It was a woman's craft and any man found casting spells was suspected of unmanliness. This made him liable to attack, even murder, by other men. To say this to him was akin to questioning his manhood.

His shoulders had slumped, and he stood staring at her. She had dropped her hands from her face, and he saw the imprint of his hand on her inflamed cheek.

"I have been too easy on you," was all he could say. "Would I had sent you home that night, before you could wreak such mischief on us all. Já, you will take our daughters; it is your right. But do not pretend you care for them.

"And I could name anyone my heir." He reached his arm out now towards Sidroc, and pulled the boy to him. "But I am glad I have a true son from a good woman to serve thus."

All was over for him, she saw, but she did not like the ending. She thought it a feeble threat, but said the next with as much force as she could muster. "If you send me away you will never see the girls again. Never."

Hrald looked to where the three stood whimpering in the doorway. They were innocent of all of this, as innocent as his son. He must trust that their grandmother would give them what they could not find in their mother. Right now he must leave them with Ingirith.

Hrald turned and left the kitchen yard, Sidroc at his side, and Oddi just behind them. He walked so swiftly that even with his own long stride the boy had almost to trot to keep up with him. When they reached the last outbuilding, Hrald stopped. He looked about him, as if dazed, then bent to his son. The ear had stopped bleeding, but the tear was a ragged one. He felt a new flush of rage that Ingirith would so misuse his boy.

"Sidroc," he said. "All will be better now. You and I will stay here, and have the life I always wanted for you." He crossed his arms over his son's back as Sidroc's arms spanned his waist. Hrald did not know how to comfort the boy, and drew on a recent day that had brought them both fright, and then happiness.

"We will return to the lake soon, and swim, continue your lessons," he promised. This made Sidroc tighten his arms around him, and nod his head. It had been the best day the boy had known.

Hrald let out a long breath, then held the boy at arm's length.

"I will bring my young brother Yrling to live with us, as I always wanted. He will be as an older brother to you, and I will learn to know him again. We will make our way." He lifted his head, looking also at Oddi.

"Go now, back to the house," he told them. They had stopped before the hut in which the fishing gear was stowed. "I am going fishing. Stay with Oddi," he told Sidroc. "She will not try to hurt you again."

"Let me go with you," Sidroc asked.

His father shook his head. "I must be alone. I need to think." He looked at the sky; it was late in the day. He rarely took the boat save at dawn, when winds were light and the sea calmest. "I will not be long," he promised. "But I must be alone now, and think."

Chapter the Eighth

WHY DO YOU LOOK UP?

HRALD did not return that night.

Sidroc had gone back to the house as his father had asked him. He splashed his face and bathed his torn and aching ear. He and his sisters were ladled a silent meal by the serving women; Ingirith did not appear. When the washing up was complete and his sisters gone off to their box beds he lingered in the kitchen yard with Oddi and the serving women. As the light began to dim Oddi walked down with Sidroc to where the boat should be. It was gone, and there were clear signs of his father having launched it. Sidroc could even see the imprint where the net basket had rested in the tall grass; the green blades were still bent from the weight. Hlaupari had come with them, and the big dog's tail beat a steady rhythm against Sidroc's leg.

The wind had risen, and now it carried a trace of salt brine to their noses. There was a shift in the fading light, and the clouds that seemed to sit behind the trees on the other side of the stream bank grew black.

"He is a good boatman," Oddi said, after a long silence. "If he met trouble, he would bring her to shore."

Oddi had at times gone out with Hrald when he was a youth. Hroft's shoulder ailed him in old age, and he would send Oddi and his son, confident in their ability.

Sidroc nodded, wanting to believe this. He knew he was a good swimmer, too.

Oddi led him back to the house. Other than the thrall and serving women still in the kitchen yard, all was quiet. Hlaupari usually slept outdoors, but Sidroc let him come in; he wanted his company. The curtains on his parents' alcove were drawn shut. When all were within, Oddi locked the front door, and slid the bar against that to the kitchen yard. Sidroc undressed and got into bed, but he did not lie down. He sat up, his back against the wooden dividing wall, listening. He sat a long time, waiting to hear the sound of his father's key in the big iron box-lock. His father always had his key with him, and the door was left locked from the inside after dark. Sidroc would hear his father's key rattling as it lifted the inner latch. His hound was on the floor boards just outside his alcove, and he knew he would bark his welcome when that happened.

At last he slipped out of bed and dressed. Hlaupari thumped his tail against the floor and rose as well. The door key was on the hook by the frame, where Oddi had hung it, and he turned it in the lock and let himself and his dog out.

Oddi found Sidroc on the bank of the stream in the morning. His hound was by his side, sitting up, and his barking when Oddi approached awoke Sidroc.

The boy sat on the damp grass, looking up at Oddi as he told him what he already knew, his father had not come back. Oddi's face turned down the stream. "He is a good boatman," he repeated. He was unable to look at Sidroc as he said it.

On the third day Oddi left, a pack on his back, to trace the stream to the sea. He might find word of Hrald, or of his boat. Sidroc wanted to go with him, but Ingirith would not permit this. She had awakened the day before to the news that her husband had taken the boat and not returned. "Would he had taken you too," was all she said to Sidroc. She had done nothing to pack up her goods, he saw that.

Her sulkiness was replaced by bouts of crying, a sudden sobbing that startled the serving women and left the girls hanging on to each other. Sidroc did his chores of carrying and stacking kindling, feeding the pigs, and penning and unpenning the geese, but otherwise spent the days at the stream bank, Hlaupari wandering though the grasses as he waited.

Ulfhildr came with him once but sitting there made her cry, and she ran back to the house. Hlaupari was never sad, and if he got restless would chase a resting fulmar from the water's surface back into the air, heading for the North Sea. Sidroc watched the birds soar, knowing they set out for open water, knowing that his father lived; but not believing he would leave him behind.

He was there when Oddi returned, and heard the story twice, the second time back in the farm yard. Oddi had walked up and down the coast for a day in either direction, looking for signs of the boat, asking any he met. None had seen man or vessel, but all told of the squall that whipped the waves to froth between the island channels and the North Sea.

Ingirith listened, saying nothing. The sea that should have taken him nine years ago had finally done so.

Oddi shifted from foot to foot as he went on. "Would you have me go to his sister, that she might know, Mistress?" He was not looking at her face, but almost at her shoes, as he addressed her.

Hrald's wife did not hear him. She had felt panic and anger and wept the most violent tears of her life in these past days. Now the surety that she was not to be driven away after all began to expand in her constricted breast. Hrald could not send her back, not now. She would not return to her parents in shame, three girls in tow.

She turned on the four children.

"You father is dead," she told them.

The children had been face to face with death before they could speak: the wrung neck of a non-laying hen, the cracked skull and slit throat of a pig, the limp plumed wood grouse and brawny deer their father hunted, the long-eared hares he snared. But to picture their father thus was beyond their ken; their faces showed it. Beasts needed to die that they might live and be fed. That he who provided for them was now also dead made no sense.

Saying it aloud made it real for Ingirith: her husband was dead. Hrald had ruined her youth, but at least he had not taken everything from her. She was free. She wanted no ill gossip, and would wait a twelve-month, but then could wed again. She would lose no time now in claiming some scrap of happiness for herself.

Sidroc was standing next to Ulfhildr, and closest to Oddi. Ulfhildr's eyes had grown round, and now were squeezing shut as she lowered her head. Her long brown hair fell over her shoulders and was caught up in her small hands as she lifted them to her face. She began to cry, quietly, but her younger sisters saw it and began themselves to weep. Sidroc could not look at them, and found himself moving closer to Oddi.

He heard Ingirith say something to the man, and saw her wave him out of her sight. Sidroc followed Oddi out of the yard.

Oddi did not stop walking until they passed the cattle shed. It was the hut Sidroc had been born in, and was now returned to its use for cows. Once out of its shadow Oddi turned to the boy at his side.

It took a while for Oddi to say anything. Sidroc, looking up at him, noticed for the first time how lined Oddi's face was.

"Master," he said to Sidroc. "I am sorry."

Oddi had always called Sidroc by his name, and did not like that he called him by the title he used for his father. It was another change, one that made him feel cold.

He could not tell Oddi what he felt, that Ingirith had lied. His father was alive. He knew this. He went out on the boat to fish and to think. He would never leave him like this; he had just told him they would go swimming soon. His father lived.

He said the only words his lips could form, the same Oddi had told him.

"He is a good boatman."

Oddi nodded once, then looked away.

Ingirith had turned and walked back into the house. She went to the closed curtains of her sleeping alcove and pulled the heavy woollen wadmal panels open. She thrust her hand beneath the box bed, reaching until her fingers touched a firm scrap of fabric. She pulled it out. There in her hand was the gaily patterned ribband her mother had bound her wrist to Hrald's with on the day of their hand-fast. It was crumpled from having been slept on, but the red and blue and green threads of the tablet weaving were as bright as the day her mother had made it. She went to the shears hanging on the wall by her loom. She pulled the ribband over one sharp edge and cut it in two. She went out to the cooking ring and flung the severed thing into the coals smouldering there.

A few days afterwards she crossed the kitchen yard after they had supped, and saw Sidroc standing alone at the corner near the grain-house, his face turned to the sky. The boy had begun to do this, as if looking or listening at something by her unseen or unheard. It irked her.

"You fool," she called to him, pulling her shawl closer about her. "Why do you look up. Do you think your father sees you? He no more sees you than the Gods see me. Or you."

He recalled all the times this woman would say something in the same sharp tone to his father, and how his father rarely answered. Sidroc said nothing.

The next day he walked to the lake, alone. He stripped off his tunic and leggings and waded in. The water was not quite as warm as it had been the first time, but the lake bottom under his bare feet was as soft. He would practice his swimming, just as his father had promised. He was not there to hold him up, but he remembered his father's movements, and words, instructing him to always keep reaching. He thrashed about in the shallow water, swallowing some of it. Then his actions began to smooth, and he stayed up more than he sank. Afterwards he sat where they sat together, and remembered his father telling him about their fylgja, their guardian spirit. Sidroc no longer knew if his father was alive or dead, but he knew what his father had told him was true.

One morning Ingirith left, taking the oxcart and thrall to Haithabu. Sidroc did not know where that was, only that it was a great trading post on the other side of Jutland. She came back days later without the thrall. But she was not alone. Following the oxcart was a horse-drawn waggon. On the waggon board sat a man and woman, the latter with a babe in arms. Sidroc already knew enough to understand these were prosperous folk; only those with silver to spare had horses.

Sidroc and his sisters watched Ingirith take them all about the place, and watched too as Oddi now set off on foot. The man and the woman were still at the farm the next day at sunset when Oddi returned.

Oddi did not have to call the boy to him. With Oddi gone Sidroc had felt a stranger in his own home, and had run to the man when he appeared, footsore and thirsty, from across the sheep pasture.

Sidroc learned more after Oddi had gone into the house to speak to Ingirith. He came out and walked to the well, drew up water from the wooden bucket and dipped some out. His throat was still dry from his walk, but what he must say needed more than water to ease it.

"You are going to live with Yrling, your uncle, and his older sister and her husband," Oddi told him.

Sidroc blinked. It was part of what his father had told him, that he and Yrling would be together. He had been to his aunt's farm two or three times, and he did not like Ful. But his uncle Yrling was twice his age and could ride and hunt, and his cousin Toki was always laughing and scamping. He said the first thing he thought of.

"Are you coming?"

Oddi nodded. "Já. It was your grand-sire freed me. I owe allegiance to his blood for three generations. You are the third."

He smiled down at the boy then. If this child before him were not also the grand-son of the man who had bought him as a boy, he would have patted his shoulder. But Oddi could not bridge that gulf, though he need not fear the child taking offence in his doing so. Likewise he could not mention that he had kinship directly to Sidroc himself. He did not want the boy to know this. He would walk the path Hrald had wrought, and let no taint fall upon the boy.

Oddi had never wed. Even thralls could do so, and their masters encouraged it. It led to more labour for the farm, though in hard times the babes of thralls were the first to be left in a scrub barren, or atop a pile of rock. Oddi had been torn from his family at twelve years of age and sold across the length of Jutland. That a good man, Hroft, had bought him did not soften Oddi's objection to bearing a son or daughter of his own who he might be forced to see sold away from him.

For a brief span of hours Oddi had thought he and the boy would remain at the farm with the boy's father, and the Mistress be going. Instead the sea had swallowed Hrald, and that was not to be. But there was comfort now in knowing he would be leaving with his niece's son, and need no longer be subject to the Mistress' scolding.

The man and woman with the babe left. Sidroc did not know they had bought the farm until Oddi told him. Ingirith was busy packing up that which she wanted to take with her into her new life.

Yrling came the next afternoon, come to take Sidroc to live with him at Signe and Ful's farm. The boy heard the hoof-beats of a cantering horse and ran to lift the hoop on the wooden gate. Sidroc had not seen Yrling for two Summers and found himself looking up at a young man. The rider had in fact no more than fifteen years, but his bearing and stance was that of a youth sure of himself. He jumped down to where his nephew stood. Yrling's hair was light brown and resting on his shoulders. More than a wisp of dark down showed on his chin and cheeks. His brow line was heavy, above eyes that made Sidroc think of a hawk, so hard and piercing were they. His leggings and tunic were no better than that Sidroc's father had worn, but Yrling had at his belt a long knife with a bright hilt, hanging in a tooled leathern sheath. He was already broad-shouldered, and though Sidroc was aware Yrling was not tall for a man, he looked big nonetheless.

"This is my horse," he told his nephew, after their first greeting. "Bought with my own silver." The saddle and bridle were worn, the brown leather cracked, but the horse itself was glossy and frisking.

Ingirith came out then, shielding her eyes against the slanting Sun. She saw who it was and turned back to the house, coming out once more with a small leathern pack.

She did not greet Yrling other than with a nod. "Here are your things," she told Sidroc, dropping the pack at his feet.

Ulfhildr and the other girls had come around from the kitchen yard; the elder girl had her spindle in her hand.

Yrling had dropped down on one knee and thrust his hand into the pack that was Sidroc's.

"Where is his silver?" he asked Ingirith, withdrawing his hand. His fingers had met nothing hard within that small pack.

"His father did not leave much," she claimed. "He was not the good husbandman he made others think he was."

Yrling, young as he was, thought she answered too readily. He narrowed his eyes at her as he stood. "This is his son," he told her, lifting his hand to Sidroc. "And Hrald would have left me silver," he challenged.

Hrald had never recited a will to three witnesses who could later attest to his wishes. Yrling knew this, or at least had been told this. But by law Hrald's son was a chief heir, and Yrling reminded his brother's widow of this now.

Ingirith considered he who stood before her, more man than boy. She did not know if Yrling could with success press his suit against her at the annual law-gathering, but she did not want to risk being summoned before the Thing next year to be publicly judged.

"Wait here," she answered.

When she came out she passed a purse of leather into Yrling's hand. He weighed it in his palm, then pulled open the oiled cord which served as drawstring. The glint of small coins and hack-silver winked back at him. He thought it close to thirty aurar, almost four marks of silver; perhaps a fair, if not generous settlement. He would make sure Ful took no part of it; it was the boy's, and his, to share.

"Oddi is coming with me," Sidroc thought to say to Yrling. "And Hlaupari, my hound."

It was Ingirith who answered this. "Take your cur, and good riddance. I need Oddi right now. He will follow when I am through with him."

Sidroc put his fingers to his mouth and whistled the dog to his side. He came, head up, sniffing the air, swishing his great tail so that the horse danced a little away from him.

Yrling was fastening the boy's kit to the saddle; he wanted to be off now so to make it back by owl-light. He was about to boost Sidroc up onto the saddle when the boy stopped to look at his sisters. Ingirith was still there, and the children hesitant to make a move before her.

"Fare you well, Sidroc," Ulfhildr managed. Sidroc could see her mouth quivering as she said this. The younger girls were sniffling, and Ingirith looked at them and pressed her lips together.

Sidroc lifted his hand to the girls, waving his farewell. Then Yrling's thick arm closed around his waist, and he was for the first time seated high above the others, looking down from over the neck of a horse. Yrling chirruped to the beast, and they moved off, Hlaupari already trotting before them. Sidroc tried to turn his head back, but Yrling's body blocked his view.

When they arrived at the farm of Signe and Ful that evening Ful questioned Yrling about any legacy the child had brought with him. They were all at table as he did so. Sidroc was sitting next to his cousin Toki, and Ful's eyes went from the lowered brown head of Sidroc to the yellow hair of his own son. Both boys were silently spooning their browis into their mouths.

Yrling had already hid the silver Ingirith had handed over to him, and told Ful so. "It was my brother's, for his son, and for me," he told Ful. The youth had a way of being direct, just skirting defiance.

Yrling's own eyes turned to Sidroc. "And he will earn his keep," he assured Ful.

There was not much Ful could say to this. Yrling worked hard himself, and had innate cunning. Ful knew it would not be long before he left to make his own way, and if Ful could profit by Yrling's ambition, he would do so.

Ingirith moved to the trading town of Haithabu. Oddi drove the oxcart piled high with all her goods, then sold ox and cart for her in the livestock yards before taking his leave. Ingirith gave no parting silver to Oddi. A more honest woman would have, for the sake of Hrald; Oddi knew this.

She rented one of the small plots on a side road, paying tribute to the King for the privilege of living there, even though she had nothing to sell. But there were both artisans and merchants in Haithabu, far more than in Ribe. Some of them must be unwed. She would establish herself there as what she was, a respectable widow. She repeated this title in her mind. She deserved to be thought as such, after what she had been through. For now she would keep the girls with her in her new life. Later she could send them to her mother if they got in the way, or if her new husband did not want them.

Chapter the Ninth

YRLING

The Year 858

THREE years had passed since Yrling had brought Sidroc to live at his older sister's farm.

Sidroc and his cousin Toki both knew ten Summers, one of the few likenesses they shared. Hrald's son continued as dark and lean as he had ever been, gangly as a colt. If his arms and legs did not seem always under his control, they served him well when he ran, for with his long stride he was fast. He also became a sure swimmer, and shared his capacity in this craft with Toki at the several ponds hard by the farm. Toki was more sturdily built, with a fine head sporting thick yellow hair, and eyes of a blue bright enough to make young girls who saw him at Summer or Jultide gatherings watch him.

Sidroc had been the only boy on his father's farm. His little sisters had been meek and fearful, kept constantly occupied by their mother. To be free now from her scolding was one thing Sidroc felt grateful for. He had plenty of chores at his aunt's farm, but now he had Toki to play and roughhouse with. He missed his father with acute longing, at times so great that he rubbed tears from his eyes. But his uncle Yrling was here, almost like an older brother.

On frosty mornings Yrling took the cousins hunting after red deer, which they downed with bows and arrows he had made. Ful hammered out the arrowheads, and the boys themselves fashioned the bow-ends, from the tips of sheep's horns, and took pride in doing so. Hlaupari was left up at the farm on such outings, so as not to alert the deer to their presence, but when they set traps for martins and weasels he proved his worth, sniffing out the snagged animals and leading them first to those traps which had proven fruitful.

These small furs were the first things of value both boys had earned. They skinned off the pelts with care, covered the flesh side with wood chips, and dried them in the barn. Ful and Yrling went to Ribe often enough in Summer that the boys need not wait long to trade them for a jingling handful of hack-silver. There were broken and bent bits of silver jewellery in what had been weighed out for them, as well as tiny coins in whole and half pieces. Toki plucked a squashed finger ring of twisted silver from this, and had one of Ribe's silver-workers open it for him on his mandrel of iron, while Sidroc claimed a whole coin, larger than the rest, bearing the profile of a man.

"Ha!" said Yrling when he had shown it to him. "That is of Angle-land, and I wager, Danish booty." He squinted at the marks encircling the stamped picture, so unlike the runes to Sidroc's eyes. "That is likely Æthelwulf, King of Wessex," his uncle went on. He turned the coin in his hand, then grinned at Sidroc. "There are many more where this one came from."

Oddi had stayed on with Sidroc out of loyalty to Hrald. He was in fact free to go, and he knew that if he asked Sidroc if he might, the boy would tell him to do so. Still, he stayed. It was true Oddi owed allegiance onto the boy, for he was the third generation, but those bonds were slight. Staying on the farm with Sidroc gave constancy to his days. He was now bald of head and bowed of back, and could no longer work as he once had, but none understood farm work as well as he. One day he would be too old to work, and then he would seek the shelter of his sister's home. Until then, Ful must pay him, as a freedman, workman's wages. This was given him most often in surplus grain which he bartered or sold on his own account.

Ful worked both boys hard, but to his credit did not favour his son over Sidroc. If anything he was harsher with his own boy, and Toki's spirit was such that no amount of birching would keep him from pulling pranks or attempting to escape any labour which, to Toki, seemed needless. "There is always an easy way," Toki was often telling Sidroc. Yrling, as uncle to both boys, took their part more than once before Ful.

"They are my blood, as well," he would remind Ful, as he shielded them from some wrathful action. The two did not forget his defence, and in fact due to Yrling there were more hands at the farm than ever before, which served to silence Ful's complaints. The prior Summer their young uncle had taken ship and gone off to Angle-land with a small group of other Danes. Ful had lent him silver to do so, and his youthful brother-in-law made good on the investment. Yrling had returned a few weeks later with his belt filled with silver, and no fewer than four thralls, two men and two women. They were like the slaves Sidroc remembered seeing Ful leading when he stopped at his father's farm, light-eyed and fair-haired. Best of all they were all young; Yrling had boasted to Ful that none could have more than five and twenty years, and so had many years of labour left to them. He kept them, all four, and as Ful still owned one of the five he had helped capture, there were now five thralls as well as Oddi for the heavy work about the place.

The farm had need of these hands, those of women particularly, for Signe was no longer robust. A dizzying sickness afflicted her at times, making her walking unsteady. At times she fainted, and became wary of going near the well for fear of falling in unknowing. Her two daughters were now grown and wed, and the farm now a household of men and boys and slaves.

In her younger years Signe had often countered Ful's severe ways, but her indulging her last child allowed Toki, willful by nature, to trade on her protection. She was mild and welcoming to Sidroc, who seemed to her almost like Hrald himself, for her younger brother had been no older than Sidroc when she had left her parents' farm to wed Ful. When he first arrived she clucked over the shabby clothing the boy had brought with him, and stitched up a new set for him, a blue linen tunic and brown woollen leggings. Toki, seeing this, demanded new clothes of his own, and the hapless woman was thus bent over her needle twice as long.

Hers was the first gentle touch from a woman's hand Sidroc could remember, and the first woman to show respect for his person. She let him comb his own hair, instead of yanking it through herself as Ingirith had done, and even praised him for the comb he had made.

The new thralls from Angle-land brought change with them. More land could now be put to the plough, and the three male thralls, along with Yrling and Ful, cleared the stand of linden and oak trees beyond the barley field. The trees were felled by axe, dragged free by oxen teams, the stumps burnt out by fire. Sidroc and Toki chopped endless boughs and branches, stacking them to dry for future kindling. The boys cared also for the sheep and cattle, milking the cows each day, and leading both sheep and cattle to fresh pastures. Hlaupari proved his worth in these tasks, nipping at the hocks of dawdling cattle, but needing only to fix his eye upon the ewes to make them move. The hound was now as old as Sidroc, and the fur on his muzzle had whitened, but though he moved more slowly, he had not lost his love of running which had given him his name.

The two women thralls from Angle-land cooked and scrubbed and swept, tended to the pigs and fowl, worked the vegetable plots, and spun thread from wool roving every free moment. Signe could still stand at her loom and weave, but in truth all three women were hard pressed to feed and clothe five men and two boys, and themselves as well.

Something else was demanded of one of the slave women, which Sidroc witnessed one day after the grain harvest.

It was early evening, his chores mostly done, the meal yet to be ladled up. He and Toki had walked down to a runnel of water beyond the cattle pasture. Snakes and frogs hid in the tall grasses there, and the sides of the water course were steep enough, and narrow enough, that the boys could test themselves, leaping from bank to bank. Hlaupari splashed through the water, snapping at rising dragonflies that dipped above the wider portions of it, and nosing in the wet growth after a fat toad. After a while Toki tired of this. He could never stay long at any activity, even one as satisfying to Sidroc as wandering by the narrow stream, and he headed back.

Hlaupari had run upstream, chasing after a water duck, and Sidroc would stay on. He had little time to be alone, and welcomed his brief ramblings with his dog. Soon he too would have to turn back, for the evening milking. He stood on the bank of the runnel, and his hand went, as it often did, to the knife at his waist. It and the dog were the only things remaining from his life with his father. There was not even a burial mound to visit, back at his father's farm. Sidroc had never known either grandmother nor grandsire, but his father had often taken him to their mounds.

Where his own father rested none could know; the sea-God Njord's underwater realm was vast. He looked up the narrow banks of the runnel; it was far too shallow for even the smallest boat, but still it brought to mind the swift moving stream his father used to reach the sea. Sidroc found himself staring into the depths of the dark-glinting water.

Water had taken his father away, and had almost taken his own life. Yet the strongest and best memories of his father were founded in and around water. At this point in his life he knew he might never see his father again. If any spoke of him, it was as one dead. Sidroc could not quite consider him thus. But the days spent with him were a long way away, and growing further off. He felt the guardian spirit he shared with his father, their fylgja, should be stronger than ever, and wondered if it were because he was bigger now himself, or if it was because she had quit his father at his death. Surely his father's luck-spirit, his hamingja, had run out on him, if he had died . . .

Hlaupari came back now, and threw himself in the long grass, panting. Sidroc let him rest a moment, then whistled. With the Sun lowering in the sky, boy and dog made their way back to the farm.

He was nearing the furthest out building when he heard a sound, a sort of gasping grunt. There, near gathered shocks of drying rye, he saw a moving form. It was his uncle Yrling, lying on the ground, his brown tunic on his back, boots on, his leggings pulled down to the backs of his thighs. Beneath his body lay one of the thrall women, facing up, her gown bunched around her chest, her eyes open, staring straight up into the dying light of day.

Sidroc had his hand on Hlaupari's neck, and his fingers now curled in the beast's fur. He felt riveted where he stood, watching Yrling move above the woman. The dog stilled under his grasp. The woman, whose name was Berthe, now tilted her chin slightly. Her eyes found Sidroc's, saw him staring at her and what was happening to her. He watched her eyes squeeze shut, her face return to the dimming sky.

He pulled himself and his dog away.

Sidroc had many times seen rams covering ewes, and cocks mounting hens as they fluttered beneath them. He had been there when a neighbouring farmer had brought his good bull to Ful's farm, and watched the huge animal rise up on his hind legs behind a young and spotted heifer, that it might bear a calf, and keep them in milk. But this, he had not seen.

He slipped into the barn, expecting to find Toki there; both cows were waiting. One had been milked, but Toki had left the basin behind, for Sidroc to carry to the spring house. For once he was glad Toki had done so. He did not want to see Toki now, nor anyone.

He stood alone in the dimness of the place. Hlaupari curled up in the straw. The unmilked cow lowed at him, but he did not move towards her. He stood, aware of the quickness of his breath and the beating of his heart, until he heard the sound of footfall on the dusty ground outside the open doors. He glimpsed Yrling, passing by, on the way to the house. Then Sidroc stepped out.

He rounded the corner to see the thrall-woman Berthe still there by the drying shocks of rye. She was kneeling on the ground, her gown now pooled around her.

He stood behind and to one side of her, making no sound, regarding her, knees in the dust. She had bowed her head. He watched her hand rising before her face, her fingers touching her brow, dropping to her belly, crossing to touch both shoulders, and joining together, palms pressing, before her. He thought her lips were moving but was not sure.

He drew nearer, and she started, but did not rise. More than a moment passed before she spoke.

"Do you too demand my body?" she asked, so softly that he must draw nearer.

Her tone was flat, and her Norse not yet easy to understand. She looked at him more closely, and as if for the first time. "You are too young."

He only swallowed, and asked something in return.

"What were you doing with your hands?"

She paused before she told him. "Trying to bless myself. Praying to Our Father." She stood at this.

"To All-Father?" He had never seen anyone make those hand movements while offering to Odin.

She shook her head. "To the True God, the Father of Christ."

Sidroc had never heard of this God.

"Does he hear you?"

"He hears everything. And even if my prayer is not granted while I still live, he will free me."

"My Uncle Yrling can free you, he alone," Sidroc offered. "Or if you gain silver, you can buy your freedom." He had heard of some thralls doing just that.

She almost smiled at this, but Sidroc already knew a smile rooted in bitterness. "The man who calls himself my master is more slave than I," she said.

He did not know what to say to this, and so said nothing. His hair had grown long, to his shoulders, and he ran the fingers of his right hand through it now, thinking on this.

"You . . . you will bear a babe now," he found himself saying. When animals mated, the females bore young.

"I will never bear the child of that man, or of any like him," she answered. Her eyes had flared as she said this. "Every touch is hateful to me."

This last meant something. He had many times recoiled at Ingirith's touch, her hand pinching, slapping, wielding the forked beating stick. He had been birched by Ful since then, but it did not seem as bad as what Ingirith had done to him.

He kept looking at her. The other thrall-woman was squat; Berthe was slender. He saw what he had not seen before, that she wore something small and black about her neck, strung on a thin leathern cord. It looked a key.

"What is that key you wear," he wanted to know. Thralls owned little or no real goods, and so had nothing to secure in chests.

Her fingers rose to it, and she lifted it in her hand. He took a step forward.

"A key, one I cut of leather."

He cocked his head at hearing this. Such a key was useless; it could turn nothing.

Her jaw moved slightly as she shook her head. "To remind me of Sainted Peter, and the keys he holds, to Heaven."

Another one of her Gods, Sidroc thought.

Berthe brushed her left eye with her knuckle. More than one tear glimmered there. She looked ready to go, and glanced beyond him. "I must go back to the kitchen yard," she told him, and left.

He watched her as she did. All worked hard on the farm, the thralls hardest of all. He saw now that Yrling had called her away from her rightful work of their supper, called her away to make her lie down beneath him, something she did not want to do. Thralls had no right to refuse anything, he knew this.

He went back to the barn to milk the waiting cow, thinking on what he had seen, and even more on what he had heard. When he sat down at table that night Berthe came up and ladled out food for all of them, not looking at Yrling, and him ignoring her, just as if nothing had happened.

Once he came upon Ful using Berthe in just the same way, and in almost the same place, sheltered from view of the house and kitchen yard. As Sidroc slowed to watch, Yrling came up behind him and shooed him away, and then himself left. But later both he and Toki heard the words, low and angry, Yrling exchanged with Ful over the episode.

"She is my thrall," Yrling said.

"Not wholly. Who gave you the silver to go to Angle-land? Part of her is mine. The part I had today."

The day after this Yrling and his two nephews were at work building up the store of firewood for the kitchen yard. Berthe and the second thrall-woman, whose name was Ebbe, were boiling water in the largest iron cauldron, ready to dye newly woven lengths of wool. It was hot and heavy work, stirring and tending the steaming fabric, and the time needed allowed just one colour per day. This morning they shook the bright yellow flowers and dried leaves of weld into the pot, then set the colour with the juice of crushed crab-apples, so that the woolens they dipped would not fade.

It took a good deal of fire to dye either wool or linen, but firewood and charcoal both were used in great quantities year round at the farm. Yrling was splitting lengths of seasoned wood, part of which was taken by the thrall-women and fed right into the cooking ring. The two boys were at the smaller chopping blocks splitting some of what Yrling had hewn into piles of kindling, and stacking it.

The oats, barley, and rye had been sown, and all the vegetables were in. Mid-Summer was a full Moon away, and Yrling was soon to leave, heading off to Angle-land again. It would be his second trip there, one which he hoped would prove even more profitable than the first, when he had returned with a purse lumpy with silver and the four thralls.

When he had come home with such treasure he had been asked more than once by the boys to relate how he had gained it all. Yrling was a Winter's child, and had seen eighteen of them now, but in the eyes of the boys he was a man, and a rich one, too. He had the horse he had owned since he was fifteen, the bag of new silver which he had shown them with pride, and the thralls. These had produced enough that Yrling need take no silver either from his own store or from Ful to underwrite his next voyage. The excess grain grown under the thralls' labour was sold in Ribe and Yrling could pay his own way to the ship owner on this coming trip. Beyond the riches he had brought back was the tale of the adventure itself, and the fact that he killed men to win it.

When Ful had gone raiding that single time, he had killed no man. It had been enough to appear with his fellow adventurers, brandishing spears before the frightened crofters whose hut they stormed. One or two folk had been hurt, but none killed; the threat of their spear points was enough. Binding their wrists and forcing them to hurry to their waiting ship was all it had taken.

Yrling and his fellows had harder work of it, or being all young, made it the harder. They struck at a hamlet of some four farms, thinking to gain enough in slaves, grain, and livestock to enrich all eight of them at once. It was dusk, the folk all within, and fire was flung on the thatched roofs, to drive those inside to flee for their lives. It would be a simple task, they thought, to surround those who came running out, forcing their surrender. It was not.

Before the first torch was lobbed a dog began to bark, then came running at them. They killed it, only to find folk flinging open their doors at the hound's death-cry. Some who came were men with spears in hand, ready to use them. Shouts and oaths filled the air. Others of the folk began throwing water on their smoking roofs, or attacked the invaders with any tool at hand.

Yrling saw one of his fellows crumple and fall under a blow to the head delivered with a spade. Armed with his spear he was surrounded by a foreign folk, men and women both, defending their lives and property, fighting for their kith and kine. He and his fellows won out, but not before he had run his spear into the belly of one man and the back of another.

The fact that he had killed two men distinguished their uncle to the boys, far more than the fact that he was three years shy of twenty when he had done so. They knew King Horik's men killed; not only those threatening his borders but those who would not pay their taxes. But those were trained warriors. They wore tunics of linked iron rings, iron helmets, and bore not only spears and knives, but costly pattern-welded swords at their sides, swords whose blades had been hammered and twisted of many plates of blue steel in far-off Frankland. Yrling had only his knife and his spear, and had joined a warrior's rank with that.

When his uncle had first told his tale, the thing that most struck Sidroc was the killing of the dog. A good watch dog was useful on any farm. The fact that the beast had been killed doing his job gave Sidroc pause. It might have been Hlaupari. He thought about the dog, and asked his uncle more than once about him, so that Yrling was short with him. It was just a common hound, one he did not kill, but another of his number; and its death by a spear-thrust had been quick. But Sidroc did not forget that the first to die had been a dog. He wondered what he would do if someone appeared and killed his own.

The three had stopped to take a break in their labours, and Yrling had drawn up a full bucket of water from the well, that they might drink and splash their heated faces. The water was cold, as well water ever is, and more than welcome. Yrling sat down on the ash stump that served as chopping block, and the boys took their seats on a round of the same trunk, upon which they had been splitting kindling.

A young rooster was strutting near the fowl house. It put Sidroc in mind of something.

"Will you make sacrifice to Thor, or to Odin, before you go?" he asked his uncle.

Toki had an answer readily enough. "Thor! Thor!" he urged.

Yrling laughed. He then looked at Sidroc. "Who do you think I should send a cock to?" His voice was not teasing, but serious as he asked his nephew his opinion.

Sidroc considered. "You Offered to Thor last year, and he profited you. But I think now, having proved yourself, you should make offering to Odin himself, so that he begins to see you."

"Ha!" returned Yrling, nodding his approval. "I think so too. Thor grants strength. But I need strength, and craft as well to win what I seek. For that I need Odin, the God of thought. It is time that All-Father takes note of me."

From the way Yrling looked at him Sidroc knew that his uncle was pleased, and a bit surprised. Sidroc now said something more, to explain how he knew what Yrling's choice would be.

"We share the same fylgja," he offered.

Yrling's lip twisted at this. Sidroc knew that such things were not often discussed in Ful's household.

Yrling had been little more than a toddling child when his father Hroft had died, but still retained warm memory of his mother Ashild. Perhaps once or twice Yrling's older brother Hrald had mentioned their inner life; Hrald who had promised to bring him home and never had. He did not like to think of his older brother. And now, of this shared spirit of which Sidroc spoke, he was not so certain.

"It is my hamingja I am more concerned with, my luck-spirit," Yrling countered. "Skill only gets you so far. You must have luck too."

"I will have both," Toki claimed.

"You will have neither, if you do not learn to work hard."

"Why work when you can take, as you took the thralls, and the silver you brought home."

"And you think that was not work? Coming alive to Angle-land was work enough, with the North Sea crossing. Then to land and find food, and scout out crofts to target. After this, the attack itself, where you have one chance to surprise and overpower the men of the place. More than once we tried a farm where many men appeared from work-yards or fields, and saw our backs and not our weapons."

Both boys always listened with rapt attention whenever Yrling spoke of his time in Angle-land. This they had not heard.

"You ran?" This was Toki, always blunt.

"Only a fool never runs." Yrling wagged his head at the yellow-haired boy. "That is why you would not live long, if you took to raiding."

This stilled Toki, but only briefly. They went back to work, and at the first blow from Yrling's broad-headed axe, Toki jested it was the head of a Saxon warrior.

Yrling stopped and looked at both boys. Eager as Yrling was for riches and a measure of renown, he would not bask in fame he had not yet earned.

"I have faced no warriors yet, just farmers, much like us," he corrected. "Some of them were good spears-men." A slight pause, as he remembered his time there. "Not as good as me."

"You will teach us spear-work soon," Sidroc asked.

"Já." His uncle was looking at him, the bright and hawk-like eyes fastened upon him. "You will come with me."

The boys turned to each other; this was the first time Yrling had promised this.

Sidroc caught his breath. He did not have the chance to speak his assent, for Toki was chiming, "Why him? I will go too!"

Yrling regarded Toki. "Ha! You have no need to seek treasure abroad. You are the only boy. This will be yours." He lifted his hand to the work yard of the farm.

"Phhh! I do not want it!"

"Do not want it?" Yrling shook his head at Toki. "This is a good farm, and it will be handed to you one day. You will wed a woman who brings silver with her, and live a good life, right here."

Sidroc had not taken his eyes from his uncle, but Toki's restless glance swept all around the farm buildings. He was about to speak when Yrling did so again.

"I have nothing," he told his yellow-haired nephew. "Only what I have earned myself. My sister, your mother, wed and came here." His eyes shifted to Sidroc. "Your father, my brother, got our farm. All I have from it is the silver I demanded from his sharp-tongued wife."

He looked back to Toki now. "And Sidroc is like me; he got almost nothing. The silver I keep for him will help him win more, in Angle-land."

"I will go," Sidroc vowed. For the first time he saw that he had been cheated of his rightful portion. Yrling was saying as much. And he had no real place here; that he had already felt. His uncle could help him to a bigger life, one in a new land of good farmland and rich folk.

"You will not go without me," Toki demanded. He had crossed his arms at his chest.

His uncle looked at him and laughed. "We will see. Only the best warriors will make their fortunes in Lindisse, in the land of the Saxons."

Toki's thoughts leapt there. "Is that where Berthe and others are from, Lindisse?"

"Já. Lindisse, on the eastern coast of Angle-land. Berthe was one of the cottar women in the hamlet in Lindisse." He glanced over at the kitchen yard, where she stood, paddle in hand, at her dyeing work over the cauldron. "The way she carried on, one of the men I killed was likely her brother, or husband."

"Were there children?" Sidroc asked. The image of the dog had again flashed in his mind, before he thought to ask this, about the young.

"Já. We left them behind. There were old folk as well; we did not kill them either."

Toki went on, as if thinking aloud. "Angle-land. Where they all speak as Berthe and Ebbe do, when they speak amongst themselves."

"Já," Yrling answered. "You should learn that tongue, have them teach you."

Toki grinned. "There are other things Berthe can teach me. Things I want more to know."

Yrling had set his axe down while talking. Now he took a short stride to where Toki stood, and with an open hand slapped his face. Toki rocked back on his heels, but in his pride would not raise his hand to his flaming cheek.

"Do not even think of it," Yrling told him. "She is my thrall." Now he laughed again. "Not that you have timber enough."

Toki's cheek grew even redder, and they all turned back to their work.

Yrling readied himself to leave. The boys had better understanding of what he was going to, and also some glimmering realisation that he might not return. The risk was well worth it, their uncle had made clear, and there was more of this new land he hoped to see. Angle-land had few folk, and great stretches of forest waiting to be cleared. The soil was dark and rich, where much of Jutland was sandy waste. Others had told him that war-chiefs and Kings kept large timber halls loaded with silver and gold treasure, and he had heard that in some places groups of men and women lived apart, with even more treasure, much of it kept on tables for all to see.

Yrling made no show of the dangers facing him, and let both nephews help him pack up his kit as if he took a two or three day trip to Ribe to trade sheep or cattle. But a young farmer heading to Ribe would not spend the hours honing and polishing his knife as Sidroc and Toki watched Yrling do, nor would he have set off with as many hours of spear-practice under his belt.

Yrling now had a shield, one he had made himself. It was a round of alder-wood planks, covered with cow-hide he had wet and let shrink to tightness. The shield was centred with an iron boss, and rimmed round with a thin band of iron to hold and protect the plank edges. The farm had forge and anvil, as all farms did, and the boys had helped Yrling in the making of the iron fittings, holding the metal by long tongs in the fire until it glowed, pumping the skin bellows to blow air into the charcoal as it reddened. Ful helped in the shaping of the boss, behind which Yrling's left hand would grip, but Yrling himself hammered out the rim iron, shaped the alder, and cut and fashioned the inner arm-sling, and the longer leathern tether so that the shield might be worn on the back. Both boys took careful note of these proceedings, and could not get enough of holding and wielding the shield themselves, even though it covered them from nose to past knee, it was so large.

To meet up with his fellows Yrling must travel to the coast. He need not walk there, as he owned a horse, but the animal must be returned to the farm. Ful would not allow that one of the boys ride his own horse, and Yrling told his nephews that he would decide which of them he would choose to ride with him, and be allowed to return alone to the farm on his horse.

Both boys were good riders, and both took care of Ful's animal, a buckskin gelding with near-black mane and tail. It was typical of many of the horses of Dane-mark, a sturdy and broad-backed creature, not much bigger than a pony, but willing enough. Yrling's horse was much the better, a sleek and spirited mare, dark chestnut, with a blazed face and single white stocking. Yrling was justly proud of her. Three years ago he had travelled down to

Haithabu and come back with her, and with the story that she was of the stock of Angle-land. Whether or not this was true, she was noticeably better than most of the horses Yrling had ever seen. She had her own part in improving his fortune, as he had bred her shortly after buying her, and the foal she had provided him with grew to a strong colt. He had kept the colt for two years, training it up, and then sold it for a pile of silver at Ribe. Toki argued that he should keep the colt and sell the mare, for why should Yrling ride a mare when he might ride a stallion? Yrling laughed at that, and shook his head.

"You see only what is in front of you, Toki, and never beyond. A good mare like mine will produce more good foals. I will breed her to the best horses on Jutland, and her blood will make her get better than the sire. And those good foals will be mine."

The chestnut mare was not a placid beast, and like many mares could test the limits of her rider. She was also noticeably taller than Ful's horse. Sidroc's height gave him the long legs to better straddle her, and he was altogether quieter in his hands with the reins. When Yrling told Sidroc he would ride with him to the coast, Toki first scoffed, then sulked.

"You chose Sidroc because he is your brother's son," he complained.

"And you are my sister's son, she who gave me a home. To me you are the same," Yrling returned. "I chose Sidroc this time; next I might choose you."

Toki was not mollified by this, and at last Yrling said, "Then you too come. Trot alongside my mare."

Yrling laughed aloud at Toki's screwed-up face, and Sidroc could not help but smile. He was proud but not surprised to have been chosen; the mare had bucked Toki off her back more than once, and he knew Yrling did not want the boy breaking his neck.

They were starting early, and Sidroc should be back in a single day, if the men Yrling was to meet were in fact at the coast awaiting him. Signe shed tears over Yrling, as she had last Summer on his first raiding trip. She did not approve of his going, and knew their dead parents would look askance at such dealings in their youngest; Hroft and Ashild were hard-working and held that goods and silver must be earned, and not at the end of a spear-point. Signe had long before this accepted that her father's judgment of Ful had been correct, and viewed her young brother's dabbling in raiding her husband's influence. Now both her own and Hrald's boy were watching, eyes round as ale-cups, and she could not counter any of it.

They set off, Sidroc behind Yrling, seated nearly on the mare's rump, Yrling's shield boss digging into the boy's chest, Yrling's packs bumping his dangling legs. Yet the sense of adventure was full about them both, and Sidroc's spirits were nearly as high as if he himself would sail. The mare too showed them, prancing and chafing under the loads she bore, and only Yrling's skillful handling kept her going forward without undue protest. Yrling held his spear upright in his right hand, and Sidroc looked out from behind him to a world split in two by the long shaft of ash wood.

At one point they stopped to water the mare at a streamlet. Sidroc slid, not too gracefully, off the beast's rump, to fall on the grass. He jumped up readily enough, and joined both horse and uncle at the stream bed. It was early enough in the Summer, and in the day, for the birds to be chirping about them, and the reeds that grew at water's edge swayed in the breeze as they drank. The peace of the place was such that it put Sidroc in mind once more of what Yrling was going to do.

"Last night," he hazarded. "Did you . . . make Offering to Odin, as you said you would?"

Yrling paused a moment. "I did, this morning. You will see the rooster hanging in the ash out in the far end of the sheep pasture." He glanced down at his hands now. Sidroc saw both were scratched; the young cock had not gone willingly to Odin.

Sidroc nodded. Ash trees were of Odin, his sacred tree. Any Offering made at its roots or hung in its boughs would find special favour with the one-eyed God.

"I will make another, that you come back," Sidroc said now.

Yrling gave out with a soft laugh. "Ful will birch you if he loses another bird."

"I would not take anything that is his, but leave something of my own making," Sidroc quickly explained. He did not know what he could make that would be worthy gift for a God, but said it nonetheless. Yrling had given him a home, and was keeping silver for him. Yrling was his father's brother, and he felt bound to him. Just as he felt bound to Toki, despite the differences between them.

"Thank you for that," Yrling allowed. "But I will come back. I must keep going each Summer, win more silver and thralls, until I have enough to buy my own ship. Then I will be able to gather men to sail with me."

He now said to Sidroc which he had said to no man. "I will win great treasure in Angle-land; silver, and land. My fame will be as great as Guthrum or Halfdan, who the Gods have smiled on in that rich place."

Yrling paused to let the boy take this in. Even Sidroc and Toki had heard of these two Danish warriors, both of whom had met rich reward in plundering the fat shores of Angle-land.

Yrling went on, his eyes now lifting above Sidroc's head to the unseen future.

"I will wed a chieftain's daughter, or even the daughter of a King of that place. I will ride a grey stallion, my sons at my side."

This last prompted Sidroc to a question. "Not a mare as good as yours, who earns you more wealth by having colts?"

Yrling grinned. "Unlike Toki, you listen, and you learn," he said. "I will have mares in plenty, but so many good horses that I need not concern myself with the getting of foals."

Sidroc nodded. Yrling knew what he wanted, and it all sounded fine.

They resumed their path, heading now due West on a trackway that passed out of the birch and hazel woods of the streamlet. A growing number of crofts met their eyes, single farms with pasturage for beasts, and those where three or more families had settled. From some dogs barked as they rode by, putting Sidroc into mind of Hlaupari, who he had tied up before he left this morning, judging the trip too tiring for a hound of his years.

Sidroc, peering around the shoulder of his uncle, saw the glint of open water rise up before them, the North Sea. Just as at his father's farm, an island sat across the expanse of water, forming a channel before open sea was reached, but the sight was impressive enough. Also impressive was the size of the single farm that sat at the end of the track, one of its fields vanishing into the sand of the beach. There lay a narrow beamed long-ship, beached, and waiting. A cluster of figures moved around her.

Yrling chirruped to his mare in response, and she tossed her head and moved even more smartly. Yrling called out, and the men at the ship, and some coming too from the house, hailed out their greeting. The pleasingly smoky smell of tar wafted from the ship, the black and shiny stuff showing on the brown hull where it had been daubed on as proof against leaks.

Sidroc found himself amidst a group of some ten or twelve men, of which he thought Yrling might be the youngest. All were eager to be off, as the tide was soon to turn in their favour. The man who owned the ship was easy to spot; it was he who gave orders which all followed. Sidroc saw at once that this man owned a sword; it was there, in its scabbard and belt, with the rest of his kit, lying on the beach. Sidroc, now standing and holding the reins of the mare, drew near it, but knew enough not to touch a man's weapons.

His uncle was the subject of some chaffing, for much of the hard work of lading was over, the water barrels already aboard, but the men wore grins as they jested. Yrling worked hastily to join them, tossing his leathern pack over the side, handing his shield and spear to a man already within. They would have to push her out, and he took his boots off too, to save them the wet. From their talk Sidroc understood that they would first sail further up the northern coast, and pick up still more men there. After that they would trim out across open water, to Angle-land.

"You marked the track well, coming," Yrling was asking him now. On their route Yrling had several times pointed out landmarks to his nephew, a split tree here, a rock cairn or field of old burial mounds there. Sidroc nodded, but at the same time felt the lack of Hlaupari. A hound with a nose as good as he would be sure to get him back. Still, his return was almost due South, and they had passed enough farms at which Sidroc could stop and ask of the folk the way.

Women and boys had come from the house now, carrying small baskets of additional foodstuffs, making final farewells. The ship captain's wife embraced her husband, and Sidroc saw he had boys of about his own age. The captain saw Yrling turn back to his nephew, and called out to Sidroc with a laugh.

"In a few Summers you will join us, bean-stalk."

Sidroc grinned at this; he knew he was as tall and lean as a reaching plant.

Then Yrling put his hand on the back of Sidroc's neck, gave his head a little shake. "Take care of my mare," he said in way of parting, nothing more than this.

"Já," Sidroc answered, not knowing himself what more to say.

Some of the men were already at the prow, pushing, and Yrling took his place alongside them. From within the ship others had taken up oars to help ease her way into the shallow water. She was not a big ship but even so Sidroc was surprised at how quickly she was in the water, and Yrling and the others scrambling over her gunwale and inside.

There was nothing other than the sleekness of her shape to give the ship beauty; her hull bore signs of patching, and the prow and stern posts ended in simple curves, and not the fearsome carved dragon-faces that Yrling had told him his own ship would bear. But the speed with which she moved out into deeper water held Sidroc's eye, and those too of the woman and children standing there watching. This ship needed no carved dragon to name her a drekar. Her purpose was clear by her speed, and the look of the men who sailed her.

The captain's voice rang over his crew, and the thick pine mast was lifted, to be set upright in place. When the sail was unfurled the ship became almost a living thing, the madder-red linen catching and billowing, thrusting the prow forward through parting waters.

Sidroc stood there, the reins in his hand, the mare nibbling at the seagrasses. The woman turned to him, gestured him to the kitchen yard with the rest of the children. She gave him buttered bread, much welcomed after his long morning.

"He is your brother?" she asked him. He saw now that the brooches at her shoulders were large and silver, and that strung from them was a thick coiling chain of the same metal.

"Nej. My uncle," he told her.

"He went with my husband last year," she went on. "When you are older, and if your father allows, you too might join him."

"My father is dead," Sidroc admitted.

"Then you will surely sail," she said.

Sidroc took his leave of them. He would have almost his full share of chores awaiting him, but he looked forward to the ride back and alone. The mare had cropped grass, and one of the woman's sons brought her a deep bucket from which to drink. Now, freed from the weight of Yrling and the awkwardly bumping packs, she stepped out under Sidroc with a frisking eagerness. The flatness of the trackways they travelled made it easy to canter, and she broke into a gallop with little urging. When she was reined in, head tossing and snorting, she whinnied in a way to tell him she wanted more. Riding her thus, alone and in surroundings strange to him, made him feel almost as if this fine mare was his very own. Ever since Yrling had first boosted him up on her saddle when he was little he knew he wanted a good horse one day. Now he wanted one even more.

He had passed one of the landmarks he remembered, a boundary cairn of stacked stones, when two horsemen came into view, heading down the track towards him. They were cantering their horses, and as they grew closer Sidroc saw from the horses' lathered necks that they were pushing the beasts. Sidroc was walking the mare now, to rest her, and pulled her off the track and into the grassland so they might pass. Instead they reined up.

One was a young man, of Yrling's age, Sidroc thought; and the other a youth three or four years older than himself. Both were red-haired, broad-chested, and blunt of face. They were surely brothers, Sidroc felt. Even the younger of them was big, making the small horses they rode look the smaller.

"Who are you," the elder one demanded, with no greeting at all.

Sidroc did not like his tone, and at once pulled himself the straighter on his horse. Nonetheless, he answered.

"Sidroc, son of Hrald." After a moment he added his own demand. "Who are you?"

"Old enough to ignore the question of a whelp," came the answer.

Now the younger one spoke, looking down the road beyond Sidroc. His hair was even redder than the other's, and his face spotted with freckles. "Une. We must hurry," he warned.

It gave time for Sidroc to turn the head of the mare. She was a far better animal than those they rode, and she had had a rest, whereas theirs were winded. He was ready to dig his heels into her barrel and leave them gaping.

Instead the older one, Une, reached forward and snatched at the rein Sidroc held. His mare whinnied and danced at the sudden yank on her mouth.

"Where did you get that horse?" he asked.

Sidroc felt a flush of fear mix with his anger; these two might steal the mare. Hanging from this red-haired ruffian's saddle was the steel handle of a skeggox, the battle-axe some Danes favoured, its wedge of sharpened metal sheathed in a fold of hard leather.

Sidroc closed his left hand over the rein his accoster held, closer to the mare's head, to relieve the pressure on her mouth, and tried to pull it free.

"Let go. It is my Uncle Yrling's horse." He said next the only thing he thought might matter. "He will kill you if you steal her. He has already killed two men."

The red-haired Une opened his hand, and pulled back. "Yrling, of Ful's farm?" he wanted to know. He began to laugh. "That is the only Yrling I know who has speared two Saxons. I ride now, to sail again with him."

Une was laughing, and had dropped his threat of horse-theft. He knew Yrling, and had taken part in the raid in Lindisse. Yet knowing all of this was not enough for Sidroc. His fear and anger still roiled within him.

"Une, there is no time," the younger one repeated. He had made a shrugging grimace to Sidroc, as if to excuse Une's actions to him.

"Jari. You scold like an old woman," Une chided.

"Jari is right," Sidroc announced. "You are too late. I watched them sail, at tide-turn."

Une opened his mouth in an oath. His younger brother Jari leaned back in his saddle.

"You see? Now you have missed them." He rolled his eyes up in a gesture for Sidroc's sake. Une was still swearing and did not notice.

Sidroc took a deep breath. Jari was not a bad sort, that was clear. He must have come with his older brother to see him off, just as he had with Yrling. As his breathing slowed Sidroc found his hand rising to rest on the knife his father had given him. It made a difference knowing it was there. Knowing the mare was not to be taken from him made the difference all the greater.

He looked over at the pair, and made his voice as steady as he could.

"You have horses," he told them, looking first to Une and then to Jari. "The ship is making a stop up the coast, at Geirmund's farm. You could catch them there."

"Geirmund's farm," Une repeated. "I will find it." He put his heels to his horse and was off.

Jari held his a moment. "I am sorry for my brother's manners," he told Sidroc, before taking off after him.

Chapter the Tenth

ENDINGS

The Year 860

IT was nearing Mid-Summer, and the time of the annual law-gathering, or Thing. Besides the hearing of complaints and meting out of justice, each Thing was a chance for local folk to trade, and to visit with distant friends and family not seen since the Winter festivities of Jul, or perhaps not since last Summer. It was also the time for young folk to mingle. Families who lived far from each other were thrown together for a few days, and youths and maids both looked forward to the opportunity to see and be seen.

There were many such assemblies throughout Danemark, and this year's was of particular importance. Old King Horik had been killed a few years earlier, felled by one of his own kin, and in his own hall. The new King, who also was Horik, lived only two years, and another man now rose to take his place. Any new King of the Danes could not be considered a rightful ruler unless the majority of freemen accepted him as such. This must be done by public affirmation.

Sidroc and Toki had only twelve years, and their voices could not be counted, but Ful and Yrling must be there. Oddi as a freedman was entitled to call out a vote, but must do so following his former master's own inclinations, so he would travel as well. Women could not vote, yet many were known to hold strong opinions which could sway that of their husband or sons. Most who held the distaff took keen interest in who should reign over them, and did not in private keep themselves silent if they could prompt their men to a favoured outcome. And all women looked forward to the Thing, with its stalls of traders and merchants displaying goods, and chances to sit chatting with other women while pairing up maids and youths for possible marriage. Despite this, only the spear-side of the family set out to the Thing this Summer. Signe still lived, but was unwell, afflicted as she was with a dizzying unsteadiness each time she stood up. She would stay at the farm with the thralls.

The regional Thing was held almost a full day away. Because there were five of them going, and would be gone at least two nights, Oddi yoked up the oxen to carry tent and food. Ful and Yrling would ride their horses, with Toki and Sidroc behind them, with the boys walking at times with Oddi to spell the beasts. Ful had three bushels of barley also on the waggon bed, ready to sell or trade.

The chief business of the Thing was always the proclaiming of new laws by the King's agent, which the designated Law-speaker would be quick to commit to memory. The local Law-speaker was always one of the most well-respected men in the area, one often of some wealth, and possessed of keen recollection and judiciousness of mind. He heard the complaints of those aggrieved, and the defence of those suspected. The crimes cited were many. Men were accused of encroaching on long-held family pasturage, of injuring man or beast through carelessness or spite, of cattle-theft, or far-worse, theft of a thrall or even a daughter or wife. Many of these crimes were settled in private and with the use of blade or spear-point, assuring a bloody outcome. This led more often than not to further violence, and ever-growing hostility. Bringing the case before the Law-speaker meant that both sides agreed his word would be final.

This year, with a new man seeking to be acclaimed King, brought more folk to the Thing than normal. The oxcart rolled into meadowlands transformed into campgrounds, a doubled ring of merchants who had thrown up stalls from the backs of their own waggons, and a centre area, filled with benches, from which the Law-speaker would hear disputes.

To the eyes of Sidroc and Toki it was as if the trading town of Ribe had been carried thence; there was that much noise, bustle, and as many new things to see. Even pounding stakes into the Summer-hard ground to string their tent was no labour, so glad were they to be part of the excursion. The tent they hung was for them and Oddi to sleep in; Yrling and Ful would claim the wooden bed of the waggon. With an oiled linen tarpaulin cast over the framework it would keep off night damp as well as any tent, and had no need for ground cloths of cow-hide. They helped Oddi gather field stones to lay their fire-ring. Lengths of fire wood were within the cart, as with so many folk gathering a ready supply from the nearby woods could not be depended upon.

Ful and Yrling carried the bushels of barley to where the other grain-traders stood. Ful would get the best price he could for them; he was always a sharp dealer. He was far from alone in using the gathering as his chance to barter for wanted goods. Hastily thrown up pens held surplus sheep and cattle, and folk milled about, picking out those they might want. Some folk had driven geese or pigs, and stood watching over them, ready to retrieve any chosen by a farmer looking to increase his stock.

Yrling now set off with Sidroc and Toki to wander the stalls. There was plenty of choice goods to catch the eye. When they neared the stall of a weapon-smith, their pace quickened, then slowed, as they stood before he who offered wrought blades, honed and ready knives, and long and lethal swords.

All free and freedmen carried a knife, and there was of course always need for them about the kitchen yard. Yet those who stood before the wares of the weapon-smith were largely of a different ilk, men and boys whose thoughts went far beyond daily necessity. The spear-points he offered were arrayed on a planked table set on trestles. Their points faced those who approached in bristling display, waiting to be fitted on an ash shaft of length to suit the thrower and the target. Some of the steel points were as long as a man's outstretched hand, others nearly as long as a man's hand and forearm both. One might kill a boar or kill a man with such spear points, and those who looked regarded them well. Most of the points were plain, but a few had received special care, and sported scrolling designs etched into the steel. Sidroc and Toki found themselves wordlessly studying their tapering forms.

On the other side of the table, hung from long nails pounded in a pair of upright boards, were six swords of varying lengths. They had yet to receive their finished grips, and their naked tangs made them even more formidable for it.

"A grip of horn, with golden rivets," mused Toki to his cousin.

"Or more steel, with copper wire beaten into it for brightness," Sidroc returned.

Thinking on what treatment their new owners would order was part of the pleasure of looking. Yrling's keen eye was also fixed on these weapons, and he and his nephews spent some little time considering the merits of each. Three of the six in particular were objects of envy.

Swords by the nature of their use needed to be good. An ill-made sword was brittle and would break in the stress of combat. A shattered blade presaged a dead warrior. The best blades were those which had the greatest care lavished in their forging, days and weeks of heating and working, hammering, quenching, cooling. Thin plates of varying steel were layered together, and under the alchemy of fire and the brawn of the smith's arm twisted over and over, and hammered flat, so that the finished blade rippled from its many thin edges glinting from one smooth and deadly face. Such were the three blades the onlookers longed to hold and heft, pattern-welded swords that caught and seemed to throw the light. One might imagine a lightning bolt in one's service with such a sword.

Yrling had a good knife, and a spear which had cut short the lives of two men. But he was far from owning any sword. Hidden back at the farm he had enough to buy a good one, but he would not spend the silver. Still, the two boys flanking him could not help but see how their young uncle's eyes latched onto the naked blades before them. Even his hand had made a slight gesture towards the board from which they hung, glinting in the Sun.

"I will win one," he said, almost to himself.

He had gotten close to picking one up from a dead warrior back in Lindisse. It was not a man he had killed but he had thought the Dane who had done so dead as well. Yrling almost was run through by the man when he stopped to strip the Saxon's body. Stealing another man's battle-gain warranted such punishment, and Yrling found himself sputtering apologies to his Danish brother in arms. He must kill his own Saxon warrior to win one.

"Next Summer," he told the boys.

They nodded. They wanted to see their uncle with a sword at his side, but knew he had shrewdness in holding out. He would not spend good silver when he could win both a good blade and glory by snatching one from the hand of a downed enemy.

They passed on. A cluster of girls and women stood before one stall, signalling that some niceties must be on show, amber beads, newly-cast bronze brooches, or some fine thread-worked linen. It was none of these things. As they neared they heard, rather than saw, what had drawn the onlookers, for the chirping song of caged birds came to their ears. They could spy the tiny creatures, hopping about in their withy cages. They were passing on when Toki paused and elbowed Sidroc, then gestured to one of the watching maids.

The maid Toki had spied was named Gunnborga. She was a new neighbour of the farm, and the boys had met her over the feasts of Winter. Her mother, who stood with her now, had lately wed their nearest neighbour, whose wife had died in childbed. Maid and mother were well, even richly dressed, in linen shifts of snowy whiteness, and sleeveless over-gowns of closely woven wool, Gunnborga's of soft green, her mother's of deep blue. Both gowns sported costly silver shoulder clasps, and were further adorned by coloured thread-work, proof that mother and daughter had leisure to bend over such needlework, and together make gay their clothing.

Gunnborga had been standing on tiptoe to see around those before her, catching a glimpse of the tamed linnets and wrens as they sang from their cages. Now she dropped on her heels and turned away, turning almost into the two boys.

Her mouth opened in surprise. "Toki. Sidroc," she remembered. The first was well-knit, with eyes the confident blue of a noon sky, and waves of yellow hair falling to his shoulders. The second was tall, lanky even, with eyes a blue so dark she was not at first certain of their hue. His face was narrow like the rest of him, and his hair dark brown, and held in two plaits.

"Gunnborga," answered Toki, his lips curling in a smile.

She smiled back at this. Her mother had turned to glance at the three young people, and smiled too.

Unlike her mother Gunnborga did not return her eyes to the caged birds. Toki began prattling away to her, asking her if she wanted a songbird of her own, and before she could answer reminding her that she had been invited to his parents' farm for the Mid-Summer fire. The man who was selling the birds now opened one of the cages to withdraw one for a buyer. This made Toki boast he could catch her a better bird than those the merchant offered. She did not try to answer this. To Toki's dismay Gunnborga was looking at Sidroc, and her smile seemed the warmer for him.

Sidroc for the first time truly regarded her. He judged her hair neither yellow nor brown, but rather that shade of dried river reeds in a strong and slanting Sun, a warm and golden hue. Her cheeks were round and faintly flushed with pink. Sidroc was suddenly aware of what Toki had known for a while, that she was pretty. He found himself smiling back at her.

Toki ran out of words for Gunnborga, and turned to his silent cousin.

"You are as dumb as a dead tree," he charged, trying with a jest to turn the maid's attention back to him. Sidroc had in fact said nothing, but this opened his mouth.

It was Gunnborga's mother who spoke. She had been half-watching the youngsters in the discreet way many mothers had mastered, and felt called to offer her opinion.

"There are some who need not speak to be noticed," she observed in a quiet voice, looking first to Toki, and then to Sidroc.

This made both boys and their uncle look at her. Even the cousins knew she was a handsome woman, and her daughter was a fresher copy of that loveliness. Yrling further knew that this woman had wed one of the most prosperous farmers in the area. Her daughter would have her pick of suitors, with the dowry she would bring.

Her remark shut Toki up. Sidroc found himself grinning. Gunnborga's pink cheek went the pinker, but her smile, as she and her mother walked away, was aimed at the taller of the cousins.

Yrling was grinning himself, as he looked to his nephews. "We know whose hand that maid will take, at the Mid-Summer dancing," he laughed.

Toki looked as if he would answer, then snapped his mouth closed. He rarely paid girls any mind, but he knew that some looked at him. Now here was one he liked, who, though she had said little to either boy, seemed to spurn him. Her mother had said aloud what Gunnborga herself must be thinking; the maid had indeed a different smile for Sidroc than for him.

A horn blew now, from a long and wooden lur raised above the crowd. The low tone from its summoning throat bid them gather by the Law-speakers post, to take the vote. They went back to stand with Ful and Oddi with the other grain sellers. The Law-speaker stood ready; he would gauge the number of assenting voices. Already standing by him and the lur-sounder were three men from the new King.

The man himself, a Jarl of great wealth, was not here; he would more likely appear at a larger Thing, but the warriors who had been sent to stand in his place and to hear the vote were impressive enough, Sidroc thought. There were three of them, standing before them in full war-kit, swords at their sides, ring-shirts on their backs, and helmets on their heads, as if to show to all gathered that this was what they might expect of the new King.

"To fight off invaders," Toki mused aloud.

"And wring taxes from us," Sidroc reminded. He had not forgotten his father telling him of how King Horik's men had seized his thralls and nearly all the livestock, leaving those left behind to starve. Sidroc could not know his own mother had been one of them, but the tone of his father's voice as he recounted what he had come home to was not forgotten.

The vote was an open one, and as simple as men calling Já or Nej. The Law-Speaker addressed the crowd, summoning all eligible to vote to come forward. Free men and freedmen stepped forward. As the Law-Speaker went on, Oddi turned to Sidroc.

"Would you have me vote for the man, Master?" Oddi asked of him.

The first and only time Oddi had ever called him thus was a few days after Sidroc's father had vanished. It was a sign to Sidroc that Oddi believed his father dead, when Sidroc himself hoped he still lived. He had not liked being called Master then, and felt there must be reason now why Oddi called him thus.

"You are a freedman," he reminded Oddi. "My grandsire made it so."

Oddi gave a grave nod. "Freed, but not free to choose. I must vote as you wish."

Oddi's eyes were a watery blue, but he kept them fixed on Sidroc long enough to make the boy flinch.

The youngster knew Ful and Yrling would cast an affirming vote for the Jarl who now claimed King-ship of Dane-mark. He had many warriors at his back, he had heard them say, and most of the smaller chieftains had thrown in with him. Naming him a King meant that his men would collect the taxes used to arm and feed his warriors. He would fight off other war-lords who tried to usurp lands, and patrol and guard the trading towns and posts so that merchants might arrive unafraid of piracy or lawlessness. There was no other man strong enough to claim King-ship, but if a majority of free and freedmen did not affirm his claim he would be turned away.

Oddi had heard the same discourse Sidroc had, and need not be told on which side Ful and Yrling would fall. He seemed instead to ask Sidroc what he wanted. The boy saw this, and it made him pause before he posed a question of his own.

"Would you choose the man," Sidroc asked. Oddi had lived a long time and under several Kings.

Oddi gave a rueful laugh before he answered. "I would choose no King at all, but if there must be one, better he be strong than weak." Oddi glanced up at the backs of Ful and Yrling, who stood in front of them. He gave Sidroc his answer. "I would add my voice."

Sidroc nodded; Oddi would stand with his uncle and with Ful and call out his affirmation.

But Oddi's words struck Sidroc. *No King at all* – how could that be, how could any folk live and prosper without a warrior-King to defend and extend their lands? Then he recalled his father telling him of an island, both rich and King-less: Gotland. He gave his head a single shake. Such a land was as remote and distant as his father himself. He did not question Oddi about his words, but did not forget about the idea of such a place, either.

They arrived back at the farm to ill tidings, though Hlaupari barked his usual welcome. Ful and Yrling were still upon their horses, and Sidroc and Toki walking with Oddi at the head of the oxen. Sidroc had bent to rub his dog's head when the door to the house opened.

Signe came hobbling out from the dim interior, supported on the arm of Ebbe. The thrall-woman's nose and eyes were running from her tears, and Signe's eyes too were wet. She looked up at the men on their mounts.

"Berthe is dying," Signe told them. Despite her weeping her voice was clear and strong. "Bleeding to death, and it cannot be staunched."

She stared at the men as they swung down from their mounts. Oddi came up to take the horses, his face downcast.

Sidroc and Toki hung back behind Ful and Yrling. Women had mysterious problems and did bleed, they knew.

Signe was speaking again, looking at Ful and Yrling. "She was gotten with child, which she tried to rid with potion of houseleek. But she could not expel the unborn babe, and it has festered within her."

The two boys saw Yrling turn and look at Ful.

"I gave her henbane seeds to ease her pain," Signe went on, "but we can do no more for her."

The men still did not speak. Signe, feeble as she was in body, straightened herself on Ebbe's arm. "She will not name the father. And I can guess why."

Signe was moving back to the door of the house, drawing the men with her, not only with a movement of her arm, but with her eyes. Sidroc and Toki found themselves drawn in their wake. They all approached the alcove near the kitchen yard door in which Berthe slept. The curtains were open. There was an awful smell about the dying woman, which hit them in a wave as they neared. Balled up lengths of linen lay on the floor about her, stained dark with blood.

Berthe lay on her box-bed, glassy-eyed before them. Signe stopped at her head and turned to the men, confronting them with the truth of what was before them.

Sidroc felt Toki turn away. But he himself continued to look at the dying woman. A light blanket covered her, almost to her throat. She lay on her back, her face ashen, her yellow hair sticking to her damp brow. Her eyes were open, but seemed sightless. To Sidroc it was reminder of how she looked, staring straight up and unblinking into the sky when he had seen her motionless under Yrling.

Signe stared at them. "Look what you have done," she challenged. It seemed meant for all of them, even the boys.

Sidroc recalled that three or four times in the past Berthe had been sick for several days. After this she had looked wan, but continued with her work. Now he understood more. Perhaps those times she was ridding herself of an unwanted child through the use of herbs.

Signe's next words to the two men confirmed this. "She has rid herself of so many of your babes. This time, it killed her."

The men were still speechless. Both of them were shaking their heads, a slight motion which Sidroc could not read. He looked again at Berthe lying under her blanket. She seemed to have one hand drawn over her chest. He wondered if clasped in that hand was the small leathern key she always wore.

A few days after Berthe had been buried Sidroc and Toki were in the barn at the milking. Neither boy had spoken about the dead woman, but her death and the manner of it had cast a pall upon the farm. Now Hlaupari, who had followed them in and curled up in his accustomed spot in the straw, began to whine. Sidroc turned his head against the cow's flank to look at him. It was happening again. Another fit.

For the past few months the hound had been taken by sudden fits of trembling. He would fall to the ground, legs rigid but thrashing, eyes rolled up, mouth open, tongue lolling. They began as this had, with a simple whine, but deepened to violent tremors. Afterwards he would lie exhausted and panting, unable to rise. Sidroc would wait until the hound's breathing steadied, then hoist him to his feet. Sometimes he fell back again, but more often than not he was able to walk, straight-leggedly at first, but then more normally. The big plumed tail never failed to thump against Sidroc's legs.

Sidroc finished with the cow and drove her with a hand on her rump back out through the barn opening. He squatted down by Hlaupari's side. He had learnt not to try to touch him when the fit was fully upon him; a number of small scars on his right hand attested to this. He could do nothing but watch, and murmur to the beast.

"You should kill him, end his suffering," Toki told him. He had finished with his own cow and come round to stand over Sidroc and his hound.

Sidroc winced to hear it, but it was what Ful and Yrling and even Signe had suggested was best. The dog was old, and his fits coming more frequently.

Sidroc looked up at Toki. The two of them had ranged through fields and marsh with Hlaupari. The hound had flushed brent geese from reeds in shallow water so the boys might let fly their arrows and try to down them. If they hit their mark, Hlaupari splashed joyfully through the waters to claim the prize, trotting back to them, head held high, with an arrowed goose in his clenched jaws. They had netted birds with the dog too, used fowler's nets propped up on tall stakes and yanked on the pull cords when Hlaupari had driven curlews into it. More than once the hound himself got netted, which always made Sidroc laugh.

The dog had been his father's, before ever it had been his. When his father had taken the boat to go fishing that final time, he and Hlaupari had waited up for him, and kept on waiting, both at the farm and on the stream bank.

Sidroc looked back at his hound, the muzzle whitened with years. The fit was lasting longer than any before. The spittle falling from the bluish tongue was thick, almost like sea foam. The noise from the throat was a whimpering cry, pitiful to the ear.

"Want me to do it?" Toki posed. He looked uncertain enough, asking this, and uneasy too. Both boys had wrung the necks of any number of fowl, strangled geese with cords, helped in the slaughtering of the big and fatted pigs. These beasts were dispatched with a word of thanks to Freyr or his sister Freyja for their lives. But they were food; raised, fed and cared for just for that end. Hlaupari was his friend.

"Thanks," Sidroc muttered, but lowered his head, shaking away the help. Yet it must be done; the dog was suffering. He could not use his knife, that knife also given him by his father.

He rose and went to the workbench there by the door. Hanging over it was one of the small axes used for kindling. He reached for it, closing his hand about the wooden handle, worn smooth as polished bone from so much handling.

He must do it quick or not at all. He returned to his dog, whose whining had grown into a series of strangled yips, the big head moving as if snapping at flies. Yet the body looked unable to stir, the legs no longer thrashing but straight as pokers.

"Hlaupari," Sidroc called. He held the blunt edge of the axe over the dog's head. He knew Hlaupari must die sometime soon, but had hoped to awaken one day with the dog soundlessly dead in his sleep. He had not foreseen having to send him.

Sidroc's jaw was clenched and his eyes swam from under his lowered lids. He hazarded placing one hand on his hound's shoulder, and with that warm fur under his touch slammed the broad end of the axe down on the head with all his strength. The crack of the breaking skull rent the air.

Hlaupari made no sound. There was a rush of gentle air from the lungs, nothing more. The head fell back, the tongue no longer moving. Sidroc lowered his chin, almost to his chest. His left hand was still upon the shaggy shoulder.

Are there dogs in Asgard, Sidroc asked himself. He had not heard of such, but Freyja herself was said to go about the Heavens in a cart pulled by two cats. Certainly if cats roamed the gold-paved ways of Asgard, hounds too must be admitted. Hlaupari would be waiting for him. He curled his fingers deeper in the fur he held.

He heard Toki moving around him and looked up. He had gotten the drag sling Ful and Yrling used to carry deer from the woods. They could swing Hlaupari's body on that, pull him to a place to bury him.

They dug together, out by the narrow rivulet that the dog had loved nosing around. Shovelling in the spadesful of dirt was the second hardest thing Sidroc had ever done.

Chapter the Eleventh

TOKI

TOKI saw Gunnborga even sooner than he had expected. There was still a week to the Mid-Summer feast and fire, but the maid and her mother came riding in a horse-drawn waggon and stopped at the farm. Gunnborga's stepfather was with them, mounted on a third horse. A serving man drove the horse waggon, and no one at Ful's farm was surprised to hear they were headed for Ribe to undertake some trading.

They had not as yet gone far, but Signe made sure water was carried for the horses, and ale for the folk. Gunnborga and her handsome mother were happy to step down from the jolting waggon for a respite. Signe was unsteady that day; if she rose too quickly she was liable to faint, and her guests walked to where she sat in the kitchen yard.

Toki and Sidroc had finished with the buckets they had hauled the horses' water in, and now lingered just outside the confines of the yard. Toki caught Gunnborga's eye, and with a jerk of his head invited her to absent herself from where her mother sat chatting with his own. She trailed slightly behind the two boys as they led her around and past the barn. There, in an unused pasture, lay the makings of the Mid-Summer fire.

"So large!" were Gunnborga's first words. She had made a little squeal at first sight of it; the mound of logs and brush rose far above her head. Mid-Summer was the most joyful of all celebrations, the longest day in the wheel of the year. It heralded the peak of the Sun's reach, and its coming decline over their days, though the long dusks of lingering daylight would last all Summer.

"And we are not done," Toki assured her. There was always dead-wood to cut and brush to be cleared, much of which was not suitable for smoking into long-burning charcoal. The great fires welcoming Spring and Summer were best for these forest offerings.

"And did you build it," she wanted to know, looking at both boys. The expectant look on her face prompted Toki to answer as he did.

"Já, we did," he said.

Sidroc grinned at this claim, and added, "With Yrling."

The larger logs, dry as they were, were heavy, and rolling and lifting them wanted both strength and care.

"Mother says I may stay up all night this year," Gunnborga now told them. Her eyes were still fastened on the brown masses of waiting wood, as if they were already flickering into flaming life.

After a long day of dancing and eating, children rapidly tired, as did the older folk at such gatherings. Often none but the young and unwed men and women stayed up to herald the new day, in a sky that only briefly dimmed. Sidroc and Toki had never been amongst those who sat, far into the night, about the base of the smouldering fire, telling tales and jesting with pretty maids. This kind of wooing would need to wait until they were older.

"I will stay up with you," Toki made bold to proclaim.

She turned to him, smiling.

"And get you a cup of mead to drink," he further promised.

Gunnborga's wide blue eyes widened further. "I may have honey-water, but not mead," she returned, in a solemn tone. Mead, potent and rich, was quaffed by older folk at such special feasts, never by children.

Sidroc could not keep from sounding a short laugh. Toki had filched the mead jug at one of the Winter's Feasts, and downed not one but two cups. Sidroc had taken a full swig from it as well, but one deep mouthful only. It had acted on them in surprising ways. After the initial sweetness Sidroc had felt a burning heat in his throat, as if he had swallowed a small coal, a heat that ended in warming pleasure in his belly. The first cup Toki downed had made him loud, and after the second, drunk with equal quickness, he had begun to look cross-eyed. It was all he could do to stagger out into the cold rain, there to retch up the drink, and the good dinner of roast pig which had preceded it. If his father had not been deep in his cups himself his absence may have been noted.

"I will bring you honey-water," Sidroc said to the girl. It was the first conscious effort he had made at any courting, this offer of his.

She beamed at him. "My mother will like that," she said.

The lady spoken of was now calling to her daughter; it was time to resume their travels. As they moved away Gunnborga waved from the waggon-board.

"I will bring her mead, and I will kiss her," Toki said with sudden vehemence as he stood next Sidroc. They had not moved far from where the fire was laid, and Toki's eyes were looking after the dust rising from the iron-bound wheels of Gunnborga's waggon.

Sidroc scoffed. "Not likely if you are rolling on the ground, sick." His cousin turned to him now.

Sidroc could not help the next. "Besides, she likes me, not you."

Toki swung at him so suddenly that Sidroc had little time to duck. He pulled his chin back, but Toki's fist still caught him on the side of his head, at the temple. For an instant he saw brilliant flecks of light where the vision in his left eye should be. The next moment he was upon Toki, battering away with both fists.

Toki was well-built and strong for his age, but Sidroc's longer arms gave him swift advantage, as did his anger at the surprise attack. The boys had scrapped many times before, ending in bloodied noses or blackened eyes. Ful and Yrling had laughed when they had caught them doing so, and sometimes both had been birched, but more often neither.

Sidroc had said nothing but the obvious; his cousin had, a few months ago, drunk himself to sickness, and their neighbour did seem to favour him. Even her mother had suggested that. For Toki to attack him over this made no sense. He gave Toki a final poke, catching him in the left shoulder, spinning him to the ground. He stood over him, panting.

He could jump on him, pin him to the ground until he begged for quarter, but did not. He just stared at his cousin, who lay blinking up at him under tousled yellow hair.

Sidroc stepped back. During the fight Toki had kicked him in the shin, and hard, and he felt the bruise to the bone there. It would hurt for days. He remembered then how a few days ago Toki had brought the drag-sling, and how they had both taken Hlaupari by his stiffened legs and swung him upon it. Toki had worked with him, digging the grave for the dog.

Sidroc's hand went now not to his sore shin, but out to his cousin, offering him a lift up.

Toki considered the hand his cousin extended to him. It was Sidroc's long reach that had bettered him. Next time he would use something to extend his own. Now he took the offered hand, and rose to his feet.

A few days later the boys were out moving the sheep to the far pasture. They both had crooks in their hands, but Hlaupari's loss was sharply felt. Even the querulous ram began trotting when the hound approached, and the ewes needed no more than a glare from his eye. Without him it took the boys some time to drive the flock to the wooden footbridge spanning the narrow dike which parted the pastures. The newly shorn sheep clattered over it, the lambs bobbing and baaing at their mothers' flanks. Then the cousins hoisted the planked footbridge up, shoving it away to hem the beasts in. This was heavy work, and both had had to run and block the sheep at times as they drove them over. Once done, they started back to the farm.

Sidroc was thinking of Hlaupari, though neither boy had mentioned him. As they walked they passed the burial mounds of the family, beyond which lay only trees. The mounds were covered with grasses, and some too piled with stones of unusual shape or colour. A little distance off and to one side sat those smaller mounds marking freedmen and thralls who had died at the farm. Berthe's mound was there, the soil still raw and brown, just like that Hlaupari lay under by the runnel of water. Sidroc found his step slowing as he looked at the dead woman's resting place.

"She is like your mother," Toki said, of a sudden.

Sidroc turned to look at him. Toki held his crook upon his shoulder, Sidroc's grasped in his hand hanging at his side. He felt that hand tighten about the shaft of it.

"My father told me," Toki went on. "You are the son of thrall."

Sidroc's protest was as swift as his words were firm. "She was a freedwoman."

Toki had ready return. "That means she was once a slave."

He seemed to know what response this would provoke, as Toki swung his crook around almost as if it were a spear. This angered Sidroc the more, and he whipped the crook he held up, knocking Toki's from his hands as if it were a staff.

Even as he did this Sidroc was aware of the truth in Toki's words. He knew his mother was a freedwoman, which did indeed mean she had once been a thrall. But the way Toki said it belied the few things his father had told him about her: that she was a good woman, and kind, and had cared for him. Toki's words were meant as insult, nothing less.

Toki's hands stung from the way his cousin had knocked the crook out of them, but he curled them into fists just the same.

"Son of a thrall," he taunted.

Sidroc dropped the crook and lunged at the jeering Toki. He gave a yell as he did so, intent on landing the first blow. Toki dodged, and Sidroc's fist met only air. Toki laughed at him, and began to speak again.

"Son of a thra – " was all he got out; Sidroc had found Toki's cheekbone.

The blow sent him sprawling, but he jumped up. Even before he had fully straightened himself Toki's hand was on the sheath that held his knife. This would defeat his cousin's longer reach. The blade flashed in the sunlight as Toki sprang at the disbelieving Sidroc.

He seemed to aim right at his cousin's throat. Sidroc raised his elbow to block the blow. Toki had all his weight behind it, the arm cocked just enough to add strength to the wrist. The tip of the knife found home beneath Sidroc's left eye, and ripped downward through his cheek.

It was not a yell Sidroc gave this time, but a deep and strangled gasp. His left hand rose to his face, clapped over the blood beginning to pour there. His right hand joined it, pressing against a slice that felt like living fire.

He rocked forward, unable to speak. The blood was such that he was not sure if he still had his left eye. He drew his hands down a little. He could see, though the eye was filmed with blood.

Toki was staring at him, but Sidroc had closed both his eyes against the pain. The backs of Sidroc's hands were running with blood. Pressed against his face as they were Toki could not see what damage his blade had wrought, but it must be great. He meant in the moment he had pulled his knife to hurt Sidroc, but now that he had, it did not give the satisfaction he sought. He felt cheated of any sense of triumph, cheated and confused. And it was Sidroc's fault anyway, he had knocked the crook from his hands, it was he who could not stand hearing the truth of his thrall-mother.

For a long moment Toki struggled, looking on his cousin. A chill rippled through him, despite the warmth of the day; a cool numbness that turned to mounting fear at what he had done. He knew he should say something, beg Sidroc's pardon for a stupid act, try to staunch the bleeding, at least run to the farm for help. But he could do none of these things. He would beat down the fear. It is your own fault, he kept saying to himself, as if he spoke aloud to Sidroc. None but your own.

At last Sidroc pulled his hands away. Toki could scarce see the gash for the blood, but it was there, a darker, welling line of open flesh running from beneath the eye and almost to the chin. Still Toki could say nothing, and Sidroc too was silent.

Sidroc could pull the knife from his own belt and go after Toki, still holding his knife in his hand. He would not, for he knew he would kill Toki if he did so.

This knowledge, swift and sudden as was his wounding, filled his breast, sweeping all else aside. If I draw my knife, I will kill you. His heart swelled in thumping heat with this awful awareness.

Instead Sidroc turned away. He walked with long strides past the burial mounds, and into the stand of oak and elm trees behind them.

Toki waited some little time before returning to the farm. When he appeared, alone, and with a swollen cheek, Yrling took note. The boys' uncle had spent the day with Ful and the male thralls, riving whole tree trunks, driving wedges to form planks. Now, as Yrling washed up in the kitchen yard, Toki neared.

"What happened to you?" asked his uncle, tilting his head to Toki's bruised cheek. The eye was showing slightly purple.

"Nothing."

"Nothing looks a lot like your cousin," Yrling answered. "Where is he?"

Toki shrugged. Yrling continued to stare at him.

Finally Toki said, "He ran off."

"Ran off?" There was not much that Yrling could think of to make Sidroc run from Toki. "What happened," he demanded again, his tone now low and grave.

"He got . . . cut."

"Cut? By your knife? Where did you cut him?"

"In the face."

Yrling pulled his tunic back on, buckled on his belt and knife. "Where did you see him go," he demanded of his nephew.

"In the wood, behind the mounds," Toki answered. He had a grudging tone that made Yrling want to clout him.

"And you left him?'

"He went off, I told you."

"Come on. We are going for him." Signe was within the house, a good thing; he did not need female fears on top of this. But Toki hung back.

"Come on," Yrling ordered. "You are twice the coward, if you stay behind now."

That spurred Toki, and they set out. The woods were too thick for a horse; they would go as Sidroc had, on foot, follow the animal trails until they found him.

Sidroc walked into the trees with no clear goal; his need to be away from Toki drove him. He felt the blood running from his chin, and his hands were both sticky with it. He stopped and pulled two oak leaves and pressed them against the wound. The blood held them there, at least for a few more steps. He had nothing to stop the bleeding with, and the plants used for this, such as earthgall and woodruff, grew back in the herb patch Signe tended; he knew of nothing in a forest which might serve the same.

He kept moving forward amongst the oaks and elms. The shade cast from their leafy boughs was broken by bright glades into which sunlight fell. Some ferns grew there, in dappled light, and he wondered if they be good for wound-care, but he went forward without stopping to pluck them, aware only of the searing pain and his growing thirst. He felt the bleeding begin to slow, then stop. The whole side of his face felt fiery-hot.

This wood was crossed with streams, most of which would have water this early in the season. He would find one, wash the wound as well as he could. The smell of the blood filled his nostrils, and more than once he swatted at flies drawn by it. The fingers of his hands felt stuck together by the drying blood; he shook them to rid them of the helpless sensation.

He found a rivulet of water. It barely flowed, and there were fine cobwebs dusted with spores from ferns floating above the still surface. He knelt on the damp mosses and thrust his hands in, shaking off the blood underwater, letting the slight chill of the wet cool them. Then he bowed his head nearer and pulled handfuls onto his face. He almost yelped at the touch of it; the rawness of the wound made even water an irritant. But he caught his breath and splashed more on. When it ran clear of dried blood he touched his cheek. He traced one finger along what he thought was the side of the cut; he could not be sure where the wound began and ended. He felt the bone under the eye, recalled the flash of the knife tip coming at it. The eye was spared, yet he knew the wound to his cheek to be a grievous one.

He sat back on his heels. Odin, All-Father, had one eye. But he had offered that which was lost willingly, so that he might gain foresight. His was almost taken from him, with nothing granted in return.

I did not kill Toki, he reflected. I did not kill my kin. Mayhap that was what was granted him, a gift he had given himself.

He bent over the water, tried to clear it with his hands. He lifted some to his mouth, thought he tasted his own blood. Some must still be on his mouth. He tried to touch alongside the cut again, as a way to see and know it. The whole length of it was pulsing, making of the pain an animate thing.

I did not kill him, he said to himself once more.

He lowered his hand, thought of what he should next do. He could rest a while longer, then rise and make his way back to the farm. But just now, kneeling in this quiet wood, he could not consider this.

He had his knife. In the pouch on his belt he had the sharp flint and iron striker he carried every day. He could find a deeper stream, a forest pool, whittle a sapling to a point, spear fish and roast them. He could make snares from slender vines and set them, catch small game. These things arose, one by one, into his thoughts, and he turned them over in his mind. He need not go back, not until he wanted to.

Yrling did not wait until he reached the burial mounds before he began whistling for Sidroc. He put two fingers to his mouth and blew out the shrill call he used, that which told the listener it was Yrling who approached. He walked so rapidly that Toki must needs almost break into a trot to keep up.

Before they chose a deer track and entered the woods, Yrling paused, lifted both cupped hands to his mouth, and called out Sidroc's name. Nothing but the buzzing drone of insects returned to their ears. He bellowed a second time, then followed that with a whistle. Silence.

They plunged into the trees, Yrling leading. They would be missing their supper, but Toki knew enough not to say anything about it. Yrling had already named him a coward, and he must prove he was not. He might have a good birching coming to him, from his father if not from Yrling as well, and must make the cut seem an accident. If he did not help to find Sidroc now, it would look the worse for him later.

It was almost dark before they returned to the place of burial. Yrling had gone as deep into the wood as he could cover, describing a broad arc through the trees and dells, whistling and calling. If Sidroc heard him, he would not, or could not, answer.

Yrling cursed the death of the boy's hound. Hlaupari would have led them to him, he was certain. As it was he could do no more tonight. Toki had said almost nothing the whole time, not even complained, which was rare. He would deal with him once Sidroc was back, not before. Now they emerged from the wood, thirsty and hungry. Winking across the gloom of coming night they saw the cooking fire in the kitchen yard, and made for it.

Sidroc had heard a distant whistle, and known it to be Yrling's. In his dulled state it washed over him, not as a summons, but as some lesser echo of his uncle's being. He had risen from the watercourse at which he stopped, and gone on into the trees, looking for a deeper stream, one at which he would make his simple camp. He had not found it. The pain of his wound, his weariness, the weight of his thoughts, all had slowed his steps. The forest undergrowth was thick where he was, and pressing forward more difficult. After a time he saw a young ash, and dropped down at its roots, his back against the straightness of the trunk.

He tipped his head on the grooved bark. It was dusk, and the leaves made only the gentlest of soughing in the lessening wind. He closed his eyes. It was then he heard the whistle, floating from afar, yet distinct, that from Yrling. He heard it once. He could rise, whistle back. He even put his fingers to his mouth. The act of lifting his upper lip brought a wave of new pain to his cheek. He let his hand drop back to his side.

The heat of the throbbing awoke him during the night. He tried once to lie flat, but it made the pulsing in his face the greater. He sat up, back against the ash, and dozed as he could.

A woman came, one clothed in light. She shimmered before him. He could not see her face clearly, but felt her beauty. He tried to speak to her, but it hurt to move his mouth. Tell me what to do, he asked, without words.

At dawn he awoke, and stood up. The pain was different now, steadier. If he lowered his head it grew fierce. He kept it up, stood there a moment with one hand on the rough bark of the ash.

She was my fylgja, he told himself. My guardian spirit, from my father. From Yrling, who called to me. I must go back, back to the farm.

He made his way, slowly but with sure steps, back along the track he had taken. He came out of the trees at a point nearer the house than where he had gone in. Oddi was out with the cows, and when he saw Sidroc he made haste towards him.

He saw his aunt, sitting where she often did, at one of the work tables in the kitchen yard. Ful too appeared, out from the barn. As he neared them Yrling came from behind Ful, and began to run to him.

It was Yrling reached him first. The look on his uncle's face said much to Sidroc. Yrling stopped before him with opened mouth, brow furrowed, his eyes locked on Sidroc's face. His grimace silently summed up Sidroc's wound. Then Yrling swallowed, gestured with his hand to come.

Oddi was next. He looked shaken, but with Ful and Yrling watching would make no move towards the boy.

Signe was trying to rise from her bench, but the thrall-woman Ebbe was holding her back. His aunt reached her arm out to Sidroc as he neared the table at which she sat.

"Hrald. Hrald," she called him. Her words were choked by her tears.

Sidroc blinked at what she said. Did he look so much like his lost father, or was she asking forgiveness for what had happened of he who had been her brother? He shook his head in answer, feeling the stiffness of the cheek.

Ful joined them, and fixed his narrowed eyes on Sidroc. He turned his head and bellowed out his son's name, then spat upon the hard ground. Toki came out from around the back of the barn, and stood where his father pointed he should stand, at his mother's right hand, facing Sidroc.

Ebbe had fetched linen and a basin. Signe had calmed enough to speak again, and now slipped a large bronze key off the keeper at her waist. "Get him a cup of mead," she rasped, in the direction of both Ful and Yrling. Yrling took it, and came back from the brewing shed with a small pottery cup sloshing with the golden liquid. He put it in Sidroc's hand.

"Drink it," he ordered.

Sidroc took a gulp. His mouth was stiff, and it hurt more to drink, but drink he did. The first mouthful was as he recalled it from Jul, the honeyed sweetness giving way to warmth as it went down. Empty as his belly was, that warmth spread rapidly through him.

His aunt had soaked a piece of linen in the basin, and now held it to his face. "It is so swollen," she breathed, when she had pulled the dripping cloth back. "It has some taint, methinks."

Her next words were for Ebbe. "A poultice of woodruff, pounded with butter," she asked.

Ebbe nodded and moved off to the rows of herbs.

Ful had been staring with unmoving eyes at Sidroc, and now gave Toki a push in the back. "What do you think of your handiwork, son?" he posed.

Toki was looking at his shoes. His father gave him another poke, almost making him trip. Toki shook his head like a bothered animal.

Ful was not done with him. "Maybe I should mark you like you marked him."

Toki jerked his head up at this, and to his father.

Sidroc felt his own eyes blaze, but he was not looking at Ful. The word *marked* was sounding in his head.

That night Toki had as well to do Sidroc's chores, the last of which was securing the hens. After he had latched up the fowl house he crossed near the open door of the barn. A figure lunged at him, wrapped an arm about his shoulders, and pulled him inside, crushing him against a strong chest. The free hand of he who grabbed him held a knife, the blade gleaming dully in the low light. That blade now came straight to Toki's face.

"Uhhh . . . " All Toki could do was gasp.

"The Gods gave you everything, Toki," he heard his uncle breathe. "How would you like to lose some of that, right now?"

Toki tried, with a violent wrench of his shoulders, to free himself, but Yrling's strength was far too great.

"I can make you two more equal, with just the tip of my knife," his uncle crooned.

Toki's eyes were nearly crossed, focussed as they were upon the point of the blade, but a short span from his eye. He could not have spoken if he wanted to; the breath was nearly being squeezed out of him.

"Even your father thinks it would be just." His uncle's voice bore a calmness that made it all the more chilling.

The words dropped like lead weights in Toki's ears. Yrling could not mean this; he could not mean that he would scar him. His uncle had relaxed his grip upon him, and Toki drew a panicked gasp of air. Then he tried to throw his head back and away from the blade, and began thrashing, flailing with his free arm and kicking with his feet. Anything to escape.

But Yrling was quick. The arm which had held Toki's shoulders in a talon-like grip now moved, and came to his face. Yrling shoved him against the barn wall. His uncle was now directly before him, holding Toki by the face, pinching his cheeks painfully with his grasp.

"You are a coward, Toki," Yrling told him. "Let us see how well you bear up now."

The blade, which had been withdrawn a short distance, now made straight for Toki's left cheek. Water ran from his eyes, and if Yrling had not been holding him so strongly, his trembling legs would have crumpled under him.

A stammering wail sounded from between his pinched lips. "Nej," he tried. "Nej . . . "

More than tears were now running; he felt the hot flow of his urine wetting his leggings, running down his leg.

"Nej, nej," he begged. He closed his eyes against the shame of wetting himself, closed his eyes against the coming cut upon his face.

He felt no touch of cold steel. Instead he felt his uncle's grip loosen, then free him entirely. When he opened his eyes Yrling was staring at him.

His uncle's eyes raked down to Toki's trembling knees, saw the darkening stain.

"Ha!" There was no note of triumph there, only disgust.

Toki shifted his head from left to right, trying to see through the gloom of the barn. They were alone; neither Sidroc nor his father were there to witness his shaming. At least Yrling had spared him that.

He looked back to his uncle. Yrling still held his knife, but lowered, and at his side. His uncle asked a question now, a harsh demand.

"What did you two fight over?"

Toki's thoughts scrambled back to the burial mounds. "His mother."

Yrling let out a short breath. "Women. Women or silver are at the heart of every fight."

He shook his head, whether at Toki's answer or Toki himself, the boy could not know.

He watched his uncle look down at the knife in his hand, watched him slide it back in its sheath.

"You are lucky, Toki. The Gods love you, and you are lucky," he summed. "I think you will not live long, because of it."

Sidroc awoke late next morning, groggy from the draught of dried cowslip root his aunt had made him drink. But he had slept, with the moist, linen-wrapped poultice covering half his face. He swung his legs from his alcove and stood, feeling his buzzing head to be twice its size.

Everything from the neck up hurt. Talking was difficult and chewing impossible. Moving his mouth moved his cheek, that cheek now split open. Signe gave him milk to drink, and hot broth to sip. He moved from alcove to kitchen yard to work table. He was weak from hunger and loss of blood and sat on the bench with his shoulders slumped. Seating himself, he knocked his shin against the trestle, that shin that Toki had kicked a few days ago when they had fought about Gunnborga. It was still sore. The hurt his cousin caused him then was so small in comparison. Sidroc's lip twisted a moment, almost in laughter.

He had not seen Toki since last night, and knew he would be about his chores, chores that he need perform for both of them. Signe made him another poultice, which he must lie down to use. He did not want to return to his alcove and climbed instead on the table. At least here he was outdoors. Despite the hardness of the surface he fell into sleep.

In the afternoon Signe studied the wound again. When she had lifted the poultice the gash was weeping, not the slightly yellowish, clear liquid of a healthy wound, but an ill-smelling pus.

She shook her head slightly as she spoke to him. "I must open it, my boy, and search out the evil in it." She bit her lip. "'Twill only be the worse, if I cannot get it clean now."

She warmed vinegar. With Ebbe pouring, Signe placed her pointing fingers on either side of the gash, and pulled. The warm vinegar drizzled down upon it. The stinging was such that Sidroc drove his fingernails into the worn wood of the table, so hard did he clutch its edges.

Tears were running from the sides of his eyes. When they finished he sat up. His tunic was wet from his sweat and the vinegar that had run through the towelling they had laid there. His aunt was fighting her own tears, but had Ebbe take her keys and bring him a swallow of mead.

"It will heal now," she promised, though her voice was unsteady with her fears. She swallowed back her next words, those she would have said for a common wound to arm or leg once the fester had been chased from it. He would not be as good as new. Her son had spoiled Sidroc's face, forever. Boys hurt each other in play or in fighting, but this went far beyond. She had not served her brother Hrald as she should have, by raising a son who could do this.

Her nephew nodded to her. He was quiet by nature, but had said almost nothing since he had returned. It hurt him to speak, she knew. With his damp hair and thin face he looked pale and even gaunt. He looked too as if he had aged overnight, like a child stolen by faeries and then restored to his rightful folk. Some boyishness had been bled out of him, she knew. He would not return fully to who and what he had been.

Later in the afternoon Toki came up to him. Sidroc had moved about the kitchen yard, but was sitting now at the work table at which he had spent much of his day. His hands were lying upon the surface of it, fingers splayed, and he was looking down at them.

Toki slowed, and stopped on the other side of the table. They were alone. Sidroc waited a moment, then raised his face to him.

Toki regarded him. He had seen the ugliness of the cut the day before. Now, though Sidroc's face was less distorted by swelling, it looked the worse. He saw the truth of what he had done.

He thought of last night, with Yrling. He thought of his shame in begging and crying and peeing. His jaw moved; he swallowed. Then he spoke.

"I am adding more brush to the fire pile," Toki said. He shrugged toward the barn, beyond which lay the waiting pile.

It was a call for Sidroc to join him.

He rose, walked with Toki past the barn. His cousin had dragged a mass of old hazel cuttings to one side. Together the boys began prodding and weaving them into the framework of logs and branches.

It took them some time to push them all in. When they had done they stood side by side, looking on the pile.

"Why did you do it," Sidroc asked, in a low voice. He had not turned to look at his cousin. His voice sounded odd, and every word he formed gave his wound another twinge. Still, he went on.

"You tried to kill me. You were aiming for my throat."

It took Toki a long while to answer. "You made me mad."

Now Sidroc faced him. He stared at Toki, with his unblinking blue eyes, smooth cheeks, firm and stubborn chin. He stared so long that Toki's own gaze faltered. The bright blue eyes shifted, and then dropped under the force of Sidroc's stare.

For the second time in as many days, Sidroc turned and walked away from him.

Chapter the Twelfth

FIRE

MID-SUMMER and its feast and fire came two days later. It was not a large gathering; farms were far-flung in these parts, but three or four of them nearby took turns hosting this ritual welcome to Summer, and fare-well to the growing light of the Sun.

Their nearest neighbour, who Gunnborga's mother had wed, had come, with his new wife and daughter, and his three children, all of which were within three or four years of Sidroc and Toki. The old couple to the East of Ful and Signe's farm were also there; they were quite alone, with daughters wed, but distant. A fourth family was a large one, with a range of hearty maids and youths, all at or nearing marriageable age; and these always had friends with them. All in all there were some forty-odd folk to cook for, though all families would make contribution to the tables in way of a side of smoky bacon, a crock or two of ale, or trays of freshly griddled and tender buckwheat cakes.

The food was of the simplest, but Signe and Ebbe tried to make good show of it. The domed oven had been kept fired, loaf after loaf of rye and wheaten bread pulled from its glowing mouth. The largest cauldron bubbled with a browis of millet, dried spotted beans, new carrots and peas, into which a fresh green sauce of parsley, thyme, and clary was stirred. Herbed cheeses, their curds washed and salted, sat in thick-walled pots. With the many long hours of sunlight, the hens were laying at their height, and honey-sweetened custards of beaten eggs and rich cream proclaimed this. Puddings of stale and shredded bread were mixed with more eggs and cream, dotted over with dried cherries and plums, and baked long in covered pans in the hottest of ashes. And the mead crock was brought out, as was a full cask of ale, the first mellowed by a year's storage in the cool spring house, the second freshly brewed, and made pleasantly bitter with ground-ivy.

Other than the needful caring for the farm beasts, which must be done Winter and Summer, holiday or no, work was set aside. It was preparation enough to carry every trestle and table out by the kitchen yard and its waiting food, to make more make-shift, from doubled boards which had recently known the adze, setting these upon saw-horses; and then roll short lengths of sawn tree trunks near, upon which more planks might be set to serve as benches.

There would be music, that of horn and drum and chimes, six-stringed harp and pipe, and singing too. Every such gathering would have at least one man, young or old, who knew the timeworn songs, and sometimes those who could make one anew. Dancing demanded music, and there would be dancing. When the fire was lit at noon, youths and maids, children and their grand-sires joined hands, to step around it in rhythmic motion. They mimicked the course across the Heavens of the great and life-bearing Sun, without which no plant could grow, no animal live nor thrive. As the music quickened, driven by beating drum or the rattling of hand-held chimes or brazen cymbals, the dancers would break their holds, pair off in smaller groups of six or eight, four or two. With laughing faces and hands slippery from sweat some would dance until they dropped, exhausted in the grasses they trampled. Even this returned life to the Earth. Every seed-head crushed under foot was given the chance to swell and sprout, push its way up to light, air and the needful Sun.

The meal would be ladled up, the ale casks tapped, and spoons raised to hungry mouths. As the day wore on young folk might walk or take sport with ball-games, bow and arrows, or other tests of skill. Their elders sat and talked, sharing news of crops or kin, or pushed amber and stone game pieces on scored wooden boards to capture the King's men.

All the time the fire burned. When first lit, in the bright light of high noon, its flame could be felt but not seen. As the sky paled and then dimmed the great logs at the base of the fire-pile showed their red and orange cores to those who came to stand about them. New logs might be flung on, young men making a contest of a perfect hit of the heavier ones. Benches were carried to encircle the flames; the young flocked to them, their elders staying within earshot back by the cooking rings. It was then that those of wooing age came into their own. Children were banished, or more often fell asleep, yawning, on blankets laid on the ground for them, to be carried away by mothers and fathers. To be allowed to stay up and greet the dawn was a privilege all children looked forward to, but few could meet.

It was this that Gunnborga looked forward to, and had been promised she might try. When she arrived early in the day with her mother and step-family she fairly ran to the pile. She saw it was even greater than when she had been here; Toki and Sidroc had indeed been busy.

She glimpsed the boys when she had jumped down from the waggon. They were making up benches from smoothed planks, setting them down alongside the long tables already groaning with food.

She saw Sidroc, bending over and shifting a round of tree-trunk that served as bench base. She went to him, a smile on her pretty lips. She wore an over-gown of yellow, which her mother told her made her look a flower.

Sidroc had loosened his braids so that his hair swung over his face. When he straightened up the dark brown hair flew away from his cheek. He had not seen her arrive, and now she stood before him.

Gunnborga looked up at him. She made a soft sound, an intake of breath. He watched her smile crumple. Her mouth twisted as if in pain, or growing fear. Her lips quavered, trying to regain her smile. She could not. Then she turned from him.

Late next morning Sidroc went to the alcove where his aunt and uncle slept. Most of the remains of the feast had been cleared away, and he was alone in the house as he went there. Under their box bed was a narrow chest of wood which he knew his aunt never locked. He pulled it out and opened it. What he sought was there, lying on the top, a round disc of smooth and flat copper. Polished with salt and vinegar it gave a good, if golden, reflection of those who looked into it. It was marred with tarnish now;

Signe did not often use it. He rubbed at it with his tunic sleeve, and carried it near the front door.

He opened the door, held the mirror up, and beheld his face. He too saw the truth of it.

His left cheek was split by a jagged rip, from eye to chin. It was all he saw.

He knew that from now on this would be the first thing folk saw when they looked at his face, the first and lasting thing.

TWO GIFTS

The Year 862

SIDROC and Toki had been sent to the farm of their elderly neighbour, to escort her to her nephew's house. Åfrid was newly widowed, and Ful had bought her farm. Both boys were sent, but only Sidroc arrived. They set out on foot, their new spears in their hands, but less than half way there, Toki left him.

"I will give you silver if you take the old hag by yourself," Toki posed. "Two aurar."

The trip would last nearly all day, what with driving the old woman's waggon to her nephew's inland farm, and the return home, on foot.

Sidroc considered. He had taken a fair amount of silver off his cousin in the past, not only to cover for missed deeds such as this, but over dice games.

"Where will you go instead?" Sidroc returned.

"Gunnborga's. Her step-brothers have that new colt."

"And you want to show off, riding it."

Toki laughed.

Sidroc shrugged in return. He ran his left hand through his hair, and glanced up at the heavens. It was early in Spring, and a steady and cool wind was blowing in a sky scudded with grey clouds.

"Go then," he answered. He had no desire to go to Gunnborga's farm, even if he were free from the task at hand. And Toki was little help when his mind was elsewhere. He would rather be alone, and give himself up to his thoughts than deal with Toki's shirking protests.

They paused long enough for Toki to pull the coins from his belt and pass them to his cousin. Sidroc was holding both spears as Toki fumbled in the leathern pouch that held his dwindling store.

"So you have no need to look upon your future home?" Sidroc asked, after he had slipped the silver in his own purse. He grinned.

Toki screwed up his face. "My home?"

"Why do you think Ful has bought Åfrid's farm? I think he means it to be your home, when you wed."

Toki scowled, telling Sidroc this had not occurred to him. Toki rarely thought ahead.

"I will no more farm than you can fly," Toki proclaimed. "And I will claim a huge hall in the land of the Angles as my home – none other."

This made his cousin laugh. "The Saxons will not welcome you with open arms."

"Nej. Yrling has shown that. But of the three of us, my hall will be the best."

"We will see. I know I will be richest." Here Sidroc gestured toward the purse Toki had just helped fill.

It was Toki's turn to shrug. "I will be back by dusk, and wait for you at the crossing so we return together."

"Make sure you are there," Sidroc warned. "I take your silver and do your work, but will not lie for you."

Toki made a face, and both boys laughed. They did so as differently as they themselves were. Toki laughed carelessly; Sidroc with knowing awareness.

Two years had passed since Toki's knife thrust. These were two years in which Sidroc must continue to live and work with his cousin, each and every day. Toki's family was the only one Sidroc had, the only folk he could live with. He had no choice, and nowhere else to go. If Fate had decreed it, he must accept it.

They parted, and Sidroc moved forward alone along the track. It was mostly open land, but not good pasture; the soil was sandy here, proof that once the sea had lapped the ridges he walked over. The gently rolling ground gave interest to the walk; most of Jutland was flat as the kitchen yard's griddle pan. For a moment he thought of Hlaupari, and how he would have liked such a walk. He gave his head a shake, pushing down a pang at the dog's memory.

Sidroc's hair was loose, he often now wore it that way. He rarely cut it, and it was long, a brown no lighter for all the time he spent outdoors. The hair fell and blew over his face, at times over his left cheek, screening for a moment the deep and ugly scar upon it.

He liked walking this landscape, liked a day free from the repetition of his chores, and most of all liked the way his spear felt in his hand as he lightly gripped it at his right side. With the point of his knife he had cut his sign into the ash shaft he held, the rune Sigel ᛋ the first letter of his name. It meant victory, and the Sun, a sign of power. The rune cut named the spear as his own.

His uncle was teaching him how to use it, but the spear already felt a part of him.

He neared Åfrid's farm. The bristle of its thatched roofs declared long years since they had been attended to, and the greening pastures were empty. Ful had already come and taken her cow and few sheep. The door to her snug house was closed, and he guessed, locked; the place had about it a silent and desolate air. Entering the work yards he saw around the end of the house a small waggon, standing horseless, but well-filled with goods. A horse, white-whiskered with age, stood in harness to one side, cropping at the long grass springing up alongside the barn wall. Some things were still on the ground at the waggon's iron-rimmed wheels, and the woman herself moved spryly about it as she loaded her final items.

He had slight recollection of her from past Mid-Summer fires and other feasts; she and her husband, being alone, had never hosted here, but were guests at the farms of others, sitting and talking with those as aged as they. Now her mouth crinkled into a smile when she straightened up and saw him. Her eyes smiled as well, small eyes of greyish hue.

"I am Åfrid," she greeted. He nodded at her, set the spear against the barn wall, and began lifting and fitting the final baskets and crocks onto the waggon bed. There was already a great deal she had stowed, including her loom, which she had pulled the pegs on and reduced to a series of long and smooth pieces of wood. She might be old, but she was full of vigour, and had a lively snappiness about her. He glanced at her with some respect, seeing how much she had done by herself.

Åfrid was reedy as a gnawed bone, her wrists and fingers thin and blue-veined, yet her face was round, almost childlike despite the maze of wrinkles lining it. That face reminded him of an apple after long storage in the root cellar, shriveled and shrunken, but still sound. Her hair was long and caught up in a grey plait, surprisingly thick, and her head wrap was of a bright green shade, almost matching the darker green of her over-gown. She had what he knew to be a fine set of bronze brooches on its shoulder straps, large ovals, well-embossed; the kind a man gives his bride the day after they are wed, and he briefly wondered if she had worn them that long.

"My hens," she said, after they had backed the horse into the traces and buckled him in. She pulled open a small sack in the waggon, and dropped a handful of grain into a dented basin. She rattled it, calling to her fowl in a sing-song tone. They flocked to her, clucking and pushing, their speckled wings partly outstretched. It was easy to catch them up and place them in the wicker cage awaiting them. Sidroc lashed it atop all else in the waggon.

Åfrid looked about her, pushing a stray strand of colourless hair back under her head wrap. She made for the house.

Sidroc was wrong; the door was not yet locked. He watched her push it open and vanish within. She must have wanted a final look. In a short time she came out. He watched her hand rise, saw her lay it flat upon the thick planks of the door. She stood still, palm pressed against it.

He had had no such farewell to his father's farm. Indeed it scarcely felt his home with his father gone, unwanted as he was. He looked away, recalling this. When he turned back she was before him, smiling.

"I give this into your trust," she told Sidroc, pressing it into his hand. It was an old key, the thumb turn worn from years of use, but the teeth, the working end, were sharp and ready. He helped her up and they settled themselves.

The horse ambled forward at the merest shake of the reins he held. Sidroc felt Åfrid was more than able to drive her own horse, but the way she grasped her mantle about her as they pulled out let him know she welcomed his help. A moment later she told him so.

"I thank you for coming for me. It saves my nephew the trip. It is enough they must take an old crone into the household." She laughed, almost playfully, at naming herself thus. "So I thank you."

He made a low sound, and gave an awkward shrug. He had been told to do this by Ful, and so far it was proving light duty. But he admired her once more, for jesting about her age. It would be terrible to be old, and he was glad he would die young, and he hoped, in glory. Not too young, he also hoped.

She had not turned back for a final glimpse; he respected that too. She had made her decision, sold the place to Ful, and was moving on. Her husband was buried here; he must be, though the mound was out of sight; she was leaving him too.

The skies above them were still grey, but the clouds less threatening. As they moved forward, following an eastward track, he asked her a question, one prompted by his being there with her.

"You have no children?" he wanted to know.

Åfrid gave a soft sigh. "Two who lived; daughters, good girls, both. They wed two brothers. But they are far away, in Skania."

Sidroc nodded. They were then overland and several short sails off. Girls were destined to wed and move away, sometimes far from their folk and farms. She had no living child near, and so now went to live with her nearest kin.

She was seated on his right, and he was aware that she was looking at him.

"How many Summers have you?" she asked.

He turned his chin slightly toward her. "Fourteen."

She did not look surprised, though others might have been. With his height, and especially his scar, folk often thought him older.

"Thinking of maids all the time," she surmised.

He felt the warmth come to his face, but hoped it did not show. Girls and women were very much on his mind; his body's urgings would not allow otherwise.

His eyes were fastened on the chestnut rump of her old horse. She began to hum a little tune, and then stopped herself to speak again.

"You are Sidroc," she began. "You did not speak your name back there."

"I thought you knew," he mumbled, uncertain. Of course she knew his name, even if they had never really spoken.

"It is good we are paired, you and I," she went on. "It is an old woman who can best teach a young man." She paused, not hiding her smile at his startle. "Not the things of the flesh – those things are easily discoverable yourself – but the greater wisdoms."

He dropped his eyes further, to the worn leather of the reins he held. He was not ready for what she said next.

"That is quite a scar you bear." This was a gentle observation, nothing more. "Who gave it deserves your thanks."

Gave it, Sidroc thought, of his marred face. Toki did it, if that was what she meant.

"It was my cousin Toki." This sharp and bitter fact sat in the air between them.

"He deserves your thanks." She repeated this lightly; lightly, and quietly.

He straightened at this madness from her mouth.

"I came close to killing him." It was spoken with the harshness he felt.

She clucked. "Yet you did not. He did you great service, two of them in fact."

He jerked his chin up. "How can you say that?"

"Your face proves the true from the false. Those fooled by showy gilt, and those who know gold. You count what you have lost, and not what you have gained. Those with true vision will . . . " she paused here, as if probing for words, " . . . still see you.

"There is no greater gift," she ended. "To be seen."

To be seen, he thought. His height made him stick out, young as he was. He was noticed, he knew. But to be seen . . .

"Who are you," he asked her, a question deeper than her name.

She laughed, in dry and cheerful mirth. "An old woman. One of the unseen. We vanish from sight, we women, when you men cease to notice us."

"I see you."

"And you may continue to see us. You are marked out, different from many of your kind."

He gave a short and rueful laugh. "Já. I am marked."

"Not that," she answered quickly. "Not that life-line you bear on your face, showing how crooked a course you must travel."

He started at this. Was she some teller of fortunes, who could look at a man's scar as well as his hand, and predict his Fate? He fell silent, turning this over, wanting to ask more, and yet wanting to return to what she had just told him.

"What was the second service Toki rendered me?"

"Ah. What you gained a moment after. You could have killed your cousin; I believe you. Yet you did not." Her words slowed, her light tone deepening at the graveness of the act.

"It takes as much courage – more – to hold back, than it does to thrust forward. You gained the sense of your own courage, your own strength."

He had turned the left side of his head slightly away during this, his chin set, eyes staring at the grasslands they slowly rolled through. He had seen his father hold back time and again from lashing out in word or deed at his wife. That same restraint must have helped him stay his hand against Toki.

He shifted his gaze ahead once more, and saw her nod, as if to herself, before she spoke again. "So the wound brought you two gifts. A test for others. And knowledge of yourself."

They rolled on a little further before she broke the silence.

"The scar you bear – you will be known for it. But that is of the skin, only. You were marked long before that; before your imagining. Before your birth."

He let this settle in his brain a moment, then looked back at her.

He could not but ask the next. "Who . . . who marked me?"

She squeezed her eyes shut. "Prow to stern . . . fore and aft . . . a woman," she recited.

"What woman?"

"Ah . . . bright. One of brightness."

My fylgja, he thought. The woman who came to me as I lay against that ash, bleeding . . .

"The ship – what has it to do with her?"

She looked down a moment. "A journey takes you to her."

It made no sense. His fylgja was with him, always. He had no need to board a ship to find her.

"Tell me more about the woman," he asked.

"Ah. The bright one." She squeezed her eyes closed. "She has you. But you cannot have her."

Then it must be the fylgja. "I cannot have her?"

"She is but young."

His fylgja was ancient; she had to be, if she had served as guiding-spirit for him, his father, and grandsire past . . .

"So it is a real woman you are speaking of?"

"She is young," she stressed, as if this were the reason for his denial.

He was looking at her from the tail of his eye now, almost unwilling to do more. Again he wondered who she was. Other women gave prophecies, but after they had chanted, chewed certain roots, drank potions steeped from herbs. Here was an old woman sitting next him, doing none of this, yet seemingly telling him what Fate had in store.

"You are a wand-carrier, a völva?" he asked, naming the title given to such a seeress.

"Nej," she objected. "Even herbs cannot summon what I see. There are men or women I near, who rouse the spirit to speak within me. Nothing more. It comes of its own. And goes."

She might be mad, or addled with age, but he wanted to hear more. He would hazard a further question.

"What else?"

Åfrid answered with a question of her own. "Who do you worship? Not just make Offering to, but truly worship?"

He chewed his lip, thinking. All-Father Odin was the choice of wise men – and those who knew treachery. Most warriors chose laughing Thor, red of hair and beard, with his mighty war-hammer Mjolnir, which never missed its mark and returned without fail to the God's hand. Loki the Trickster meant disaster, which seemed to touch everyone but he himself. He was lucky and deserved respect, if only for the damage he could wreak. But Loki could never be his choice; he did not want to fear who he worshipped. Baldr was the God of light, beloved by all, and Bragi had the gift of poetry and song, and wed to the lovely Idunn; but with his face, Sidroc could not find a model in such as these. At last he spoke.

"Tyr."

"Ah. Tyr. The God of Law. You have known great injustice, and his arm will guide you. A good choice."

Sidroc had never heard Tyr referred to this way before, but it made sense to him. Tyr was a warrior God, but a thoughtful one. When Fenrir the giant wolf allowed himself to be bound by a magical thread that gnomes had woven, he demanded that one of the Gods place his hand in his mouth as a pledge. Only Tyr would do so. When Fenrir found he had been tricked, he bit off and swallowed the God's sword-hand. Yet Tyr bore his loss without complaint. He understood the justice of his forfeit. Deceit had been used when none was promised. One might indeed consider Tyr the God of Law for this.

He felt she was studying him, and when he looked back to her, she spoke again, with another question. "Bethink you, though, of any God who might choose you, and honour them."

He felt the puzzlement showed on his face. How could a God choose one on Midgard? It was too much to ask. But the old woman was going on, answering for him.

"One day you will want Freyja on your side."

Freyja. Völvas were always dedicated to her.

He took this in. Freyja, that wild beauty, Goddess of lust and battle, giver of life, protector of all beasts of the field, she who as an equal to Odin himself welcomed slain warriors into her gemmed hall in Asgard.

"How do you know all this?"

"I do not. But I feel much. Because Death is near me. She has, I feel, once grasped you by the ankles, young as you are, tried to pull you down."

His father's fish net pulling him under. He let out a breath as he nodded.

"Yet you live," she went on. "And you nearly died."

"Já, almost."

She was staring at him, as if she would brook no half measures.

"What saved you?'

He was ready with his answer. "My father."

She gave her head a decisive shake. “Not who. What saved you.”

This was another, and quite different question, he realised.

It came back to him in a flood of sensation, the fish net tangling round him, the rough feel of the small and tight knots of its mesh as his fingers tried to beat it away, the cold saltiness of the water filling mouth and nose. The pull of the heavy net-weights. The sense that the more he struggled the surer the net coiled about him like a spider’s web, trapping him under. He thought of how he freed one hand and reached it out above the surface of the cold waves.

“My arm. I reached my arm up. My father could catch me then.”

“Out of Death’s pull.” She nodded. “You will make your way with that arm. And with your grasp.”

My arm, he thought. Always be reaching, his father had told him, the day he taught him to swim in the lake, the day the sea had nearly taken his life. By reaching he could stay afloat, propel himself through the water, tame it, make a friend of his enemy.

“Make my way,” he repeated, liking the sound of this. He spoke with real conviction now. “I mean to be a warrior, go raiding, and win treasure.”

“And I think you shall,” she agreed.

“My grasp?” He looked at her, for more. Did she mean the sword he would soon hold? Or something larger – glory and gold, that he would seize?

She looked at his hands, folded about the thin leather of the reins.

“Your hands are large and well-formed. You will close those hands around much of worth. But only because you have first grasped what you want, in your mind." A small pause, then a quick release of breath.

Her pale eyes went to his face, now turned to hers, and her words came slowly. "And much you will discard." Then with a shake of her grey head, she ended. "Woe betide those who stand between you and your desire."

All the long walk back to the farm Åfrid's words were sounding in his head. It was not only the odd nature of what she had told him, but the telling of it. She spoke to him as if he were already a man, gave him her full notice and attention.

He wanted to believe what she had said, even though half of it he could not understand. Circling in his mind was her mention of the woman, the bright one, who had him, but who he could not have, because she was too young. Too young? Some maids wed at little more than fourteen, the same age as he was now. What could Åfrid have truly meant – not ready? Perhaps. But maybe she spoke of his fylgja after all, who was both young and old at the same time; she must be, if she had been the guiding spirit to his kin for many generations, but was also the most beautiful woman he could imagine . . .

It was wholly dark by the time he neared the farm. If the sky had not cleared, with a half Moon hanging in it, he might have had a hard time finding his way. As he approached the crossing he whistled, and Toki whistled back. He saw his cousin stand up from the stone way-marker he had perched himself on.

"What took you?" were the first words from Toki's mouth.

"If you had shared the walk with me you would know," Sidroc returned, as they fell in together.

"Your neck is not broken, so I reckon you stayed on the colt's back," Sidroc offered next. "If he let you near him, in the first place."

"I am a better rider than you," Toki protested.

"Ask any horse," Sidroc scoffed back.

Chapter The Fourteenth

THE WARRIOR'S BARGAIN

YRLING, true to his word, had placed spears in both his nephews' hands, the iron heads not forged by Yrling nor Ful but by a true weapon-smith. Under Yrling's guidance the boys had cut and smoothed the straight and long ash poles which would serve as shafts. These sprung bolt upright from the trunk of a mid-sized ash tree beyond the cattle pasture. A few years ago Ful and Yrling had chopped it down with axes, then sawn the stump flat. With its roots sunk deep in the soil the ash sprouted with vigour, a circle of straight pole-like offshoots rimming the sawn-off edge of the trunk. Such coppiced ashes produced the best shafts for spears, for the round shoots had lively spring to them, far better than any sawn and shaped from a plank. Each boy was given two, a carrying spear for hand-to-hand fighting, and a shorter, lighter throwing spear, with a smaller iron head.

Yrling and the cousins had cut the stakes a whole year in advance, to give them time to dry, and laid them in the hay-loft in the barn; once fitted they must not shrink and loosen from the spear-head socket. After the shafts were crowned with the tapered heads, the boys held them as a King does his scepter of power. The carrying spears were much taller than the boys; man-sized in fact, for Yrling had trust in their strength, and saw no reason to deny them true men's weapons. Then their practice could start.

They began not with the dark and lethal tips, but by holding the shaft in both hands across the body, like a quarter-stick. Yrling had them spar, pushing and blocking with the poles, forcing the other to give ground through sheer strength, or by a sudden downward thrust at the foot with the blunt end. Strong wrists and shoulders were demanded of such training, as was a solid but fluid stance: knees bent, weight slightly forward. After this came throwing practice, hurling the lighter spear from a standstill and from a run at targets they created of rounds of wood, and straw-stuffed woollen bags strung hanging from tree boughs. Their uncle kept them to this; next year they would begin practice of actual thrusting fight, both two-handedly, and from behind a shield on their left arms.

Both cousins were strong, and avid learners, and Yrling pushed them. Even Ful could not begrudge the time they spent in such training; chores needed to be complete beforehand, and watching the youngsters and their uncle he secretly admired the skill he saw there. These three were destined for a larger realm than Jutland. As long as Toki returned to take over the farm, he would not stand in his son's way on the path to treasure.

The boys felt it too. Yrling had consented to take them both with him to Angle-land, and they wanted to be worthy of that promise. Yrling had sailed three times over the last five Summers, bringing back with him varying amounts of silver, weapons, and slaves. Much of the weaponry and all of the human treasure he took up to Ribe to exchange for more silver. He now had a good sword of his own, one picked up in battle from a slain foe, and owned a steel helmet as well. But he wanted a ship. He had only one-and-twenty years and would have to wait, for to buy or build a ship and outfit it for the North Sea crossing was a rich man's role. Yet Yrling was determined to hold the steering oar of his own drekar, and to look down the length of his dragon ship knowing all the men aboard it were those he had picked for their boldness and enterprise.

At the Thing, the Summer law-gathering that year, Sidroc saw two of those men. Once again, his Aunt Signe was not steady enough to go. Ful was feeling poorly in his joints, and did not relish the jolting of the waggon nor the hard bed it offered. No vote of Kingship would be taken, so Oddi was not needed, and he stayed on the farm with them and the thralls. It was Yrling and the cousins who went, Yrling driving Ful's horse and waggon bearing their camping gear, Sidroc on his uncle's mare, and Toki mounted as well, as Yrling had one of his mare's offspring he hoped to sell there. It was a three year old filly, a lighter chestnut than her mother. Riding there was a thrill for the boys; only the well-to-do had horses, and they were sorry Yrling was determined to sell the filly. As they entered the crowded grounds where the Thing was called, they saw youths who looked up at them, and in envy.

They were still pulling up the tent when two on horseback approached them. All three of their horses were now staked at their campsite, freed from saddles or harness. The two men who rode up to them reined their own horses in, and looked the mare and filly over. The third horse, Ful's gelding, was much like their own, a sturdy and willing enough beast. But the mare and her daughter were long of limb and had fine heads.

Sidroc, on his knees pounding a tent stake, was facing them, and after giving the sharpened stake a final blow, stood up. He still held the broad-headed steel hammer in his hand. The two who sat their horses looked at him.

They were large figures, one bigger than the other, and red of hair. Sidroc recalled both the riders and their horses. The elder one screwed up his face, as if trying to place Sidroc. The younger one began to grin at he who stood watching them.

"He wants to buy, this time," Jari assured him.

Sidroc gave a laugh. Toki, who had been hammering in the stake to the ridge line of the tent, now came and joined him. Yrling appeared from over by the waggon, carrying packs from it, and called out to the horsemen.

"Une! I heard you did not return."

Une snorted his laughter, and he and his brother got off their horses. "Not me. But Gye was killed, and we lost the ship to the Saxons who did it. It took us a few days to find Danes who would carry us back."

Gye was the ship captain with whom Yrling had sailed to Angle-land, all three times he had gone, the same man who Sidroc had met. Yrling had not ventured out this year, and his face showed that Une was the first to bring him this news. Sidroc had clear memory of the man, of his sword and ship, and the way he had named him bean-stalk, and said that soon he might join them. Now he was dead. Sidroc thought of Gye's wife, she who had given him and her own young buttered bread to eat.

As Yrling and Une spoke about this, Jari came up to Sidroc. He was as tall as he was, and much broader. His face was covered in freckles and his front teeth were slightly crooked, a youth's head set on a man-sized body. Sidroc watched Jari's blue-green eyes flick to the scar on his cheek. Jari swallowed, and to keep him from asking, Sidroc spoke first.

"Did you go?" Sidroc asked him, making a slight gesture to where Yrling and Une stood talking about the ill-Fated trip.

"Nej," answered Jari, though he grinned in a way that showed his pride in Sidroc thinking he might have. "My father will not let me go yet."

"Maybe you and I will go together," Sidroc offered. "My uncle will have a ship one day, and I will sail with him."

Toki had come up to them, and Jari was now looking at him.

"You will have to prove you are as good a fighter as me," Toki proclaimed. "Only the best warriors will sail with us."

Jari laughed good naturedly, but Sidroc spoke.

"It will be Yrling, not you, who chooses who is to sail," he reminded.

"And I will choose who I challenge to fight," Toki returned.

Jari stepped forward with surprising quickness in his large body. He grabbed Toki by the arm, laid hand on his shoulder, leaned into him and flipped him over on the hard ground. Jari was still smiling as he did so. Une and Yrling joined Sidroc in laughing at Toki lying flat on his back in the dust.

"Jari will fight you anytime," the red-haired youth answered, looking down at him.

Toki got up from the ground and slapped off the dust. With all watching he could do nothing but offer a cracked smile back at he who had bested him. He would not risk further laughter at his own expense.

Une's eyes shifted over to Sidroc. He was one of the biggest men Sidroc had ever seen, with a chest that looked an ale cask, and wrists the thickness of Sidroc's upper arm. The dark red hair and drooping moustache he sported suggested a fiery temperament. Une's eyes narrowed as he regarded Sidroc. He looked then to Yrling.

"I thought of stealing your mare, that second year we went out with Gye." This admission was offered in a light tone.

Yrling's eyes widened. He had not heard of the small adventure his nephew had suffered, upon his returning to the farm.

"But this one – " and he raised his hand to Sidroc – "made sure I knew whose animal it was." Une was smiling now, looking at both Sidroc and Yrling. "And the forfeit for stealing her."

"All say nephews fight best with uncles," Yrling answered, with his own grin. This pairing of nephew to uncle deepened the bonds of kinship, tying the uncle's sibling closer to him as their son took up arms for the greater family. Kinned warriors fighting shoulder-to-shoulder were ever formidable.

Une had returned his eyes to Sidroc, and gave a low grunt. "It looks like you have already made the warrior's bargain," Une told him, studying his scar. "You are willing to pay the price for fighting."

Sidroc kept himself from flinching, both under Une's searching gaze, and his words. He knew it was a form of praise that fell from this big man's mouth, and in response he held himself the taller, and lifted his chin. The scar was ugly, but not to Une.

From the tail of his eye Sidroc could see Toki on his right. It would be like Toki to pipe up now and lay claim to his deed, looking for praise himself. Instead Toki cast his eyes down on the ground from which he had just arisen. His mouth twisted, whether in shame or envy Sidroc could not know.

Yrling took a step forward, his hands on his hips, and regarded them. "When they are ready, both will sail with me," he said. Toki would not be stayed, that was clear, even if he had the farm awaiting him.

"Já," Une agreed. "And if I still walk Midgard by then, Jari and I will join you."

Yrling tossed his head and grinned at this; Une, skilled with his battle-axe, had known good luck in fighting so far. He then asked, "Did you come alone?"

"Our folks are here, camped across from the Law-speaker's circle." Une pointed with his hand. "They brought mead," he ended, with a sly smile.

"Then we will see you at dusk," Yrling laughed.

Later that night he and his nephews left their horses behind without concern. All would be safe in their absence. Theft was the most grievous of offenses, and no one would risk plundering at the Thing, where the law was heard, and justice sought. Before they banked their cook fire Yrling took some little time in combing out his hair, straightening his clothes, and wiping the dust from his boots, things which his nephews noted, and in their small ways, echoed.

It was not hard to find Une and Jari's campsite. Their father, a prospering farmer with more than sixty head of cattle, had two wives and many children, and most of the family seemed to have made the outing to the Thing. Campfires winked from all around them as they made their way in the deepening gloom, but they headed for the largest. A booming male voice guided them; Une's father making jest, filling up another crock of mead from the cask he had brought, making all welcome.

Nearing the fire, they saw one distant beyond it, from which strains of music wafted. After giving their greeting to their host and his amber-adorned wives, the younger of which had a babe at the breast, they made for the smaller beacon of light. The hulking form of Une was readily discerned, the dark mass of his back to them as they neared. Ever-smiling Jari sat next him and waved them into the circle, into which a number of small siblings was also gathered. Most sat cross-legged on the ground, a few on stools and short benches. There was just enough coolness to the night to make the fire pleasurable, and the bright and ruddy half-light it threw on the faces of the young around it cast its own attraction. Une had already secured a small crock of mead, and now dipped three shallow wooden cups into it, passing them to Yrling and his nephews. The boys were likely the youngest there handed the strong drink, and accepted their cups with quiet gratitude.

There were as many maids as youths flanking them, and Sidroc saw his uncle scan the faces of the former as he sat down. Some of these must be Une's sisters or other kin, so caution was needed, but others would have been strangers, drawn by the music and laughter from their family's own camps. A few of the maids looked up as the three joined them, but their eyes swiftly returned to the youth who sat opposite, strumming a long, oval-bottomed harp of wood, set upright in his lap.

The harpist played well, with surety in his touch, and the melody that arose under his fingertips was sweet. His voice was lacking, though, wavering and strained, and he could not well follow his own tune. After a song or two Toki, having downed his cup of mead, arose and went over and sat beside him. He gave a glance at the harpist, then began to sing in his stead. He had in fact a fine voice, of a timbre rich and silvery, high in pitch, and yet the voice of a young man and not a maid. At once all eyes shifted to Toki, his face alight with song.

One could not but look at him. Toki, even at fourteen years, had the kind of manly beauty that both women and men will notice, and maids pause at. The fairness of his skin; the sharp colour of his eyes, gem-blue and bright even in the fire's heat and haze; the wealth of long yellow hair streaming down from his white brow were all things to capture a woman's eye, if not her heart. Add to this his voice, one unexpected in one so young, a voice of tenderness and even yearning. When he finished his song he gave a smile, one which could have melted a far harder heart than in the breast of any female who surrounded him. It was not meant to do so; Toki smiled because he himself was so well pleased with his song.

In the morning Sidroc and Toki took a roam around the many merchant's stalls. Behind the waggon of a seller of iron pots they spotted a knot of youths, kneeling on the ground, casting dice across planks of smoothed wood, and whooping at the results. At least three or four of the dice throwers had been amongst those gathered around the fire the night before. The harpist was one of them, and his instrument, half revealed in a leathern pack, lay off to one side as he tossed the dice.

To judge by the pile of silver at the harpist's side, his play had been good; the hack silver and coins at his knees was twice that of the other player.

Both Sidroc and Toki liked gaming with dice, and they stopped to watch. The harpist made two more good throws, and the other player, sitting back on his heels in disgust, watched his wagered silver be pulled over to the harpist's growing pile.

The harpist was crowing with his win, and glanced about the faces of those watching.

"I will play you for your harp," Toki said, moving forward.

The harpist's surprise was clear. The offer was from one a number of years younger than he. He remembered Toki well from the night before, and had to admit the songster deserved the attention he had received around the fire. He might be a better singer than he, but now he could put him in his place at gaming. He gestured Toki into the circle.

Toki squatted down on his heels. First he picked up the dice, smooth cubes of walrus tusk ivory, and shook them in his fist by his ear, to ascertain they were solid. He had seen Yrling do just that when playing with strangers.

The other boys jeered, but Toki paid them no mind. For wager he took the ring of twisted silver from his little finger and set that next the harp. The harpist looked down at Toki's wager. "The ring is not equal to the harp," he pointed out.

Toki squinted up at Sidroc. His cousin knew Toki squandered almost every bit of silver that came into his keeping. Still, Sidroc found himself pulling at his own belt, and setting a few pieces of broken coinage atop the ring. Sidroc did not need to mutter to his cousin that he had better win; his look did it for him.

Within four tosses the harp was Toki's.

Sidroc had taken no part, but had watched the play with careful eyes. The dice were not his cousin's, and there was no way for him to cheat. But Toki's hamingja, his luck-spirit, was always strong. And Sidroc already knew that no winning streak went on for long; mayhap it was time for the harpist to lose. Still, Bragi, the God of poetry and song, must have wanted this harp for Toki.

"Bragi favours you," Sidroc said, as they walked away, the harp in his cousin's hand.

"And now the women will too," Toki laughed back.

"Once you learn to play it," Sidroc reminded.

On the ride back to the farm Yrling was well content. He had sold his filly to a copper-smith for a large cluster of bent and broken hack-silver, and whole and half coins. He had seen Une, knew that he lived, and talked with him about returning to Angle-land next year, should they find a captain they could trust. Until he had command of his own craft that is what he must do, sail on another man's ship. He thought Une and his brother Jari would one day serve as a core group of warriors to surround himself with. With his own nephews that made four men, ready to throw in with him once he had his ship.

His two nephews did not share his high spirits. They were leaving the freedoms and excitements of the Thing behind them, for a return to the drudgery of daily chores. These must continue on until they were old enough to flee Jutland with their uncle. Sidroc, driving the waggon, was lost in thought about this. It would be long years before he could sail to Angle-land; that was the barb in the arrow. He still had the whole coin of the King of Wessex, that which Yrling had told him was Æthelwulf. He had kept it, apart from his spending silver, in the same pouch he carried his flint and striker in. He often took it out and looked at it, recalling his uncle's words that a great deal more silver awaited in the lands of the Saxons. He wanted to be old enough now to go. With his height he almost looked it. Then he reflected that he had no shield, and did not yet have the skill he needed with his spears. The one thing that gave him satisfaction was recalling Une's words to him, telling him he had already made the warrior's bargain, and could accept hurt. It was the first time he had heard any words about his scarred face that did not make him wince within. The scar marked him, it was true, but marked him as one to become a warrior. It made him remember that old woman he had met in the Spring, Åfrid, who had told him that there would be those who could truly see him.

Toki, beside him on the waggon board, had his new harp in his lap. He quickly learnt that to strum the six strings to begin or end a song was one thing. To pick out a pleasing melody and sing along with it was quite another, and more challenging, task. He plucked away at the strings, trying to find a melody there. He felt angry enough at times that he wanted to hurl the thing out onto the packed ground they rolled over. Yet the harpist coaxed music from its wooden body, music which made those who heard it stop in admiration. He must too.

Once back at the farm both boys were restless and distracted. Toki, intent on mastering his harp, spent enough time at it that his chores, of which he was ever careless, grew neglected. Ful could no more curb his temper as could his son, and one day, finding Sidroc alone at work splitting kindling, called Toki to him, to birch him. Toki had been careful to set his harp down and in a safe place on the work bench in the barn, but knew his father had heard him playing while Sidroc chopped. Now father and son confronted the other, Ful grasping the birching rod in his fist.

Toki looked at the man before him. As his father raised the switch to lash it against the back of his son's legs, Toki reached up and closed his own hand around Ful's wrist. He stepped towards him, wrenching his father's arm back. The birch switch dropped from his father's hand.

Ful looked open-mouthed at Toki, and stood as if frozen. A moment passed, in which Toki feared his father was enraged and would attack him. Instead Ful began to laugh. He had now more than fifty years, and had gained no wisdom. But he saw his son had overpowered him, and fairly. He would put the best face on it he could.

"I have been looking for this day," Ful said.

Toki blinked at him. He knew all too well the sting of the birch rod from his father's hand, and acted without thinking in stopping that hand. His father stood grinning at him, even though he was holding his wrist where he had twisted it back. It was clear now they were nearly equals.

Sidroc had paused in his work at the tree-stump, and stood watching this. He had not gotten a birching from Ful in more than a year, but he did not go out of his way to warrant one, as Toki did. Maybe it meant his cousin would grow up some.

But Toki, thinking on it, realised that if he had only acted out earlier he might have avoided several good beatings.

Chapter The Fifteenth

WHAT RIBE HELD

The Year 865

THIS year the Mid-Summer feast and fire was held at Gunnborga's farm. Sidroc had seen her many times since his scarring, at the feasts of the Winter's Nights festivals, and at each Mid-Summer. She was grown into a most comely maid, and when they met she was able to nod and quickly smile at him before dropping her eyes or turning them elsewhere. He would nod and do the same. He had never gone, as Toki had, to her family home to spend a day. Gunnborga was Fated to wed a man with a farm as good as that she lived on. Sidroc knew this, and he had no land. But that was not why he avoided her. He did so because he read in her quick glance that it was hard for her to look at him. Now though, her mother and step-father were hosting the feast and fire.

Four families were there, that of the hosts and their several offspring; the members of Ful and Signe's farm; another family whose unruly group of children increased by the year; and a family coming for just the second time. The land which had belonged to the elderly Åfrid was now being farmed by them. They were a tenant family in need of house and fields, and Ful had installed them there on what had been the old couple's holdings, which they had so far made profitable. They were also a large and active family, of both youths and maids nearing, or of, marriageable age. Sidroc and Toki knew that Yrling had at times this warming season ridden there to see the eldest daughter.

It was a Mid-Summer's day of unusual fineness, dry and clear-skied, and the feast had been one to remark on, as Gunnborga's folk were both rich and given to generous hospitality. With such a large proportion of young folk there, the guests, after all had downed the whole roast pig and a deep kettle of milky cod stew, parted, leaving the numerous young circling the fire they had earlier danced about, and their elders back at the kitchen yard, picking at a few stray bones as they talked and drank amongst themselves. Ale had flowed freely for all, young and old, and as was custom, a crock or two of mead was brought out as well. This was, as ever, imperfectly defended, so that the young were sure to make off with a jar or two dipped out of it, carried back to their own fire to be passed around; but this was indeed how the young learnt to moderate their thirst for strong drink, bad heads or no in the morning.

The feast was well over, and the Sun dropping in the sky when a waggon rolled down the dusty track and into the farm yard. Those about the fire had in fact heard the laughter and singing from the waggon before the doubled team of oxen could be seen, for the broad wooden waggon bed was packed with youths and maids. No fewer than four more walked alongside, flanking the patient oxen and pulling at long stems of blue or white wildflowers springing from the grasses by the track. A group went out to meet them, Gunnborga's step-father foremost, and several of the younger men quitted the fire to join in the greeting.

The rowdy group had at its core two brothers from a farm lying further to the East; their own parents' proceedings had not been deemed festive enough and they had set out earlier in the afternoon, pausing at various farms, collecting the young with the goal of stopping at the better gatherings. Several of the revelers were known to Gunnborga's step-father, and to their cheers he welcomed them with little more than a laughing wave before retreating to his own kitchen yard. He sent a small cask of ale their way, gratefully received by those already circling the fire, but the flower-bedecked newcomers had as well a crock of their own. This they lowered with care into the midst of those by the fire. Its appearance was greeted with hoots of glee, as all thought it mead. It was set on a hastily pulled-up bench and the wooden lid lifted.

It was instead rare Frankish wine, far more precious and potent than honeyed mead. It had landed at the trading post of Viborg in the North of Jutland, was traded for, and now carried here by the revelers. None of Gunnborga's guests had tasted it, but once one of the two brothers who had brought it began dipping it out, all fell silent as they swirled the dark red stuff in their mouths.

Toki had been sitting on one of the few benches at the fireside, his harp in his lap, strumming and singing. Like his cousin, this was Toki's seventeenth Summer. His playing was now such that it made just accompaniment for his voice, and both earnt the admiration of those flanking him. He had not forgotten the harpist from whom he had won it, and how all eyes had been fastened on him when he played. Now those eyes were on Toki, and to have so many maids look smilingly at him when he strummed and plucked made the hours he had struggled with the harp well worthwhile. He had set the thing down to accept his cup with all the rest, but now, having swallowed the ruby liquid down in almost a single draught he was moved to place the harp on his thigh and begin again.

Some light still hung in the sky, softening a day filled with dancing and feasting. Behind the crackling logs of the fire lay a field of tall grasses, dotted with wildflowers. All knew that soon one or more couples would rise and make their way there.

The giving of self on the still-warm Earth was more than a celebration of the life-giving power of the Sun which today they honoured; it returned the couple's own life-force into the soil. All life sprang from plants; no beast nor man could live without greenery and the animals so nourished. Young married couples might slip away and drop together amidst the screening stalks of nodding grasses, celebrating their love, giving of each other in hope of bringing forth a child from this special coupling. And those men and women who had no intention of wedlock nor babe might, under the spell of the heat, the endless sunlight finally dimming, and the stimulus of strong drink also clasp hands and lie together in the fragrant grass.

Yrling was seated with a group of other young men; they had been throwing dice in the dimming glow of dusk. Now, for want of light, and under the influence of the Frankish wine, most of them settled in to hear Toki. Yrling's eye went to the cluster of young women who had arrived on the waggon. Some of them were clearly coupled with the youths they arrived with, but three or four others were not shy in returning his smile. He did this with care, for the elder daughter of the tenant family was there about the fire as well. They had spoken together as the younger folk had gathered for the fire, and before that also at the feasting tables, but he made no show of it. He had no intentions on the girl's future; she had thrice favoured him by lying with him in a shady glade beyond the farm, and he meant it to go no further than that. Nor could it, in her family's eyes. With no land to inherit, it was well known he would have to make his own way. He knew what way that was, a ship of his own, a drekar, setting out across the North Sea to Angle-land and treasure. The secret he shared with the girl of their brief trysts would remain just that.

He did not even know if the girl, Frideburg by name, was still about the circle; there had been coming and going about the group, knots of young men and women forming, breaking off, moving back to where the settled married folk sat, or off to one side where the youngest, like Gunnborga, huddled. His gaze returned to the females from the waggon. When he smiled a second time and gestured to a young woman in a pale blue gown, she rose.

Toki's song aided him; it was mournful and lovestruck, and Yrling had almost to stifle a laugh looking at his young nephew's face, upraised in a passion of longing as he plucked the final notes.

Yrling was already before his blue-gowned target, who had been sitting with two other young women, whispering and laughing into each other's ears. She who rose before him did so with a little lurch, which she tried to hide, but then laughed the more at. She had set her empty cup on the ground and then upset it with her foot, and she laughed ruefully at this as well. As Yrling took her hand he saw Toki had risen. Another of the strange women, seated not far from where he had been playing, had come to Toki, and now stood before him. She like so many had been looking raptly on as he sang. Toki wasted no time in answering her summons, and set down his harp.

Sidroc, sitting cross-legged on the ground amidst other idle youths, saw first his uncle and now his cousin take the hand of a willing young woman, and lead her away from the fire ring and into the darkening field. Sidroc had drunk ale at the feast, mead here at the fire, and then, like all who wanted it, downed a cup of the dark and potent wine. His head felt fuzzy, but cleared to an almost awful acuity as he watched Yrling and Toki claim women and move away with them.

Another couple rose, and followed. Those left behind sent the celebrants away to a low chorus of whistles and chiming laughter. Some turned smilingly about, looking at who might be next, or in invitation to one they had earlier admired. But eyes soon returned to the retreating couples, walking slowly through the tall grasses, hands clasped or arms about waists until they both knelt and were lost to view. Those left about the fire fell either silent, or lifted their voices to petition for more wine. Gunnborga got up from where she sat with three other demure maidens and with flushed cheeks walked back with them towards the kitchen yard and the families there.

Laughter drifted from the field in which the couples had vanished, brief laughter that must be ending in kisses, and more than kisses.

Sidroc took a breath and looked about him. The spotty-faced youths near him were several years younger, and grinning like fools. He looked over at the two women who remained after Yrling had chosen the one in blue. There was no doubt they were half-drunk. He could rise, walk to them, watch their faces as he approached, try the one that seemed likely.

He could not. To be refused before so many others, even if the onlookers be deep in their cups and unlikely to recall it later, was a risk he did not feel up to taking. And it was not, he knew, the witnessing of it that would be the worst part, but the refusal itself. He imagined the women looking up at his split cheek. Their eyes would go to it and it alone. He pictured them recoiling, even mayhap laughing at him in their drunken giddiness.

He shook his head to himself. He knew this would be Toki's first time, and would like to claim that for himself as well. He could not risk it. He began to rise, unwilling to sit there any longer, thinking that he might head back to the farm. He would hear Toki's boasting on the morrow.

As he rose he noted a woman, walking alone and at a distance in the field. He turned his back on her and the fire.

A female shriek of anger turned him back. Like all others his eyes were trained on the grassy field, growing ever dimmer in the low light. He saw the woman bend toward the ground. He heard then a male howl, and more shrieks.

Everyone at the fire was standing now, and some starting out across the grass. They stopped when the woman made straight for them. It was clear she was in no peril, but why she had screamed they could not guess. Then Sidroc saw a male figure rise, back to them. It was Yrling, and the woman he was with was hastily, and with loosened hair, taking the long way back to the fire, holding the skirts of her blue gown in her hands.

Yrling walked forward uncertainly, even staggering. His hand was clapped over his nose. He was staunching a flow of blood with a bunched up square of dark linen, perhaps the blue-gowned woman's head wrap.

A group of men, summoned by the unhappy racket, had now quitted the kitchen yard and came striding towards the younger revelers. Their host, Gunnborga's step-father, was one, as was Ful's tenant-farmer. The woman who had earlier been walking alone in the field came straight to the latter.

"Frideburg! What happened," her father demanded, looking from her to the straggling figure of Yrling.

"I hit him with his weapon belt," she said, with no small touch of triumph. "Found him out in the field like a randy goat."

Her father's eyes boggled at her. All knew couples might take to the fields on this night, and interference was awkward, even an embarrassment. There was no particular shame in such festival coupling, but the thought was unwelcome for a father, who, like himself, took pride in the thought of sending his daughter still a maiden to her husband.

Yrling had now caught up to those awaiting him. "She broke my nose," he said. His voice had a higher pitch than was usual, and more than a little complaint sounded in his tone.

"Why had you cause to do this?" her father asked her. It had taken him a moment to recognise the victim of his daughter's rage. Yrling was kin through marriage to Ful, at whose behest he had a good farm to till.

Frideburg, now that the shock of discovery and the twinned thrill of revenge had died, was forced to slow her thoughts and measure her words. What she answered now would make a great deal of difference in her life, and in Yrling's.

Eyes shifted, going to Yrling, to Frideburg, and then to the men she stood with. These were but farmers, and none carried a sword, but all wore knives, and the girl's father had his hand upon the hilt of his own.

Yrling was standing alone, and had now lowered the bloody cloth from his face. Sidroc found himself moving forward, taking a stand at his uncle's right shoulder. Yrling glanced at him and gave a slight nod. Sidroc cast a quick look over his shoulder; Toki was nowhere to be seen. They both knew he was still in the field.

The wronged woman, a girl of not yet eighteen years, spoke with care.

"We have exchanged a few words," is what Frideburg said.

Her coolness took her father aback.

"Words? Nothing more? What kind of words – vows, or pledges?" He must know how far he need press this.

"Have you been wife to him?" he now demanded.

She drew herself up, stunned that her father would ask this before so many. If she told the truth, Yrling might be forced to wed her. If he refused, there would be bloodshed this very moment.

She looked to Yrling, blood still dribbling from his nose. He was not a good match for her, she had feared, but it was his eyes that had attracted her, those hot eyes, smouldering under heavy brows. They were suggestive of power. And he had ambition. He had an air of authority about him, despite owning no land. Now with his bloodied face he looked defeated, almost foolish.

"Nej," she declared. She would not force a hand-fast with this man. Two nights after he had last lain with her, she had caught him with another woman. And he had no land. She could do better. "I will not take him. There is no need for me to do so."

These final words seemed to seal the girl's innocence in the eyes of her father. He gave a small sound, almost a snort of relief. His eyes passed to Yrling, waiting to see if he would pursue any claim against her assault, as was his right to do for unprovoked attack. But Yrling stood silent. Satisfied, Frideburg's father, not wishing to plumb further depths, gestured her to him. They turned to the house.

Sidroc heard, and almost felt, the heaving breath leave Yrling's chest. He was now taller than his uncle, and he turned to him. His uncle's nose looked as if it had been knocked off-centre. He watched Yrling lift the bloodied cloth to it again, saw him wince as he dabbed at the side of it.

"The warrior's bargain," Sidroc told him. One must be willing to forfeit for one's actions. He saw the shadow of a grin break upon Yrling's face, and grinned back.

"So?" asked Sidroc, when he and Toki were alone next day.

Toki did not feign ignorance. He could not, for a slight flush crept over his face, warmth he could feel.

"It would have been better without that shrieking Frideburg," he admitted. "The one I was with got scared, and almost jumped up."

It had in fact been a hurried scramble, once the ruckus had sounded. It had begun well enough, despite his groping uncertainty; but she had laughed. He felt a twinge of near-deflating shame at that, but the urge of his body drove him despite his sense of ineptness. When the shrieks were heard, she did in fact try to flee, and he found himself pinning her down until he had finished. He was glad when she hurried off.

"What was her name?" Sidroc wanted to know.

Toki shrugged. "I never asked." And he never wanted to see her again, after what happened to Yrling.

Sidroc kept looking at him.

"It was – good," Toki finally said.

This was bald enough that Sidroc assumed the opposite. Toki's eyes were shifting to the right, as if he tried to think of more to say.

"She was nothing special," Toki went on, as if he had means for comparison.

Sidroc could not stifle a short laugh.

"At least I had a woman," Toki defended.

Sidroc recalled the brazen way in which she had risen, come to Toki, and presented herself to him.

"Or she had you," Sidroc returned.

The following week Ful sent the cousins out to move the sheep flock from the furthest feeding ground. The far pasture was hemmed all around by a ditch deep enough to form a kind of dike. Across this ditch, forest bordered on one side. The dike helped drain the grassland, and kept the sheep from wandering. To enter, Sidroc and Toki had to push a heavy wooden platform across, to span it. Both walked with their herding crooks, and Toki had also a short numbering stick hanging from his belt, marked off with a line cut for every sheep there. Twenty animals warranted a score, a much deeper cut in the wood. There should be two score and eight sheep to move.

There was abundant grass within this far pasture, and even a small copse of trees for shade. Sheep had ever done well there, but when they began to number the animals against the marks on the counting stick, they came up four sheep short.

A walk about the edge of the moated pasture found no beast trapped there, but on the side butting the forest they spotted a plank of wood lying on the other side of the dike. The plank was half-concealed, but trampled grasses were near it.

They looked at each other. Then Sidroc backed up, and took a running jump at the chasm, landing on the other side. He picked up the plank and shoved it over, and Toki joined him.

Bent grasses and parted, shrubby growth presented a track, and wisps of cream and charcoal-coloured wool clinging to low-lying branches told them sheep had lately passed.

They moved forward, quietly as they could, and in single file, Sidroc first. The sheep had been driven off, and whoever had done so was likely to be ready to fight.

They went on some way. The track began to follow a stand of small birches, through which the light of a glade could be seen. Sidroc heard the sheep before he saw them.

He stepped out into the glade. A rough pen, from newly hewn branches, had been thrown up, behind which were ten or twelve sheep, snorting and moving about. A fire-ring, equally rough, had been formed by small stones, and held but a few days' ashes. Two packs of well-creased leather sat near the cold ring, ready to be shouldered. It was a camp, hastily built, and having served its purpose, was now being hastily abandoned, for a man who had been bending amongst the sheep now stood up, his hand on a rope he had slipped over the neck of a ewe. He looked in startle at Sidroc, then jerked his head behind him towards an opening in the trees, betraying the fact that he was not alone.

Sidroc, though, was alone. Toki had lagged behind.

From where he stood Sidroc was close enough to see the head of a ewe that looked out at him. She bore the single ear-mark, a notch at the tip of the left ear, which Ful used on his flock. Another ear-mark was on the beast, as well, and Sidroc could see the second, lower notch was freshly cut.

Sidroc's eyes went from the ewe's head, back to the man. He was young, five-and-twenty, perhaps. As Sidroc studied him he parted the stakes of the sheep pen and stepped out. Now another joined him, stepping from the trees, an older man. Father and son, or uncle and nephew, thought Sidroc. Both were unwashed, with tangled brown hair and unkempt beards. Their clothing was worn almost to rags, and no woman had seen to the tears in the knees of their leggings. Both bore long knives at their waists.

All remained silent, and Sidroc did not move his eyes from the men. He heard Toki coming up behind him; his cousin had caught up.

"Those four are our sheep," Sidroc said as greeting to the two he faced. He pointed with his crook to the pen.

There was some little strength in his voice. Theft of livestock was a serious crime, and this a blatant flouting of the law.

The two men stared back at him with unblinking eyes.

"They bear our mark," answered the younger.

"A mark that is fresh, and on our animals," Sidroc returned. "We will take them now."

"What do you want," the elder one said, as if he did not understand. He came nearer Sidroc. Sidroc was taller than either of them, but they were both broader, and grown men.

"Our sheep back. The four ewes with the notch at the tip of the ear are ours." He would not call this man a thief if he could avoid it.

Toki would, and did. "You are thieves," he hissed.

Sidroc saw him from the tail of his eye; Toki's hand was on the hilt of his knife.

Sidroc took a slow breath. He was not going to get cut for the sake of the sheep. While the two men eyed Toki, Sidroc lifted his gaze a moment to the blueness of the sky, showing through the leafy growth of the trees about them. He would try words first.

"Surrender them now," Sidroc told them, "or we will be back on horseback, and with dogs, to hunt you down. Do not think you can run. When we find you, you will lose more than sheep.

"You have no choice," he finished.

"I do," said the older of the men, swinging his fist at him.

Sidroc dodged back and to his left. The swing left the man off balance, so that he nearly stumbled. His target was quick to straighten up.

"Take off your knife," challenged Sidroc. Toki hooted, and the younger man did as well. They were already unbuckling their belts, sliding their knife sheaths off. Sidroc and Toki dropped their crooks next their discarded knives and squared up before the two.

It was, like all fist fights, no holds barred. Kicking, grappling, tripping, even biting were all allowable. It was the first real fist fight for the cousins, a magnified version of every such weapon-less scrap they had ever fought with each other. They had grappled with Yrling in practice, but never with the passion of connecting blows. They used all their agility and every part of their limbs. When the younger man was bent over recovering from a punch to his face, Toki jerked his knee up at the man's brow, sending him backwards and sprawling. Sidroc's long reach allowed him to grasp the older man's forearm, and with a forceful swing flip him over and onto the ferns of the glade.

The two they faced were older and stronger, and had no doubt practice in such fighting. They kept coming after the cousins, and landed hard blows against them. But what Sidroc and Toki lacked in strength they made up in speed. And they were angry, and in the right.

They had another advantage over the thieves. The two they faced were weary; a furtive life cannot long sustain a man.

In the end Toki had a growing lump on his forehead, and Sidroc's left ear got boxed so his head rang. But Sidroc's fist connected, and heavily, on his final swing, hitting his opponent full in the jaw. The man staggered back, coughed, then spit out a tooth and a mouthful of blood. Both he and Sidroc stood, panting. They watched Toki dive for the younger man's knees, saw him knock him down to pin him, then pull his arm behind his back until he yelped that he yielded.

Nothing more was said. Toki jumped up to his feet, and he and Sidroc stood silent as the two backed away. The cousins picked up their knives and crooks. Together they kicked down the flimsy pen wall, waded into the sheep, and found their own. With one before and one behind they ushered the beasts back through the wood to where the plank lay waiting.

Only when the ewes rejoined the flock did they speak. Their blood was still racing, and they were proud of what they had done. Both of them were dirty and sweat-stained, and both had fists that ached.

"Back with dogs and horses," Toki repeated with a grin. One of his sleeves was ripped, and Sidroc's tunic was torn half-off.

"You are not the only good teller of tales," Sidroc answered with a laugh.

Later that Summer, Ful, Sidroc, and Toki made the trip up to the trading town of Ribe. Ful had excess of early grain to sell, and was looking for a second team of oxen, two already paired. It took half a day to reach there. A shallow moat, one left broken at intervals, marked the boundary of the river town. Crossing over with their ox-drawn waggon they were sent by the guard to a vacant plot on which to make their camp; one of the King's own men would be by later to exact a fee for the privilege of selling there. Once the oxen were unyoked Ful took up position by his grain sacks. Sidroc and Toki were free to wander.

The trip to Ribe was made only once or twice a year, rare enough to make it a treat for the cousins. Neither had been to the greater trading town of Haithabu, but the planked walkways, guttered trenches carrying away waste water, and other amenities of a place as thriving as Ribe impressed the eye. There were more goods gathered for sale than at the Thing, and buyers from many parts, not just those come to their local law-gathering. The ships landed at the wooden piers or hauled up on the river shore were alone worth their attention. Their curved hulls served as backdrop to the final row of stalls and workshops, and Sidroc and Toki studied them, some of which looked swift enough to serve double duty as war ships.

Coloured glassware from Rhineland sat on linen-shrouded tables in booths. Neither Sidroc nor Toki had ever held a beaker of glass in their hands, but it was easy to imagine the pleasure of seeing swirling ale or mead within one. Skillfully-worked amber gaming pieces, polished to a warm and golden glow, were lined in ranks next drilled beads and cylinders of the same stuff. Silver and even goldsmiths displayed glinting baubles for rich men and women. Oiled linen awnings protected those drinking ale from the noon-day glare, while the aroma of grilled fowl drifted from one who offered the hungry a savoury repast. But they walked about with purpose. Sidroc wanted to look for a knife.

He still wore at his side that given him by his father. It was the only thing he had left as token of the man, and despite the fact that he had made use of it every day, it was still in good shape. But it was small now for him. He needed a man's knife, and resolved to buy the best he could. There were always weapon-smiths at Ribe, including one who lived there all the year round. Others came for the trading season, setting up their forges Summer after Summer on the same site, hammering out spear points, knife blades, and swords for merchants to buy ready from the anvil and quenching-cask, and to carry off to distant parts.

"Will you sell the old?" Toki asked, as they looked over the blades at one forge. He might trade on it for the new knife, save himself some silver.

Sidroc lifted his head for a moment from the knives they looked at. Toki had owned several knives. He had broken the points of two, lost one, and was as careless with his newest.

"Nej," Sidroc answered, almost under his breath. He would no more part with the knife his father had given him than he would with the hand with which he held it.

He chose the blade he wanted, filling up one of the smaller dishes of the smith's hanging scales with hack-silver to do so. It was the costliest thing he had as yet bought. Yrling had paid for the spear-points for their spears, something they both knew they owed him for.

It was not pattern-welded; he would have to wait to afford such a knife, but it was well-made blue steel, and took, as the smith showed him, a razor-fine edge. The grip was of dark brown ox horn, coupled with brass rivets, and handsome indeed.

He parted with more silver at the stall of a worker in leather, for a sheath to fit. This was of cow-hide, deeply tanned, and Sidroc had the woman who had cut and stitched it stamp it with two of her many steel dies, a running pattern of tiny arrowheads and squares. The new knife slid within with ease, yet was held firmly. But not until he was back at their waggon did he slide the worn sheath housing his first knife from his belt.

He did not wish to part from it, and had already thought of how he might wear the smaller knife. He took the low boot from his left foot, unwrapped his leg-wrappings, pulled up the calf of his leggings. He would strap his father's knife to the outside of his left ankle. Covered by his leggings and leg-wrappings, it was barely discernable. He stood up, walked around. He felt the knife, but it in no way hindered his gait.

Toki had been looking on. "Could be handy in a fight," he noted.

Sidroc nodded, but knew it was not a weapon that could be got to quickly. It was rather something secret, to be kept in reserve, like the memory of his father himself. "I would look disarmed, even though I am not," he told his cousin.

The plot they had been given was on the main trading road, and not far from the moated opening they had entered by. Ful had already sold half his rye, and was feeling well pleased. As soon as he had sold the remaining two sacks they would repair to one of the brew-houses, take refreshment, and then set out looking for the oxen he sought. As they awaited this, Toki climbed up upon the waggon board, and drew his harp from the leathern sack he carried it in. He set it upright on his thigh, and began to strum, and then to pick out a melody.

Ful was not in the habit of praising his son, but even he must admit that Toki sang as well as any he had heard in brew-house or farmstead. He took a kind of perverse pride in the fact that it was Toki's devotion to his harp that had made the boy take the birching switch out of his hand.

Sidroc too could not gainsay that Toki was blessed by the God Bragi, though the innocent look that sometimes alighted on his cousin's face as he played made him want to laugh, so false was it. Still, he had more than grudging admiration for his ability.

As Toki played, a waggon, drawn by two horses, came through the town gate, and turned towards them. The waggon was flanked by two mounted men, armed with spears and shields. It was not uncommon for those purveyors of precious goods to travel thus, with armed guards. As the waggon neared they saw three who perched upon the waggon board, a man of above middle age, who held the reins, and two young women, sitting next him. The one sitting closest to the wheel was exceedingly pretty, with light brown hair dropping in waves from under her head wrap, lustrous eyes, and a nose both straight and delicate. Her full lips curved readily into a smile as Toki's music reached her ears.

She tilted her face to him, and Toki saw the second woman raise her hand, stopping the waggon. This second maid was almost as plain as the first was pretty, but she too bore a smile for him, which he returned. Both were quietly but well dressed. If they were sisters, the one had certainly received the full measure of beauty for them both. He went on with his playing, enjoying their smiles. He ended his song with a flourish, both hands active on the throbbing strings.

The driver called out now, his grey beard wagging as he did so. He had listened to the air with nodding head, seeming also to enjoy the music. "What, my fine fellow! You are an able skald, in need of a tunic of silk to match that voice of yours. Then you could play for the King himself."

Toki laughed, but the man went on. "Come to the stall of Balle, and see the fineness of silks my waggon bears."

Toki's father, swift to take note of any of wealth, chimed in. "We will seek you out, Balle, as soon as this good rye is gone to its new owners," he promised. There was as little chance of Toki ever wearing a silk tunic as there was as his playing before any King, but it was ever a good thing to place oneself in the company of the rich, even for the briefest of time. And few merchants were as rich as the buyers and sellers of precious silk.

Later the three of them, coming back from the cattle pens in which Ful had selected his new team, did in fact come upon Balle. An awning of yellow had been extended from his waggon, and propped up by tall poles. Beneath it was set a table laden with bolts of brilliant cloth. Balle stood behind it, and off to one side the pretty maid was busy stacking smaller lengths of silk. The other maid was seated on a stool at the end of the table, in full view of all who passed. But she looked quite different.

She had changed her woollen gown for one of surpassing loveliness, for it was all of silk, the rich blue colour of the sea under a perfectly cloudless sky. She was in this way an example of the merchant's rich wares, and not a few folk, men and women both, paused to look upon the treasure she wore. She composed herself to sit in the Sun, so that it might play upon the expanse of her skirts pooled about her. The blue silk gown was indeed eye-catching in its tightly woven and glistening beauty. The maid clearly enjoyed this, perhaps feeling the many admiring glances were meant for her, and not merely her garb. It was a gown that would flatter even a maid who, like this silk merchant's daughter, had few attributes of loveliness about her person.

Balle called out when he saw the three approaching, and the blue-clad maid stood up. Her round face broke into a broad smile as she watched Toki near. She interrupted herself long enough to order the other maid, whom she called Gunhild, to bring stools for their guests. So the pretty one was no sister, but a serving woman, they saw. Once they were seated behind the table with her father, the daughter resumed her place at the end, mindful of her role. But she had shifted a little, so that she might glimpse Toki, seated on one side of her father.

"Our home is near Viborg," Balle was saying in response to Ful's question, "but I make the circuit of all trading posts on every island of Dane-mark; Skania, too." He had called for ale, and the serving woman was quick in returning with it from a brew-house close by, a boy wheeling a hand cart and setting a crock of it aside on a stool made ready to receive it. The pretty serving woman dipped it out, but now that she was face to face with Toki, and so near her mistress, did not hazard gracing him with her smile.

Balle found a ready listener in Ful, and the two youths attended as they downed his ale. The silk merchant had no fewer than three wives at home, with many grown children, all of them settled. His older sons acted as agents for him in the silk trade, forwarding the precious stuff along the way from the fabled lands far to the East in which it was spun. His numerous daughters were wed into solid families throughout Dane-mark.

As Balle spoke, he noted that his daughter, despite her maiden modesty, could scarce keep her eyes from drifting over to the yellow-haired singer of songs. This girl was his youngest, Ginnlaug by name, and one of easy disposition. Finding good husbands for her seven older sisters had not been easy, despite the rich dowries he could provide; he had near run out of worthy men. Now, as he and Ful conversed and drank, he began to consider his guests in a different light. A sharp man of business, he had long recognised that the maid lacked the comeliness of her sisters. He knew he might need seek further afield for a good match for her.

He shifted the talk from himself to Ful. Where is your farm, he wanted to know, and then looking over to Toki, who is his mother? Ful, flattered by his interest, was ready with his answers. The boy's mother is from one of the best families on the coast of southern Jutland, he claimed.

Ful then saw the silk merchant looking sidelong at Sidroc, an unspoken question as to whether he had any share in the farm.

"The son of my wife's dead brother," Ful named him. "Who I have taken in and raised.

"The farm," he ended meaningfully, "will go to Toki."

Balle seemed truly interested now, and indeed all three young people were now glancing at each other in turn.

"And of your farm?"

Ful was more than glad to boast how he had enlarged his holdings. He numbered thralls, freedmen, cattle, sheep, geese, grain yields, detailing far beyond what he was asked, all to impress this rich man. "I came today to sell our surplus rye, and have bought a second team of oxen," he reminded Balle.

As the talk went on it was not difficult for either Sidroc or Toki to realise its import; and indeed Toki grew more and more uneasy. The round-faced maiden was simply beaming at him, and his father was nattering away.

The talk of the older men slowed, and there passed a meaningful look between them. Of a sudden Balle arose from his stool.

"Ginnlaug," he said, gesturing with his head that she arise. "Your legs need stretching. And a walk through the trading streets will mean more folk will see your silk. Gunhild will attend you, and I am sure young Toki and his cousin will be happy to escort you."

In this way Toki found himself paired with Ginnlaug, as brilliant of gown as she was plain of face, while Sidroc walked next the pretty Gunhild.

"Mind that you walk slowest next the gold and silver smiths; spice sellers, too," prompted her father as they moved away. Ginnlaug only laughed, and sweetly too. She well knew where rich buyers would be found.

Balle watched his youngest move off with this treasure on her back, safe in the knowledge she would be careful with it. To Ful he said, "She wears it for display, for I hope to sell it too; but does she not look well in it?"

Watching the splendour of the retreating gown, his son walking next it, Ful must admit she did.

As the four young people made their circuit through the trading roads Toki said not a word. At several points the thoroughfares were crowded, but the sight of Ginnlaug's silk gown caused many to pause and make way for them. They were a striking couple indeed, and if Toki's handsomeness was not well paired with the maid's plainness, at least her gown was dazzling. Just behind them came another couple, with a maid of true loveliness, walking at the side of a young man tall and lean. This pairing was less strange, until one glimpsed the long scar marring the man's face; it made jarring contrast to the beauty at his side.

Sidroc too was silent, and Gunhild kept her eyes upon her mistress' back. The only one who spoke was in fact Ginnlaug, for when a man or woman cast an admiring eye upon her gown, she was quick to direct them to the plot where Balle, the famed silk merchant of Viborg, was now showing his wares.

On their return the silk-clad maid led the cousins down a side way they had not before noticed. A few cloth merchants were there, sellers of woollens and linen, and perhaps she wished to show herself to them. As they passed one building of timber a man stepped from the door. The group was already moving on, but a shrill clanging turned Sidroc and Toki around. The man they saw was curiously dressed, in a plain brown tunic so long it looked almost a woman's gown. His brown hair was short, and cut in such a way that the top of his head was nearly bald, though the hair grew thickly enough, like a fringe, elsewhere upon it. The clanging came from his hand, for he shook a cup-shaped piece of metal, so that it rang out loudly.

"What is it?" Sidroc said aloud. The noise was shrill and clamourous.

Ginnlaug knew, and Gunhild too showed no surprise.

"A Christian. I have seen him before. His name is Anskar. That is his temple, and the bronze in his hand, a bell. He is calling others to come and pray with him."

"A Christian," Sidroc repeated. He remembered the thrall woman Berthe, and how she worshipped Christ.

"The King gives him leave to do so?" Toki asked.

"Já, já, for many of that belief come from Frankland, and they needs must pray to their Gods, just as we do."

"So, a good business to let him be," Toki said.

Here Sidroc and Toki found their eyes meeting, then going back to the simple and small hut where the man Anskar stood, shaking the noise out of the bronze cup he held. Yrling had told them the Christians of Angle-land had treasures in their temples; he had heard of other Danes finding great weight of silver lying in the open on tables there. But this hut was so humble as to make it hard to believe anything of value lay within.

They moved on, and by the time they returned to Balle's waggon the silk seller and Ful were ending their talk.

"We will be here three days. Go home, speak to your wife about it," Balle was saying. "Come back within that time, we will talk more."

As they took their leave, Ginnlaug dropped her eyes before Toki, hoping that when she raised them he would be smiling at her. He gave a hasty nod and turned away.

"We have met your match," Ful told his son as they reached their own waggon. He was in high spirits, rubbing his hands together, and grinning broadly.

"My match?"

"Já, this Ginnlaug. There is no better bride than a rich man's daughter."

"Bride? I cannot wed now; I want to go with Yrling, to Angle-land," Toki answered.

"Já, you must have your adventure; that is understood. But wed first, get settled. When Yrling is ready then you can go with him on his raiding trip. You will see Angle-land, then you will return."

Toki had opened his mouth, but his father cut him off.

"He is a buyer of silk," Ful stressed.

"And he wants to buy me too," Toki returned.

"There is no better match for you. Who indeed would you choose?"

There was in fact a dearth of suitable maids in the area, at least maids who could bring Toki real value in bridal-goods. Gunnborga was one; she was not only winsome, but would be richly dowered. Whenever they met she was polite to him, but even Toki understood she did not favour him. At any rate, Gunnborga was already promised to a cousin of her mother's, a man undoubtedly far richer than he.

"Someone like Gunnbor – " Toki began to answer.

"Gunnborga, Ginnlaug, there is little difference," Ful retorted.

Toki snorted. "Ginnlaug is as homely as a turnip," he complained.

If Bragi favoured him with a fine voice, it followed that the God should also allow him a wife of loveliness similar to his own: Idunn, she who kept the golden apples of youth for the Gods. This silk-seller's daughter his father eyed for him had the face and form of a root vegetable.

Ful was forced to consider this. "Já," he allowed. "But her silver will be beautiful. And," he went on, "in the dimness of your alcove it will not matter. Keep your eyes closed if you must."

This fatherly advice fell short of easing Toki's concerns. "You ask too much," he shot back.

It was all Sidroc could do to keep from laughing aloud. It would be a long time before he could afford a wife, but at least he was free from Ful's plots and plans.

Ful was already envisioning the coming of Ginnlaug to the farm. "You will make your home at Åfrid's old place; Ginnlaug will expect being mistress of her own farm."

Toki remembered, with almost a sick feeling, Sidroc teasing him about this; his cousin had been right. He knew Sidroc was just at his left but could not look at him; it would confirm the snare he was being led into.

His father was going on. "Já, she will want to begin in her own house. And she is sure to come with a raft of serving folk."

At this Toki jerked his head. "The pretty one, too?"

Ful thought a moment. "Be wary. Women dislike you sleeping with their own servants. But a second wife – that she can have no objection to."

"I do not even want a first wife," Toki protested.

This was no argument. All men and women wed, save those who were unsound in body. Toki knew he must wed, and make as good a marriage he could. His father countered this, and with no little impatience.

"Why are you blind to your good fortune? If you wed her, you will have silver enough to keep a second wife, one you can choose for her beauty."

So it went on, nearly all the way home.

"When?" Toki finally asked, in way of assent. They had neared the farm. "When will it be?"

"As soon as we can. It is too good to pass up."

Chapter the Sixteenth

HAITHABU

TOKI'S hand-fast was set for the beginning of Blót, that month named for the blood that flowed from the sacrifices offered to the Gods. This last month before the onset of hard Winter was also marked by its feasting, as all beasts which could not be kept over on sparse fodder were also killed, and their meat salted, brined, and smoked to serve over the long and dark Winter months. Blót was thus ideal for celebrations, and deemed to be a propitious time for the joining of young couples.

This was three months away, but the farm was already preparing. Toki in particular was at work. The tenant family with their troublesome daughter had been sent on its way, much to Yrling's relief, and Toki and two of the male thralls were readying Åfrid's old farm to serve as bridal home for Ginnlaug, the silk seller's daughter. The distance was great enough that Toki moved there as he readied the place to receive his bride. It marked a decided change in the lives of the cousins, as Toki moved closer to this threshold of manhood.

Sidroc and Yrling were busy at the farm, aiding Ful and the remaining thralls, but after the last grain harvest Yrling surprised his nephew. He invited Sidroc to join him on the three-day ride to the great trading port of Haithabu, on Jutland's eastern coast. Yrling had travelled there once, and wanted to return. Ship-builders were there, and those artisans who crafted every needful thing for sailing vessels, from whale-skin and braided hempen line, to wool and linen sails. He wanted to take a serious look at all this, even though he was not yet ready to buy.

And there were further attractions to the place, which he went on to share with Sidroc.

"There are certain women in Haithabu," Yrling told him. "We will go and visit them."

Sidroc knew what this meant, and could not keep a slow smile from spreading across his face.

His scar went crooked as he did so. He had worn it now for five years, but it still had the red and angry look of one newly healed. Yrling's own face had suffered by his broken nose, but in its own way it made his visage the more hawk-like, a set of piercing eyes over a raptor's beak. Some may have thought him more attractive for it. But few would have counted Sidroc handsome, even without his marred cheek; and though they had never spoken of it, Yrling was right in assuming his nephew had yet to know the embrace of a woman. This was one thing he could help him to.

Sidroc said nothing, just nodded his assent, and Yrling gave a laugh.

They would ride there, taking Ful's horse as well, which Sidroc would ride. Their bed rolls and hide ground cloths were strapped to their saddles, but they would stop at farms for food; any would feed them for a bit of silver. Sidroc welcomed a break from the tedium of farm work, and before him was the long ride on horseback, and the prospect of sleeping out under the night skies in countryside new to him. Then there was their goal, and what it might hold.

Haithabu was due South, and then clear across the width of Jutland, right to the barricade of the Danevirke, which they would skirt when they came to it. Sidroc knew this is where his father Hrald had come and bought the good salt from Angle-land that took him across the Baltic to Gotland. As they walked their horses at the foot of the Danevirke he was aware he trod the same path his father had so many years earlier. But Sidroc was on a horse, and when they approached the sword-bearing guards at their posts along the base of the barricade, they looked up at him. True, he carried only a spear, and his shield slung over his back by its leathern tether, but he was at Yrling's side. The two of them looked fully warriors, he thought. One day he would have fine clothes, a sword of beaten steel in a tooled sheath, and the horse tossing his head under him would be a stallion of great worth. As it was they warranted a glance, more than given those on foot.

Yrling owned a sword, and a good one, but he was not wearing it. Instead of strapping it on, Sidroc had watched him pack it in his leathern pack, and tie it to the iron rings of his saddle.

"You will not wear your sword?" he had asked then.

Yrling shook his head. "For show?" His grin faded. "I should not need it here on Jutland, and the wearing of it can bring more notice, and so trouble, than I care to court."

It was this thoughtful cunning that Sidroc admired in his uncle. He carried the weapon with him, should they need it, but would not flaunt it.

It was late in the trading season and the crowds not as thick as found at Summer's height, but there were still more folk than Sidroc had seen, even at the largest of the Things he had stood at. Once they passed through the gates in the tall palisade they could walk their horses on the larger planked roads. They edged their way past rows of stalls laden with baskets of cabbages and carrots, sacks of grain, small pots of honey, crocks of linseed and whale-oil, tables where shorn fleece and sheep skins lay heaped. Iron pots and pans clanged from overhead hooks, simple buckles and fittings for horse harnesses and bridles lined one man's table, and an old woman had piles of animal teeth from sheep, goats, and cattle, drilled for use as fastening toggles.

Seeing a group of women clustered at the tables of one stall put Sidroc in mind of why they had come. He went over to what they looked at, made a decision, and slipped his purchase into his belt before catching up to Yrling, nearly lost to view in the throngs closing around him.

Folk of many lands traded here, both walking the pathways and standing at attention in stall and booth. Snatches of speech unknown to them floated to their ears, as did Norse in many accents. Rus traders from the shores of Lake Ladoga, garbed in peaked caps and the full and pleated leggings of their kind, held up pelts of brown mink and white fox, or cradled tiny coffers bearing healing resins and aromatic gums from foreign trees. Svear traders were there, with stacks of dried stockfish, and shining ingots of pure copper. Most numerous of all were buyers and sellers from every part of Dane-mark's many islands. A large number of those at workshop bench or treading the roads were women, working at the sides of their husbands and grown children, offering woollens or linen, carving combs from red deer antler or ox horn, selling boiled eggs from baskets slung over their wrists. There was a brightness to their countenances that surprised Sidroc. Some of them, both young and old, rimmed their eyes with some sooty substance, making them stand out; and some young women had a rosy sheen on the lip. Some sort of beeswax, he thought; and as they made their way through the crowds it did make him look the longer at them for it.

Their goal was the frontage of the fjord on which Haithabu lay, where all the ships tied up. Some were docked at long wooden piers, others hauled up on the reed-lined shore. Boat builders and the repairers of boats were there, as were tar-merchants, rope-makers, coopers hammering up casks, and those smiths whose specialty were ship rivets and pulled nails.

Once at the frontage, they got off their horses, and led them. At the end of one pier was a space clear of work shed or warehouse, a space apart, and not yet empty. Two tall wooden carvings rose from the packed ground, and behind and before them were the smaller posts holding tined forks and open-work boxes marking a Place of Offering. The carvings were painted depictions of the heads of one-eyed Odin, All-Father; and of green-clad Freyr, guardian of ships. The great heads were the size of bushels, the painted eyes fixed and staring. All trading anchorages in the Norse world had such, a place where landing merchants might give thanks for safe passage, and offer what they could of loaves, bread, or a live cock fowl to ensure good trading. The richest merchants might even send for a piglet, and spill its blood in order that his goods might find ready buyers.

This noon there were none bowing their heads before the images of Odin and Freyr, but the speckled feathers of a newly-killed fowl spoke of one who had recently dedicated it. A dog, likely stray, sat beneath it, with lolling tongue and hopeful eyes.

They gave a nod at the carvings, and moved on with their looking. Most of the ships before them were broad-hulled merchant ships, knorrs; or smaller fishing boats whose bulging nets returned full of cod, herring, and sea trout to help feed the masses of hungry tradesfolk. A few, though, were drekars, war ships, and these were the vessels the two lingered before. All raiders were also traders; booty must be sold and bartered, and there was no greater trading post in all of the Norse lands than Haithabu.

Those built for war were fashioned for speed, longer and narrower than either fishing boat or trading knorr. Their tall pine masts could be swiftly lowered in bad weather, when rowing up narrow, tree-hung rivers, or while fighting ship to ship. All it took was the pull of the mast lock at its base to guide it down by the lines arising from prow and stern to the mast's peak. Stout oars powered by strong backs propelled the ship in light winds or when every knot of speed was needed. In the back, near the stern, the greatest of these, the steering oar, shot over the starboard side and into the water. The tiller that slotted into the steering oar was held by the captain himself, or his trusted helmsman.

The curving prows and sterns of the ships they looked upon rose high and proud above the decks. A fearsome carving of an open-mouthed dragon or fanged creature might front the rising prow stem, and there too a wind-vane of chased copper would swing, ready to tell the helmsman how fast and from where blew the winds he sailed into.

On one they saw, standing up against the straked sides of the prow, an upright iron bar ending in a spiked curve. A stout and heavily tarred hempen line was knotted through an eye at the top of the bar. It stopped Yrling when he saw it.

"How rich is he," he muttered to his nephew, "to have such an anchor, all of iron?"

Most boats and ships used anchors of stone, wedged between a yoked fork of wood, and tied in. But this war ship boasted one far easier to handle, of iron. It had Yrling shaking his head in wonder.

Even unladed, the ships were never left unguarded, and for the brief duration of their port stay a few heavily armed men would always be aboard. As Yrling and Sidroc walked along the line of ships, such men peered over at them, looking up from some task they bent over on the deck, or standing, arms crossed over chests, at prow and stern. Some wore swords at their sides, and bracelets of twisted silver upon their wrists, and one man bore a necklet of gold. A few cast what Sidroc knew was an appraising eye upon them. None spoke.

"If we wanted to join them . . . ?" Sidroc asked his uncle in a low voice, once they had moved away.

"I would choose the likeliest ship, one that showed its captain took care about it, and its lading," he was told.

Yrling glanced back to the crowded roads of the trading town. "Then I would ask where their captain was drinking. Seeing him would tell me more, about him, and the men he chose to raid with him."

Such a war-chief would be surrounded by his best men, as they took their leisure over ale or mead. It would mean approaching them, revealing their interest in being taken on. It could end in scorn, or blows. Men were killed at common brew-houses, and with some regularity. But those fighting at Haithabu, or any royal trading town, faced penalties so steep that few disputes broke out.

Sidroc looked his question to his uncle, wanting more.

"He would size us up," Yrling went on. "Ask who else we had fought with. Where we had been."

"What would you say about me?"

Yrling swept a glance over Sidroc, head to foot. A man's outward form was his hamr, the shell to contain his hugr, his essence and mind. In some men the hugr could even be that of a wild beast. Yrling could not guess much of Sidroc's hugr, but his outward shell, his hamr, was impressive enough.

"I need not say much," he told his nephew. "He would look at you, your size. The scar would tell him the rest of what he wanted to know."

The scar would tell him the rest, Sidroc thought. The scar my cousin gave me at twelve years of age.

For years he had been taken for being older than what he was; at seventeen he looked five years more. It was his height, and he knew, the scar. If men wished to believe he had earned it in some desperate struggle, let them.

"You would wear your sword," Sidroc asked, thinking of Yrling standing before such a captain.

"Já, there I would. And tell him of Lindisse."

Yrling had been there three times, and had some knowledge of the coast, and its river inlets leading into likely settlements to raid.

"If he liked the looks of us, he would ask for silver."

Lading a ship for a raiding trip was costly business, and each man must pay a share. Sidroc knew that proven men paid less than those new to the captain they sailed under.

"Which you will one day do," Sidroc prompted, thinking ahead to when Yrling was master of his own ship.

It made a grin break upon his uncle's face. "Já. But you need not earn more; your share is already safe with me, that which is buried with my own silver."

They spent some time at a sail-maker's, where a bank of women stood at wall looms, beating up a tight weave of creamy-hued fabric from twinned woollen and linen thread. Some of the narrow lengths that grew under their shuttles and weaving swords they would dye in shades of madder red, woad blue, or weld-flower yellow. At the long tables on the other side of the shed more women worked, leathern thimbles on their fingers, stitching. The lengths they bent over were sewn and sometimes inter-woven into a broad square many ells long, a strong sail to billow and drive the ship that bore it through the watery furrows of a foaming sea.

All who worked within the sail-maker's shop were women, including the owner herself, one of middle-age who took care to answer Yrling's questions, and show him the two sails upon which she and her weavers and seamstresses worked. Next to the ship itself, the sail was the most costly part of outfitting any craft, and one which must not fail.

They left the workshop. Yrling lifted his face to the sky; the Sun was now past its highest point.

"Now for the other females we came to see," he told Sidroc. They headed further down the banks of the fjord, to where the curving palisade wall enclosing Haithabu ended at the water's edge. There was a gate there, a smaller one, for it led to no true road. Yet, as at the other portals in the palisade, there was an inner pen, at which one might surrender beasts or goods, and walk unencumbered within or without the walls of the trading town.

"We will leave the horses here," Yrling announced. They were nearing several well-armed guards who kept watch over both gate and the goods left in their keeping.

Sidroc was quick with his question. "Why?" His uncle had told him the women they sought lived on the other side of the wall. That being so, they would make a stronger impression, appearing before them on horses.

Yrling cast a look at his nephew's crestfallen face and answered.

"We will go on foot. If we ride, the price may be higher."

All Sidroc could do was nod. He saw the wisdom in that, but was no happier about the loss of show.

They gave their horses into the care of the guards stationed there.

"When do you return," they were asked.

Yrling looked through the opening and down a long row of fishing huts strung along the river bank. At some men worked, spreading nets on racks to dry, tarring boats or line, or flaying new caught fish. At the far end of the rank of huts a streamlet ran, with a small footbridge spanning it, and a cluster of further huts. It was these Yrling looked to.

"We are going fishing," he answered. "But we will not be long."

The guard looked down the line of huts and grinned back. "Fish of all sorts to be had," he agreed.

They passed out of the gate, spears in hand, their shields on their backs, but leaving the rest. They walked past the row of working fishing huts, and came to the streamlet and its bridge. It marked entry to another world, for the rank of huts that lay on the other side were all occupied by women.

There was a line of ten or twelve small huts, all of weathered brown wood, much like those of the fishing men they had passed. But by these no nets were strung to dry, and no small boats hauled up.

A little way deeper up the banks there was a fire ring, just as there would be in a kitchen yard, and standing over it was an iron cooking frame, with a cauldron. There were tables and benches ranged about this. Closing the distance, they saw the brightly-clad figures of a number of women, both sitting on the benches, and walking about. The hue of their gowns caught the eye at once, woollens which had been double-dyed in shades of blue, green, yellow, or red, worn with shawls equally bright in contrasting colours. As they neared, those who wore them looked so many brilliantly plumed birds.

Sidroc had been aware of whores in Ribe, for a few women walked alone there, or lingered, half-drunk, at certain brew-houses. Men had passed knowing looks when they came into view. But the women before him were much the prettier, and some of them looked young enough to be maids.

Being early in the day, Yrling and Sidroc were alone as customers. They saw no other men, save for one. On a stool at a discreet distance sat a burly fellow with a long curling yellow beard, his feet up upon a small cask. A spear lay on the ground by his right, and a shield was propped up against the left side of his stool. A guard, of course; these women had silver, and should any man visiting get out of hand he was there to ensure their safety.

They were now close enough to truly see the women, and see also the eldest of them, seated at a trestle table covered with a long cloth of deep red linen. She rose in greeting, pushing herself up from a plush cushion shrouding the rough bench she sat upon.

"I am Odindis," she told them, "and we welcome you." She was at middle age, and herself still comely. She was much more quietly dressed than the women who surrounded her, in a woollen gown of pale grey, set off with dark bands of tablet-weaving. What was striking was the string of small and lustrous pearls strung between the silver brooches at her shoulders. She almost looked a great lady, a King's wife, or consort to some war-lord of renown. Like some of the women they had seen here in the trading roads, the depth of her eyes was enhanced by the sooty stuff rimming them. Yrling, regarding her, was struck by the fact that she dressed thus for her own pleasure, and not for that of any man.

Uncle and nephew nodded at her, not unaware of her eye gauging their own clothing, weaponry, and demeanour.

She smiled now, and with head inclined to the women who flanked her. She let the two glance about the benches, and the faces that smiled up in welcome at them.

At one end of her table a metal bar was fixed, suspended above the ground, and from it hung a balance scale with its two dishes, lest any forget this was a place of business. She stooped and brought from beneath the cloth-covered table a single lead weight, and laid it upon one of the dishes. She had determined what to ask.

"Balance this weight with silver, and you may each take your pick."

These words were quietly spoken, but thrilling none the less.

Both men looked around at the women before them. Most of them were fair of hair, in every shade of yellow, from tow to deep amber. One had a ruddy tint to her locks, and two, fawn-brown. It was a third, with the darkest hair, who caught Sidroc's eye.

Yrling had stepped closer to the table and its waiting dish. He pulled his leathern purse from his belt. The pieces that dropped from his hand were mostly bits of broken silver jewellery, easy to see if they had been plated or not. Only with a short length of plain silver coil did she take a nail and scratch it, to ascertain it was true metal. He kept adding until the two dishes balanced in the air.

Odindis then lifted both silver-bearing dish and weight, and they vanished beneath the table covering, where she must keep a strongbox. She opened her hands, in gesture that they make their selection.

Yrling scanned the circle and did not hesitate moving towards one of the first his eye had fallen upon, a comfortable-looking woman with abundant yellow hair. Her plump cheeks dimpled as she smiled. She rose.

Sidroc's eye had returned to the dark-haired one. She was clad in a gown of blue, with a red shawl pinned over her slight shoulders. Her skin was white, her hair so dark as to be near black; dark enough to make him wonder if her folk had not been from some other clime. She smiled up at him.

She was paid to smile, he knew that. But her eyes of gentle blue held his a moment longer than was needed.

He nodded at her, and smiled back.

Yrling and his choice were already vanishing within the hut she had led him to. Now the dark-haired one crossed to another door, Sidroc just behind her.

There was almost nothing within but a broad and low bed, made soft with feather cushions. In the gable end of the peaked roof the shutter of a high window was open to the sky, giving light. A small table held a basin and jug, nothing more. No bench or stool on which to sit; clearly sitting was not expected. A row of wooden pegs pounded into the wall awaited what clothing did not find its way to the floor boards.

She closed the door behind them, and he set his spear in the corner by the door frame, and his shield on the floor next it. Almost as soon as she had shut the door she began undressing, unpinning and dropping her red shawl. With the toes of one foot she pushed off the first of her charcoal-coloured shoes. Sidroc saw now they were not of leather, but soft felted night-shoes of boiled wool, such as those worn indoors to protect the feet from Winter's cold. They came off easily, and she stood in her naked feet, for she also wore no stockings. She was grasping her gown by its skirts to pull that off when he stopped her with a question.

"What is your name," he wanted to know.

She let the gathered fabric fall back to her bare ankles. "Alvild."

"I am Sidroc."

This surprised her; few men gave their names, and few asked hers. Despite the scar on his face, it was not hard to summon another smile for him.

She pulled off her gown and shift in one action and stood before him naked. She let both pool on the floor by her bare feet, an act that in its freedom and wantonness excited him the more. Some deep laughter wished to break from his lips; it was so wonderful. Her breasts were small but round, the nipples small too, and pink, that same pink of her lips. Her arms and legs were slender and shapely. His eyes fell to the shock of dark hair where her thighs met, aware he held his breath as he looked. Her body had true loveliness, and to have her stand before him, utterly unclothed, and smiling, was nothing he had expected.

She turned slowly before him, so that he might admire the firm and decided curve of her hips and rump.

He began pulling off his own clothing, scarcely feeling his fingers at his belt, the toggle of his boots, unwrapping his knife on his left ankle. His hands were upon her now, the softness of her skin yielding under the tips of his fingers. In a deft move she fell, gently, upon her back on the cushions of the bed. The covering was of linen, smooth to the skin, almost as soft and smooth as the flesh she offered to him.

He felt fear of hurting her, crushing her; there was a delicacy about her, despite the firm animal strength in the arms she cast about his back. She seemed to sense this, for she murmured, "You will not hurt me."

All whores knew tricks allowing them to shorten their time with the men who had bought their services. With Sidroc she used none of them. He took such pleasure in her, without swagger or pretence, that she had no wish to. She would give him full value, and more.

When they lay quietly he found himself just looking at her. It was warm in the small hut, and a bead of moisture had formed between her breasts. His finger went to it. Every part of her rewarded his touch. He spoke to her now, his voice just above a whisper.

"Why do you do this?" he asked.

Her answer was low, but forthright. "I am of thrall stock. The woman Odindis bought me, made me a freed-woman. I work for her now, but I am free to leave."

"Will you, always?"

"Nej. When I am too old for men to choose me, I will wed, if I wish. I have a share in all the silver she collects on my behalf, and that will be mine. I will have enough so that I will still look good to many men." She gave a light laugh at her words. "Or perhaps I will open some stall and trade goods, and not my body. I may even do as she does; buy young girls and profit from them."

He found himself nodding at this, admiring her clear-headedness. It prompted her to speak again.

"As a thrall I had to work hard in fields and house each day, and then lie with my master wherever he wished, and with no silver to reward me. Here I need do nothing, but be nice." She smiled. "It is much the better life for me."

He was sitting up now in the bed, his back against a few of the feather cushions piled against the wooden planks of the wall. She was curled, almost kneeling, next to him, so that they faced each other.

Alvild asked a question of her own. "Why do you wish to know these things? My name – and my story?" Her brow creased a moment, as if she truly considered this.

"And you have told me nothing of yourself," she went on. "Only your name, but that is more than I usually learn."

He was aware he had no answer for her; he wished to know simply because of who she was, and what they had shared. This was perhaps not reason enough, and instead he gave a shrug.

"Who do you worship?" he asked now. "Who is your fulltrúi, who you have given yourself to?"

No man had ever asked her that, and she found herself blinking her surprise.

"Ah . . . Frigg."

He took this in. He thought it might be Freyja, who gave her love so freely, but it was Odin's wife, the Queen of Heaven, the patron of marriage and childbirth, whom she prayed to. Still, like her wild sister Freyja, she was protector of women; that would be enough.

"And she listens to you?"

Alvild laughed gently. "I have two pretty gowns, and growing silver. No man beats me, no woman chides me. Odindis is strict with us, but she is just. I think Frigg hears me."

He nodded at her answer, which seemed a good one. She was making her way, knew what she wanted, and why.

A cloud passed in the sky, dulling the light streaming in from the high window, making him think of what lay outside the confines of these four small walls. They had been here a good while, he was aware; Yrling must be outside, awaiting him. He had no desire to leave, to quit this place or her company. He drew breath, slowly and deeply, allowing the impress of this new sensation to flood his mind, letting the warm air fill his lungs. The small house held their scent, the gamey musk of man and woman together, a scent he now knew he liked. Just to look at her naked body was enough to make him wish to stay.

He forced himself up.

He swung his legs off the bed, rose, began to put his clothing on. She watched him as he strapped the knife against his left ankle, pulled on leggings and boots. He took his belt from a peg on the wall, and she watched too as he reached into it.

He had paid his silver, but some men gave her a little extra, if they were well pleased.

"This is for you," he said, holding forth a scrap of cloth. It was folded over and tied with a twist of straw.

She plucked at this, and opened what he gave, stuck into the piece of wool.

Three bronze needles. It was no cheap trinket; if other men brought her gifts it was showy trash. This was something useful, something that looked beyond the means of her livelihood. He saw that she was a woman, in her way like any other; and need sew and mend her clothing.

Of a sudden a tear welled in one of her eyes. She blinked it away. "Já. I sew, like other women. I thank you."

She set the folded cloth on the little table. Her gown was a pile of blue wool on the floor. She had done her work, and could pull it on now. Instead she faced him, another smile on her lips.

"Lie down," she invited, calling him back to the bed.

When they finally emerged, Yrling was indeed waiting, sitting, cup in hand, at the table with Odindis. It was the rule that the woman left the hut first, so that Odindis might see that all was well with her, but Alvild and Sidroc walked out together. Alvild was smiling, and went straight to another hut which served as kitchen shed, returning with a cup of ale for Sidroc.

Odindis, looking on, ended by telling both men, "You are welcome back, any time."

Yrling and Sidroc reclaimed their horses and joined those walking Haithabu's trading roads. They were both hungered, and their noses led them to the side road where cooking sheds and brew-houses abounded. Entire meals could be had at the latter, but they were dear. After having spent such silver they were content to go from stall to stall, finding loaves at one, a slab of roast pig at another, and plums and early pears at a third.

They stood with others at a baker's, whose domed ovens, set back on the earthen plot, belched forth steam each time the small round-topped doors were pulled open. On tables before them were laid round loaves of rye and oaten bread, plain and seeded with walnuts or hickory nuts. Meat pies also were there, still steaming, and giving off a savour which drew folk closer. Many were at work at this baker's, men and women at back tables kneading and cutting dough, others pulling forth iron pans from the two ovens, and youths carrying ever more wood for the never ending fires. Three women stood in front, just behind the tables on which rested the finished, cooling wares, ready to take a sliver of silver and hand over a loaf in return.

One of these women neared them across the narrow trestle, ready to hand them what they wanted. Sidroc raised his eyes from the loaves he looked at to see Ingirith.

Yrling saw her too, and jerked his head back. His lip twisted in a way that once more made fresh his dislike of the woman. Ingirith saw this, and her eyes dropped to the table, then back to where Yrling's nephew stood.

Ten years had passed. It was clear by her face that she was startled by the sight of him. He wondered later if he looked like his father, come back to life. And for Sidroc too it took a moment to truly believe it was her. She seemed so small – shrunken, really. He remembered when she had stood above him, pulling his arm, whacking him with the stinging beater she favoured for cleansing bedding and punishing young ones.

She could not harm him now.

He stood looking down at her, a short, slightly plump woman with fading yellow hair. The fingers of his left hand rose unbidden, to the lobe of his ear, which she had torn.

"Sidroc," she finally said.

Her eyes dwelt a moment on the ugly scar on his cheek. A small breath came from her, a puff of air. Her face was moving, an uncertain look which ended in a faint smile. She was biting her lower lip, studying him.

Her thoughts and memories were her own, but he wondered if she were not a better woman. Perhaps forming loaves and handing them out to those hungry for what she had made had struck up a spark of generous feeling in her breast. At any rate no scorn showed on her face.

He would not use her name; he could not, after the grief she had caused his father, and the pain to him. But he must speak, if only to recognise the connection between this woman and his lost father.

The names of his half-sisters rose to his lips, almost surprising him; he had not spoken them in so long.

"Ulfhildr, Thyrvi, and Äse – are they here? How do they fare," he asked.

She wiped her floured hands on her apron. She had been taken by surprise at seeing him, and now by the honest concern in his voice.

"Äse is here, with me. Ulfhildr is wed, and farming, not far from my parents' farm. Thyrvi is with her; Ulfhildr will have a child soon."

He realised they had left home young, these two, but perhaps life with their mother made them eager to be on their own. He nodded at this news.

Ingirith kept looking at him. She could not quite bring herself to share that with the baker she had wed she had a fourth child, yet another daughter. Indeed, she found it hard to say anything at all.

She had, since her first marriage, taken obstinate pride in her capacity for hard work, giving short shrift to those who failed to measure up. But living in the great trading centre had blunted the sharper edges of her nature. Haithabu agreed with her. The folk she lived amongst were many and diverse, and even given the repetition of the baker's trade, each day brought fresh faces to see and accents to hear. If she was as yet unable to take real pleasure in herself and others, she could at least take some satisfaction in deciding to come here.

"Why come you to Haithabu?" she asked at length.

Yrling was quick to answer. "Trading."

They spoke a short while longer. When they selected two loaves she refused their silver, placing them in their hands, and biding them good journeying.

Toki's envy was high, when he learnt of Sidroc's trip to the fabled town of Haithabu.

"What did you do there," he demanded.

"Looked at ships. Spoke to a sail maker.

"And – there are certain women in Haithabu. We went to visit them."

THE SHIP

The Year 868

"WE will go, this Summer," Yrling said.

Neither Sidroc nor Toki needed to be told of what he spoke. Yrling had just returned from a trip to Ribe, and must have determined that by Summer he would be ready to sail for Angle-land, master of his own drekar.

"My ship is being built, the sail woven. I have two months to gather my men, and lade the ship. Then we will go."

It was after the evening meal, which had been taken within the farm house. A light drizzle was falling, and a few thralls worked about the kitchen yard. The three men were there as well, under the roof of an open shed, for what Yrling wanted to speak of, he wished to do away from the house, and in private.

We will go, Sidroc thought. The door leading to his new life was at last cracked open. He had feared it would not be this Summer, but the next; Yrling had not shared with them his plans. The one hint had been the recent stress Yrling had placed on weapons training. The three of them had not only spent long hours sparring with blunt-tipped spears, but taken turns with Yrling's sword, hacking away at the iron rims of their shields and splintering the boards so that each needed to be replaced twice.

Even Toki was quiet, after his initial whoop of joy. He had looked for this day, almost as much as had Sidroc. The past three years had brought much change, and little had turned out as Toki had once expected. At twenty, he was the father of two children, and his own father was dead. Ful had not lived to see his son's hand-fast with the rich Ginnlaug.

Ful was killed not two months before the feast day, but it was neither man nor beast who had brought him low. He had been felled by the bough of an elm tree. He had gone, with his son and Sidroc, into the forest to find a likely elm, one whose water-resistant wood would be cut into planks to help shore up some diking in a low and marshy pasture. They would not chop it down at once, only mark it for felling once the leaves had fallen.

They came upon such a tree, even greater in size than Ful had hoped, and he rubbed his hands as he spotted it, deciding the Fate of the mighty trunk. But the eldest of the Norns, those pronouncers of destiny, was watching. She was Skuld, ultimate collector of debt. This is the wise crone who snips the Thread of Life, and Skuld had other plans for him.

As Ful was marking the stately tree for its death, the elm did what elms are known for, the sudden dropping in full leaf of a healthy bough. That which struck him was the thickness of a man's thigh. Sidroc and Toki were brushed back by the reaching branches, but only scratched. They jumped up to lift the bough off the groaning Ful. He was badly crushed, and though they carried him alive to the farm, died the next day.

It had been, in its way, a violent death, and was a shock to both cousins. One moment Ful was standing near them, gazing at the massive trunk, gauging how many planks could be sawn from it. A few heartbeats later they were struggling up from a green and leafy prison, the main body of the bough having just missed them. They had nothing to lay Ful upon, and must take him up by shoulders and feet and thread their way through the trees and back to the farm. Yrling was not around, having gone to a neighbouring farm with some cattle; and Signe, when she saw her senseless husband, fainted so heavily they feared her dead as well.

Toki let the elm stand, and did not tempt Fate by returning to it. The hand-fast went forward. Both fathers had given their word, and if the feast was not as gay as it might have been, Ginnlaug did indeed bring a fat purse of silver to her new husband, and carried as well as gift to her mother-in-law a panel of red silk to adorn her sleeping alcove. Though Toki had made some effort in preparing a home for Ginnlaug, they never lived there at the distant house, for now with his father's death, Toki was made head of the farm. Signe could not run it alone, she was ill; and so the new couple moved into the house Toki had been born in.

Ginnlaug had proven a good care-giver to her mother-in-law Signe, and the serving folk she brought with her were hard workers. She had been too clever a maid to have brought the pretty serving woman Gunhild with her, which had at first aggrieved Toki. But as it was, knowing that within a year or two he would leave with Yrling on a raiding trip, he was in no hurry to invest the silver his bride had brought him in a second wife. He began to see the wisdom in growing what treasure he had, and this stayed his desires. Besides, he had his hands full. Ginnlaug was gotten with his child almost at once, and soon another followed, a boy, which is what mattered to the farm.

Now, as the rain pattered on the wood roof screening their heads, uncle and cousins spoke of what needed to be done before they left. Ginnlaug had been aware of Toki's impending adventure, and almost as if she had been privy to their speech, began to call from the house. Toki lingered a few minutes more, and left, grinning with the knowledge that soon he would embark on a voyage of such daring.

Yrling and Sidroc watched him hurry away though the rain. Then Yrling turned to Sidroc and spoke.

"Your silver. I have put it all into the ship."

Sidroc took this in, and without speaking. He saw his uncle had more to say.

"Those I take on, I will ask for silver, for provisions. But we may land with almost nothing, save the ship itself."

Sidroc found himself nodding at this admission. He had little of his own, so to begin on foreign shores with almost nothing seemed no special hardship. But he saw his uncle's concern. They would have to win all they could in their first few raids, this was clear. And Yrling was untried as both leader and ship captain. He need seek more men to sail with him, and fight with him. Sidroc knew he might not be able to ask for as much as those captains who had with success sailed to Angle-land and won booty.

He thought for a moment of the silver. Yrling had showed it to him, several times. It was all he had gotten from his father's farm. His share of those fields had been turned into silver, and buried by his uncle, and now his uncle had poured it into a ship. That was the magic of silver; it could take many forms.

"We will land with our arms," Sidroc said in return. He lifted his hand, fist clenched as if it held a weapon. Everything they would win must be wrested with their strong right arms.

Yrling was pleased with this. "And you will get your silver back," he promised.

Sidroc went the next morning to Oddi. They had begun to keep goats, and Oddi, with his steady and quiet way, was favoured by the beasts. The nannies pushed forward when he neared to be first to have their ears scratched, and he did the milking of them. Just now the new kids had dropped, so no milk was robbed from these young. Oddi was standing at the birthing pen looking over them when Sidroc approached.

As he neared the old man Sidroc felt again how aged he had grown; he knew he had the better portion of sixty years. He had been part of his grandsire's life, of his father's, and then of his. For all their long history, it felt awkward to now tell him what he must.

"I am leaving this land, Oddi; Jutland and Dane-mark, both. I will go to Angle-land, and not return."

The old man was blinking at him.

"You are no longer bound to me," Sidroc went on. "You are your own man, and free to go."

Oddi was still staring at him. "Já, I will go," he said, so slowly that Sidroc thought he discovered this thought only now. "My sister still lives, I heard tell of that, not long ago. She is up past Ribe."

"Who does she live with?"

"Her daughter. And my niece," he found himself saying, but could not add, She who is your mother.

"Then you will have a home," Sidroc said.

"Já. I will have a home."

Oddi made bold to ask a question.

"You will slave?"

Sidroc thought a moment. "I will not come back. I have heard enough of Angle-land to want to go, and stay. If slaves are taken, it will not be me bringing them here."

Oddi gave a nod.

"Ribe," Sidroc considered, thinking of what awaited his aged friend. "It is a long walk."

Again Oddi nodded. "But there will be waggons, and carts passing, which will take an old man aboard."

This was true, Sidroc knew. And Ginnlaug was a woman who felt no one should go hungry. He pictured Oddi staggering under the food pack she would fill for him. He would have food enough, to eat, and to share.

Sidroc had something ready for him, caught in a tiny pouch of leather, and held in his fist. He had counted over the silver he had at hand, and taken one-third portion of it to give to Oddi, as a parting gift.

"For your service to my father," he said, lifting Oddi's weathered hand and pressing the purse into it.

Oddi came close to speaking then, but his memory of Hrald stopped him. Hrald had never told this boy he shared a blood-tie, however faint, with his former thrall. He would honour that silence once more.

"May the Gods see you on your way," was the blessing the old man gave.

Indeed, despite the misfortune in the young man's life, Oddi thought the denizens of Asgard did take note of Sidroc.

"Oddi is leaving," Sidroc told Toki later that day. "Going back to his kin."

Toki's mouth opened. "I need Oddi. He must stay here, help run the farm while I am gone."

"He is free to go, and he will do so, soon," Sidroc returned. "The thralls know enough. And Ginnlaug – no one is sharper with silver than she; she is her father's daughter in that."

Toki did not share Sidroc's estimation of his wife's ability, and he showed this by the way his lip twisted at his cousin's words. How could a woman who had been cosseted all her life, whose prize possession was a head wrap of silk, be trusted to run a large and active farm?

"Many women run farms when their husbands trade, or raid," Sidroc pointed out. "Balle, her father, was away months at a time."

Ginnlaug may have lacked comeliness, but she was sensible, and more than capable about the place, and with the thralls and serving folk. She was also not without feeling. Toki, if he thought of such things, would have no fear for his mother's happiness with Ginnlaug mistress.

"And Ebbe need brew much less ale, once you are gone," Sidroc added as a gibe. Since Ful's death and his own marriage, Toki had ended nearly every night drunk.

Toki did not seem to hear this; his thoughts reached back to an old resentment. "This is my father's doing," he sulked.

"Ha! If he had not forced you to wed, you could not go at all; you must remain and care for the farm. Instead you have a rich wife and so leave her, and your mother, in comfort."

There was not much Toki could answer to this. As it was he hoped they would leave before Mid-Summer's Day and its feast. Ginnlaug relished any chance to be seen with Toki, and they had hosted many a gathering at her behest since they wed. She need not know he planned to take his time returning.

The next month Yrling went ahead to Ribe, moving there to oversee the completion of his ship, and to find men. Signe shed tears over her younger brother's leaving, and Sidroc and Toki found it hard to watch him mount his mare and ride off alone. All the grain was sown, but sheep-shearing remained to be done, and there was no need to join their uncle in Ribe until his ship was afloat. Indeed, it saved silver to wait, for food was costly there.

As in every late Spring, certain tasks of the season awaited. Roof thatching that had lifted over Winter must be set aright, beating it back in; wattle fences weakened by wind or beasts must be renewed by re-weaving; and chopping and stacking firewood, the endless task of their boyhoods, still beckoned. The busy days fell, one by one.

The day before they were to leave for Ribe, Sidroc left the house in the grey mist of dawn. He saddled Ful's old horse, then went to the fowl pen. He snatched at a young cock and stuffed it into an oiled linen sack, so that only its head arose above the pucker of the drawstring. He tied this to the saddle ring, slung his shield on his back, tightened the tether, and took up his spear. Then he swung up, and put his heels to the barrel of the beast. They trotted out of the farm gate, heading due West, and to the sea.

Sidroc did not often look at the sea; the farm he had lived on for the last thirteen years was just far enough inland to make owning a boat a trouble. But he held close in his breast the memory of his times on the water with his father; and knowing where he was headed, and for what ends, felt called to go there now. He had a dedication to make.

Trotting along the westward road he passed a farm or two in the early going. The road turned North, but he went on his westerly path, by smaller tracks and then through grassland. He had his spear in his right hand and guided his horse with his left. He felt the weight of his shield, and the leather strap across his chest that held it. The young cock warbled and gave a stifled crow as they set off, but was otherwise still.

There had been little wind when he left, as happens often in the early hours of the day, but as the Sun began to climb he felt a freshening breeze, carrying to his nose the salty smack of the sea. The blue haze which was the sky resolved itself from the darker blue of the water. The grasses before him gave way to shrubby growth, and he picked his way through it to a beach of soft brown sand. The offshore islands were out there, sand bars, really, and he walked the horse along the beach a way, until only open water met his eyes. He got off his horse.

Across that water, far to the West, lay Angle-land. He could not see it, but he knew it was there. He would make Offering here, facing his goal, and dedicate himself to what lay ahead.

His father's words came to his mind. Always be reaching, he had told him on that day he had taught him to swim, the day in which he had grasped his outstretched arm and saved his life in this North Sea.

He knew what to reach for, what he wanted: Angle-land and treasure. But no man could venture to such a goal unaided.

He set down his spear, pulled his shield off, and laid it at his feet. He loosened the cock from its sack, and holding it by its struggling feet, raised his arms. He was alone before the Heavens. Only the gentlest ruffling of the wind could be heard, and nothing moved save the nodding heads of the sea grass. No bird, neither gannet nor fulmar, oared overhead. The sea-path to Angle-land lay open, empty and beckoning. The Sun was glinting off the water before him, showing ripples golden and shimmering, making almost a bridge of light to the paling sky.

"Tyr!" he cried, to get the God's attention. "Look at me!"

His voice rang over the empty landscape. No one lived but he and his God.

His hand went to his knife, and he drew it as he lowered the fowl to the sand. A thrust at the throat sent the cock to Tyr. He stamped his left thumb in the warm blood and put it in his mouth, taking part in the Offering. Then he straightened up and again lifted his arms to the sky, bloodied knife in his right hand.

"I have no father but you," he called. "Make me your son, Tyr. I give myself to you."

The light breeze picked up of a sudden, blowing at his hair and tunic, as if Tyr had heard and was sending him an answer.

His shield was at his feet. He had painted the leather-covered face in a spiral of red and black, radiating out from the iron boss in the centre of the round. He turned the shield, looked at the inside, above the hand grip in the boss. He had already carved the rune Sigel ᛋ there, the first letter of his name. Now he knelt and carved in another rune, for Tyr ᛏ on top of the Sigel [bind-rune].

This bind-rune would be his. He and the God were one.

The next morning, packed and eager for the road, Sidroc and Toki made their farewells. They would travel on foot, for Yrling had ridden his good mare, meaning to sell her there in Ribe to bring him final silver, and the farm horse must of course stay behind. The packs they shouldered had each a bedroll of wool-stuffed linen, the latter waxed against fleas; a ground sheet of cowhide to guard against damp; bread, soft ewe's cheese, and half a cold roasted capon for the walk; and a change of clothing. Sidroc's wool leggings and linen tunics were of the simplest; but that which Toki wore and carried were of finer make, his tunic edged round with bands of tablet-weaving, his leg-wrappings equally bright, demonstration of Ginnlaug's care for her handsome husband's appearance. They carried no cooking gear with them, for Yrling was seeing to all such things.

Toki had left Ginnlaug weeping at the door, and had given quick pecks to the two babes he was leaving her with. Toki had slipped his harp into its fitted leather bag, and had that foremost in his larger pack, that it suffer no hurt. Ginnlaug wondered briefly at his taking it on so short a trip as this; could not he live a Moon or two without his music? But singing, and drinking too, was when he seemed happiest, and she would deny him no pleasure; mayhap he might even compose a song of her while he journeyed. She was smiling through her tears at him as he and Sidroc said their last farewell, to Signe. The old woman was seated as she often was, at the table in the kitchen yard, the faithful thrall-woman Ebbe standing just behind.

Sidroc stood before Signe, and bowed his head. She had given him a home, he knew, and was grateful for it, flawed as it had been. A poor marriage and her fainting-illness had left her a worn and pallid shell, but looking upon him, her voice, cracked though it be, was strong.

"You will not return here."

"I will not return," he agreed. They had not spoken of this before, but he was glad she had discerned it.

Signe closed her eyes, tight, and now said, "Hrald."

Sidroc had one thought at this. I will not be lost at sea, as my father was.

Her son Toki stepped forward, and she looked on him. His long yellow hair was loose, and despite the stricken look on his mother's face he was grinning, as he often was.

"I fear your going," she managed, "but you will return."

Toki was ready with his answer. "Já, I will return, when I can. You have plenty here, and Ginnlaug to help." He bent and wrapped his arm about her for a moment.

The two cousins turned then, slinging their shields over their packs, lifting their spears.

They had not walked far when Sidroc broke their silence. He was thinking of the farm folk gathered behind them, waving them off.

"You will not return, either," he decided.

Toki laughed. "Of that, you are right."

The ease of his reply hung in the air.

"If you do well in Angle-land, you can send for Ginnlaug and the children," Sidroc posed.

"Já," Toki agreed, after a pause. "But she dislikes the sea. She sailed to Skania once. Short as that was, she did not do well. The voyage to the land of the Saxons would not agree with her."

Sidroc said nothing to this. The shallow mound that covered the bones of his dog Hlaupari was the only cherished thing he left behind. All he laid claim to was on his back. Toki walked away from his farm, his wife, their two babes, and an aged mother. He gave it up so lightly.

Early as they started, the walk took all morning. The Sun was overhead when they passed over the planked road spanning the dike around Ribe. Sidroc's low boots, already worn when he set out, suffered from the distance. Once inside the palisade they passed by the plot on which three Summers ago they and Ful had stopped, where he had sold their surplus rye, and where Toki had met his wife. Today a large waggon was there, its bed arrayed with heavy soapstone pots.

They went on, moving past stalls and booths offering hides and pottery, passing women selling cheese-stuffed loaves from arm baskets, and the King's guards moving slowly about, collecting fees or quelling arguments. They made their way to the shipwrights at the river bank, and Yrling.

They found him easily enough. His ship had already been floated, and he moved within the hull with several others. The warm and smoky smell of pine tar wafted from their work, for they daubed away, stuffing any small gaps in the straked oak planks that made up her sides with a mixture of tar and twisted wads of woollen fleece. The ship was barely out in the shallow river, held in place by lines to the end of a massive post, and Sidroc and Toki dropped their packs and spears and clambered aboard over the steep gangplank.

Yrling greeted them, a wooden dauber in his hand, a smear of black tar across his brow. Jari straightened up from where he had been kneeling within the hull. He had a blob of tar smudging his red hair, and a ready grin when he saw Sidroc and Toki. "Now that we are done, you are here," he chaffed, as tar-stained hands were scrubbed with tallow and sand. Though the heavy work of rigging and lading remained, Sidroc, walking the narrow deck of the sleek craft, envied Jari even the tarring, wanting to know the vessel as closely as he did.

It was small for a drekar, six-and-twenty oars, but there was no denying her beauty. Despite her graceful form Yrling had given her a fearsome name, Dauðadagr, or Death-Day.

The mast was up, to give more room for the caulking-work, and even without a sail the ship looked both able and ready to plough the watery distance she would soon be tried at. She was almost all of oak, save the tall and smooth pine mast, and the spar to which the sail would be fixed. The gleam of her rivets and newness of her wood, unblemished by worm-hole or scar, suited most of her youthful crew. Both prow and stern beams rose above the hull in graceful arcs, the stern to coil in on itself like a tail, the prow to fittingly hold the carved head of a gaping-mouthed dragon.

Nestled in the stern, not far from where Yrling would stand at the steering-oar, another carving had been installed: the face of one-eyed yet all-seeing Odin. One eye socket was blank, reminder of the God's forfeit for a drink at the well of wisdom. The other was a chunk of quartz, which flashed and sparkled in the afternoon Sun. The God himself would look over the crew, and look forward over the seas to the lands they sought.

Besides Jari, there were eight or ten young men who Sidroc and Toki had never before seen, all working on or about the ship, or at the little tented camp on the river shore that served as base. Others were about Ribe, or had gone home to return with their packs and weapons.

"Une is at the sailmaker," Yrling told his nephews after they had stowed their packs. "They are nearly ready with it; we will go see."

The sailmaker Yrling had dealt with was a family of weavers and stitchers, father, mother and grown children all at work in the covered shed, standing at floor looms or bent over needles. Yrling's sail was indeed almost done, a mass of interwoven panels of bleached white and bold-dyed madder red panels. A stitcher bent over it, reinforcing with heavy thread a bottom edge grommet from which a hempen line would fix it to the spar. Even lying in folds on a long trestle the bold red and white sail caught the eye.

They found Une at another of the tables, his thumb in his mouth, sucking the blood from the needle-prick he had just given himself. The father of the business was looking on, shaking his head, when they walked in.

He turned from Une to Yrling and asked a question as greeting. "And would you know how to mend a rent in the sail?"

Yrling was quiet just long enough for the man to make up his mind.

The sailmaker took the scrap of linen sailcloth from before Une, and laid another small piece over the tear it bore. "This is how you must sew it. Fold the edges of the patch over, and stitch through those, into the sail. The mend will be stronger, and the patch not fray, and fail, if you do so."

Yrling recalled the time, sailing with Gye, that a careless move with a spear had punctured the sail. He recalled too the speed with which one of his fellows had mended it, lest the rift in the fabric grow.

They all took turns with the mend, Yrling, his nephews, and Une as well, until the sailmaker was satisfied. He would be sending along a spare length of cloth when he delivered the completed sail, along with waxed thread and large-eyed needles, and all must be placed in able hands.

Over the next few days they added a heavy layer of stone under the decking as ballast; took possession of the striking two-hued sail, lugged to them in a hand-cart; rigged the shrouds on starboard and port to hold it in place, carried on the newly-carved oars, and began the lading. Yrling, Sidroc, Toki, Une, and Jari slept aboard the ship at night, the others in the small tents on the shore. They kept a cooking ring to complete their camp. Any of them could roast fish on sticks, but one of the men, Bjarne, proved an able hand at stirring up savoury stews of shredded pig, barley, and new peas. He even waded into the shallows to pull up wild cress, that he might crown each bowl with its fresh greenness.

It was Yrling's silver feeding them all now, and in these final days he and Une were much concerned with the taking on of dried cod, and arranging for several score of loaves, boiled eggs, a crock of butter, and cask of ale to be carried to the ship just before they weighed anchor. That anchor itself was not yet procured. Unlike the one of iron he and Sidroc had seen and admired at Haithabu, Yrling must content himself with one far simpler, which he fashioned himself from a yoked piece of wood he got from a waggon-maker and a large wedge-shaped stone he scavenged from the river bed.

Before she had felt free waters beneath her Yrling already felt pride in his dragon ship. Everything he owned, save his weapons, had been put into Death-day. Hardest of all to part with was his fine mare, which he had traded for silver here in Ribe. He had owned her thirteen years, and she had produced five colts and fillies for him, all of which had profited him by their sale. To sell the mare herself was akin to the loss of someone dear to him; and Yrling, deprived young of both his parents, did not easily form attachments. He trusted Dauðadagr, this new and mightier steed, would bring him even more good fortune.

One lack concerned Yrling more than any other. His ship was one of six-and-twenty oars, but he had gathered only twenty men. Three of the twenty – his nephews and

Jari – were untried as seamen and warriors. Five were those who had sailed with Yrling before, on Gye's ship, and looked now for new adventures; these were men he could trust. The other twelve he had found himself. Though he had made no secret of his destination and his aims with shipwright, sailmaker, and various artisans supplying him, few adventurers had found their way to the river frontage where his new ship tied up. It was Yrling, going to brew-house and meal sheds, and walking the trading roads, who found himself eyeing likely looking fellows, asking if they sought treasure in Angle-land.

Eight men he could trust and twelve unknown to him was not the ratio he had hoped for. The simple truth was he had found it more difficult than he had wagered to attract more of Gye's former crew to sail with him. Gye's last venture had ended in disaster, with Gye dead and his ship captured. Une had made it back, and was more than ready to venture out with Yrling, but others who had returned had reason for caution.

At least on land the spirit of the crew was good. One noon, a day or two before lading was complete, they sat about the cooking ring, having eaten the bean and sausage soup Bjarne had spooned into halves of oat-flour loaves. Bits of tough sausage casing had been flung into a pile of refuse not far off, and now two half-wild cats were digging at it.

"We must have a cat, to keep our food sound," Jari judged, thinking ahead to the foodstuffs they would carry. He had certainly watched rats scavenge through the very same pile of refuse that the two cats were now pawing through.

Jari continued to eye the two felines. The black and white one looked scrappy and a good bet; it might even have extra toes, for good luck. He looked to Yrling, and then to his own brother. "Une has been to sea with rats; nothing is worse."

Toki lifted his eyes from the harp strings he was tuning, and jeered. "A cat! We are not setting up house-keeping, we are raiding. Next you will want a cow and some hens."

Jari took this more seriously than was meant. "A cow takes up too much room. But hens would mean fresh eggs."

Laughter arose from all, save Jari, who warned them if they got hungry at sea, he should not be blamed.

Sidroc laughed with the rest, but kept on thinking. He turned to his uncle. "A fishing net," Sidroc said. "Men adrift have lived, if they can fish."

Yrling nodded his assent. A small net could be cheaply had, and what Sidroc said was well true. A few near him fell silent, considering life aboard a dismasted ship.

This talk of food spurred Une's own thoughts, for now he asked, "For cooking kit?"

"We will carry it, já. But there will be no fires aboard the ship," Yrling answered. "We can eat cold food for four days."

"Four?" repeated Une. He shook his head. "Five, if we are lucky."

"We will be lucky," Yrling declared.

The sea-God Njord must have been listening, and scoffed.

Toki had taken a large purse of silver from the farm, and indeed his wife had almost pressed it upon him, so that he might know more comfort. Silver was ever hot in Toki's hand, and he had not been in Ribe two days when he parted with most of it. At a weapon-smith's he spied a sword, pattern-welded, its bluish blade deeply etched, the grip encased by some rare black wood, the pommel of that grip ending in waves of thin silver set into the steel. There was no waiting with Toki, no reasoning that a good blade could be had for half the silver, or even won at the price of his courage and skill from some Saxon warrior on a field of battle. Yrling sported a sword, and he would have one as well, and so he made the beautiful thing his own.

Then he needs must have a belt and scabbard, and he and Sidroc found themselves at the same worker in leather who had fashioned a sheath for Sidroc's new knife a few years ago. It was blue-dyed leather that Toki chose, adding to the bright show of the new sword. It took the woman two days to fashion both scabbard and hanging-strap, and Toki carried the naked sword with him to her stall, just so he might slide it into the woad-rubbed scabbard, throw it over his shoulder, and then walk as slowly as might be through the crowds on the way back to the river bank and Yrling's ship.

His cousin was again with him. They were due to push off in the morning, if the wind was fair, for the tide would be in their favour just after dawn. It was a cloudy afternoon, and a fresh breeze made it feel cooler than an early Summer's day. As Sidroc waited for Toki to pay the leather worker he looked about. He was aware, as he scanned folk moving from booth to booth, that he might likely never see Jutland, or any part of Denmark again. If those here in

Ribe's trading roads glanced up at him, it was oftentimes to look quickly away again, unaware of such thoughts.

As he had grown older, people stopped asking about the scar on his face. When he was younger strangers would often look, then ask how came he by it, as if they deserved to be a part of its story. As he grew taller that tapered off, then ceased. It was his height, he thought, but mostly his scar. His look was a menacing one, he knew. Folk glanced at the scar but no longer questioned him, as if they had a right to the story.

Sidroc stood, his back to the leather maker's booth, looking out. At first he did not notice a tall, thin woman staring at him. He did not know why she looked at him; he had never seen her before. She was old; at least she looked old to his eyes. She was poor, and simply dressed. An undyed head wrap was tied over her grey-streaked brown hair. Her eyes were fixed upon him. Her mouth moved, and her left hand rose slightly, as if towards him. She held the hand of a small child with her right, and other children were about her. She kept looking, taking him in. Yet she said nothing.

Toki finished, and Sidroc found himself returning her look for one moment more before turning away.

Jorild remained looking after him, knowing she had seen her son.

She had come to Ribe for the day with her nephews and nieces; it was a treat that made the long walk worthwhile. After leaving Hrald's farm Jorild had never wed. Between fields and house she had made herself useful at her cousin's farm, tending to the cows, washing wool and spinning, helping to care for the children, and spending increasing time as well caring for her aunt, Gillaug, who now was grown old.

Her uncle Oddi, lately returned, had told her much about her boy. She knew how tall he was, and also that his face had been marred by his cousin's knife. And her uncle had told her that Sidroc had resolved to quit Jutland and seek his fortune in Angle-land.

Now standing there, she had no doubt it was her own son. He looked like his father, who she knew from Oddi had been lost at sea years before. Yet Sidroc looked his own man, looked, even at the age of twenty years, to be growing into the name she had bestowed on him, that of a great war-chief.

It seemed a blessing, or boon from the Gods that she could see her boy now, as he headed into a new life. To see him, tall, strong, and vital before her, was some return for all she had suffered in losing him.

The children who surrounded her grew restive, but Jorild did not move until the tall form vanished from view. She had at last again seen her son. Her eyes were wet, but a smile was on her lips.

THE NORTH SEA

FROM the hour they cast off, they were the sport of Njord, the sea-God.

Yrling had offered two geese at the carved and painted likenesses of Odin and Freyr; secretly hoping as he dispatched the birds that the succulent flesh he surrendered would not be regretted in a few days by a hungry crew. He gave thought as well that Njord got nothing, though it was into that God's hands he must commit his ship and men. While on land one gave Offering to those Gods of Heaven and fields, that was custom; and he would trust that Odin and Freyr would grant both protection on the journey, and increase at its goal.

Even then, standing there flanked by his nephews and with most of the ship's company looking on, rain began splattering about them, heavy drops that left coin-sized circles on the hard ground. They boarded and pushed off, dropping oars into a river dull with the grayness of dawn.

They had lifted the new red-and-white sail a few times, admiring how its interwoven stripes caught both breeze and eye; but in the river channel and with growing crosswinds, Yrling ordered it stay furled against the spar. He stood in the stern, hands on the tiller of the steering oar, as all took up oars. This was their first time pulling together, and Yrling had those new to the skill take up the oar with the practiced men behind and before them. The rain had begun to pelt, and Yrling had not donned his new oiled-skin tunic and leggings, so soon all were wet. Une sat nearest him, so that he might be in ready earshot, and Toki opposite on the port side. All, save Yrling who stood, sat upon the chests that held their kit; the knee-braces of the hull serving as blocks against which to brace their feet. Sidroc took up a place at broad amidships, where his height was better served. Jari was across from him, on the port side.

They had been eager to cast off Ribe and its constraining river, but as they did so the weather turned its back on the newly-launched drekar, presenting it with rain so chill that all forgot it was the first month of Summer. They need sail up the river to its outlet into the North Sea, skirt the sandy barrier islands, then take a northerly tack to catch the prevailing currents to help spill them South and West across that vast sea to Angle-land.

Emerging from the river mouth they all saw what they had set off into. That sea now was a foaming expanse of chopping, curling white-caps, the wind whip-sawing back and forth, but with a steadier under-wind beating them back whence they came.

Oaring in such conditions exhausted both strength and patience. Yrling scanned the skies through the rain, searching for a glimmer of light that told of coming clearing. He saw none.

They beached on one of the barrier islands, and spent two days there in rain and wind consuming their stores, before the skies lightened and they could move on. They built a camp of sorts the first day on the sand in the lee of the ship, stretching oiled tarpaulins from the gunwale to stakes they drove into the sand with the blunt ends of the war-hammers three of them carried. Beneath was shelter enough to allow Bjarne to strike and light a fire from twists of sea-grass. Driftwood, scoured from the wave-beaten sand, seemed wet through but dried with little coaxing, allowing them a bit of warmth to toast loaves and melt the soft cheeses and butter they scooped from crocks.

Around such a fire the score of them talked and jested. Their progress had been arrested at first setting out, but turning back to Ribe to await favourable winds was never in their captain's plan.

The first night was made easier by Toki's prowess at the harp. He set himself up in a corner of their lean-to and pulled it from its bag, striking the strings so that they thrummed under his fingertips. He sang songs that all knew, of the giant race, the Jotuns, those devourers who the Gods had need to defeat before the world could come into being; and of that Trickster Loki, Jotun blood-brother of All-Father Odin, ever causing grief but also bringing laughter.

A number of bawdy songs fell from Toki's lips that night, some of his own devising, speculations about which of the Goddesses would bring greatest pleasure. These gave rise to debate amongst a few of the men, some holding that sleeping with any Goddess was far too dangerous an endeavour to reward the risk. Toki's songs thus proved diversion, and loosened their own tongues. That first night, hove to on the sand bar, driven by rain under the dripping tarpaulin, they then began to speak of themselves, trading stories of what past adventuring had cost them.

Yrling knew fewer than half these men; Sidroc and Toki, only Une and Jari. One, known solely as Gap – for his upper two front teeth were missing – had sailed with Yrling before. His absent teeth did not keep him from grinning, an effect that to Sidroc looked like the opened gates of a palisade wall. Of necessity Gap bit off food and chewed on the side of his mouth. And Bjarne lacked most of his right ear. All, even those who had been witness to it, heard how Gap's teeth were knocked out by the butt end of a spear, and of the Saxon seax that cost Bjarne his ear.

Eyes then went around the circle of men, and several stopped on Sidroc.

"And you?" This was Gap, who whistled slightly as he spoke.

They were expecting Sidroc's story; even Une and Jari were looking at him. He was silent.

His eyes shifted slowly to his left, to Toki, who had earlier put away his harp. Sidroc said nothing, wondering if his cousin would laughingly lay claim to the act, as the fruit of a friendly fight. But his cousin too was silent.

It was Yrling who spoke. "I was there, soon after the deed. The one who gave that cut was worse marked than Sidroc."

Toki, eyes down, was now busy picking dirt out from the grooves of the grip of his knife. Sidroc too had dropped his eyes a moment, and when he raised them saw all looking on him. His uncle's words seemed to do him honour, one Sidroc knew unearned, just as he knew the same words were meant to privately castigate Toki. Yet Yrling's true meaning was shared only by the three of them.

Talk shifted from hurts suffered to contests, and warriors, which lived on in memory.

"Who has seen a berserkr?" Une posed, a question answered by laughter, or the shaking of heads.

"Seen one, and lived?" Yrling challenged. "If the bear enters a fighting man, those he faces are not likely to tell the tale after."

Bear, wolf, boar – all these mighty beasts might take possession of a warrior who was so favoured by the spirits. In body he would look a man, but the beast's hugr – essence – would suffuse his being, giving him powers beyond mortal fighting men, and animal cunning too. To be so possessed gave a warrior almost invincible ability, carrying him to a realm of expanded senses yet narrowed focus. The essence of the spirit beast was constricted into a channel, deep and clear, flowing into the warrior's consciousness. It took possession of his human form – his hamr – spreading throughout his body, and thence to his limbs, to direct their action. Sometimes a man's voice was taken over, sounds issuing from his throat never before heard. Other times he might fight in silence, the whirlwind sweep of his weapon and that of his breathing the only sound.

Pure rage alone could not take a man there; in fact, such wrath was often the key to recklessness and an early death. The awakening of the hugr was a deeper arousal, like that of the bear who each year went to its den under the ground, a seeming death lasting months, to arise in Spring to new life.

Most gathered under that dripping tarpaulin hoped they might be found worthy to attain such a state; such warriors won rare repute amongst their brothers. Yet there were dangers too in this possession, a kind of madness that could make a man fight with indiscriminate fury.

Only let me fight like Tyr, Sidroc thought; with an arm that does not fail me, and discernment too.

Later, both Sidroc and Jari quit the slight shelter of the tarpaulin. One must sit beneath it, and their legs needed stretching. There was naught but scrub-growth, sea thorn and the like, springing from the sand where they had beached, and walking on the barren flatness both felt the taller for it. The rain fell only in scattered drops, but the wind was fierce upon them, and both clutched their woollen mantles closely to them. They walked leaning into the blow, side by side, not unaware that each was watching the other from the tail of their eye.

"I am taller than you," Jari said, for no reason. Sidroc stopped and sized him up. He shook his head.

He turned on his heel and they stood back to back. With lifted hands they tried to determine the taller. It was indeed Sidroc, but Jari was close.

"I am still growing," Sidroc claimed. He could not know this for certain, save that he recalled his own father telling him that he himself had had a late growth spurt.

Sidroc could not pin this telling to an exact moment. He felt prompted to say it nonetheless. Once out, he felt for a sudden moment the presence, in his breast, of his fylgja, nodding her head in assent at his words, Já, that is correct; that is true.

Jari took it with ease. He was certainly broader; a chest like a barrel, a neck well able to hold the large head and abundant fiery hair. "We will be tall enough to face any," he said into the wind, as they turned back to the ship. "You, Une, and me. We can put Sif between us for protection."

He laughed, and Sidroc did too. Sif was the name Une had once called Toki in jest; he had watched Sidroc's cousin combing out his yellow hair, delaying him in some task about the ship, and teased him with the name of the yellow-haired wife of Thor. Toki had not taken well to it.

After two damp nights on the sandy spit of the barrier island the blast abated enough that they could once again push off. Hoisting sail made all glad, and the ship fairly lunged forward in seeming eagerness to be at last underway. They must travel northerly first, up past the tip of Jutland, and from there cast out, working with the currents, letting them carry them down across the North Sea to their target. They cleared the last of their native land, and staring on the dim green and brown line of it some on the deck looked forward to their return. Three at least did not, and though Yrling, hand on the steering oar, said nothing, he followed the gaze of his nephews' eyes. He read in their faces the cool satisfaction of final farewell.

Yet winds remained contrary, and with it the work of keeping the ship on its southwesterly course. When it grew dark enough to spot the North Star they could check by its gleam they headed South and West; but the lengthening northern days made it hard to see. Yet the Sun refused them its bright beams, and the ceaselessly grey skies denied them a clear benchmark. When for a generous moment or two the Sun grew strong, it would cast a slender shadow from the pointed spindle of the wooden Sun-board Yrling held up, and from which he must determine their course. They had now seen no land, and no other craft, for three days. The ship was a brown sliver of wood, blown along by its red-and-white sail on a grey and ceaselessly rough white-flecked sea. Une and others had made this journey before, but Yrling now led these men. He must serve as his own kendtmand – that man who knows the secrets of open-water sailing.

Both gannets and fulmars ranged far out to sea by day, but returned to shore at dusk; they were truth-tellers of land ahead, and when they were sighted Yrling knew to turn his back on them, keep heading across the expanse before the prow.

The food was cold, parcelled out so none were ever full, and fogs and frequent rains assured that none felt dry or warm. And some were sick. Sidroc, used to going out in a small boat as a child, felt it not, and Toki too was blessed with a strong stomach. But a few of the men, including those who had before made the crossing, found their bellies lurching with the roll of the waves. These could barely keep down a bit of stale bread, so it freed up remaining stores for those who laughed at their brethren clinging to the gunwale. But the ale in the big cask was beginning to sour, and must be drunk up before it became unswallowable.

"Rat!" called Bjarne one dull morning. He had been placed in charge of the food supplies, and opening the chest that held the remaining loaves was startled by a brown rat that leapt out at him. He flung his knife at the lithe creature, startling one of his fellows, Asved by name, by whose shoulder the blade flew. But the rat vanished behind one of the casks of water. Asved, who had narrowly missed being punctured by the knife, stood cursing the thrower. But Bjarne was busy turning the food chest. Sure enough, there was now a hole gnawed clear through the wood of it, near one of the bottom corners. The rat had had its full, and many of the loaves were left in crumbled fragments.

Jari leapt up from where he sat near the mast. "I told you," he challenged all, with not a little triumph in his declaration. "No cat – and we have a rat."

A few of the apples, but lightly secured in a sack, had before been found to have been gnawed, but the men had laughingly accused each other of taking a bite and returning the rest of the fruit. Their bread was a more serious matter, for between the creature's teeth and the scat it had left, it had despoiled much.

Une, looking on his brother, was forced to admit aloud he always had good sense, and regretted they had not scooped up a clawed hunter when they could.

There was no cornering the pillaging creature, though Jari, Bjarne and a few others shifted casks, chests, and packs where they were lashed, in an attempt to capture it. It darted about, a streak of sleek dark fur, until it vanished down a narrow slot in the decking, beneath which lay the ballast stones.

The rat, unwelcome as it was, served as momentary distraction, one which Yrling felt the need of, though no one regretted the loss of bread as much as he. Short rations ever led to short tempers. All were suffering from the first, and nearly all from the second. Their cheese was gone, but butter they still had, now with less bread on which to spread it. The dried cod was meant to have served them when they landed in Angle-land, and could fire a cauldron and boil it down. They had a few apples and some boiled eggs, and now must hack up the dried cod and chew small chips of it. It was of leather-like hardness and salty enough that it only increased thirst. One cask of water had been exhausted, and when Yrling warned the men to slow their drinking of the second, a few of them looked at him with glowering eyes. No one had a gaze as hard as Yrling; his heavy brow line gave his eyes the cowl of a raptor, but he saw how some of those he glared at clenched their fists in wordless protest.

In truth they had been too many days at sea, with little to eat, continual damp, and no land in sight. The winds meant that the sail was always up, and full. But once the mast was lifted and sail unfurled, any four men could tend to the actual sailing, with one as look-out, which left an idle group of wet and hungry men with time to grumble. Yrling was loath to yield the steering oar to any but Une, with short stints for Sidroc and Toki, that they might learn the feel of the tiller. That night as he wrapped himself in his blanket on the decking under the carved visage of Odin, Yrling bethought him that in the morning he might order the fishing net to be unrolled and dropped. He would not go so far as to allow fire on his new ship, but the moist flesh of raw fish would be better than barely chewable flakes of wind-dried cod.

That next morning, their seventh out, no net was cast. All who slept were jolted awake by a sudden swell, which caught the ship, carried her up, and dropped her into a trough. Une was at the steering oar as Yrling staggered up and out of sleep. The fog and cool mist of the night was gone; the sharpening wind had driven it off. The sky was overcast, unchanging, an unbroken leaden gray. The sea roiled beneath them, and another few swells found wave tips slapping over and inside the hull. Yrling yelled out orders as the sail was hastily dropped and furled.

The rain began, in confused flight. The wind sent it down upon their heads as if to batter their brains. It then thickened and froze, shifting so that particles of hail came at them from the side in sheets, smarting their faces and bare hands as hornets might. Indeed it felt the ship herself was under attack, and she betrayed this in her movement, bucking as a stung horse might, rising and falling, canting to port and then to starboard. The bow lifted, driving the painted dragon head seemingly straight above them, then plunged so that carved Odin in the stern grinned over them as they clung to anything that kept them from being flung overboard.

Une stood with Yrling at the steering oar, four hands and two strong backs on the tiller. The frenzy of the sea was such that there was no keeping her bow heading into the swells, for waves crested on all sides, pouring water within. The oaths of men scrambling for handholds as they were dashed against the hull were lost in the whistling of the wind. Tarpaulins were blown from where they had been stretched over the bow, ripping away the slight shelter they had provided. Yrling had not been able to afford a stout netting of hempen line, cunningly knotted to cage his cargo; all had been secured by simple lines lashing down their stores. These had been disturbed, and then imperfectly re-fastened, by the chase after the rat, and now fell loose. The wind mounted in its fury, shrieking about the scrambling men. Freed chests and casks rolled wildly. Sidroc, trying to reach a loose bucket which neared where he held the base of the mast, saw even the coiled fishing net be picked up in the wind and fly over the gunwale. But the bucket came within his grasp. He was able to scoop at the cold water soaking him, joining those men who had grabbed what vessels they could in their bailing.

One thought was in Sidroc's mind as he struggled, on his knees, to hurl bucketsful of sea water back into the angry depths: I will not rest in Ran's bed tonight. He was not alone in this determination, even if for some it was little more than mere hope. Ran was a Goddess of the Sea, one known for her greed in pulling men down to their deaths in her sea-net.

They crawled, shivering through the churning salt water that engulfed them. Any sudden roll of the ship might fling them out, and those who found lines near them hastily tried to secure themselves. Twice when Sidroc reached the gunwale he found the deck dropping away from beneath him, and the bucket he grasped dumped its sloshing contents back over him before he could toss it over.

More than one man howled out prayers. Sea-God Njord heard, and seemingly took pity. The gale released its grip on them. Stinging hail melted to hard rain, and the battering winds slackened. At length the ship slowed in her tossing. Buckets, cooking pots, even bowls were used to lift and fling the sea water out from whence it came. They all worked numbly, soaked and even trembling with cold, to rid the ship of the channel of sea water they stood in, water at first as high as the calves of their legs, and still up to their ankles. Other than a random oath they barely spoke. Nearly all the men were bruised from being thrown about the hull, or hit by wooden chests and barrels. One sat dazed, having struck his head against the spar.

It was only when most of the water running along the keel had been scooped out that one of the men spoke.

"Where is Tönne," he asked, to all and yet to no one. This was Gizur, a good bow man who Yrling had picked up within Ribe. Gizur had straightened up, and was standing near the mast, his wet clothes dripping. He looked up and down the length of the drekar.

Tönne was gone. He was a friend to Gizur, but little known to the others. Now all saw he had been swept overboard.

They stood, and grasping the gunwale for steadiness, scanned the seas on all sides. The water was too rough to see much beyond the nearest waves.

"Tönne!" cried Gizur, a call answered only by the creak of wood beneath them, and the slapping of the waves against the hull.

No one spoke. Yrling had one thought, recalling his act of sacrifice at Ribe: that Njord did indeed exact an Offering.

Few slept that day, and then only from exhaustion. All were still wet, with no way to dry out until the Sun might show itself. Their possessions were soaked, those of them who had not lost them overboard. The scant food stores were ruined, the remaining loaves a soggy, salt-water soaked mess, caked in one corner of the chest which had housed them. Bjarne, looking at this, doubted that even the rat would be tempted. A few apples, rapidly browning, were found, rolling about the knee-braces, and precious few boiled eggs. These were counted out and divided so that each man got one egg and half a mealy apple. This was their only provender that long day, though some chewed also on the tough flakes of dried cod. By lucky chance the remaining barrel of water had remained sealed; they would not die of thirst, Yrling had declared, in attempt to rally their spirits.

In the long dusk Yrling heard the men muttering. He stood at the steering oar, looking out over them in the gloaming. The sail was still furled tight against the spar; mayhap they could lift it in the morning; the wind had calmed so he no longer need fear for the safety of sail or mast. They had been battered and blown so far, they must sight land on the morrow. He wondered if they might have overshot all Angle-land, and that Frankland lay before them; he was certain they were still heading on a southerly course, and it was not beyond reason that the currents had carried them more South than West. Whatever land they sighted, he knew he must make for it. He had no choice.

Yrling stayed long at the oar that night, letting Une sleep until he himself must meet rest. He wrapped himself in his damp blanket in the very stern under Odin's eye, and fell into sleep, one no less profound for the trouble he felt. It was nearby voices, loud and rising, that roused him. Dawn was breaking on another grey morning, but the air was dry. Yrling sat up to see a line of men before Une, who held the steering oar. Yrling stood up.

Une was blunt of speech, and now loudly upbraided those who had come in challenge to face them. Yrling saw Gizur foremost.

"What is this," Yrling demanded, stepping to Une's side at the tiller. His action reasserted his claim as captain and ship-owner, and his words were more growl than question.

"Free Danes, who hold that you do not know what you are doing," came the angry retort.

"We have no food, and soon no water," said another.

"And Tönne is dead," said a third. This was Gizur.

Yrling looked to him. Gizur was smaller than any of the others who had signed on for the adventure, but sinewy and fast. Like many smaller warriors, he was a master of the bow, and had showed this to Yrling when they had met, sending a well-fletched arrow whizzing through the air to strike a protruding post-end at the top of Ribe's palisade wall. This won the attention of the nearby guards as it met its mark, forcing both Gizur and Yrling to look coolly about them and walk away as if innocent of the offending arrow's origin.

Now five of his twenty men stood angrily before him, and one of them was Gizur. Yrling knew how swiftly mutiny could spread amongst ship-bound men; he had heard the tales. He was no less hungry than the rest, but it was he who led them into this, resisted turning back to Ribe at first setting out, allowed them to spend the extra days beached on the barrier island, eating what was needed now.

The five standing before Yrling were empty-handed. The spears were secured along the hull where they had been all voyage, but all wore their knives. If any had tried to pull a spear the time for words would have passed.

Yrling let his eyes lift to those who now ranged behind the five challengers. Sidroc, taller than them all, was first he spotted. He had been awakened by the noise of dispute just as his uncle had. He had lain awake a long time before sleep had finally come, listening to a murmured but growing dissent about him.

His nephew stepped closer, almost behind the five, awaiting any sign from his uncle, that he come forward and stand next him. Yrling gave none. He would not force a confrontation, if none was needed.

Now as Sidroc moved closer to its source, he became aware of Jari flanking his shoulder. *You will be my brother*, Sidroc thought, thinking of the moment they would fight shoulder-to-shoulder. He did not expect it to be against other Danes, on his uncle's own ship. Yet there Jari was.

Sidroc flicked his eyes to Toki, like all the men now standing and staring at the group in the stern. He would have liked Toki to have glanced his way, telling him he stood ready, but Toki's blue eyes were fixed on those staring down his uncle.

Yrling had also spared a moment to look at Toki. Most of the men already liked Toki, he knew this. But he knew Toki to be reckless, and his yellow-haired nephew did not like either Une or Jari. Yet Yrling must wager that Toki would join his cousin and stand by him in any dispute. The bond of blood must be stronger than Toki's petty dislikes. Yet he saw Toki cast quick looks from side to side, as if gauging the depth and seriousness of the dispute.

Une, already at his side, would not fail him, this he knew; and of Sidroc, untried as he was, he had no doubt. Jari was also untried, but huge, and if he was like his older brother, would be fearless. And Jari had taken up with Sidroc.

Gizur spoke again. "Tönne is dead," he repeated. The flatness of his tone suggested that Gizur looked not to cast blame, but instead sought explanation.

Yrling had man-craft enough to read this. He lifted his hands, as if holding the enormity of the sea. His next words were as firm as he could make them.

"Njord exacted his due; that is all. The ship is sound. We are nearly at Angle-land."

It was not quite enough.

"You do not know where we are," one of the challengers countered.

"We will reach Angle-land today," Yrling declared.

Or tomorrow, he thought. He kept his face from showing this concern, kept his hawk-like eyes moving from face to face.

He and Une were the only ones facing the bow, every other man was turned towards them. Thus it was Yrling who saw the other ship.

It had to have been caught in the same gale as they were, and in the chop of the water was hard to see. It was in fact the action of its yellow-dyed sail being raised, and filling with wind, that made Yrling notice it; it stood out against the greyness of the seas. He was at enough of an angle to it to name it for what it was, a Danish war ship, a drekar, one of thirty or more oars. It moved smartly along, all unwitting that it had been spotted.

Yrling began to laugh. Some of those who faced him gaped. He lifted his hand, forefinger extended.

"We are going to take that ship," he announced.

All whirled about, some almost turning into Sidroc and Jari as they did so. Eyes which squinted against the morning light saw the ship Yrling spotted.

"Hoist sail," he called. "We will stay behind and to her port side, unseen as long as we can."

Men sprang to action. "Unloose the spears," Yrling went on. "If all goes well we will not need them, but have them at your sides. Shields, off from the gunwale. Hide them well in the prow; cover them with hides.

"Fill every bucket, every pot with sea water, have them ready so that at my call you can cast it back, as if we floundered.

"Gizur. Sidroc. Toki," he called next. The three came to him, one who he knew as a crack-shot, the two younger untried. One life had already been lost; he must show that he would risk his young kin to win this ship.

With Une at his side he detailed his plan. They would near the ship, pleading distress. While Yrling engaged them in talk at the stern, they would close the distance as much as they could.

They had but one grappling hook tied to a length of hempen line, and one gaff, its iron hook broad enough to catch the inner edge of another ship's gunwale. The grappling hook could be thrown a fair distance, but the reach of the gaff was only as long as its wooden shaft. To Sidroc would be given the task of throwing the grappling line, and pulling the two ships near. Toki would be called upon to extend the gaff and help pull the hulls together, closing the distance between them.

"You will be amidships," Yrling told them. "We will come up alongside. I will be at the stern, where their captain should also be. I will be calling to them; they will be looking at me, and your throw may be able to catch them by surprise."

His nephews stared at him, open-mouthed, alert, hanging on each word. They were being singled out for tasks, which if well achieved, could greatly aid the scheme's chances of success.

"Já," breathed Sidroc, a single word of assent conveying the distinction he felt. Toki too uttered agreement, his blue eyes flashing as if he already pulled upon the gaff.

Yrling nodded back at them. Their exposure would be great; he saw this. They would need both hands, each of them, to do their jobs; could hold no shield nor weapon if the suspicions of the other ship were roused. He turned to Gizur.

"You will stand behind me, behind me and Une. We must look unarmed; but hidden behind us they will not see your bow. I will step away suddenly, and you will send your arrow into the captain's heart."

Gizur gave answer in a single exhalation of breath, an "Ah!" that showed his approval of such a daring plan, and his own part in it.

Their sail was now billowing full as they bore down on their target. Men were dipping buckets and cauldrons over the side, re-filling them with the same cold salt water that they had laboured mightily to free the ship from yesterday. A new and humming energy rose from the ship, one felt by all, an energy that sharpened the senses and directed all action.

Yrling's eye fell on the dragon head crowning the prow. It was a separate piece of wood, its base slotted to fit between the prongs of the rising beam of the bow. He had paid a Ribe wood-carver a whole handful of hack-silver for it. Like all mast-heads it could be removed for safe-keeping from storm or theft. This dragon had seen a gale and come through admirably, but Yrling knew he should hide it now. A ravening dragon did not serve his purpose.

He left the steering oar to Une and moved with Sidroc to the bow. Sidroc stood on a chest, reached up, and with a wooden mallet tapped the pin which held it, so that he could pull the carved head free. He lowered it into Yrling's waiting arms.

Without the gaping mouth of the dragon foremost, the aspect of the ship was changed. "Now we look almost a fishing boat," Yrling said. Their shields, now stowed inside the ship, would not betray them either. Yrling went on so all might hear. "But she is still the Death-day," he told them. Yrling now pointed to the stern, and the carving of one-eyed All-Father. "And Odin watches us still, expects our best."

They were close enough now to have been sighted by the yellow-sailed ship. But they offered no war-whoops, sent no arrows through the air to assail them. They could see the figures on the war ship standing and at the ready.

From a long way off Yrling began hollering at them. He had resumed his place at the steering oar in the stern, and bellowed across the waves. As he did a few of his crew began tossing water over the gunwale, and making good show of it.

"Tar!" cried Yrling, to his counterpart on the other ship. "Captain and brother, we need tar!"

They sailed up to the war ship, a ship of fully thirty oars, as boldly as if their lives depended on it. Each side of their target was hung with the shields of the men within, an impressive display of discs painted red, blue, black, and yellow.

"Tar," called Yrling again, making his need known. The men before him flung out buckets of water, proof of their distress. If they could not re-caulk their ship, they would sink.

"We have fish!" he cried out, as inducement. The storm both vessels had been through was great enough that this story might be believed: they were but a stout fishing craft, blown far off course, taking on water, but full too of fish. They could well pay for a small cask of tar.

They were near enough to see heads turn, and talk exchanged at the steering oar of the war ship. Whether the war-chief thereon planned to aid them with tar, or seize their ship for the fish he thought it held, Yrling did not care. They only needed to grow close enough to enact the rest of his plan.

"Captain and brother, give us tar!" Yrling called. "Cod and herring will be yours."

They were now coming alongside, and looked out on an able-looking crowd of men. Their captain stood, as Yrling did, at the steering oar, easy to pick out by the fine tooling on his dark leathern tunic, and a broad and bright bracelet of silver on the wrist that steadied the tiller. He was above Yrling's age, of thirty years or slightly more, his flesh well set on his bones, with a long, light brown beard and hair of the same hue resting in plaits on his shoulders.

Yrling looked to Sidroc, standing at the broadest part of the ship, his hands holding the coiled line of the grappling hook. He was partially screened by Toki, at whose feet lay the gaff, ready to be taken up. As Yrling had hoped, all eyes were on he himself, calling out as he came up even with the stern of the other ship.

Sidroc watched the distance between the two brown hulls narrow. He would have one chance to hurl the hook and catch it within the nearing warship, and he must be able with a solid pull to bring it at once within reach of the gaff Toki would extend. He nodded to his cousin, who moved off.

Their crewmates who seemingly bailed water were also back near Yrling, ranged nearer the stern, catching the eye of those who watched from the war ship.

Sidroc let another moment pass. He took a long and slow breath. *Tyr,* he called within him, *make true my arm.*

Sidroc stood alone, allowing clear aim for his throw. He reared back and let loose. He saw the black iron claws of the hook fly through the air, the hempen line tied to it sailing after. He watched it vanish over the hung shields, behind the straked planking of the other ship's hull. Then he gave a yank. The sharp points of the hook found home in the oaken planks of that hull. He pulled with all his might.

Toki was now at the gunwale, lunging forward, gaff pole fully extended. Oaths and calls arose from those amidships on their target, cries of surprise at the flung hook. Yrling, at his oar, called out again, eyes trained on the war-chief.

"Cod and herring I have for you," he taunted.

The other captain looked down his own ship to see the line tethering it. He was beginning to speak when Yrling and Une stepped apart, and Gizur, arrow nocked and waiting, sent an arrow into his breast.

Cod and herring and something more, thought Yrling.

The face of the war-chief still wore his scowl of surprise. The impact of the arrowhead made a thump, a muffled echo of the heart beneath it which it had suddenly stopped.

The captain rocked forward with the roll of his ship, and fell, face down, over his own steering oar. A shrill two-part war cry was sounded near the fallen man, and those nearest him gave out with yells of protest. Metal flashed as a sword was drawn. But Yrling already had a light throwing spear in his right hand, and all too quickly sunk it in the body of a second man.

An instant later the two hulls smacked together, Sidroc and Toki able to bump their ship up broadsides. It knocked some of the men on both ships to their decks, but Yrling and many of his crew were over the sides and swarming the other drekar. They had rapidly taken up spears, and those who had swords had the naked blades extended. Yet they felled no more men. The astonishment on the war ship was so great that they met little resistance; both their captain and his second in command were dead, sprawled in a bloody heap beneath the tiller.

Sidroc, having leapt over, spear in hand, stood with Toki and Jari, staring at the men they had overcome. This was a ship they had taken sudden possession of, through the audacity of their own captain. The treachery was such that those on both sides who witnessed it would in years to come laugh in admiration. Indeed, they may have done so then, if Yrling's men had not been light-headed from hunger and the sudden rush of action.

No one was laughing now, not even Yrling, who had been grinning at the war-chief when the arrow was fired.

"Who is his kin?" Yrling bellowed. He was standing over the body of the dead captain. "Tell me, or more will die."

Even under this threat no voice was raised, no hand pointed. At last one yellow-haired man spoke, he from whose throat the shrieking war-cry had issued. The man had brandished a spear perilously close to Yrling's head, but it now lay on the deck where he had dropped it in surrender.

"He had no kin aboard, and no brother at home."

"And this one?" Yrling returned, prodding the body of the second man with his foot.

The yellow-haired man shook his head, nej.

Yrling was satisfied. The thirst for vengeance would be slight. He studied the man who had responded. He had perhaps a year or two more than his nephews, and had a broad, open face, one which did not look overly troubled at this new turn of events.

"Brave enough to fight. Smart enough to speak," Yrling answered. "What is your name?"

"Asberg."

"And where do you make for, Asberg," Yrling asked next.

"Any part of Anglia," came the answer.

"You have made this trip before?'

"Já."

"Now we sail to Lindisse," Yrling confirmed. "We are two ships, ready to tear Saxon treasure."

"I am Yrling," he called above the heads of all. "And fitter to lead you than they who lie dead on this deck."

This was met by a silence which was broken by a practical query. "Have you really fish?' one of his new crew asked.

"We have nothing," Yrling was forced to report. "We lost all our food stores in the blow. What you have we will share out." A pause, as a rippling murmur grew amongst the men. "Angle-land is very close," he asserted.

It was Asberg spoke next. "It is just ahead; we will see it by dusk."

Yrling's own men, both on Death-day and upon this new drekar, gave out with a hoot of approval.

Asberg's ship had a metal wind-vane on the tip of its mast, one from which ribbands streamed, thus showing from whence the winds blew, and with what speed. He looked to it now, so that Yrling followed his eyes. Those ribbands were snapping in the stiff breeze. "It blows West," Asberg said. "We need only follow it, and we will be carried there before dark."

"Then we will eat tonight, and on land." Yrling's voice fairly thrilled with this claim, and his men offered up a cheer in response.

First he must take full possession of his new ship, and could not do so with the bodies of the dead at his feet. Stripping a warrior's body for battle-gain was the final act of a victor. But it was one done in the company of one's fellows, oftentimes busy with the same task. Only rarely was a body stripped before those of the surviving vanquished.

He knelt at the bodies before him, turning the captain over so the face now looked into the blankness of the grey sky above. With a twist of his wrist he pulled the arrow from out the captain's chest. He had already seen the silver bracelet the man wore, but in turning the body a thick line of braided silver showed above the collar of the tunic of leather. He reached for that first, pulling from over the man's head a chain from which hung a true prize.

It was a silver amulet, a large and beautifully worked hammer of Thor. It almost spanned Yrling's palm, such was its size. The bright shaft of it, and the two blunted hammer heads flanking, were covered over in minute balls of silver spiraling over the whole. These caught and almost threw light all along the surface, so that heavy as it was, the hammer seemed to dance and shimmer. It was solid silver; he weighed the heft of it in his hand. Gizur's arrow had happily missed the prize, and it was undented. Yrling took another look at it, then slipped it over his own neck.

He unbuckled the weapon belts next. Each held a good blade, he could see that from the care lavished on the hilts. A small purse of leather was there, secreted inside one of the belts; all this he set aside.

He pulled off the leathern tunic. The front of the man's linen tunic was soaked with blood, the dark green of it showing a muddy red-brown. But the leathern tunic itself had only the single puncture and a dark patch of wet on the inside. The tunic he handed to Gizur as reward for his work.

"With a sheep's fleece under it, you will fill it out nicely," he jested to his marksman. He then pulled off the bracelet of silver from the dead man's right wrist and placed it as well in Gizur's hands.

This captain had been rich, and everything on him worthy. Yrling pulled off even the man's shoes, which were new and sported toggles of amber.

He regarded all he had taken, knew that the man's shield and spear must be near and of equal fineness; he would claim those as well. But Une was standing there, and Yrling lifted the sword and belt to him. Neither spoke, but Yrling's gesture made clear it was his gift to his second in command. Une had a sword, though his skeggox with its wedge shaped edge was his weapon of choice. A battle-axe suited his size, but he was glad for the new sword. In the circle of battle-gain Une could now keep or trade for it.

Yrling turned to the second body, far less rich in what it held, but yielding things of value nonetheless.

"Toki. Sidroc," he called, in a low tone. They stepped forward. This man wore a sword, the most costly possession of any warrior, unless he sported gold. Toki had parted with much silver to buy a sword back in Ribe, but Yrling must be even-handed to both nephews. The man's knife was a good one, and though he bore no silver at neck or wrist his purse rattled with it. He thus passed the sword belt to Sidroc, and the knife and purse to Toki. In this way they knew battle-gain before they had ever yet killed a man.

Yrling rose now. He and Une took up the shoulders and feet of those dead, and cast them over the side into the grey and swirling waters of the North Sea. One and then the other splashed into those cold depths. They were nearly in view of Angle-land, and these two had not lived to make land.

He turned back to the deck, the big hammer of Thor glinting round his neck. He looked over the greater prize he had seized, this dragon ship and its men. The ship was older than his, and like its men, tried. Its cargo was roped in with the kind of knotted mesh that he lacked on his own; its crew had not suffered the losses his own had. Now he must win these men's loyalty, prove at once he would deal fairly with them.

"Men new to me. You have lost nothing. All that you owned is yours. And you have gained a new, and better war-chief."

He let this settle. The act of stripping the bodies and casting them overboard sealed his dominion over the ship. He had won by craft and brazen courage, traits valued by all raiders. Now they must move forward. He looked to light-haired Asberg.

"You will stay on this ship, Asberg. I name it Yellow-sail, for that was what caught my eye. Une will serve as captain, and I put my nephew Sidroc with you as well." Yrling looked behind him and chose a few more from his own men to join the captured ship, Jari amongst them.

He then turned to the remainder of the captured crew. "Half of you, bring your kit and come aboard my ship."

The men moved about, dividing themselves, heaving their kit over the still closely joined hulls. Sidroc had at once strapped on the sword he had been given, feeling the weight of it on his hip, yearning to draw it from its scabbard and look at it, knowing he could not do so until later. He stayed on the new ship, was handed his two packs, then stood as men passed back and forth, Toki and Yrling last of all. Toki too had put on his new belt, so he wore for the moment two knives. Other than the slightest grin their uncle had given them when he had called them forward and bestowed their rewards, Yrling had said nothing to them. He said nothing now, as he prepared to clamber back into his own ship. Toki gave his cousin a nod and a grin, and once on the other side withdrew the gaff and pulled it back into Yrling's ship. Sidroc had likewise resolved to keep the grappling hook with him, and stood a moment at the gunwale, coiling up the line to it as the distance between the craft widened.

He had watched first Gizur and then his uncle kill a man. Yrling had killed several men, this he knew; when he was still a boy Sidroc had listened in near awe as Yrling told of the first Saxons he had speared. But the telling of it, and the witnessing of it were two different acts. And these two were not the Saxon enemy, but Danes like them, making a perilous journey to seek fortune in a distant land.

He saw the great daring in it, driving his ship right up in a plea for aid, knew that daring was what fitted Yrling to be the captain and war-chief his uncle wanted to be. But Sidroc felt the treachery behind it.

You must trust no man, he told himself. He heard his own voice, hollow but clear in his breast. Trust no man.

ANGLE-LAND

THE morning brightened and wore on. The ships kept within close hailing distance to each other, and for the first time Sidroc was able to see and admire his uncle's vessel as it ploughed the sea-furrows. The red-and-white sail of Death-day was puffed full, and on its deck were now more men than oar-slots. Not that rowing would be needed, in the wake of the storm there was still plenty of good wind. At times the dark water offside that sail reflected shimmering red-and-white squares on its endlessly moving surface, something he had not seen from its deck. Considering Death-day from a distance, Sidroc felt it akin to looking on a horse of value. On its back you had the pleasure of the ride, the beast's spirit and strength. But a different satisfaction could be wrought from standing to watch that horse move and prance, filling the eye with its beauty.

He had taken up a place near Une at the steering oar. Jari had positioned himself in the prow, and with the sail full was thus sometimes out of sight, but not out of earshot. Yellow-haired Asberg was also near the steering oar; he had jumped up from there when Yrling's ship had approached. Earlier he and Sidroc had both watched as

Yrling's ship pulled away, and watched too as the dragon head was slotted back into the bow beam, declaring its true intent upon the seas. Now the two sat almost side by side, their backs supported by their packs resting against the hull.

Before taking the tiller Une had called for a pail of sea water, which he had dashed against the blood pooled on the decking where he would stand. Even tarred as the wood was, some blood had seeped in the worn planking there. Both Sidroc and Asberg found their eyes drawn to the stains.

Asberg looked up at where Une stood at the oar, hand on that tiller which his own captain had lately held. Then his eyes dropped again to the bloodied decking.

"He did it well," Asberg conceded. He spoke of Yrling's deception; Sidroc knew this.

Sidroc only nodded, but Asberg went on

"You are his kin?"

The question gave Sidroc pause. It was much the same Yrling had asked of all aboard when he took this ship. Yrling had already named him nephew. To remind Asberg of this might set himself up as a target for revenge. He found himself looking at he who sat at his shoulder, and Asberg looked back. Asberg's unclouded blue eyes suggested other than vengeance.

"Yrling is my uncle," Sidroc told him.

Asberg nodded. "He has doubled his holdings, and more than doubled his men, with one arrow, and one thrown spear." He rolled his shoulders a moment, then went on. "Thor made it so," he decided. Then in justness, he added, "But your uncle – he did it well."

Sidroc found his eyes lifting to the greyness of the sky for a moment, then looking back. "Já," he allowed. "He did it well."

They sat in silence a while. Sidroc shifted and saw Asberg studying his scar. He did not think he would ask about it, as indeed he did not.

Instead Asberg asked a different question. "Where is your home?"

Sidroc gave the shortest of laughs. "I have no home. I hail from Jutland, the western coast. My new home will be in Angle-land, where I do not yet know."

"All of Angle-land is good," Asberg offered. "I have seen some of Wessex, and of Lindisse. Green fields that love the plough, and forests of oak as we never have in Dane-mark."

"Also treasure," Sidroc laughed.

"Já. Their temples are filled with it sometimes. Men in gowns live there, make devotion to a table set with candle holders of silver, and silver cups too."

"Yrling knows of those men," Sidroc concurred. "And they will not fight to keep it."

"Nej. They will not fight. They will beg and make signs with their hands, but carry no knives nor spears." He thought a while, as if in remembrance. "They have serving men, sometimes, who will kill for them, and for the silver on the tables. One must be wary."

"Já," Sidroc nodded. One must be wary.

Asberg was as good as his word. Before dusk had deepened into night a long and dark line of land could be discerned by the sharpest-eyed amongst the men. Calls and hoots of relief went up from all.

They neared land, seeing no other ships upon the water, and coasted along looking for a likely beach to run their ships up upon, one deserted where they could camp the night. They must rest, Yrling knew; get their land-legs back, eat what they could, and in the morning set out to find a river to sail up, a farm to raid. Their greatest need was simply food. He was now in charge of nearly fifty men, and he must feed them all.

They beached, side by side, on a narrow swathe of white sand, a thick stand of fresh-leaved saplings springing from the soil not far off. They jumped off the ships into a skim of water; the tide was receding. Before they even began handing down the cooking gear Yrling called out, gathering all to hear him.

"Men of Jutland, and of Laaland," he began, for that low and flat place was the Danish island where the second ship had set off from, "we are now on Saxon shores. If any amongst you would try their hands as lone-wolves do, go now. But recall yourselves that a pack of wolves can run down the biggest game. I will make my mark here, and those who fight with me and for me will know great treasure in silver, weapons, and women."

A few approving whoops were sounded, a few exhausted cheers. None made move to leave, though one muttered loudly that roast pig and ale was what they needed now. What was spooned up into their lifted bowls was boiled salt cod, poured over the few stale and broken loaves the captured ship yielded. Still, it was hot, and both ships had water enough to wash it down with.

They sheltered their fire with a tilted screen of hide ground cloths, not wanting to attract any from sea with an unwitting beacon. By its light Sidroc at last withdrew the sword Yrling had awarded him. Jari and Toki sat with him, with the new Asberg not far off.

It was a good blade, as befit he who had been the second man aboard. There was no flash about the dark leather-wrapped grip, or curved pommel, but the blade itself was pattern-worked, and possessed of the spring and strength of the many thin layers of steel it had been forged from.

Sidroc could hardly believe his good fortune. He had his spear and knife, and had known he must fight with these, hoping to kill a man who wielded a sword, and thus be able to claim it for his own. If he could not he would need to win enough silver and treasure to trade another Dane for one. Both of his weapons were serviceable, but this sword better than either spear-point or knife, having been, like all blades of its kind, hammered, twisted, and re-hammered. Now with this sword he felt himself already well kitted out, for he had as well his good shield, which he had made himself around an iron boss brought last year from Ribe.

The sword was a little shorter than he might have wanted; that was its only flaw. Still, his long arms gave him great reach as it was.

"Manne was not as tall as you," Asberg said, as if he had read Sidroc's thought.

It was strange to hear the dead man named, and Toki and Jari also looked to Asberg. Sidroc was not alone in wondering if Manne had been a friend to he who spoke this.

They slept on the sand in the lee of the ships. There was nothing to break their fast with, no food to warm, and no drink save water. Yrling determined he would take one ship, his own, in search of food, leaving a strong guard on the second, to await their return.

"I take thirty with me. Une, Toki, Sidroc, Gap, Bjarne, on my ship. Twenty of you will stay here, to guard Yellow-sail. Asberg is in charge." This distinction was a signal one, a sign of trust he placed in this new man. "Jari, you remain as well."

Jari looked surprised, but not disappointed to be marked this way. His very size would be a deterrent, if any of the new men amongst them attempted to make off with the ship.

"The rest to go, to be drawn by lot," Yrling went on. "Pair up, choose straws, sort yourselves. We will be back to feast together."

This was done, and Yrling's ship underway as swiftly as could be managed, given that all wanted to join the raiding party. Yrling saw several men bargain for and buy the long straw which would give them passage on it.

They pushed the ship out into water enough to float her; the tide was at an ebb and it took work. Those sailing clambered onboard. They used their oars to reach deeper waters, then Yrling ordered the sail lifted to catch a breeze just beginning to freshen. They struck out, sailing a northerly track up the coast, looking for farm or village. The dawn was rapidly proving by its spreading golden fingers that the day would at last be fair, and the Sun began beaming at them over a scrim of clouds still lodged on the horizon.

A river mouth presented itself, one wide enough to promise good water for some distance. Grassy banks alternated with stands of osier and other water-loving growth, and they passed as well thick groves of mixed hardwoods, spreading oaks and elms, with ashes keeping their distance as they are wont to.

They sailed a long way up before they spotted any sign of human habitation. What met their eyes at last was a small hut, like unto those shepherds use during lambing-time, when they stay always with their flocks. No sheep were near it now, but they could not be far from the farm from which those sheep must range. Around a slight bend they saw a settlement, no less than that, for the cluster of low timber and thatched buildings must make up three related farms. Pasture land fronted it, on which several milk cows grazed or lay, working their jaws. A worn path led from river bank to settlement.

It was more than Yrling could have hoped for, almost a reprise of his very first raid in Angle-land nearly ten years ago, and one for which he hoped a cleaner end. They must strike fast and with fury; with three households there could be a number of able-bodied men.

The farmstead was more than two hundred paces off, he judged; the river must flood, and often, for it to have been sited so. They would need to leap from the ship, run as rapidly as they could along the path, before the men within were roused and armed.

"No war-cries," Yrling told them, as they readied their kit. He wanted no losses from his own men, and surprise was the best way to ensure this. They threw the stone anchor onto the soft mud of the bank, and dropped overboard.

In fact it was women they saw first. Three gowned figures were working in the rows of a vegetable garden fronting one of the animal sheds, hoeing out weeds. One of them lifted her head to see a war ship, men clambering from its hull.

Sidroc was still splashing though the water when she screamed, a gasping cry of alarm. He was moving forward, his shield on his left arm, his spear in his right, his new sword on his hip. Now it begins, he told himself. I am on a raid. He blinked his eyes at the buildings ahead of him, aware that more than one woman was screaming now, aware too of movement coming from around the back of the houses. He was pounding down the pathway, passing the placid cows, running in a group of heavily armed men towards these farmer folk. Jari was back at the captured ship, not at his shoulder. Yrling was ahead of him, flanked by Une, and Toki was near too. He heard their breathing as he heard his own.

One of the women had lifted her hoe as weapon. The other two had vanished. Only now having gained the fore-court of the first house did Yrling's men give voice, led by he himself. They bayed like hounds, fanning out to face the men who came running out at them from kitchen yard and barn. Some had the tools they had been using in their hands, rakes and spades and pikes; but not a few had had time to run for and grab a spear where they must be kept ready by a door. They were of all ages, some mere youths, others aged, but most were men hardened by farm-work. Now their faces were contorted in rage as they braced themselves against the onslaught. It was hard to gauge how many they were; perhaps twelve or fourteen.

It was complete slaughter. If any owned them, none of the men of the farm had time to take a shield upon their arms; they used both hands to thrust their weapons at the invaders, whether spear or pike. They were cut down by the threes and fours with swords and spears, the remaining men surrounded and speared like cornered pigs. They were so outnumbered that it was mostly over before all Yrling's men had even reached the pounded dirt where now the Saxons lay heaped and dying. Anguished cries came from some of them, cries stopped by the quick thrust of spear-points driven into bodies already rent and bleeding.

A stillness followed, broken only by the hard breathing of Yrling's men. Sidroc's spear had been extended, but it had not found home in any flesh. He had made a few thrusts, driving the defenders closer together, but the more experienced around him had leapt to the point of vantage and delivered the killing blows. He stood with the rest of them, staring down at the bloodied mass at their feet. None moved.

All the men of the farmstead were dead. The realisation seemed to flow through Yrling's warriors.

On the other side of the nearest buildings, women and children could be seen fleeing, running for their lives through the work yards. They headed towards the back fields to the woods. More than one had a child in her arms.

"The women – get them!" cried one of the men.

A group of them dropped shields and spears and gave chase. Sidroc stood unmoving, to watch two men tackle the nearest woman, knock her to the ground, watch as one of them held her down by her arms as the second covered her body with his own. Shrieks and screams forced his eyes to a second woman, caught by a lone man, saw him yank her to him, heard the sharp slap across her face which stilled her cries. A moment later two more men were there, pushing her down between them. Toki was one of them, and before he dropped down he saw two females run past.

He looked to Sidroc. "Get yourself one," he yelled.

Sidroc found himself running after the women, brandishing his spear. They were not screaming, but silent as they ran. By their form and height they might be mother and daughter. The elder turned her head to look where a cluster of warriors surrounded one of the women on the ground. She saw Sidroc, almost on her heels.

"Go, go," he ordered, in their own tongue. "Go into the trees, as far as you can. Run."

She saw his step had slowed. He was driving them off, driving them away from where their female kin were being raped, and mayhap murdered.

He stood a moment at the edge of the trees, seeing the blue gown of the elder vanish in the shrubby growth; she had been pushing the younger ahead of her. He turned then. At least five women were down on the ground, pinned in the stubbly growth of the newly-mown hay field. Three times that number of men crawled about them. Children running with them, or who had been in the women's arms sat crying. A few toddling young stood nearby in gaping and blank-eyed silence.

Sidroc saw Yrling and a few others come out of one of the houses, sacks in their hands; other men had been ransacking the bodies of the dead, seeing if any carried things of value. Knives and shoes were pulled off, and every spear the defenders had used was collected, but other than this the yield was slim.

Yrling scanned the farm yard, put his fingers to his teeth and whistled. The men in the hay field came straggling back. One woman was seen to rise, and walk haltingly toward the trees, before falling again to the ground. The rest lay still, though muffled moans told they still lived.

One of the men led a young fair-haired girl, sobbing, her hands tied with a leathern thong, blood upon her face, her gown half ripped off her white shoulders. Her shortened, awkward steps made clear the pain inflicted on her tender and torn body. They stopped before Yrling, and she trembled so it was hard to know how she kept her feet. Toki was trailing behind them, and Sidroc wondered if this was the girl he had helped fell.

Yrling said, "Leave her." The man who captured her was one new to him, from Yellow-sail. Yrling knew no more than his name, Bue.

"But she is so pretty. The best of the lot," came the answer. "You said we would win women."

"And you have had your fill, now." Yrling cast a quick eye on the girl, her mouth bleeding and swollen from having been slapped into submission. He looked to the man Bue who held her. "We are not slaving, not yet," Yrling went on. He did not want any extra mouths to feed before he had a proper camp. "Food and plunder is what we seek."

The crying girl had gone mute at the sight of the dead men she had been led past.

Bue was loud in his demand. "I caught her first, and she is mine."

This time Yrling's hand was on his knife hilt as he answered. "Leave her."

To decide this he himself took his knife and cut the thong binding the girl's hands. She took a step back, then another, before she turned to the field and ran to a figure still lying there.

Bue's own hand raised slightly in protest, then lowered. He did not do more than spit on the ground in response.

Another of the men looked about, then touched a torch into the cooking-fire, and flung it with a whoop onto the roof of the nearest building. Almost at once the thatch began to smoulder.

"No more!" Yrling yelled. "Smoke will be smelled a long way off. Food now, and what treasure they have." He let his eyes sweep over the men nearest him.

"Get the fowl and sheep, as many as you can," he ordered. "There are pigs too." They must leave the cows, but sheep and pigs were both thrifty keepers and quick to slaughter.

"Meal. Grain. Gather what you can from the storehouses," he told others.

This was a farm not unlike those Sidroc had been raised on, larger and more prosperous to be sure. To range about its sheds and store rooms, hastily plucking hams from the smoke house, filling baskets and buckets with barley and rye from the grain bins, catching up the ewes in the milking pen, felt almost like despoiling his own home. Yet he did it, with a quickness and decision that belied the fact that he had killed no man, taken no woman.

The shared spring house held crocks of butter and soft ewe's cheese, and they found two casks of ale. Root cellars were rifled for cabbages and apples. The fowl houses were full of eggs, and a few geese had been snagged as well.

They took all they could carry. They found a hand wain, and in the growing smoke of the burning house stacked it with these things, while others led and pulled what pigs and sheep they could corner to their ship.

Then they were off, oaring down the river, moving with speed. The trip back to the sandy beach where the others awaited felt half as long as that setting out. Handing down the sacks of grain, struggling geese and bulky sheep, they all were laughing. Even Sidroc felt a flush of triumph; they would eat soon, and well.

Bjarne and two other men set to work, slitting the throats of two of the ewes, collecting the blood to stir into a huge pot of barley, cutting up turnips and onions carried from the root cellars. Slabs of the sheep flesh were roasted over the fire, the rest cut into chunks and set to boil with the grain and vegetables. Neither ship had salt, both stores having been wetted through in the storm, but chips of the salt cod lent savour to the whole.

They huddled, cross-legged, about this feast, draining both casks of ale in short order. Spooning the mess into his mouth, chewing on the roasted meat, still running with juices, Sidroc ate as one famished, as indeed he was. The dwindling supplies on the ships had been parcelled out in equal measure, leaving the largest men the hungriest. Watching how Jari, Une, and Gap devoured their food, with an almost savage intensity, told him how he himself looked. He had never been as hungry as he had been during the length of the long voyage. He had worked to master the pangs, and when that was not possible, to ignore them. Now he could give free rein to this most basic of bodily needs.

Almost no man spoke during this riot of consumption. Bjarne, stationed closest to the fire, wielded both ladle and fork, and any man coming forward a second, third, or fourth time saw him ministering to their wooden bowls as if it were their first taste.

Sidroc was sitting across from the man Bue from Yellow-sail who had tried to bring along the girl. Toki was at his side. As Toki scraped his bowl clean with his forefinger he turned to the man.

"Almost as good as that woman," he said, with a grin of doubled satisfaction.

Bue gave a hoot, then cast a rueful glance to where Yrling now stood at the cook fire. He was still angry about the loss of her.

Toki saw Sidroc looking at him, and grinned the broader. Sidroc stood up from where he sat and took his bowl to the rippling water at the edge of the beach. He swirled a handful of sand within to scrub it, then dipped it full of sea water to rinse. Other men were there as well, doing much the same. As he bent over the water a series of images filled Sidroc's mind.

He thought, for the first time of the whole voyage, of Toki's wife, Ginnlaug. The plainness of her good-natured face was followed in his inner eye by that of the old woman, Åfrid, who had told him he would one day seek Freyja's favour. The indistinct countenance of this Goddess of love and lust flickered in his mind. A new image came to him, that of the smiling and dark-haired whore, Alvild of Haithabu. She gave her body so willingly, had been so generous in bringing him into manhood. There had been other women too, since her; some he had not needed to pay, women he had coupled with at festivals; all of whom he had enjoyed. Their faces were followed by a far earlier memory, of the thrall-woman Berthe, captured from this great island, and how as a boy he had seen her lying motionless beneath Yrling and Ful.

The final impress was no image at all, but the jarring echo of the women of the farmstead screaming as they were being held down, shrieks only silenced by the blows of those who overpowered and ravished them.

Disgust and wonder both filled him, just as the rich food and strong ale of the dead filled his belly.

THE FIRST WARRIOR

THE Moon had waxed full, and waned. They had spent the better part of a month in Angle-land. Before Yrling killed him, they had learnt from a terrified goatherd that they landed in the Kingdom of Anglia. This news fixed them on their course. Since then they had been on the move, working a northerly way up the coast, never camping more than two nights in a single place.

Now that they scoured the coasts they were always ready for battle. War gear which had been packed away on the long North Sea voyage was kept at hand. Only while rowing or sleeping did those who owned swords remove them, and the spears which had been tightly tethered for safety were now held in open wooden brackets along the inside of the gunwale. The round and brightly coloured shields hung in easy reach on the outside of that same rail, giving cover under sail. They steadily coasted, tracing the contours of the new land. Silently oaring up inlets at dusk, they hid the ships overnight amongst standing sedge-grass or the hanging boughs of over-arching branches. At dawn they were again off.

The hilliness of the place surprised Sidroc the most, steep cliffs, rolling knolls and downs as he had never seen on the flat expanses of Jutland. Even at the edge of the North Sea the land could rise, looming to impressive heights. And the forests were as Yrling, and then Asberg had told him: dark with trees, hardwoods towering until they blocked the Sun. This was a new part of Midgard to his eyes, wild and empty. Even the ground itself looked different to Sidroc, soils red with clay or black with richness, not the thin and sandy stuff that covered so much of southern Jutland. The fruitfulness of it was ever before him, even in the waste lands. Marshes ran with deer, and flocks of water fowl blanketed the waters and nested in the waving reeds.

Provender was ever their main concern. They had come for treasure, but food stores needed constant replenishment; few war-chiefs could keep their men if they went hungry. Their initial raids were all on farms, and all played out in similar fashion to the first. At times they could gain what they sought without rousing any within timber hut. In the gloom of dusk Gizur or another of the better archers would drop cattle where they stood. They would haul the beast out by a line tied about the hooves of its hind legs, an effort taking several men. Once pulled to the shelter of trees, the carcass was hacked to manageable size, and carried back to whatever camp they had made that night. There it was flayed into thin slices and imperfectly smoked over a fire of smouldering oak branches, upon which their large cauldrons were overturned. Later when the meat was dropped into boiling broth it would truly cook, but this quick smoking would keep it from going green until then.

Their raids on farms filled their bellies but gave them scant silver. They could pick up spears from downed men, and some amongst them pilfered the angle-edged knife, the seax, as well. This was the everyday knife and weapon of all men, that which had given its name to the Saxons. Unlike the straight knives of the Danes, the men here wore their blades hanging across their bellies, and not from one hip, as did most Danes. The blades were good, but these were the weapon-tools of farmers, serviceable but plain. Only the trained warriors of these kingdoms would carry seaxes with silver wire cut into the grip, or have a gemstone crown the tip of the pommel. They had as yet met no such men. Yrling knew they must soon engage with real defenders, but until he felt his men solidly united behind him, was not eager to speed that day. And treasure in weapons was ever the hardest fought to win. What Yrling truly sought was a temple, in which the Christian God was worshipped. There the men and women dedicated to that worship kept their silver and gemstone treasure. He knew one lay at Beardan, up a broad and marshy river he headed for in Lindisse, which they made steady progress towards.

The farmsteads they struck at were all small, sometimes lonely huts, never more than the holdings of three or four intertwined families. Every farm had at least two cows, a handful of sheep, and a stoutly-fenced pen with dusky-coloured pigs rooting within. On occasion they saw the long-legged horses that graced this new land, but with their ship to return to, they had no need for them.

Raids in the dim light of dusk proved best; nearly all folk were within doors, or working about the kitchen yard. Most were thus grouped closely together, the easier to surround and overcome. Firing a house when all were within made it easy to pick off the men as they ran out. But weapons were also close to the defenders' reaching grasp, spears kept ready by their doors, cooking pokers and butchery knives at hand in the kitchen yard. Two of the raiders died the first half-month. One of the men from Yellow-sail was knocked senseless by an iron pot hurled by an old woman, then stuck through by a youth wielding a long-tined roasting fork. Another of Yrling's men, from Death-day, took a deep gash in the calf of the leg, given by a farmer as he lay dying. The farmer had force of life enough to lift his knife and hack as the invader passed near him. They were able to carry him back to the ship, but the wound went hot and the man died, writhing in pain, within days.

And Sidroc killed a man, his first. He felled him at his uncle's side, Yrling downing the man, and then with a jerk of his chin telling Sidroc to deliver the death-blow with his spear. No farmers had swords, and spears with their long reach were the best offence against men swinging plough-bats or hoes.

It was at a single small holding on the banks of a river they had sailed up. That these were fishing-folk was proclaimed by the flayed bodies of salted fish, hanging ghost-like on their drying racks by owl-light. The man Sidroc would kill came running from a shed with a long and lethal scythe, summoned by the shouts of his family. The razor's edge of the scythe swung perilously close to Yrling's spear-arm, but using his shield as cover Yrling twisted and dropped, driving the point of his spear head into the man's left thigh.

Sidroc was just at his side for cover, but did not expect his uncle to yield the kill to him as he did. It was a heart-beat's pause before he sprang forward with his own spear, thrusting the struggling man fully back and onto the hard ground, then ramming with all the might in his spear arm. The arms of the man flailed, that holding the scythe opening as the worn wooden shaft of it dropped from his grasp.

Sidroc was looking down his spear shaft as he drove it, seeing his own hand, large, strong, unscarred, and more than capable. Whatever that hand had done in the past or might do in the future, this was what it did now, take this life. It felt an action solely from his hand, far from his head, far from his own beating heart. He watched his spear point still the heart of this man on the ground before him.

Such a hit in the breast would kill a man quickly. What Sidroc did not expect was the man's eyes locking with his own as he leaned in on the spear. He did not expect that he would feel the forceful expelling of the man's dying breath on his face, nor read both fear and fury in the man's lined visage and outstretched hand. That hand reached towards where a woman screamed, before dropping lifelessly into the dust.

Sidroc pulled his spear out, the slight sucking sound of its withdrawal silenced as soon he stepped back. Yrling had said something to him, something in approval, but was already gone. He himself looked about, turning back to the work yard they had invaded. Toki had chased a man across the sheep pasture and Sidroc saw his cousin's spear extend and pierce the man's back as he neared him. Asberg, screaming out his two-pitched yell, had flung his own spear at another as he fled, downing him.

Jari and Une were together, the two giant brothers fearsome as they faced three men, each of whom clutched spears. Once again the farmers lacked shields or any protective kit. As the brothers moved in behind their own shields, spears bristling forward, one of the three they faced turned his back and ran. A thundering laugh issued from Une, and he and Jari jumped forward. The remaining two broke and ran, making also for the line of trees, ever-darkening as the Sun dropped behind it. They let them go, following those women and children who had already fled thus, and set to work rifling the place for food.

That night Sidroc felt different. As they had after every raid, they made a new camp, this one found by retreating to the coast and taking shelter at the river's mouth. Hours had passed since the attack, but the churning energy which had arisen in his belly was taking long to subside. Yrling had said nothing to him about the kill, nor had Sidroc spoken of it. But looking on the embers of their cooking fire recalled him to the dark gleam of the dying man's eyes. He turned his gaze down to see his right hand closed of itself around an invisible spear shaft.

His arm and shoulder still felt the tenseness of his killing thrust, and something more than the man's ribcage splitting under the point. There was a taste in his mouth, one akin to metal, which made him almost think he had gritted his teeth so that he had bit his own tongue; but it was not that. This taste rose from his belly, which was still tight and cold, despite the warm food he had just eaten.

It was battle-sickness, the aftermath of violence seen and done. And he was still unused to the sheer surprise of it, of seeing how men went down, how men died, how blood spurted from hacked limbs, and now the surprise at what he could do.

They were off the next morning, a dull one, sailing up the coast. A light rain was beginning to spatter the decks of the ships when they sighted a palisade wall of upright timbers not far from the water's edge. The wall and what it enclosed lay on a narrow and projecting spit of land, upon which beat an active surf. The paling was not much above man-height, and the wooden roofs of three or four small buildings could be seen behind. If it was a coast-guard, a fort this size could not house more than a score of men, perhaps less. The guards so stationed were there to defend against warriors from others of these Saxon Kingdoms, and from Danish raiders just like themselves.

A horn began sounding from within. They thought they had been spotted, but then over the narrowing distance of water they heard loud and active war cries. A watchman seeing them would sound the alarm, but the battle yells puzzled them. As they rounded the spit they understood.

At the gates of the palisade wall a knot of men had gathered, charging at the upright planks of the doors with a felled tree trunk. This battering ram was thicker than any man's two hands could encircle, yet not so bulky that the eight or ten who wielded it could not run it with considerable force at the faltering door. Others of the invaders stood back, armed with bows, releasing a flurry of arrows at those defenders who hazarded taking a shot at the battering crew from the parapet walk behind the walls.

None within Yrling's ships failed to recognise their brethren.

Yrling, at the steering oar of Death-day, made swift decision. The Danes attacking at the gate were no more than twenty men. He had nearly fifty. They would beach and swarm ashore. Whether they would join the attackers or overtake and put them to the sword he did not care. All he saw was a fitting target, its gates already being breached. He would make good on their dauntless act, turn to his own advantage the efforts they made.

He called out to his men from where he stood at the steering oar. "Odin smiles," he assured them with a grin, and jerked his thumb behind him to the carving of the one-eyed God. "Our brothers open the door. Let us walk in before them!" The answering cries were loud and eager, and the two ships, propelled by the pounding surf, made for shore. Spears were pulled from where they lay ready in the brackets against the hulls.

Arrows from the parapets had found their marks in two of the number handling the battering ram, and two of the Danish archers had run to make up the company hammering at the gates. With less cover a third man was hit and went down. Yrling's ships were grounding on the shingle beach when the gate gave way. He and his men were armed and now ready to leap down into the shallow water and attack.

Death-day and Yellow-sail were nearly side by side. Sidroc was upon Death-day, and jumped from her canted hull. He landed in calf-deep water washing over the hard and shifting pebbles of the beach. His spear was in his right hand, his shield still slung on his back, the better for balance as he leapt down. He saw Jari almost fall as he hit the shingle, then recover with a grunt as he straightened. Yrling was somewhere behind them, and he could see Toki's long yellow hair ahead, flanked by Gap and Bue. The sounds of splashing water, of the breathing of men jumping and running, filled Sidroc's ears.

They all ran, an onrushing stream of men, towards the opening gates of the fort.

An issue of men had stormed from those gates, men helmeted and wearing ring-tunics. The first rank held long spears, aimed at the attackers from behind their round shields. The second rank of defenders held shields and swords.

So here at last they met true warriors, those called thegns in the tongue of the Saxons. These were the men of the local war-lord, or mayhap even those of the King of Lindisse, set here to guard the coast. They were bearing good arms, as well as protective gear any of Yrling's men would covet. And being rich, there might be silver at their necks and wrists.

As they neared the palisade the bright and unmistakable clash of metal ringing upon metal washed over Sidroc. Louder than this clanging were the oaths of struggling warriors, and the screams of those who had been hit. The horn was still sounding, a keening alarm over all. Sidroc knew he was running but scarcely felt his feet.

He had killed for the first time the day before, and was not yet settled in himself. Taking that life had changed him; his blood running hot and cold in his veins in the hours since. Yet he knew now how readily he could be pushed. He could kill the farmer with the scythe, and all like him, because in their outrage they were trying to kill him. Yet he had used a spear to kill a man with a thresher.

This was different, different and better. A thrill of excitement shot through him. These men before him were not farmers protecting homes and families, but warriors from the hall of some war-lord, or King. This is what he had come for, to face these men, who were trained and ready to fight. To prove that he could be their match.

His war kit did not come close to theirs. He had his good spear, and a shield he had formed himself and in which he trusted. At his waist was the knife he had bought in Ribe. Then there was his new sword, one from a practiced warrior who had been felled through treachery by his uncle. It had not tasted blood while in Sidroc's hand.

For protection he had a tunic of leather. And strapped just above his left ankle, his boyhood knife hidden there, for surprise.

He lacked helmet and ring-shirt; these Saxon warriors wore both. They might protect the body and head from glancing blows, and one day soon he would own them, but just now it mattered not. He had his young body, his height, his speed.

He felt a surge in his breast, a warmth shooting up from his still-cold belly, spreading upward like a licking flame. Was it his fylgja, his guardian spirit, making herself known to him again, or his luck-spirit, his hamingja, urging him on, assuring him of victory? He felt almost twinned, with this new energy within him.

A movement at the tail of his eye made him turn his head. He found Jari near, and looked to him. Jari's jaw was clenched but his eyes carried the glint that Sidroc thought must be in his own. Their eyes met. With a nod they agreed, Já, they were ready. And they were nearly upon their target. Even if they must fight through these strange Danes they would win through to battle the Saxons.

As Yrling's men neared those fighting they fanned out, three men deep, to half surround the contest. The Saxons, facing them, gave voice in yelping protest, causing several of the Danes to turn their heads to see what came up behind them. The distraction caused some of the attackers their lives, as the thegns sprang forward, and spears found home in Danish flesh.

Yrling was now in the foremost rank of his men, forging on, Une and Bjarne at one side, his nephews and Jari on the other. The first man, Dane or Saxon to turn on him he would fight. He leapt over the fallen body of one of the attacking Danes and found himself face to face with a Saxon thegn, wielding a sword. Yrling's onrushing spear point collided with the man's shield, knocking it away from his torso. Yrling uttered one word, crying out the name of his ship, Dauðadagr, Death-day. A moment later that spear sunk into the thegn's breast, splitting the heavy ring-tunic, puncturing the handsome leathern one beneath.

The choice had been made. Yrling would go for the Saxons first, knowing the Danes arrested in their attack saw his choice.

It was a fevered and disordered struggle before the gates, bloody and confused. The Saxons had rushed out at a dwindling foe, only to find their numbers more than doubled from the two beached dragon ships. The Danes who had begun the attack were just as startled. Engulfed as they were between the thegns and the new arrivals, some stood motionless for a moment, unsure of who to fight. Yrling's act of beating into the front rank of the Saxons and killing the first one sealed their decision.

The rain had continued, growing from a light spatter of large drops to a finer but much steadier fall. The bare and trampled ground before the gates was slick and growing more so; the discarded battering ram tripped one man, and others slipped in the mud. But Yrling now had more than sixty men at his back, and they swept into the work yard of the small keep. The brazen horn, blowing all this time, at last fell silent.

The garrison did not yield easily. More warriors awaited them within, and archers still upon the ramparts of the palisade did what they could to pick off the invaders. Within the walls lay the hazards posed by buildings, animal pens, and low fences, and the challenge of fighting in the tight quarters between them. The Danish archers took aim at their Saxon counterparts, while warriors with spears and swords faced off by twos and threes. Crowded as it was, a few thegns on horseback, appearing from behind the largest of the timber buildings, spurred their whinnying mounts through the clusters of men fighting. They galloped out the broken gates, their horses hurtling over the sprawling bodies lying there.

Their flight had parted Sidroc from Jari, and from his uncle too. Yet the man he was facing gave ground steadily before him. The Saxon held sword and shield, and Sidroc with his spear was troubling the man, jabbing and ducking, using his speed and agility to drive him back. The Saxon's only hope was to land a solid blow against the spear shaft, severing the head of it, but Sidroc kept the spear always in play. The Saxon edged his way between two small buildings, store houses of some sort, with Sidroc goading him on. Halfway down their length the Saxon turned and fled, vanishing around the gable end of one. Sidroc leapt after. He came almost face to face with another Saxon warrior.

If Sidroc had not raised the point of his spear as he neared the end of the shed, it would have driven into the man's right shoulder. As it was the Saxon saw the point early enough to fling the shield covering his torso up, forcing the spear higher into the air. He let out with a sound like Ha!, and met Sidroc's eyes with a glare.

The man was of some five-and-thirty years, well-knit, with a breadth of shoulder conveying the strength in his arms. Glinting eyes shown through the eye holes in his helmet, and the lines about those eyes suggested he had stared down Death more than once. His face was creased by rough weather and years of hard fighting. Behind his shield lay his ring-tunic, a few mashed places in the links testifying to blows received and survived. The sword he held in his right hand was aimed at Sidroc.

With that sword foremost the Saxon jumped at him, forcing him back between the two sheds.

Sidroc had one instant to decide. In these tight quarters he did not think he could bring his spear to bear against such an opponent. This man was battle-hardened, and likely possessed cunning to match.

He let fall the spear from his hand and opened his shield enough to allow his reaching hand to pull his own sword from its scabbard at his left hip.

The Saxon sprang at him.

It was Sidroc's first real fight with a sword. He had sparred with the borrowed sword of Yrling, and in the last month practiced with Jari and Asberg with a weapon newly made his own. Now he faced a man older and stronger than he, one who had fought for years with the weapon he held. The thegn came at him with the practised skill of the trained killer he was.

Sidroc knew to look for certain patterns in the opponents he faced, a rhythm of strokes high, low, and high again; a preference for the uppercut to knock the protective shield away, followed by a sudden down stroke to catch the unguarded wrist. He knew some men might have a lightness of foot that kept them in almost constant motion before him, and others a resolute and ox-like stolidness that made fighting them feel like facing a mountain.

What he had heard tell of did not serve him now. His head emptied against the Saxon's attack. This man had years of warring behind every thrust and slash of his sword, every block and track of his shield. Even the stream of taunts falling from the thegn's mouth were additional assault; he had sworn at and belittled many men before cutting them down.

Sidroc felt himself completely overmatched. He was on the defensive from the first, at once regretting his decision to discard his spear, yet knowing this Saxon with his expert sword work would have made a swift end of its shaft. Sidroc had not himself won the sword he now gripped, and he held it without the surety of skill such knowledge would have brought him. All he could do was parry each thrust as they fell, covering his body with his shield. The thegn's blade beat against the iron rim, leaving deep gashes in the leather-covered face of it. The few swings and thrusts he managed to land on the thegn's own shield seemed feeble. His youthful speed and his long reach were all he could bring to bear. His back was to the rest of the yard and though he heard the sounds of combat behind him, he could see naught but the man before him. Where Yrling or Jari or even Toki was he could not know. He was alone.

The flame he had felt in his breast as he ran from the ship had damped into a chill, one that curled throughout his body as if ice lodged there. His hamingja, his luck-spirit, was stirring within him, stirring and rising. He felt it leaving him now, his luck fleeing, running out on him.

He had wanted to go as a raider, win treasure, and die in glory. The few things he had won so far he could find little pleasure in, beyond that of food to keep him full from day to day. And dying before he had won real treasure, while meeting his first true warrior, was not a glorious end.

He could not long withstand this thegn's attentions. His luck was turning, and would not aid him.

The Saxon seemed to read his thoughts. As Sidroc slowed in his movements, retreating into himself, the thegn's offense too slowed.

Sidroc found himself casting his eyes upwards, as if for answer. Between the thatch of the low roofs an expanse of grey sky loomed, one from which rain no longer fell. They said a warrior marked to die saw one of the shield-maidens summoning him, inviting him to Asgard and the bright halls of the Gods. He saw nothing there.

Yrling and Une both had told him that the Saxons took hostages for ransom. If he was not being called to die by the shield-maidens, his other choice was to live.

He stepped back from the Saxon, a decided and resolute step back. He felt himself raise his sword almost straight before him, saw the Saxon's questioning face vanish a moment as the blade blocked Sidroc's view. He tipped the sword back down again. The thegn stopped, gauging him through narrowed eyes. Then Sidroc dropped his sword in surrender.

It fell at his feet, on the muddy straw they had been fighting on. The noise it made was no more than a dull thud. Yet it was Sidroc asking for life.

A slow grin began forming on the thegn's tight mouth. He made a small sound, a grunt of satisfaction, or of amusement. His eyes went to the sword lying before him. It was a good one.

He stepped closer, his own blade still extended. His eyes raked over Sidroc, a young and green warrior who had now discarded both spear and sword. With his sword the thegn waved him further back, then slid his own weapon into the baldric hanging from his chest. He stooped to pick up Sidroc's dropped sword.

The moment he began to bend, Sidroc saw his chance. The thegn had not made him drop his shield, and under that shield was his knife, hanging at his hip. The man had just closed his reaching fingers around the hilt of Sidroc's sword.

Sidroc's right hand went to his knife scabbard. He lunged forward on one knee, naked blade extended, and thrust it into the thegn's chest, riving apart the iron links of the ring-tunic.

There was a jerking movement of the man's head. Sidroc wrenched the knife out. The Saxon fell back, almost as if sitting, before crumpling to his side on his shield.

Sidroc took a step away. He drew breath, hard to do with his tightened throat. His eyes again rose to the grey heavens. He had seen no shield-maiden. He would be called one day, but not so soon as this. He looked now at his knife, the long blade of it skimmed with this man's blood. He lifted it and wiped it on the wet thatch of the roof.

He re-sheathed his knife, and stood a moment longer. He did not know if he had been trembling as he drove his knife into the thegn's body, but he felt rock solid now. He drew another breath, deeper, fuller. His empty hand rose to his own chest, and he laid it there, palm open, almost where he had hit the dead man with his blade. He was not feeling for his heart through the thickness of his leathern tunic, but for his luck-spirit, his hamingja. It seemed to have rushed back in, returned to him.

The shrillness of Yrling's whistle called him back. Sidroc retrieved both sword and spear and walked into the yard of the fort. He saw a figure dressed in the way of a serving man edging his way along the inside of the palisade, saw the man reach it and dash out, following several others who had fled. No arrow nor flung spear hindered them. Those inside and still alive were turning to other things.

Yrling stood near the largest of the buildings, a timber hall of stout and sturdy make. He still held his unsheathed sword, but had set his shield against the upright planks of the hall. The carnage before him was considerable. Perhaps a score of men lay dead or dying within the walls, and half that number without the breached gates. The Saxon thegns amongst them were easy to spot. Their weaponry marked them at once; the swords worn high on their chests from now-empty baldrics, their knives hanging across their bellies. And all bore ring-shirts. The Danes, both Yrling's and the strange crew, were an altogether more ragtag lot.

Sidroc stopped at the edge of the yard, scanning those who stood and those who lay on the muddy ground. Yrling looked hale. Like all of them his hair was disheveled, his face wet with both sweat and rain. Sidroc saw Asberg next, spear in hand, straightening up from where he had been poking at the downed body of a Saxon, felled with that same weapon. Asberg lifted his spear in a kind of salute to him, and grinned at Sidroc. After what Sidroc had just undergone, Asberg, with his light blue eyes and broad and open face, seemed a friend of long standing, and Sidroc grinned back.

Jari was there, turning from where he and his brother Une stood by a trampled wattle fence from which geese had fled. Jari had a bloodied head but otherwise looked unhurt. And Sidroc saw the remains of the troop of raiders who had begun the attack, standing, weapons still raised, and looking at he who had whistled them to attention.

Yrling was speaking now. Having won the place, he too must address those Danes they had aided.

"Brothers new to us," he began, and looked at four or five who stood nearest, weapons in hand. "Who leads you?"

The response was slow in coming. At last one spoke. "We have no leader. We sailed with Gorm from Aros in Jutland, but have left him to go our own way."

"So you have no ship," Yrling said. They had seen none, and now knew why.

The strangers had demand of their own.

"Whose men are you?" one tossed out.

"The men of Yrling," he answered. "And I am that Yrling – Yrling of Lindisse."

"You sound from Jutland to me," came a voice from one of the strange Danes, and indeed, all his men had looked to him as he named himself thus.

"Já. I was Yrling of Jutland, but now will carve out holdings here in Lindisse. One day I will be Jarl here."

He kept his eyes on the newcomers as they took this in. His voice was steady, his white teeth flashing as he spoke. "It was bold work you set for yourselves, taking this keep. And the Gods were with you that we came along when we did."

This was more than simple boasting. With only a score of men the attackers would have been hard pressed to have won out against the Saxons. It told Yrling how desperate they were, to attempt such a strike. If Gorm's men had been outnumbered by the Saxons, they were even more so by his own men. He paused a moment to consider. He could threaten that they join him, or die, but Yrling had some little pride in his skill at man-craft.

"There is a debt now, which you owe us," he chose to tell them. "One you can fulfill behind me."

The Danes thus addressed spent some time glancing at each other. They had not perhaps left one war-lord to take up so soon with another. Yet they had suffered heavy losses in this attempt against the coast-guard; continuing on with so few men made success at any other raids unlikely. And they were hungry.

"I will join you," said one, who had yet to speak. He made good on his words by walking to stand next Yrling. One by one his fellows joined, until all who still could stand made declaration in this way. There were three-and-ten of them. One had a bad slash on his fore-arm, but other than that their hurts were slight. Yrling looked on them with satisfaction, and sheathed his sword.

They must now count their own losses. Gap was going around the yard, spear in hand, making certain all the Saxons were dead. A quick thrust to the breast of any that groaned or seemed to breathe assured that. He stopped at one body, from which a low and strangled moan issued. It was one of their own number. Gap waved Yrling over.

The man before them, Asved by name, had been one of the original twenty who had left with Yrling from Ribe. Most remembered how Bjarne's knife, thrown after the rat aboard Death-day, had barely missed Asved, and recalled how he had sworn at Bjarne before beginning to laugh.

That rat had not been seen since landing on the shores of Angle-land, but now Asved was dying. He had taken a deep wound to the lower belly, the wool of his leggings dark with running blood. Yrling looked down on him. Asved's eyes were tightly shut, his face knotted by suffering. He could not live much longer, the rasping gasp of his breath told that. Yrling shook his head, and re-drew his sword as he bent over him.

"Asved," he called, in a loud voice. "Now I send you to Odin!" The man's eyes were still shut, but Yrling knew he heard him. It was a promise he kept with a swift thrust of his blade at the man's heart.

"To Odin," echoed several. Like all the other Danes who had fallen, his had been a warrior's death, one to celebrate.

They had lost but six men from Death-day and Yellow-sail, a slight price to win such a prize as what lay before them. And for the six that had died, more than twice that number now joined their ranks.

Those who lived were tired, sore, and thirsty, yet there was no time to lose. Thegns had ridden off; more would be back, and soon. As they numbered the bodies, they found four-and twenty dead Saxon warriors, more than Yrling had expected. Each of them bore worthy war-kit, and all of it was now theirs.

"Everything. We take everything," Yrling told his men. He had lifted his right hand, gesturing to all within the palisade. They turned first to the battle-gain from the dead thegns, each man seeking out those he had downed.

For Sidroc it meant returning to the narrow path between the two small outbuildings, and to the body lying there. He set his shield on its rim against one of the timber walls and squatted down on his heels at the side of the dead Saxon. He knew what to do, start with that of greatest value. For Sidroc this was the man's steel helmet, still upon the head. He pushed the man over on his back, pulled at the legs to straighten them. He lifted the helmet off, his eyes tripping briefly over the opened grey eyes of the man he had killed. He put the helmet directly on his own head, felt the warmth still held in the padded leathern interior of it. Looking through those large and slanted eye-holes for the first time framed what seemed a new world for him.

The ring-tunic. A pool of blood, showing almost black against the iron rings, marked the entry point of Sidroc's killing thrust. It stained the brown leather of the sword baldric on the man's chest. He fumbled for the buckle, found and unfastened it, pulled the weapon and its scabbard away and to one side. The thegn's seax must also be freed, with its separate belt. He did not take time to draw the blade out and admire it; he knew it would be good by looking at the care taken in adorning the grip. Swirls of red copper wire had been hammered into carved grooves, making the grip gleam even in the grey light.

To claim the ring-tunic itself he must pull the man's arms over his head, and wrestle it off. His hands were bloodied by the time he finished, but he had the heavy thing rolled up. The rent his knife blade had caused he would have mended; until that day he would wear it himself, once the blood was rinsed from it.

Nothing at the wrists, but a handsome silver chain at the neck, one braided of many strands of silver. Remembering Yrling's act after capturing Yellow-sail, Sidroc slipped the chain over his head as soon as he had yanked it over the man's face.

The leggings were held by another belt, but no purse would be there; this thegn's silver would be within the hall in which he slept, and thus be forfeit to Yrling. But the brown belt itself, stamped over with dark circles and squares from a small die, sported a large buckle of bronze, and Sidroc pulled it loose. The thegn's black boots too he wrenched off; his own were split in two places, and the farmers they had killed wore shoes little better than he owned. Those on the feet of this Saxon were almost new, made of thick leather – goat hide, Sidroc thought – and were long enough to fit him.

He had worked quickly, aware of the beating of his heart, the warmth still felt, however faintly, from the thegn's body, aware too of the noise of hoots and crows of triumph coming from the yard, the calls of others doing what he himself had just done. He gave a final look at the body he had despoiled, then turned from it.

What he did not already wear he dumped in the thegn's shield. He swung his own on his back and carried his battle-gain out to the yard.

The ground there, of blood-stained and churned mud, was littered with the half-naked bodies of Saxons. All the Danes who had died had been carried to the wall of the largest building. All were still fully dressed, their weapons laid on their chests or at their sides. They must be left behind, and would be sent to Asgard, weapons and silver intact. Odin, All-Father, or that Goddess of love and lust,

Freyja, would be ready to welcome them to their waiting and respective halls.

But the living must look to their next meal. Yrling and Une had been ranging in and out of the timber buildings, stuffing leathern packs with any valuables their reaching fingers closed upon. Sidroc joined the rest pillaging for food. Two large hand wains were wheeled from one of the outbuildings, into which was heaped anything they could lay hands on. Storehouses had bins of early grain, the remains of last year's dried beans and peas, and half-empty barrels of shredded smoked meat. A springhouse sunken into the soil yielded pots of fresh cheeses and butter. A small wooden box lined with crinkled sheet lead held salt in great flakes of snowy white. Loaves of precious bread, that which the men craved, were swept from the rack on which they had been cooling near the cooking ring, and other loaves plucked from the hot pans in which they still baked. One locked storehouse had its door broken down by the blows from a battle-axe. Within were pottery crocks of mead, to add to the crocks of new-brewed ale already taken from the back of an open shed. The two who carried them out cried out in gladness at their find.

Such geese and fowl which had not escaped were grabbed, a prize worth the pecking and scratches they gave. The wains, piled high, made two hasty trips to the beach, their contents held upright by the guiding hands of the men who won the goods. On the final trip they all gathered their battle-gain.

Yrling himself would fire the place, and was at work at the cooking ring with rush torches. It was his final act of triumph against the Saxon guard, and he took more than a little pride in the deed. But beyond sealing his victory, it was the funeral rite of their lost brethren. Whenever possible raiding Danes burnt their dead, freeing the life-essence at once. He flung the rush lights one, two, and three onto the wooden and thatched roofs of the fort. Damp as it was, the oil-soaked torches still caught, flaring into brilliant if smoky flame. All were watching, now crowded into the broken gateway as the fire spread. The bodies of the Danes left behind, composed, armed, awaiting the after-life, lay in stark contrast with those of the defeated thegns.

Yrling must show that all who fell in his service would be so honoured.

"Our dead will fly to Asgard in a moment," he claimed aloud, assurance to the living.

Sidroc had been looking too. Some of these men he had come to know fairly well in the past weeks. He knew it was not only their injuries that made them unrecognisable now. He felt as if he looked on the corpses of strangers, so different were the dead from the quick. He could not let himself think that his body could also be lying there.

They loaded the ships, pushed off, oared away, a brilliant and smouldering beacon marking the path they had taken.

That night Sidroc awoke in the dark. The camp they made was on the firm banks up a narrow river, a camp they would abandon after first light. He always slept soundly, but he awoke with a suddenness that made him wonder if all was well. They had feasted and drunk much ale, and all had also two cups of the strong honeyed mead they had won. He felt none of it now. He lifted himself on his elbows. By the light of a slender and waning Moon he could make out the forms of two of his fellows as they stood, keeping watch. He lay back down in the near-blackness. Closing his eyes his brain was full of an image, that of his last look at the plundered body of the thegn he had killed. He was a warrior who had been the picked man of the lord that set the coastal watch. The man had ten or fifteen years on him. He had a wife somewhere, and children too.

Now the thegn's fine silver chain was hung around Sidroc's neck; his boots lay near to Sidroc's feet. He had asked the thegn for life, and had repaid the man's granting it with death. It was akin to what his uncle had done, sailing up to the captain of the yellow-sailed drekar and asking for help, before sending an arrow into his heart. Both men had made mistakes, mistakes that led to their deaths.

This was to go a-viking, Sidroc reflected. To abide by no law on land or sea, to live wholly by one's wits, to seek every advantage, no matter the means. What he had first thought treachery was in truth cunning, without which no man could survive. Yet it was long until sleep again found him that night.

NOTHING

YRLING kept the men of Death-day and Yellow-sail on the move. They might spend several days oaring up a river, exploring its narrowing stream, striking at what farms lay within easy reach of their waiting ships. But they always returned to the North Sea, and their steady northern way up the coast of Lindisse. It was a kingdom both sparsely peopled and poorly defended. And it was far enough from Wessex or Mercia, the stronger kingdoms to the West, that a band of some sixty Danish raiders striking there would elicit little interest from Kings Æthelred of Wessex or Burgred of Mercia.

The demands of keeping them in food meant a strike at almost every farmstead they spotted. The knowledge that fleeing survivors would find their way to some lord's hall to summon help kept them sailing on. Crossing from the borders of Anglia to Lindisse had aided them, as no king's men could pursue them across kingdoms, but the haste in which Yrling and his men moved meant unavoidable waste in the foodstuffs they captured. They gorged on meat before it could go bad. The flesh of fowl, sheep, pig, and cattle was roasted, or boiled up with whatever grain they could carry off. Smokehouses might yield hams or a haunch of deer; and eggs, if they could be carried off safely, were prized. As they had found at the fort of the coast-guard and at earlier strikes, a cask of ale or even crocks of mead might be discovered. More than once Yrling issued threats to those who tried to claim such for themselves. Better they all get a swallow than a few men end up drunk, or dead from fights over it. It was the same with women; he wanted no fighting. He could not stop the men from having their full of any women they caught, but never allowed women to be brought aboard his ships.

As his men began to know each other friendships and aversions formed. Men paired up as fighting partners, and trading partners too, for what booty they had taken. Certain men would not eat or even stand next to others, though Yrling sometimes made a point of sending such to perform a single task together, to keep any rift to manageable width. The man Kjeld from Yellow-sail had angered Gap by ridiculing his whistling manner of speaking. Thus Kjeld and Gap were told to join Yrling as they ripped up the floorboards of a particularly thriving farm, hoping to spot a sack of buried silver. Bue, who had, for no seeming reason, taken a dislike to Jari, was sent with him to tackle and spear a huge blue-black pig.

Jari was younger brother to Une, who was second in command, so Bue's dislike put him at odds with both brothers. But Toki and Bue had taken up; they shared the same reckless spirit and loud and jesting taunts. Both Toki and Bue had love of dice, and after studying their play Sidroc found he could often best each of them. Their daring would not still their hands even when their luck-spirits had wandered; they would play and lose with an almost defiant pride. Sidroc gained much from them, both in the way of hack-silver and the better things they had stripped from the bodies of the dead, good shoes, belts, woollen mantles.

Still, when it came time to run against the gathering men of a place Toki would form up near Yrling, sometimes flanking him with Sidroc and Une. Jari would be close, and the quiet Asberg, who they all saw was nimble with both feet and spear, was a welcome member of their line.

One of the men they had picked up at the coast-guard fight had special skill, one not in the way of fighting. Aki bore on his left wrist the pricked-in design of a coiling snake, one he had made himself. The snake even sported overlapping scales, so skillfully was it wrought, and as the design lay under the skin no ash-and-lye soap could scrub it off. All the men admired it, perhaps none more than Sidroc. One late afternoon, after they had eaten, Sidroc saw Aki at work on his own wrist and came to him.

Aki was seated on a log, his kit on the tree stump. He had two small pouches opened before him, a scrap of linen dotted with tiny blood marks, and an awl like a thick needle in his right hand.

Sidroc watched as Aki poked the punch into his skin, wiped away the welling bead of blood, and sprinkled the hole with a mixture of powered, dried woad, and fine copper dust. Both would lend a blue colour to the design, and the woad, being both a dye plant and one used to staunch bleeding, kept the many small holes from weeping too much. Right now Aki was adding to the detail on the snake's scales, rubbing small pinches of the dye-stuff into the tiny wounds he gave himself.

He glanced up at Sidroc, as the latter knelt down to get a better look.

"The punch is iron," Aki told him. "It helps fix the colour, the iron holds it."

It made sense; dyers often used iron shavings as mordant to hold the coloured dye stuffs in the fabric they boiled.

"I would have a beast, too," Sidroc said, after watching a few more jabs. "Can you do it?"

Aki blinked up at him. There was still much light in the sky to work. "What would you have?"

"What I have never seen – a dragon. One such as stories are told of. On my chest."

Aki laughed. "It will be large, and it will hurt. But I will do it."

Sidroc pulled off his tunic and lay back, and Aki began. First he used shears to snip Sidroc's dark chest hair close to the skin. After this Aki outlined the design with the point of a burnt stick from the fire ring. The drawing began just beneath the collar bones, and fanned out almost to the shoulders. Then with his pouches of fine coloured dust before him, he got to work with the iron awl, kneeling at Sidroc's side.

The pricking did indeed smart. As soon as Aki had made ten closely-spaced punctures, he sprinkled the pigment over the bloodied holes, rubbing it in well.

"What are you doing first?" Sidroc asked. He could see none of what was going on, only feel the progress of the jabbing into his skin.

"Always start with the head of any beast," Aki answered, with another laugh. "You do not want the body writhing about, looking for its brains."

Aki laboured until the light began to fade, and his eyes tired from the fineness of the work. "We will do more tomorrow," he told Sidroc. "It will take three or four days to finish, but the outline is there."

Sidroc too was ready for a pause from the ceaseless puncturing. A number of other men had wandered by, looking on at the progress, jesting at how reddened was the linen scrap Aki used to blot up the blood. Sidroc had no mirror-disc of polished silver, but Aki had a small one of copper. When he stood up Sidroc held it before him.

The first thing he saw was his own face, one long and narrow, marked by the deep scar travelling the length of his left cheek from eye to chin. He quickly canted the copper disc to his chest.

There lay an outline of a serpent-like dragon, with fangs never seen on either snake or wolf. The dark blue body of it coiled about the upper part of his chest, and the tail ended in a barb as fearsome as were the fangs it led with. The bruising and soreness he felt were well worth such a beast.

"I have red ochre, too, for the eyes," Aki was telling him, tilting his head to where his pack lay.

Over the next few evenings Aki laboured over the design. He had asked as payment the handsome chain of braided silver Sidroc wore. Instead Sidroc gave him a stack of small silver coins for his efforts, whole coins stamped with the visage of the kings of the place, finds on the bodies of those he had killed. Yrling had a scale set, and the coins were equal in weight to the chain taken from the Saxon thegn. He could not give or trade anything from this first battle-gain he had earned; all from this first man he wanted intact. Yet Aki deserved rich reward for the dragon, now made part of Sidroc's own flesh, and he was glad to give the coinage as he did.

It was said that dragons lived forever. Sidroc knew he could not, but this beast writhing on his chest gave silent witness to his own new life. He had thought he was going to die, or at best suffer the shame of falling prisoner. The shield-maidens had not pointed at him, and he saved himself through his craft. A spiralling dragon springing into flight over his heart suited his sense of re-birth.

"Sif!"

This was Une, calling out to where Toki stood on the margin of a small stream, combing out his still-wet hair. "Leave off combing your hair of gold, and gather wood with us."

The oath Toki flung back at his summoner only made Une laugh. Toki did take pride in his long and yellow hair, and Une had often teased him by calling him after Thor's golden-haired wife. But Toki slid his comb of ox horn into its wooden sleeve, jammed it into his pack, and scrambled back to the other side of the stream to join those plucking dried branches from the woodland floor.

Summer was at its height and with it the heat. It was the morning after a strike at a cluster of three farms, and though they had begun roasting the pigs they had carried off as soon as they arrived back at their camp, they had need of much more fuel to aid in the quick cooking needed before the flesh began to grow green.

The last tubs of butter they had were rancid, but with no bread to smear it on its loss could be dismissed. The farmstead of last night had been a poor one despite its size, its milk cows scrawny and likely dry, its rye and barley stores paltry. The ale they had found in a brew-shed was already souring. Even the four pigs they made off with were lean, and with nothing to lard the flanks as they roasted would be dry and tough.

The smell of smoke, reek of blood and the discarded entrails of the pigs all permeated the clearing they had settled in. The mingled odour of slaughter and fire was one more layer of the stench they lived with. The men themselves stank. Toki had not been alone in going for a wash. He was careful of his hair and did in fact spend as much time as a woman combing it; but the grime of so much sleeping out and rough living marked each of them. Common to all were ragged hair and beards, fingernails black with embedded dirt and blood, bodies sore from swift travelling and much fighting. Their teeth were easiest to keep up, for slender green twigs could be snapped from any tree and used to rub teeth and gums. Some still had combs, just as Toki had carefully kept his own by, or tweezers or tiny ear-scoops of bronze to clean their ears; all the kit that any free man would use about his person. But much had gotten lost, either during the storm aboard Death-day, or in the everyday movement from camp to ship to camp again. On the water they were crammed together on the decks of the two ships. They beached to make a strike, then with all speed took ship to safety, where they might eat and rest as they could.

Their clothing too had suffered. With no women amongst them, there was none to keep their tunics and leggings in good order, and to scrub them with washing-lye and pound them clean with wooden bats. Indeed, of these things they had none. Rips and tears went unmended. A few of the men were handy enough with needle and thread, using that kit provided by the Ribe sail-maker to make clumsy patches; but most depended on stripping the bodies of men they had killed to gain the clothing they needed.

It would be thus until Yrling found a place worthy of laying claim to. Then he would have a hall to fill with the men who now followed him, and women too, and thralls to do the work they did themselves. He would know the place when he saw it, one far enough inland to keep raiders such as himself from easy access to what he had won. Until then they would range up the coast, striking inland as far as rivers provided good farms to target, then returning to the North Sea for another day's venturing.

Each night a watch was set of two men, relieved when the dark was at its deepest by another two. All shared in this guard duty, even Yrling, whose turn this night it was. When he was awakened by the man he was to relieve he went and joined a yawning Bjarne in his slow pacing about the camp site. Though the fire had burnt down to reddened coals, a half and lowering Moon hung in the skies, lending its light. Yrling and Bjarne had not been long at the watch when a rustle in the spreading branches of some young quickbeams made them both jerk their heads. They hoisted their spears, ready, but gave no alarm lest it be only a fox. Yrling took a few strides to the fire, poking it up with a cooking iron to give more light. Then he and Bjarne stood still, waiting. Out from the narrow track between the shaking quickbeams stepped Toki and Bue.

The scowl on Yrling's face betrayed his rancour even before he spoke. These two must have crept off during the first watch of the night.

Toki had not remembered that his uncle would be taking the second watch, and his eyes opened wide at the sight of him.

"Uncle." It was clear from Toki's voice the sight was unexpected. But Toki's tongue was ever glib, and he determined his best defence was to speak first.

"We went back, looking for silver," he said.

Those sleeping nearest were already rousing. Yrling's taut response made them all lift their heads. Sidroc was on the other side of the clearing, but stood up.

"You went back. To the farm we struck at," Yrling repeated.

Toki had his spear in his hand, and now set its butt end on the ground, as if tired. "Já," he agreed. "And if we had found silver, we would have brought it to you."

This claim did not assuage Yrling's ire. His words were low, but the veins in his neck were starting in anger.

"That farm was my strike. You cross me by sneaking away, to loot it alone." Yrling now let his eyes flick to he who had emerged with Toki. "Bue," he said. He had no high opinion of this one from Yellow-sail, and in naming him nearly spat out the word.

His eyes went back to his nephew. "You are more stupid than I knew, Toki. Anyone could have met you there, warriors summoned by those who ran. If you had been caught they would force you easily enough to tell where we were. Your greed put us all in danger. And for what – you found nothing."

Toki's spirit would not be easily daunted, not before so many men watching him. He grinned. "We carry back nothing. But we found women." He paused just a moment.

"Some had returned." Toki's grin increased, and a few of the men looking on offered up gleeful hoots.

His uncle did not share in their approval. Toki's lust, either for silver or for women, had endangered him.

"A woman will cause your death, Toki," he warned. "But if you bring added danger to me, I will kill you myself before that day."

The tone of voice in which this threat was issued silenced the sniggering surrounding them.

Even Toki straightened up, his grin fading from his face. He had been looking unblinkingly at his uncle's shadowed face, but now his eyes slipped to the faces of others. It was awkward for all. Uncles often fostered their nephews, deepening the family bond with their sister's sons, thus tying her kin more closely to the male line she had married into. It was more common for uncles and nephews to set off, either trading or raiding together, than it was for fathers and sons. And it was almost unheard of for an uncle to threaten his own nephew, yet they had all witnessed it. Most of these men liked Toki for his daring, his skill at the harp, his jesting and bawdy singing. Now he was being shamed by their war-chief. But they knew Toki had endangered them.

Toki looked across the fire to where Sidroc stood. The entreaty in Toki's eyes was all too clear to Sidroc. He could not defend his cousin's act, yet the threat hanging in the air must be addressed.

Every angry man felt his anger just; Sidroc knew this. And surely most of the men here agreed that Yrling was right in his ire. Toki never saw himself in the wrong, both Sidroc and Yrling had long experience of that. But he must try to shift the tension around the guttering fire. Sidroc would ask his cousin a question, and see how he made answer.

"Toki." His voice was low, but carried strongly over the glowing bed of coals to where Toki stood by the trees. "Do you know why you have angered your war-chief?"

More than a little petulance was in his cousin's response. "I was not caught back there, only here," he answered.

This admission of wrongdoing was as close as any might get from Toki. Sidroc heaved a quiet sigh, and hung what he could on it.

"Já. But you were still caught. Do not forget that."

They were off in the morning, pointing the prows of the ships North, rounding a vast curving landmass of forest. Late afternoon revealed a small cove with a sheltered place to beach. The next dawn found them awakening to explore the margins of the sandy strip. They were, as ever, hungry. There were several narrow tracks through the trees; one or more of these could lead to a nearby farmstead, hidden from sight by the greenwood. They pulled the ships a bit higher up the sand in answer to the rising tide. As he always did Yrling left men as guards, a total of twelve to keep the ships safe in their absence. One he pointed to was Bue.

More than fifty of them, spears and shields in hand, made their way up the broadest of the tracks. Bringing up the rear were Asberg, Jari, and Sidroc, last. Not knowing what they might find, they wore nearly all their armaments, despite the heat; swords and ring-shirts for those who owned them, helmets too, a knife at every waist. Une did not venture out without skeggox in hand, and a few others also carried this fearsome battle-axe. With as many men as they now were, sometimes little or even no fighting was needed when they appeared thus armed at the woven wattle gates of a farm. The families oftentimes fled upon seeing them, running only to gather babes too young to walk. But this was not what they found when Yrling and Une, at the lead, stepped through the stand of trees into a fronting pasture.

A farm it had been, now burnt nearly to the ground. A few blackened and still upright timbers marked the buildings of it, as did the margins of the remaining wattle fences. Whether their brethren had been here before them, or some cooking or smithing mishap had claimed the place they could not know.

They all filed out from the wood, looking across the high and uncropped grasses of the pasture. Yrling decided to near the ruins, and they spread out, keeping close watch on the more distant trees behind the holding. As they drew closer the smell of charred wood wafted to them. The fire could not have been long ago; a few days at most. Why the folk of the place had not returned to begin their rebuilding was a mystery, one Une voiced.

"They are dead, or taken as thralls," Yrling supposed. They were now at the long edge of what had been the largest structure. No warmth rose from the pile of flaked and ashy roof supports covering the earthen floor of it. Small handfuls of time-bleached thatch, singed short, lay amongst them.

They lifted a few of the burnt joists, trying to see sign of a treasure-hole which had once been dug in the ground, one that bronze or silver bits had been secreted in. They found nothing.

They gave it up for what it was, a ruin holding nothing of worth. They would head back to the ships and be off; they needed food.

They retraced their steps, the leafy hardwoods over their heads making dim the way back to the beach. The forest floor they trod was mossy, thick and springy underfoot, and their legs brushed against the curling fronds of ferns as they traversed the narrow track. It was not a bright morning, and all about them took on a hue of soft green, shading to the deep browns and greys of rock and tree bark. The cool and green wood seemed a place utterly apart from the despoiled farm behind and the pristine and waiting blue-grey sea just ahead.

They stepped out on the beach. Death-day and Yellow-sail were gone.

Yrling and many others whipped their heads, checking to be certain they had come out upon the right cove. Another glance back to the sand told them they had.

Several bodies lay there, and they ran the distance to them. Just beyond, disturbed grains betrayed the trampled footprints of many men around the long and straight skid marks of the keels and hulls of two ships.

They scanned the horizon. No drekars in sight, but the cove they had beached on sat within a broad and curving promontory. Their ships might be just beyond that.

There was naught but stunned silence for the long moments required to take this in. Then Yrling let out with a stream of oaths that pierced the stillness. Only those too staggered to speak did not join him.

When he could draw breath he let out a final howl, his face tilted upwards to the heavens.

When he returned his gaze he found Jari and Sidroc at two of the bodies, turning them over. Asberg knelt at another, pulling the arm away from where it had fallen across the face. Yrling and Une strode over to them. A fourth body also lay there, one further off. All showed signs of combat. Most still held their shields, though they had been stripped of their spears and knives, and the two who owned them, of their swords. Gap was one of these, the body furthest off, his opened mouth revealing the lack of his front teeth.

Yrling cudgelled his tumbling brain, recalling who he had set on the watch. There had been five from Death-day, and seven from Yellow-sail.

"Bue." This was Toki. Bue was not lying on this beach. All the dead were men from Death-day.

Treachery had been repaid with treachery.

A call from the edge of the sand near the encroaching trees made them all look. It was one of the newest of their number, who had joined up with them at the fight at the coast-guard. He had discovered something, and was looking down at it.

They clustered about. A number of smooth grey beach stones, palm-sized, had been laid out with purpose. One long line was crossed at an angle with a shorter line slashed though. It formed the rune Nyd ᚾ.

"It was Gorm," the man told them; Gorm the war-chief from Aros whom they had abandoned. "He marks all his strikes with it."

Those left as guards had been discovered by his passing ship. They had been given the choice to fight, or steal away with the ships. Bue and seven others had chosen the latter.

This finding prompted action from Yrling.

"Gorm of Aros," he shouted, raising his arms in the air and facing the empty sea. He pointed his thumbs to direct his curse. "One-eyed Odin sees you! May Dauðadagr take you to your grave!"

Some of his men looked a long time at the rune-message, as if the mute stones themselves could tell more than the bald facts of the theft. Yrling took but a single, second glance at it, anger churning in his breast.

Nyd, repeated Yrling. Need; hardship. It stood also for Nothing. That was apt. They were stranded, and with no food stores, kit, or supplies. All they owned was what they had carried into the wood with them – their weapons. And their hunger, which also remained.

THE WARRIOR'S BARGAIN

THEY ranged about on the empty beach, exposed and vulnerable. Other than the bodies nothing remained. Yrling always made certain that any gear they had camped with was packed away before the raiding party went out, so that on their return they could the more swiftly load the booty they had taken onto the ships, and be off. There was nothing to salvage. The fire-pit with its cold ashes looked an empty eye.

They stood bereft, taking it in. The ships had been home to them. Every scrap of comfort they had known was now lost. Blankets, mantles, spare clothing, extra weapons, and the little food they had carried over from the last raid, the supply of henbane seeds they used to quell the pain of wounds; all was out of their reach. Their very means of travel was gone.

Each man cast his thoughts to what he had lost in this outrage. Some, like Asberg from Yellow-sail, had lost their ship twice, and now for good. A few stood looking down at their persons, as if gauging what was left to them. Sidroc, staring out at the blankness of the sea, found himself recalling loss of the beautiful blazed-faced chestnut mare. Yrling's final sacrifice to pay the last sum of silver due on his ship was giving her up.

"My harp," Toki muttered.

"And your comb," Une added, for it would have been in Toki's pack, gone with all their goods.

"Bue served you well," Une ended. There was no triumph in his voice, only the grim recounting of a simple fact.

Toki gave a short laugh at this. "No worse than I would have served him," he admitted.

They must move on, find food. Yrling did not want to stay to gather brushwood to fire the bodies of the dead, yet they did so, hauling the four bodies side by side, striking sparks from iron and flint. These had died in his service and in that of Odin, to whom he had given himself. He must send their bodies to All-Father's hall in Asgard to keep faith with that bond.

They set off, the Sun now high overhead, the smell of burning spreading like reaching fingers after them. They would skirt the sea. The forest was deep, and their one foray down a track through it led only to desolation.

Food was their pressing need. Three of their good bowmen had bows and arrows with them, but finding deer in mid-Summer would not be easy; the stags would be upland, the does still hiding their young. They knew boar ran here, but had no hounds to search them out with. All had seen wild ducks and geese, but it would take a score to feed the fifty of them. They had spotted no berries, and the apples they found were still tiny and sour. At least fresh water was never far away; the land was scored with flowing streams. But water alone could not keep them moving. A river could offer fish, captured in a weir of woven roots. It all took time, which they did not have. Yrling knew their best bet was to stay on the move until they came across a likely strike.

They spent the day following the coast, and slept that night as they could upon the sand, their bellies grumbling. They set out again just after first light, finding the forest to their left running down to shrubs and then to marsh. The water was brackish but they drank it. They moved slightly inland to firmer footing, and picked up the smallest of tracks where it led from the forest. The track grew to a path, and widened until the scars of wheel ruts marked it. They were cautious now, lest any be taking the same route, and kept themselves within the line of shrubby growth. The Sun was at its highest point when they heard the sound of a man, singing.

They froze behind the leaves which hid them. The path twisted and turned, losing itself to sight between the tall growth of waving reeds on one side, and osiers on the other. Then they saw him, a single figure seated astride a dark brown ass. He was gowned, almost as a woman would be dressed, and singing a song both unmelodious and unintelligible to their ears. The man was the poorest of riders; his elbows up almost about his shoulders, his knees splayed out so that he did no more than perch upon the top of his wood and leathern saddle. The ass, for its part, kept turning its long and furry ears as if in protest to the man's song, but other than that went on smartly enough.

All knew to make no move until Yrling signalled, and he did not. They let beast and rider pass unmolested, themselves unseen.

When he was out of sight they stepped out upon the packed ground he had passed them on.

"He came from someplace," Yrling noted. "We will see from where."

They moved forward, on the path itself and almost at a trot. Their spears were in their hands, but their shields still slung upon their backs. The marshes on one side of them continued to firm, the water becoming a true channel. The setting gave Yrling hope. Rounding another bend in the path they saw from whence the rider had issued.

A settlement lay ahead. The palisade surrounding it was no more than a stockade fence, meant to keep wandering livestock out, and the gates to that fence were wide open, almost as if in welcome. Outside the stockade were pastures on which sheep grazed, and milk cows lay in the slanting sunlight. To one side were fields, furrowed in rows of grain and vegetables, where men, some dressed in long gowns, and some in the way of ordinary folk, worked, bending over their hoes and mattocks.

Even better, the top of one building within was crowned with an iron frame work, one rod of iron upright, the second crossing it through. The sign of the Christians. Here was all they could ask for, Yrling knew.

"The Gods have led us," he said. "This is one of their temples, with holy men. This place is called Beardan. There will be treasure within."

This would be easier than they had dreamt possible. They could sweep in the open gates unopposed. Their hunger coupled with their excitement made them feel giddy, their empty bellies tightening even further. Almost to a man their shields were swung around and taken up in their left hands. Gizur and the other archers were ready, their quivers within easy reach of their fingertips, their bowstrings taut.

They quickened their pace but kept their silence, knowing soon some of the field workers would see them and call out alarm. In fact so intent were the men on their hoeing that they were less than fifty paces away before one straightened up and gave cry. The raiders ignored them. Spears ready, they had formed up in lines of four and five, few enough across to be admitted through the gates in a single rank. The file behind those first four ran ten or twelve deep, a river of rushing men. Yrling stepped through first, flanked by Une, Jari and Sidroc; with Asberg, Bjarne, Toki, Gizur, and all the rest just behind.

The work yard had more of the gowned men within, men wearing the long plain brown garb the ass-rider wore. These were the holy men, monks they were called. There were also men in ordinary leggings and tunics which all Saxons wore, serving men perhaps. These were at work with the monks, sawing boards by the side of the stockade, wheeling hand wains piled with fire wood, and stepping with astonished faces from the smaller outbuildings.

The raiders streamed in, their mouths now opening in fully-voiced war cries, their fists brandishing their uplifted spears as they came. The look of confused terror on all who they met gave a reckless glee to those who stormed in. There were no guards to oppose them, and those living here bore no weapons. Even the serving men who wore knives were slow to draw them, and the gowned monks were completely unarmed, nothing hanging at their waists save for long cords of hempen rope ending in a small cross of two wooden sticks.

Some of the men within ran out of sight, behind sheds or storehouses. These made their way along the stockade and out the gates when the raiders were all in, joining those who had been working in the fields before they fled.

In the centre of the enclosure, at the very heart of it, stood a squat gable-peaked building the like of which none of the Danes had ever seen. It was made of cut stone blocks, closely fitted together. Its roof was neither mossy wooden boards nor bristling thatch, but sheathed over with dully gleaming lead sheets, the costliest roof any building could bear. It was all proof against fire, in its stone walls and lead roof, and proof too of the value of what must lie within. The other buildings were timber and wattle and daub, as would be found in any keep or farmstead, but this stone building, marked with the iron framework of two crossed rods on its roof, surely marked the treasure-place.

The door of this building now opened from within, and they watched gowned men run to it, and into the dim interior. Those in the first rank of the raiders saw the monks as they scurried to take final position before a high table built of stone slabs, a table upon which lay a wealth of gleaming silver. This silver sat on a linen cloth of purest white, trailing over the slab ends of the stone, its own smooth brightness heightening the pale glow of the treasure upon it.

A man, older than the others, gowned and with the top of his head shaved clean, stood before the high table, arms outspread as if he could by force of will deter those running at it. An arrow from the bow of Gizur dropped him before any outstretched spear could touch him. A younger monk, shrieking, swept past the fallen elder, and crying out words that none who knew the tongue of Angle-land could follow, grasped at the tallest piece of silver on the table, holding it before him.

It was that Cross of the Christians, their sacred sign. He held the heavy thing before his chest, thrusting it forward at Yrling as if it were a protective shield. He did not remain long on his feet. The men who had crowded in were now everywhere.

Sidroc, off to one end of the stone table, stopped another monk who had snatched something from its surface, and now clasped it to his breast. Sidroc held his spear before him, his round of alder wood shielding his body. The man he stopped had nothing save what he cradled to his heart. The monk was young, a few years at most older than he, slight and bony. He was not, like many of the others, crying out gibbering pleas, but it was clear he thought he was looking his last on a human face. The face the monk saw was that of a lean young Dane of great height, one with a cheek badly scarred, who wore his dark brown hair in two long plaits.

"Give it," Sidroc found himself telling him, in the tongue of the Saxons. He could not kill this one, unarmed and unresisting as he was.

The man blinked at him. Spear still pointing at the monk, Sidroc let go his shield, dropping it to his knees. He reached out his hand, summoning the man to surrender what he cradled.

The man was quaking, his body trembling like a leaf in a bitter wind. Around them the cries and shrieks were abating; monks lay on the floor where they had fallen, pierced by spear points or arrowheads.

He did not let go, did not obey Sidroc's order. It took a mere snatch of Sidroc's free hand to wrench the thing away, pushing the monk back the few steps to the stone wall as he did so.

"What?" asked Toki, suddenly at Sidroc's side. His yellow hair had fallen all about his shoulders, and his teeth were flashing as he grinned at his cousin.

Sidroc showed what he had won, the most curious piece of silver he had ever beheld. It was formed in the shape of a human hand, fingers and all, and was of the same size of a human hand. It ended at the wrist joint, which was set round with a rim of white pearls and gemstones of blue, as if a cuff on a richly decorated sleeve.

"A vessel of some kind," Sidroc said. It was weighty due to the silver, but he could feel as well it was hollow within.

The monk he had taken it from was still flattened against the wall, eyes large, staring at them.

Toki jerked his shield towards him in question.

"I cannot kill a man who will not fight," Sidroc told him.

Toki made answer with both spear and voice.

"I can," he said, plunging his spear into the monk's chest.

The oath Sidroc uttered was spoken with stark vehemence. The monk was his capture. It was almost as if Toki had tried to claim the silver hand. He found himself baring his teeth at his cousin, turning away from both him and the dying monk, now crumpled at the base of the wall.

He shoved the silver hand under his belt, retrieved his shield. He faced back into the body of the temple. His eyes rose from the stone floor and the monks lying there to the dark crooks of the timber roof joists. He glimpsed, from the tail of his eye, Toki move away as well.

Sidroc had seen much of needless slaughter in these last weeks. To practise that here, amongst men protecting objects of magical intent to their Gods, men who could not be provoked to fight back, seemed foolish and possibly worse. Tyr, the God of Justice, was his God, his fulltrúi, and he could not believe that Tyr would approve of such butchery.

He shook his head; it was all he could do. His uncle was kneeling at the side of the oldest monk, sprawled at the foot of the stone table. This one bore a cross not of wood, but of silver, and Yrling was cutting it from the cord that had tied it to the man's waist.

Jari and Une were at the table, gathering up what had sat there. Besides the tall silver cross, retrieved from the floor, there were two candle holders, also of silver, and each holding tapers of beeswax. There was a small chest of some kind, also chased in silver, and a choice goblet, silver with a flaring foot of gold.

His uncle was standing now, looking on this. Sidroc went to him and added the silver hand to the pile. His uncle greeted it with a grunt and a nod. He lifted it, gave it a shake, and heard the faint rattle from within. He saw the seam line about the pearl and gemstone cuff, pulled at it. Out dropped tiny splinters of dried and brown bone. They stared at them, poor fragments of a once real hand, encased in splendour, and now lying on the veined stone floor. If it was some kind of magic, they would let the fragments lie. But Yrling once again gave Sidroc a nod before he refitted the end; of all that was taken this hand was of special note.

The linen cloth draped upon the stone table was splashed on one end with blood, looking like berries in the snow. It still served well to wrap all these up. It was a heavy armful Yrling walked out with.

The action within the stone treasure house was over almost before it began. Only the men in the foremost ranks were needed, freeing the others to range about the little settlement. The first flush of conquest had ended, and richly, and now the gnawing hunger felt by all reasserted itself.

The kitchen yard was off to the right, set off by goose pens and fowl houses. Not a few of the men were there now, clustering by the cook fire and by the work tables near to the domed ovens.

The first thing they fell upon was fish, rows and rows of it, freshly roasted and impaled on green skewers. The kitchen yard was lately abandoned by the cooks; meal time must have been near for these monks. Some of the long skewers hung still above the fire, while many others had been set to cool on an iron rack propped up by stones. They were the young of some fatty fish, bream perhaps, the curling scales shining with heat, the flesh firm, moist, and of delicious savour. There was bread too, and in abundance, enough for each man to have his own loaf; bread must form a large part of what these holy men supped on. This was eaten with a relish even greater than the fish, the crusted loves broken open, dipped into crocks of soft sweet butter lifted from the cooling depths of the sunken store house. Cheeses were there as well, tangy and flavoured with green herbs. They stood there about the cooking rings and the work tables, tired, filthy, lifting this all to their mouths, the filling of their shrunken bellies making them almost forget the mound of silver treasure they had just won.

The well held sweet water; if there was a brew-house they did not find it. Nor was there any meat they could uncover, no smokehouse with deer haunch or hanging hams. Late peas and early beans might be found in the vegetable gardens; time for such foraging they had none. But they filled baskets with eggs, both hens and geese; and wrung the necks of as many fowl as they could. They took as much cooking kit as they could carry, not the largest iron cauldron, but several smaller ones, and toasting forks and spoons.

Then mindful of the need for haste, they scoured the rest of the buildings. They must take everything upon their own backs, but packs of leathern and oiled linen were found piled in the storerooms. One house of timber which seemed an ordinary hall showed itself a honey comb of tiny rooms, each holding a single cot and stool.

"Sif!" called Une to Toki, who had entered one such room together. Toki was about to swear back at him, when a grinning Une tossed him a well-made comb of wood, found on a low stool. Every monk had a comb, and each had also small shears, ear scoops, bone-handled razors and oil, and a linen towel. They had need for all of it. They plucked shoes from under cots or from the feet of the dead. They stuffed away rolled blankets, filled as many packs as they could with oats, barley, and rye; found a sack of hazelnuts and another of dark dried cherries.

In one building, set round with tables, lay a locked chest. A strike with Une's war-axe revealed what it held. Four nearly square objects lay within, boxes they looked, decorated with silver lids holding clear crystals, carnelians of ruby hue, and blue stones of a richness like lapis. They were wondrous to behold, as was the thought of what might be hidden within. Pulling them out Yrling saw they were not boxes. The silver lids were hinged, but within were leaf after leaf of animal skin, thinned and smoothed to a creamy shade, and covered all over with scrawling designs in black, red, and blue. They had their own interest, but the whole was heavy, and they set to work ripping the silver and gemmed boards from top and bottom.

Another chest revealed more finely woven linens, these stitched with coloured thread work, and also narrow strips of the same, as highly decorated as the trim on any great lady's sleeves and hem. All these were rolled and stuffed into leathern packs. To his great delight Toki found a harp, one slightly smaller than his own but far more richly decorated, the light wood stained yellow, the body of it bearing drawings in black of coiling beasts. Even the pins holding the strings were worthy, carved from pale walrus ivory made to look like the heads of cats. Something of this value he must offer to his uncle, and did so, holding it out to Yrling. His uncle, busy packing away booty, only laughed, telling him he expected a Saga-tale made of his exploits in return.

Then they must be off. They would have liked to have stayed there; closed the gates, rested, eaten their fill once more now that the sharp edge of their hunger had been dulled. But so many men of the place had fled there were bound to be warriors after them, and soon. Those who had made such strikes before knew Christian places of worship were built on the silver of local lords.

"He cannot be far away," Yrling told them as they shouldered their packs.

Not a single woman had been seen, and one of the men asked why.

"The holy men of the Christians forswear them," Yrling told him, an answer greeted in jeering disbelief. But Yrling was the happier he did not need to contend with that distraction.

They stood grouped in the middle of the yard before the stone temple. Every door of every building, large or small, hung open; all had been entered, and much of what was found within was now upon their backs. All of the dead monks had been felled inside the temple, and apart from the clusters of brown and white feathers blowing about the trampled enclosure to the fowl pens, no sign of violence met the eye.

Yrling saw Sidroc's own eyes lift to those crossed bars of iron topping the gable of the roof. The shape so formed was almost that of the runic letter Nyd. The rune held another, deeper meaning which had been difficult to think on, seeing their ships stolen, looking at the stones so arrayed. It also suggested endurance to see through the trial. Here, rather than Nothing, they were thinking, this place held true treasure.

They set off, the gates gaping open in their wake. There were oxen, and carts too, they left behind, but such were far too cumbersome and slow for the speed at which they must travel, and the narrowness of the trackways they must take.

The road continued along the side of the encircling fence, turning inland and away from the sea. They took it. Behind the settlement they found the source of the fat bream they had gorged on; the marsh waterway, narrowing to a stream, had been dammed in a deep pool, from which captive fish could be readily dipped up.

The road beyond was wooded on both sides. Sidroc looked down it. "If there is a war-chief coming with his men, they will use this road," he guessed.

"Já," his uncle seconded. "And if they are horsed, Odin smiles, or at least winks. Let us see if we can meet them."

They kept on, but need not wait long. The sound of bridle hardware, of the light ringing of metal on metal, and the hoof-fall of horses met their ears.

"Hide yourselves. No sound, no movement, until I signal," Yrling told them, his orders a harsh whisper. They slipped into the trees on the left side of the road, so that those who passed would have their weapon-hands on the other side. He kept himself and his nephews and Une and Jari at the furthest point of his hiding men, so that when they sprang out, they would hold the rear.

A troop of Saxon thegns, riding almost at a canter, came into view. One man fronted the rest, seated upon a grey stallion, and behind him his men rode by twos. They came at enough speed it was hard to count them, but it seemed a score of warriors bore down the road. They had spears held upright in their hands, and their shields upon their backs. The war-chief in the lead was kitted out as a King might be, for the crested helmet he bore upon his head had been chased in gold. It looked something wrought by dwarfs, long-skilled in forging magical armaments. The skies were clouded, but the helmet glinted even in that dull light. Coming at them, it caught and held the eye.

Yrling had his three good archers strung out so that one was with him, nearest the end of his hidden men; one in the middle of the line, and the last at the other end. If each archer made a hit, at beginning, mid-point, and end of the coming file, the confusion amongst the Saxons would be great. Yrling must hold off his battle-yell until the war-chief was well past, and the final horsemen before him.

His yell was never sounded. A cry came, but it was from Toki, leaping forward just as the war-chief reached him. The golden helmet was too great a lure; Toki must have it. He sprang forward from the leafy growth and flung the spear towards the chest of the lead man.

It was perfectly aimed, and thrown with such force that when it hit, the front legs of the great stallion the war-chief rode buckled beneath him. The horse snorted and gave out a shrill whinnying call as his rider pitched head first over the arched neck. Almost down on its knees, the stallion rose, shaking off the body. The horses of the two warriors just behind reared, and one of the men lost his seat and fell to the pounded surface.

The road erupted, coursing with plunging horses, men springing out from the trees, and flown arrows. The oaths dropping from the mouths of the horsemen were as naught to those flying from Yrling's lips. There was nothing to do but rush out in reckless disorder. Horses were large targets and easy to hit, yet horses were what they most needed. They aimed their spears high, knocking the riders from their saddles as the men tried to control their mounts. The shock of their war-chief going down first, the bumping and rearing of the cantering horses, so suddenly halted by the attack, and the spear points thrusting from many men on foot broke the thegns into a wheeling scramble. Those at the end of the file were well out of it and could have turned and fled, but they did not. Spurring their horses, they rode to where they saw the grey stallion of their leader, now rider-less.

It was a grave mistake. There were in fact only nine-and-ten of the thegns, and the Danes swarming them numbered more than fifty. Between the riders who had been thrown from their horses and those who had been knocked off, all were soon unhorsed.

Strung out as Yrling's men had been, it was at first impossible to surround their foes. And the thegns, stunned as they were by the ambush, fought with desperate drive. They had their shields on their arms as swiftly as they could close their hands around the handle in the centre boss. Some had dropped their spears in being unhorsed, and had pulled swords from the baldrics high on their chests. But these men, despite having horses, did not sport the war-gear of the men at the fort of the coast-guard. Only a few had steel helmets. The rest wore caps of hardened leather, fitted over with thin supporting iron bars. More had ring-shirts, but not a few had suffered some hurt in being knocked from their mounts.

Still, the fighting was hot, and Saxon steel found home in more than one Danish body. These were again trained warriors, not farmers swinging haying forks, or the holy men, pleading and defenceless, whose temple they had just bloodied. And their lord had fallen, he who had armed and likely horsed them, he to whom they owed allegiance unto death.

Sidroc had sprung from the tree line with Yrling, Une, and Jari, as astonished at Toki's act as were they, but backing his action up, as they were forced to do. As the frightened horses and storming men swirled about the edge of the road, Sidroc had been swept further down its length, running to confront the thegns in the packed midpoint of the melée. After using his spear to topple a man from his horse, he leapt forward and free of the rearing beast's front legs and was able to plunge the point of his weapon into the thegn's back as he lay insensate on the ground. Pulling out the point, the butt end of his spear collided with something. He craned his head to see that he had struck the shield of a Saxon, sword drawn, moving in on his back.

The butt end of a spear did not provide much purchase. He did what he could, ramming it with strength downward at the man's feet. He missed the instep but the thegn started, and Sidroc, with a ripping motion pulled the spear up with speed, knocking the man's shield a little away from his torso. The thegn covered himself with his sword, but Sidroc, turning fully, was hand-over-hand with his spear, tipping the long and lethal point forward, puncturing the ring-tunic at the thegn's right shoulder. That hand opened, the sword falling from it, as the thegn took a deep step backward, landing on one knee.

The man's head tipped back, the leathern cap falling from it. His eyes were a dark greenish-blue, and closing, as Sidroc leaned his weight behind his spear shaft and made another, more grievous hole in the iron rings over the heart.

He straightened up to see Bjarne and Asberg finish off a staggering thegn, quick thrusts of their spears striking at the man's belly and back at nearly the same instant. Asberg was facing Sidroc, and pulling away from the shared kill with Bjarne, called out a word of praise to Sidroc for what he had seen him do.

A horse, bolting and dragging its downed rider with it, made Sidroc jump back. A glance up and down the road told that the battle would soon be over. The cries and battle-yells of warring men, and the distressed whinnying and calling of their beasts had fallen away. The horses were now stamping and snorting as they circled in a small clearing off the side of the road, tossing their heads and worrying their bits. Reins trailed on the ground, and some had lost their saddles or wore them askew over their lathered flanks.

To one side of him Sidroc saw one of the men from Yellow-sail go down, his shield splintered into four pieces under the hacking of a helmeted thegn whose sword work was as fast as his arm was strong. The Saxon warrior was well-protected, wearing a ring-tunic as well. After delivering a killing thrust the thegn sprang away, seemingly fleeing.

Many of the men upon the ground, Saxons and Danes alike, were beyond any sound. Those who still lived tried to raise themselves to their knees, find a weapon, crawl to safety.

It was that last stage of any contest, when time began to slow. Sidroc found himself drawing breath, deep lungs-full of it, not the panting gasps which had powered his movements just minutes before. He was whole and sound. He had killed two men. Some of their own number were dead, but their losses were scant next to the destroyed troop of thegns.

Looking down the road he saw big red-headed Jari straighten up from the kill he pulled his sword from. A moment later Jari was no longer alone. A Saxon thegn ran to him, and Jari found himself engaged anew. Sidroc was heading for him when he heard Jari's scream. He could not see what had happened, only that Jari had dropped his blade. Sidroc was not alone in watching this. As Jari staggered backwards another red-haired Dane appeared, running with all speed to aid his brother. Une favoured his skeggox as weapon and it had bitten into Saxon flesh several times this day. The steel handle of it was long, giving him the same reach as the sword the Saxon swung. Both men had shields and both were sure in their ability.

As Sidroc neared, he saw the Saxon facing Une was the same he had earlier seen face the man from Yellow-sail, destroying first his shield and then his life. The thegn no longer wore his ring-tunic. In the extremes of combat warriors sometimes flung off their protective ring-shirts, to save their strength and give them speed. This thegn had been one of them.

Sidroc knew him to be the same man, ring-shirt or no. It was his expert sword-work that marked him, that and his helmet, one whose eye-protectors were boldly set off by projecting eyebrows of steel.

It took four blows from the Saxon, as Une countered with shield and a single swing of his battle-axe. The thegn got in, hammering high on Une's shield, the steel of the blade clanging against the iron rim of the wooden disc. Then that blade retreated for a single heartbeat before rising again to strike Une's head at the ear.

Une's helmet flew off, skipping through the air like a stone thrown by a boy onto water. He made no sound, only toppled sideways and to the ground. Sidroc was nearly there and felt the impact of his large frame as he landed. As Sidroc reached the spot he shook off his shield and helmet, dropped his spear, and plucked at the skeggox lying at Une's feet.

Jari, seeing all, was sitting in the road, the howl now coming from his throat sounding like that of a dying hound.

The thegn fled, sword extended, down the road. Sidroc leapt after. He was burdened with his heavy ring-shirt, slowing him, but an unaccountable vigour coursed through his long legs, powering him forward in great springing steps.

Gripping Une's weapon he chased the thegn, then paused to steady his arm and let fly the axe at the retreating Saxon. He uttered a single cry as he flung it, calling out the name of Tyr. The skeggox left his hand, stopping only when it sank into the thegn's back, between the shoulder blades. The head of the Saxon snapped back, the arms flailing as he crumpled face first to the hard surface of the road.

Sidroc took a sharp inhale of breath. He ran back to where Jari sat, passing Une on the way, glimpsing the bloody mass that had been his head. Jari was now silent, rocking forward trying to stand, holding his right hand in his left.

He held his bloody hand uplifted, but his eyes were fixed on the spot where his older brother lay sprawled. Jari's face was white as milk; even his freckles had paled, and his ruddy hair looked the redder on his blanched brow. He seemed unable to speak. Sidroc now saw what had made him drop his sword. The Saxon had got in a blow on the grip, severing the first two fingers of Jari's right hand, just at fist level.

The stumps were bleeding, but not badly; Sidroc could see the bone so revealed. He pulled his knife and ripped at the tail of Jari's tunic, cutting a strip with which to bind the maiming. As he worked to wrap the hand he saw, off to one side on the road, Jari's two fingers, the tips of them unbloodied.

Jari saw them too, his eyes leaving the mound that was his brother, to look at the two digits severed from his own body. There was horror in seeing them, and his eyes were as round as a child's. They wore the stilled look of the fevered, or of the dead. Sidroc began to fear he might go mad with shock of what he had witnessed, and what he had lost.

Jari's sword was not far off. Sidroc rose from where he had been squatting at his side and went and got it. He lowered himself back down, sword in hand, to look in Jari's glazed eyes.

"It is not over for you, Jari," he told him, his words low and urgent. "Here." He lifted Jari's left hand, made him take the sword hilt in it.

"Close your hand around it. You will fight as a Tyr-hand, kill many men this way."

The big head bowed, looking down at his left hand, a sword hilt lying in its palm for the first time. He looked back at Sidroc.

"Close your hand," Sidroc ordered.

The fingers of that hand curled around it.

Sidroc's own hand rose to his hair. His plaits were undone and he swept the dark strands away from his face. His eyes lifted to the sky, as they so often did when he looked for answer.

Jari lived, and he felt certain would fight again. But Une was dead.

Sidroc's first memory of Une was of a hothead who tried to steal his horse, the mare that Yrling prized and had left in his keeping. When he knew who Sidroc was he had laughed about the threat, showing Sidroc even at that young age how swiftly a single fact could change everything. Later Une was the first man to look him in the face, judge the scar on his cheek, and commend him for having already made the warrior's bargain, of risking injury for gain. In his way Une had given Sidroc a fresh identity, a new way to think about himself. Now Une had made the bargain himself, and for the last time.

Sidroc saw Yrling and Bjarne walking towards them. He made move to rise, glad to see that Jari tried to do the same. Sidroc took Jari's sword and helped him to his feet. It was the work of a few moments to unbuckle Jari's weapons belts, and rehang them, his sword scabbard on his right hip, his knife now on his left. He steadied the scabbard so that Jari himself could slide the sword within.

"Une is dead, and my fingers are gone," Jari told Yrling as he neared. He held up the bandaged hand, the shape of it telling all too well of the stumps beneath.

Yrling swore softly, almost under his breath. Une was a savvy warrior, fearless and strong, his size alone a deterrent. He was Yrling's friend, and second in command. Both Yrling and Sidroc would miss him. But Jari's loss had been far the greater, his elder brother dying after coming to his defence.

Yrling walked, flanked by Bjarne at his side, and Jari and Sidroc, to where Une lay.

He had fallen where the force of the blow had sent him, onto his left side. They took a glance down, and then away. It was hard to look at. The sword had struck the mid-point of the ear in its ascension, splitting the skull, revealing the brain-pan.

Yrling looked further down the road, to the body of the Saxon. Even from this distance it was clear it was Une's war-axe cleavered in the man's back.

They made their way to him. Yrling spent several moments looking down, studying the thegn's body. Both arms were splayed out, the legs akimbo. The axe head was buried deeply enough in the back that the leading edge vanished, the steel handle rising at an angle in the still air. Blood pooled on either side of the thegn's ribcage, the brilliant red of it staining his dark tunic brown. His helmet lay an arm's length ahead, where it had rolled off.

"Who killed him," Yrling wanted to know.

A lift of Sidroc's chin gave him the answer.

"And with Une's skeggox," Yrling noted. He gave a nod of his own at this act of justice. He looked down at the man. A wry laugh escaped his lips. "You have destroyed his linen tunic, but his ring-shirt is back there, where he threw it off. That is yours. His sword too."

Their eyes went to the naked weapon, just out of the reach of the outstretched fingers. There was no doubt of its worth. Everything about this thegn was of a quality matching his skill. The sword hilt was inlaid with silver wire, and the pommel also silvered. The blade itself was the real treasure, pattern-welded with so many layers of beaten bluish steel that they looked ripples of an endlessly receding tide.

There was something else about this sword, and Sidroc, who had watched it at work, felt it strongly as he looked down at it. The hand that had wielded it had great skill, a skill which might travel into cold metal and make it skillful of itself. This blade had slashed many men, and likely over many years. It had today taken Jari's fingers and

Une's life, and before it had done this the life of the man from Yellow-sail.

It had maimed a friend and felled another. The sword was Sidroc's to do with as he saw fit; he could snap the blade and kill the weapon as it had killed Une. But he could not serve it thus. This sword was like a half-wild horse which broke a man's neck. One did not kill the beast for that.

He walked past the dead Saxon, picked up the sword, claiming it. The skeggox would be given back to Une, but it was Sidroc's to pull from the back of the man he had killed with it. Yet he stopped and looked to Jari, gesturing that he be the one to pull his brother's axe from his killer.

To do so Jari must use his left hand. He bent over the body of the Saxon, closed his grasp upon the smooth steel shaft of the skeggox, and pulled. It was the second act he had performed as a Tyr-hand.

Jari nodded at him as he straightened up, the axe held firmly in his fist. He who he looked at could read much in Jari's eyes.

Sidroc had avenged Une's death, and Jari's hand. If he could give Jari hope, that was something worth the having, as well.

Toki now appeared before them, a smear of blood on his face, but the golden helmet on his head. He had passed Une's body on the way. In answer he spat on the ground.

"Sif," he breathed, knowing that yellow-haired Goddess' name would never more be attached to him.

"You," Yrling said, as Toki neared. "I would take the helmet, if you had not earned it. Do not cross my orders again."

"It was Odin," Toki returned. "Odin filled me, told me to do it."

Yrling took this in. It was hard to let anger rule him when things had turned out well; the death of Une was a blow, but mayhap he would have been called anyway. Toki was ever taking risks and this one had paid off. Killing the Saxon chief first and in front of all his men had upset any balance in the contest.

"No man knows how the Gods will point," he ended up telling his nephew. "If Odin guided your spear, so be it."

He looked along the length of the road, at his men alive and standing, at all the many thegns dead upon the road. "We have lost few men, and have won horses."

Their task now was to strip the bodies of the thegns, and to gather their own dead. Six of them had fallen. There was no time to build a pyre, and no dry wood with which to light it. But the stream and its boggy marshes was a fitting place to consign the bodies of their brethren. They carried the bodies to the reeds, set out their weapons on their chests and by their hands. To be left on or by water was almost as good as burning. Water could carry the spirit as surely as a ship could carry a body. It was Yrling and Sidroc who took up Une's body, and Jari who laid his weapons out, the skeggox at his brother's stilled right hand.

Then they must get off the road. They put Jari and the rest of the wounded on horseback. To speed their own walking they slung as many packs as they could on the saddles of the other beasts, and set off into the woods.

FOUR STONES

SUMMER reached its peak, and began to wane. The brilliant hues of marsh and forest deepened and then mellowed, softening as the weeks fell by. The great and arching canopies of elms and ashes loosed their leafy cover, and the unyielding oaks, always last to surrender their leaves, saw them blanch from bright green to pale brown. Rushes went gold where they sprang from the shine of muddy banks. Fogs and mists that shrouded lakes and lay above the stillness of meadows thickened. The days grew noticeably shorter, the Sun more hastily making its transit across skies blue or cloud-scudded. The nights turned colder, sharply so, and the damp of even the milder days felt chill.

After the victory at Beardan a new confidence and urgency filled the men. The horses they had won allowed them to send scouts about the countryside, searching out richer targets, larger farmsteads. Une's death meant Yrling must find others with whom to entrust his plans, and Sidroc and Toki had grown in importance and responsibility, always flanking their uncle in any action as his chief body-guard. Bjarne, Asberg, and Gizur were ever in this first rank as well, having survived unscathed through many raids, and distinguished themselves doing so.

Jari too came forth, not to stand in for his slain brother, but as one reliably found at Sidroc's left. The loss of Une had stunned him, and the loss of his sword-hand served as constant reminder. A kind of coarse tissue knit itself over the severed bones, closing the wounds, though with only thumb and two fingers intact the hand was at first of such limited use that he despaired of being fully able. Then Sidroc fashioned a new and larger grip on the inside of the steel boss on Jari's shield, one which his maimed hand could more readily grasp. He also took the forearm sling and re-hung it at the right side, for Jari's red-and-blue painted shield sported a kind of coiling cat on its leathern face, and could not be held upside down for sake of the design. Jari did not yet feel confident in any real sword work as a Tyr-hand, but with his spear in his left began to feel he might do great damage.

Of their number who had suffered hurt in the encounter at the abbey, Jari's was the only lasting injury. All must be able to fight, travel swiftly, fight again. There could be no weak links. They fought in an endless effort to keep their bellies full, and for their just share of the pile of silver treasure roped to the pack horse always following the stallion that Yrling now rode. That treasure could not be shared out until they had attained a hall.

There was much to hold them content against that day, for all the men had gained plunder. Toki, with his gilded helmet, wore his greatest prize each time he fought. And Sidroc, in the sheer number of men he had downed, found himself the possessor of goods the value of which had been beyond his ken a year ago.

He had won no fewer than four swords from warriors over whom he had triumphed. He had continued to use the one his uncle had given him aboard Yellow-sail; continued until he killed the Saxon thegn who had killed Une. Then he took that sword with its silvered hilt as his working weapon. It was not only the sheer beauty of the thing, but the fact that it had dropped from the hand of a swordsman as skilled as that thegn. It had been his favoured weapon and was now that of Sidroc. The rippled blue steel of the blade bore marks, not runes, but marks he could not read. An outline of an animal too had been etched there; a fish. Sidroc had not considered a fish any sign of power, but thinking on it, saw how apt one might be for the sleek and flashing beauty of this blade in motion. Knowing the Saxon had marked the sword this way gave it more allure.

Of treasure in arms it was his chief spoil. He also favoured the man's helmet with its standing eye-brows of steel, but kept as well that from the first warrior he had felled, the one whose silver chain he had claimed.

Beyond this he had gained three closely-linked ring-shirts, the worth of any of them above his reckoning. It was one of the pieces of war-gear that was easier killed for than saved for, he knew, and he had pondered this oddity when he had first seen its truth. He kept the largest of them, the better to fit his rangy frame. The others found ready takers amongst his brethren who lacked them, always eager for a layer of linked steel rings to lay over their tunics of leather. He traded with other men for what he wanted and needed, often clothes and always shoes and low boots, which he went through quickly. He had won as well much jewellery, large circular pins of bronze with which to fasten the neck of a thick woollen mantle, and smaller, finely worked pins of silver. Of silver too he had taken from the dead or won in trade the carved clasps and keepers of buckles, broad wrist cuffs and narrow circling arm bands, necklets which ended in animal heads, and finger-rings of slender twisted silver rod. He kept all this by in a pig-skin sack, building his store of portable treasure.

The act of lifting spear or sword against another man was now couched in the surety of his skill. He belonged here, an adept warrior amongst brethren. When the stakes were so high it did not take many victories to begin to think winning came as it should to him. He had proved himself as a warrior, to his own watching self, to his uncle, to the men he fought alongside; and most vitally of all, to his full-trúi, Tyr. He had given himself to Tyr, and felt himself now worthy of that God's eyes upon him. Each time he slipped his red-and-black spiral painted shield on his left arm, his eyes fell on the bind rune he had carved within, uniting his sign with that of the God [rune]. Slipping his forearm into the sling, closing his hand around the grip in the domed centre boss, it looked back at him. He never lunged forward, weapon at the ready, without first calling out the name of Tyr, asking for his notice, dedicating his skill to him.

He began to know that eyes other than the God's were sometimes on him. He could now, by his presence, by his look, force an opponent to pick another to square off against. After any contest, when they had won food and drink and silver plunder, boasts went around the fire they gathered at. Often those of greatest prowess said the least. Others spoke for them, making of their actions Saga tales of no little glory, one all the war-band shared in. More than once Sidroc was spoken of this way by his brethren.

To be a warrior of repute was what he had come for, that and the treasure he was now beginning to acquire.

The sense of command he now felt sprang from the first thegn he had killed, one taken more by his cunning than his knife blade. He would need both to survive, and to thrive, and he had been taught that in this first warrior kill. That triumph could have been instead his death, and the dragon on his chest was reminder of this. He gave more silver to Aki, who continued to work at odd times on pricking the dragon there. He darkened the outline along its lithe body, and the fangs descending from the gaping jaws were made solid blue, the act of much painful puncturing to render them thus. Aki had used his red ochre to mark an eye of red, completing the beast.

The weeks wore on, from strike to strike, the war-band always seeking greater plunder. But treasure in steel or silver could not keep them moving. Only food could do that, and it was becoming more difficult to find.

During deep harvest time the farms that they struck at had offered up their greatest gains. Store houses were full to overflowing with barley and rye, and wheat too from the richer holdings. Grapes, apples, pears, and medlars sat in baskets, ready to be laid by in cold cellars, or sliced and dried in the still-bright sunshine. Butter was being salted by farmwives to make it last longer into those months when the cows could give nothing so rich. Sometimes a pot of thick and golden honey might be found, the discovery of which caused almost as much glee as good ale or even mead. Yet whatever they carried off in stolen bounty was not enough.

Treasure though he had gained, Sidroc had never known hunger as he had these past few months; none of them had. All of them had been raised on the land, and lived by the rhythm of the seasons. Late Winter and early Spring were ever lean times on any farm, whether in Dane-mark or Angle-land. The stores of smoked and brined meat were by then exhausted, grain bins almost empty, hens not yet laying. Nothing fresh, green, or succulent had been consumed for months. The arrival of the first peas was celebrated, relished as a treat by all. Yrling's men had known this kind of annual privation, their entire lives. It ended in a burst of abundance: cows giving rich and fatty milk from which butter could be churned, ewes yielding tangy milk to render into cheeses. But the kind of nearly daily want they had all suffered since arriving here had been unknown to them. They gorged on what they took, followed sometimes by days of gnawing hunger.

Bjarne was still in charge of their food stores, a difficult task given the number he must keep at least half-fed. To augment what was carried off from farms they foraged lamb's lettuce, clary, dill, and cresses, to shred upon the endless bowls of boiled grain which was their daily fare. They plucked wild berries and apples and plums as they travelled. But these things were coming to an end, as the days grew both short and dark.

And more Danes joined them. They met them on the road, some stragglers cut off from a retreating body of raiders; others the disaffected who had abandoned their war-chiefs, as the men they had met at the gates of the coast-guard had forsaken theirs. There were also those who had been driven off by their war-chiefs, just as Yrling drove a few of his own away.

The number of horses in their train grew as well. Yrling had claimed a stallion for his own, and let his nephews next take their pick; they were all good riders. Others were also awarded mounts, as Yrling saw fit. Once a few of them were horsed it was easy to steal others, and whenever they were spotted in pasture or paddock they swept through and took them. These beasts, long legged and long necked, were much the better of the stubby ponies of Jutland, recalling in their fineness Yrling's prized chestnut mare from here. They had need of their swiftness, for they must keep driving onward.

At times they found old stone ruins to camp in, roofless walls rising to an empty sky. Other nights were spent sleeping in the shadows of the mounded barrows of the great chieftains of the past. Yet of real shelter there was none.

However hidden they might stay, other Danes began seeking them out. They were enough strong now, over eighty men, that they would camp several nights in succession in the same forest glade or shrub-bound clearing, any place that offered water for their horses and themselves.

On one such night, they settled in a wood, heavy with now-bare elms and ashes, through which a stream coursed. Their meal was still cooking, the first of the day, barley and smoked pig simmering in a collection of small iron cauldrons over their fire. The light was just beginning to dim in the skies when they heard a whistle through the trees, loud and full of purpose. They were all upon their feet, almost in a single motion, when a voice cried out, one in their own tongue.

"A Dane seeks a Dane," it rang.

Their weapons were at the ready as they turned to the trees from whence the called issued.

"Show yourself," Yrling answered, his sword drawn, and Gizur with a nocked arrow at his side.

A man stepped forward, with six others ranged behind. They kept their distance, and held their spears at the ready. They had fair war-kit, to a man; and each had as well a pack slung from his back, telling those they approached all they owned they carried.

The one in the lead spoke. "I am Gudmund of Laaland, seeking Yrling."

"Who you have found," Yrling answered. He was not unaware of the distinction, which came as a surprise. He had won some little fame already, so that others sought him out by name.

The seven before them looked able enough, hale and whole. The uncertainty of their reception meant that even their helmets were upon their heads, but they all sported them, as well as ring-shirts. These were no beggars.

"Come in, brothers," Yrling told them, gesturing with his drawn sword that they near. Room was made for them, and they approached the centre of the encampment where Yrling and his chief men stood. There was no ale to offer, their meal not yet ready to be ladled up. But blades were re-sheathed, and the newcomers set down their packs and stood amongst them, looking about at the faces of Yrling and his men. The smell of the boiling barley rose about them, and by the way their guests need force their eyes away from the source of the aroma, it was easy to see they were as hungry as their hosts. The horses were off beyond, many standing at the stream, noses lowered to the water. The newcomers took these in, as well.

Yrling let them look, and then spoke.

"How did you find us?"

"As many head of horse as you have are easy to track," came Gudmund's answer.

Yrling gave a grunt in response. He was more than aware that the greater his troop of men became, the more difficult it was to conceal them. Hoof prints were left in soft ground. Any good tracker could find an entry point where they had led their beasts into the densest of forest growth. Horses even in single file broke twigs and branches, left behind scat.

"And why are you here?" came his next question.

Gudmund was ready with an answer. "To throw in with you." He let a moment pass, one in which the eyes of all were upon him and the six he spoke for. "We have fought with some of the best. But Winter comes, and we are only seven."

These newcomers lacked just what Yrling and his own men lacked, shelter against the coming cold.

"And what do you bring me, other than more bellies to fill?" Yrling posed next.

Gudmund took no offence, but his answer was ready. "You will not often find arms like ours," he began, looking about at the six he headed. "Beyond that, I can lead you to a keep here in Lindisse that will be worth the having."

Gudmund paused long enough that Yrling gestured with his hand to go on. His guest now had his shield on his back, and hooked one thumb in his belt as he told his tale.

"There is a Saxon lord a two days' ride from here, Merewala by name. His hall is known as Four Stones; the base is built of rock. His holding is a large one, with forest as well as plains. He has been too strong to take, but with this many men . . . "

"You have seen this place?"

"Já. I was one who walked the base of the tall palisade by night. The gates are the strongest I have seen, defended inside by a high parapet. But there is a small door in the back of the palisade. It opens to the kitchen yard; I could tell by the noise within."

There it was, target and plan in one. A sham attack at the palisade gates would divert attention from the real attack at the rear, through the kitchen yard door.

"What more do you know?" Yrling asked next.

Gudmund glanced at those flanking him. "Three of us were outriders, and spent more than a full day watching the keep. But the place was too strong for Tume, the chief we fought with. We returned, told him all we had seen. He would not show himself, turned his back on it."

"So you turned yours on Tume," Yrling summed. He was listening, head tilted back, arms folded. Gudmund went on.

"Merewala has fame among the men of these parts," Gudmund offered. "His grown sons are dead, but his warring men are many; thegns they are called here. Also he has a daughter; she is a princess of the place."

Yrling's eyes shifted to Gudmund; this man knew much.

"The village fronting Four Stones has folk beyond number living there. Part of all they raise and grow they give to Merewala."

There would be no want of food in such a place. This alone would seal his decision, but it seemed Four Stones had much more to offer him as well: a ready-made hall and garrison, even a woman for him to wed, assuring the village folk's allegiance to their new Danish lord.

"A two days' ride," Yrling repeated. He looked again at Gudmund and his companions, fit, hardened, and risk-taking enough to present themselves to him. "As reward you will flank my chief men, be the first to storm the place."

This declaration of coming action was met by all listeners with acclaim, voices and arms raised in assent.

Later, as they spooned their supper into their mouths, Yrling thought to ask the well-travelled Gudmund another question.

"Do you know of Gorm of Aros?"

Gudmund shook his head. "Who is he?"

"A thief who will soon die, by my hand, or Odin's will," came the answer.

Yrling knew Gorm was likely long back in Denmark, with his stolen ships. But at least this knowledge was some satisfaction. His own fame had reached Gudmund's ears, and nothing of Gorm.

Two days on horseback brought them to the threshold of the hall known as Four Stones. They did not push their animals, for each was heavy laden, most with both man and goods. But being as many as they were allowed them to ride openly on the pounded clay roads Gudmund led them to. For any of those who had stood with Yrling on the deserted beach, swearing over the loss of their ships, this was no small moment, to now be of a moving force large enough to fear none.

They had reached deep in the heart of Lindisse, a land of tree-covered hills unspooling into the distance, of broad plains showing themselves verdant even as the chill of Winter lay there. Signs of the approaching keep were clear. The road grew broader through use, but no deeper the ruts, showing Merewala's care. The red clay under their feet began to rise, and this was sign to Gudmund that they leave it, take to the wood skirting the pastures that would soon lie before them.

They did so. The Sun had passed its highest point in a day both clouded and chilly. They entered the trees on foot, pulling their mounts deep enough within the bare growth to be hidden from the village they now glimpsed through the screening branches. They could at times see folk about, digging up late turnips or skirrets, or working in their wattle-rimmed crofts. The houses within each were small, but sturdy-looking enough, and the number of sheep and cattle in the common pastures was beyond ready counting. On the far side of the road, and close to the fortress itself, a small pond lay, its grey surface shifting in the breeze that ruffled it. At times a dog barked, but none betrayed them by racing across the fields in discovery of those who made their slow progress through the trees.

The palisade surrounding the hall and its buildings did indeed impress. It was twice the height of that of the fort of the coast-guard, a massive and blank face on the village. A doubled gate for entry sat at the end of the clay road they had abandoned. Those gates were closed.

No warriors were about, either outside the gates or upon the parapet, but the fact the gates were shut in midday was proof of the wariness of those within. Still, the village folk went on at their daily tasks, unconcerned, so no warning of danger had been issued.

They moved on, needing to draw their horses deeper into the trees to keep themselves hidden as they neared the side walls of the enclosing palisade. The ground dropped away, as if the back of the keep were set on a ledge of some kind. But before they retreated fully into the wood, Gudmund was able to point out the rising of ground just past this, where the door opening into the kitchen yard lay.

Finding water was easy; a spring of some sort ran from the ledge Four Stones sat upon, and they followed it until it opened into a clearing large enough to admit them all. Much daylight was still in the sky, put to good use by four of them sent to fell and fetch a tree suited for use as the battering ram they would need upon the morrow. It was a young ash they chose. Lopping off the branches they left several carefully spaced and sturdy bough-ends as hand-holds to help in propelling the shaft forward and against the door.

They lit no fire that night, as near as they were the risk of discovery was too great. They had boiled up barley that morning just for this reason, and now ate it, in cold and congealed lumps, as they made what all hoped was their final camp under the stars. Such a meal, eaten by men who know that some of their number would not live to see another dusk, is best enlivened by ale. This night the chill water of the spring was their only drink.

Yrling had already detailed the plan to all. One third of them would set off, back through the trees in the morning, gain the road, and come at a gallop down it. The main body of his men would stay with him, at the keep's rear, waiting to burst through the small kitchen yard door.

The scheme had its hazards, particularly for those breaking in. No more than two could enter through the doorway at one time, making it far easier for his men to be picked off by warriors within. The breadth of the main gates would allow for as many as a rank of ten to enter, but Yrling did not feel Fate would favour them with the chance to cross over that broad threshold.

Now Yrling would pick those men to lead the group riding through the village.

"Toki. You and Bjarne will lead the men at the front gates. Stay well back, in the village, as if you seek only food stores. See if you can draw them out."

Leading this group was an honour objected to by Toki. "I want to be with you at the back, and gain entry first."

Yrling was not to be swayed. This nephew was rash, dangerously so.

"Then we both run the risk of Odin speaking to you, and you disobeying my orders. And perhaps you will die this time because of it, by the hand of All-Father. Or my own."

This silenced Toki, though his eyes darted left and right along the circle of men he sat with. His gaze came to rest on Sidroc, who he knew would be part of the assault at the rear door. Sidroc's eyes, a dark flint blue, met his cousin's much brighter ones for an instant before turning back to their uncle. Sidroc had learnt much over the years from Yrling, and this single small decision was in his eyes a good one.

Toki did not ken his own value as part of the decoy; his uncle saw this, as did Sidroc. Toki could be counted on to make great show of his sham attack, tearing down the road of pounded clay, waving his spear above his head, war-whoops ringing from his throat. It was the way he preferred to meet any enemy, calling as much attention to himself and the attack as possible. His uncle had found the perfect role for him.

Yrling continued his directive to Toki and Bjarne. "If you can draw them out, get them to open the gates, then begin to run, so they give chase. The fewer within the keep when we enter, the quicker our work."

Yrling now addressed all.

"This fortress will be well defended," he noted.

All Gudmund had told them seemed true, and after seeing the height of the palisade he had no reason to doubt any of what their lately joining brethren had said.

"Once inside, secure the place."

The assurance with which he gave this simple order lay rooted in the confidence he held in the men gathered about him. The task would be difficult; they would achieve it.

His thoughts moved on, beyond conquest to reward.

"The princess of the hall, the daughter of Merewala – do not touch her. She will be my wife."

Some of the men's eyes flicked through the gloaming towards the walls, unseen through the trees that sheltered them. Their war-chief's pronouncement sealed it. This then would be the end of their many months' wandering.

"No fire," Yrling went on. "Four Stones is mine. It is our home; Odin will make it so. And I will be Jarl." He had been standing as he spoke, slowly pacing before his men as he thought.

He stopped now, swept his eyes along the men he fronted. Then he lifted both arms into the air of the dimming day, and made his vow. "Odin will have an ox in Offering for his help."

The pale streaks of a chilly dawn began to lighten the sky as the two parties set out.

Toki, Bjarne, and the score with them moved off through the trees, to work their way back to the road from whence they would make their run at the village. Gizur too would be one of their number. He had proven he could aim from a cantering horse with a trueness almost matching that from a standstill.

The others, more than sixty men strong, formed up by pairs. Six were chosen by Yrling to carry and wield the ash trunk which would batter down the door. As soon as it was breached Yrling and Sidroc would step through, followed by Asberg and Jari. Gudmund and his men would come on their heels. All others would follow, two by two, a doubled column which once inside must be ready for any obstacle, in a place entirely unknown to them.

They crept out of the trees, working their way down the dropping grade behind the palisade, until they reached level ground and the small door Gudmund had told them of. It was stoutly built, strapped over with iron banding, with hinges safely on the inside to prevent tampering by any without. They gathered by it, those who would hoist the battering ram ready to lift it against its strength.

From the other side they could just hear the sounds of the awakening kitchen yard, a muffled clatter of moving griddle pans, and a voice too, seemingly of an old woman, singing to herself, perhaps as she stood over the pot she stirred.

They waited, it felt, a long time, though the slowness with which the sky lightened told them it was not. They must not act until Toki and Bjarne had drawn the warriors within to action.

A horn sounded, in some mid-distance, a sharp and sudden rent in the dawn stillness. Outside and at the rear of the huge enclosure as they were, it was still unmistakable, and all snapped to attention at its summons. Yrling silently gestured that the men who had been reaching for the ash trunk leave off until he signalled. They must wait, not betraying their presence, behind the kitchen yard door. Only when they were certain the attentions of the warriors within were focussed on the threat to the village outside the front gates could they themselves act. Merewala's warriors must be given enough time to be drawn away by the sham attack.

The sounding of the horn alarmed all in the kitchen yard. In the silence that followed the woman who had been singing left off. Cries and gasps were heard. Yells rang out, the sudden movement of scraping metal. Doors slammed.

They kept waiting, picturing the action within. As early as it was, all would be confusion inside; some just tumbling out of their alcoves when the horn alerted them.

The horn again. This could be a rallying-call, a troop of men now ready to storm out the gates after those invaders in the midst of the village.

"Now," ordered Yrling. He and his chief men moved away from the door.

Sidroc had time to turn to Jari and Asberg, who would be just behind him.

"Fight well," he told them, something they had before said as they headed into a contest. It was hope and blessing both.

Sidroc's sword was drawn and in his hand, that blade of blue steel from the thegn who had killed Une. He looked at Jari, spear in his left hand, blue-and-red shield on his right, the cat on it dancing in an endless circling dance. It took getting used to, seeing a man's shield held in the right, just as the darting action of a spear point coming from the left could surprise you. Surprise always served a warrior well. Jari may have lost some fingers, but had gained this.

Asberg too had chosen spear today. He had neither Sidroc's height nor Jari's size, but was blessed with a nimbleness of movement that made facing him as a spearman a daunting task. He had spent no little time sparring with Jari over the many weeks Jari had been reborn as a Tyr-hand.

They nodded, each to each, all three; touched the rims of their shields together.

The palisade loomed before them. The taking of this fortress would be their greatest challenge yet. Sidroc gave another look at the two. Any of them could die, or all. He felt moved to say one thing more.

"If not this hall, then Asgard."

The eyes of the three again met. Those who would die would await their brothers there.

Six pair of strong arms ran at speed with the heavy ram, colliding with the iron-strapped door. A recoil from the stoutness of the oak the door had been built with did not mask the sound of shattering wood; the door was old. It took one more attempt to pierce, great splinters bristling forth as the ram was withdrawn. Axes hewed away the boards, then reaching hands gripped and pulled what remained apart. A single board on the hinge side was left standing.

Yrling and Sidroc leapt through, the others rushing in behind them.

The cooking folk, alarmed by the warning from the palisade gates, had already taken up the tools of their trade as weapons. Now the invaders were in their very midst. A strong-armed cook held a butchery knife, the brawn in his arms showing he had full skill in using it. Bakers, both men and women, snatched at long and lethal oven pokers. Kitchen women used to stirring cauldrons of earthy vegetables and grain wielded long-handed ladles, toasting forks, and griddle pans. Slaves of the keep, hauling wood or scraping out cold ovens, stood open-mouthed, but reached for any stave of wood or piece of iron to defend themselves.

The war troop ignored them, stopping only to down those who would impede their progress. Some folk ran in fear. Others showed defiant love of their hall and their lord, made clear in the way that they threw themselves in the path of the invaders, flung pots or burning brands of firewood at them. Men and women, free and slaves both, were swept down, falling in an upwelling of shrieks and oaths.

Sidroc was aware that Jari and Asberg had moved up with him and Yrling to form a single line as they ran through the kitchen yard. With their spear points foremost his two friends were like the thrusting tusks of a boar, flanking uncle and nephew.

Then Asberg staggered against Sidroc, almost tripping him. Yrling and Jari were slightly ahead and kept on running. Sidroc should go on too, keep pace with his uncle.

He did not. He regained his balance, turned to see Asberg on his knees upon the ground. Just behind him Sidroc saw the cause of it. A simple stone, one that likely ringed the cooking fire, had been hurled, and with good aim. Asberg's helmet was still on, but by the way he hung his head it was clear the missile had struck him there. Gaining on them was the cook with the long butchery knife, a blade as sure to kill a man as quarter a beast.

Asberg was able to raise his head slightly, no more. Behind the iron openings of his helmet his eyes were dazed. "Stand, stand," urged Sidroc, all he had time to say.

The cook had lifted his arm above his shoulder, ready to fling the knife at the target of Asberg's back. But before the man let fly the knife, Sidroc jumped behind the kneeling Asberg, to face the running cook. Bracing his shield arm before him the blade struck it low, its point puncturing the hardened leather cover and burying itself a little way into the alder wood of Sidroc's shield. It hung there, vibrating, until Sidroc knocked it free with the flat of his sword.

The cook got no further; Gudmund and his fellows were just behind. And the knife meant for Asberg's back now lay on the pounded soil of the hall yard.

Sidroc turned to Asberg, saw how he shook his head as if to clear it. "Come," ordered Sidroc. Using his spear shaft as a staff Asberg rose to his feet. The butchery knife lay there, harmless, and there was a new mar in Sidroc's shield of red-and-black. A bob of Asberg's yellow head was all the thanks he could muster.

They moved off together, through work yards filled with running warriors, shrieking women, and crying children. Yrling and Jari were just ahead, pausing to look left and right between buildings. They caught up to them there. The hall of Four Stones was on their left, easy to mark from its size and its rock walls. It was built part way up of blocks of creamy sandstone, capped with another floor of upright timber, upon which sat a roof thickly thatched. Just opposite it was a building of nearly equal size, all of timber, but sporting a roof of dull grey lead sheets, such had crowned the monk's temple at Beardan. But the treasure of this building was its horses, for it was a stable-block, and a mass of men were clustered at its opened doors and by the adjoining paddock, saddling their mounts or swinging up upon them.

Directly before them, past both hall and stable, stood the palisade. Its broad gates were wide open. They could see the parapet running above the gates, upon which men stood, looking out, and looking back at the disorder behind them.

As Sidroc and Asberg gained the spot where Yrling and Jari stood the horn sounded a third time. This was a different note, doubtless calling back those men who had ridden after the village attackers.

Yrling threw a look over his shoulder, left and right, to see his men filling in around him. They came from behind buildings great and small, skirting workshops, running, spears and swords foremost, along the inside of the great palisade, which had in places small structures built up against the planks of it. The confusion about them was great.

The warriors of Merewala were dressed and equipped just as the thegns of the coast-guard and the defenders of the abbey had been. But they had been surprised by a doubled attack, one struck at dawn when many were still abed. The shock of the invading assault was everywhere apparent. Some of the defenders were still in the act of outfitting themselves, buckling on weapons belts, even pulling on shoes. Those first horsed had been sent after the invaders in the village, but now many more enemy warriors were amongst them, and in the fastness of the keep.

The horn kept sounding the order of return, for through the gates a number of horsemen still in the village were seen to turn their mounts, only to be now pursued by those they had ridden out against.

Of those clustered before the invaders one man stood out. He was at the mouth of the stable, in the act of placing his foot in the stirrup of a great chestnut-red horse. Other warriors were about him, all on good horses, but none matched the worth of the red stallion this man was mounting. The horse's head was being held by a stable man, but it did not keep the beast from tossing its arched neck, and neighing in alarm at all about it.

It did not take Yrling or any of his men more than an instant to name this rider as Merewala, Lord of Four Stones. Grey hair, still abundant and long, streamed from under a helmet fitted with a standing crest on which a boar of steel ran. A beard, also grey and thick, lay upon the looped rings of his ring-tunic, one polished so that every link shone in the rising beams of day. Despite hair and beard there was nothing feeble about him; of his fifty-odd years each were worn well. He may have lost his sons but nothing had softened him.

Merewala now saw them. He pulled his foot from the stirrup to face a line of Danes, here before his very hall. He quit his horse and stared at this affront, the men who had been ready to ride with him doing so also.

Yrling was flanked on one side by sword-bearing Sidroc, and the other by Jari, wielding his spear. Two men of great size, on either hand of their chief. The Lord of Four Stones took them in.

Utter outrage broke on Merewala's face. As he took a step towards the invaders, Yrling screamed out his battle-cry. Oaths and the names of Gods fell from the lips of all his men. Sidroc called out Tyr's name. Asberg, still shaken from the head-blow, found his thoughts steadied behind his two-part war-cry.

Merewala pulled his sword from his baldric to meet the onrushing sword proffered by Yrling. The act of grasping his weapon, revealing it to those he would send to their deaths with it, wrought a kind of spell on the older man. Merewala's face contorted in a fearsome grimace that even the half mask of his helmet could not disguise. Sidroc, looking on him and the hand that grasped the sword, was recalled to the story of a weapon so thirsty for blood that it could never be re-sheathed without killing a man. Merewala's rage was of that ilk.

Such fury told the men he rushed towards that this might be a warrior who could transform himself. His outer form, his hamr, was but his earthly vessel. Some warriors and shamans were so touched by the Gods they could call on another form granted to them, their hugr, their deepest essence. Merewala looked this moment an úlfshugr, one who had form as a man, but the nature of a wolf. It was the wolf who ruled him now.

The two lines of warriors lunged at each other. About them horses which had been left in the act of being saddled or mounted wheeled and turned, shying and whinnying. Sidroc glimpsed Merewala's thegns galloping back through the opened gates. Right on their heels was their own troop; even at this distance Toki's gilt helmet could be picked out. And Gizur rode at his side, bow extended, planting arrows in the backs of Merewala's retreating men, knocking them from their horses.

After this Sidroc saw no more than the weapons of those Saxons he faced. He had, he thought, been fully tested in the past. The conquest of the fort of the coastguard, and the victory over the thegns at Beardan had set him against the seasoned veterans of many contests. Now he saw that few he had faced had the prowess of these men of Merewala. Surprise or no, they fought with a skill and determination that had marked the best of those they had overcome.

These thegns of Four Stones had as well their anger to fuel their actions. The same outrage that Merewala betrayed was shared by all of them; this was their home under attack.

The same need – that of a home, for shelter from the coming depths of Winter – powered the attackers. There might not be so rich a target in all of Lindisse, and now it was within their reach.

The fighting raged in a blur of movement about Sidroc. For the first time in battle he did not feel the pounding of his heart, or hear his own laboured breathing as he slashed and hacked his way through the men he faced. He had screamed out the name of Tyr as he had begun, but after that he kept a silence as profound as it was deadly. Something moved in him, some reserve, some animal power of his own. His right arm felt an extension of his sword, he could not feel his own fingers closed about the hilt. He and the blade became as one, cold steel made warm in his strong and ardent grip.

Later he would think of this and wonder if Tyr himself had entered his arm. There was something beyond him, made his, as he fought.

Rising from a man he had delivered a killing thrust to he saw Jari, moving off to his left, and Asberg, at the end of a doubled line of warriors, spearing those who were unprotected on their flank. Yrling was before him and to his right, squared off in combat with Merewala. Sidroc saw Jari and Asberg move to either side of Yrling, fending off with their spear-work the closest body-guards of Merewala, so that he and Yrling remained locked, together and alone.

Sidroc could not look long; two thegns sprang forward at him, one on either side. They were a spearman and swordsman, of unequal height, adding to the challenge of facing two men at once. The taller held the spear. A broader and altogether more powerful man gripped a sword. Their round shields were well pocked with signs of the biting blades they had resisted.

The spear came up at Sidroc's head with lightning speed. He swung his own shield up, pivoting on his heel away. He had his sword extended as he whirled; he might catch the swordsman with it to his right. Instead the swordsman's own shield met his blade along its edge, as the thegn behind that shield lunged at him. Sidroc was knocked off his feet.

There was no danger so great as being knocked to the ground in battle. There a man could fall prey to a spear thrust or sword hack issued by any warrior who neared. A man so downed could fall prey too to being trampled upon by accident, or purposely having their life crushed out of them. Sidroc fell, the slowness of his motion through the air belying the smacking solidity of his landing.

The contact with the hard ground opened his throat. He was down, and never so vulnerable for it. He gave a roar in denial, a roar of dissent. As he did so he watched the spearman take aim, ready to plunge his spear point into his prostrate body.

Sidroc's yell channeled his quickness. He had fallen on his back between the two thegns, his sword dropping from his hand as he landed. By putting his left foot on the ground and bending his knee he was able to traction his movement to twist his body. He gripped his shield with vice-like strength, pulling it over his torso as best he could. With his empty sword hand he grabbed the calf of the swordsman and toppled him forward, almost upon him. The spear point driving down on him met the body of the thegn, and not his.

He heard the gasp of the thegn he had pulled down, and the oath of the spearman over them.

Sidroc was on his knees in an instant, freeing himself from the dying thegn. His sword was partly obscured by the man's body. He could pluck at one end of the guard and pull it out.

The tall spearman gaped in disbelief at what he had done, his fellow convulsed, back arched, on the ground before him. He had withdrawn his spear point, but it had already chased life away. The spearman leapt closer, anger clouding his face. Sidroc was still rising to his feet when he slashed his sword across the tops of the man's unprotected knees.

The hack was deep enough to fell the man. He dropped forward, a doubled issue of blood pouring from his legs. Sidroc, now fully up, needed only a moment more to thrust his sword blade into the spearman's back. Both thegns lay still, and nearly atop each other.

He shook his head to clear it. Downed, he had caused the death of two thegns, and almost at once. Let your opponent help you, he thought.

His hand was warm and wet, slick with blood which spurted from the slash he had delivered. He wiped it best he could on the wool of his legging.

Yrling and Merewala were framed in the doorway of the stable, filling the yawning opening as they fought. Jari and Asberg were still there, engaged with those of the body-guard that lived. Sidroc would go to them, see if he could tip the balance. He would not intrude on his uncle's contest unless he saw Yrling falter. Taking the strides he needed to near he felt no little awe for these two warriors, hacking away all this time without giving ground. They traded blows, blocking with their shields, at times feinting with their blades in an attempt to deceive the other. The Lord of Four Stones was of an age to be Yrling's father, yet the passion with which he wielded sword and shield in no way placed him in the shade of the younger man.

An unexpected feint by Yrling allowed him to get in a touch, and more than a touch. His blade made contact with Merewala's forearm. The old warrior screamed out his wrath. His leathern tunic beneath his ring-tunic covered only his body; on his arms the linked metal lay only upon linen. A seam of bright red blood now opened on that strong forearm.

Bloodied, Merewala fought like a cornered wolf. He jumped forward at Yrling, sword flashing, teeth bared, veins in his neck throbbing. An instant later he stood as if frozen. His face, flushed red from ire and exertion, went grey. A bloom of leaden hue spread from his neck, up his chin and cheeks, and under the eye holes of his helmet. If the wolf was in him, perhaps he was coming forth, and he would shape-shift before them all.

But no, the hand of the Lord of Four Stones, still clutching his sword, rose to his chest, then his throat, mouth opening, eyes agog. The old warrior was not ready to stop, but his heart had known enough. He swayed, and with a shudder, fell to the ground.

Yrling had stepped back, eyes fastened on the toppling lord.

Sidroc, now at Yrling's side, watched, transfixed; they all did. Merewala's men gave up a wail in answer to the falling of their war-chief.

There was, mayhap, no need for Yrling's sword-thrust. The man was dying of a failed heart, having given his utmost in defence of Four Stones. Yet Yrling must be certain; there must be no doubt. He would not rend the fine ring-tunic; the mercy-thrust was at Merewala's throat.

Yrling straightened up over the body. The Lord of Four Stones was dead.

Those watching, even those fighting, gave pause a moment, eyes moving from the body of Merewala to the Dane who stood triumphant over it. This was the new lord.

Their war-chief dead, their hall overrun, the thegns took their final stand. They fought in clusters of three or four, numbers easily surrounded and dispatched by the ever-circling invaders. The broad palisade gates were still open. None of the thegns broke and ran for it; there was nowhere to run to, no lord to honour, fight for, or be rewarded by. They fought on in stable and work yard, by cooking ring and animal pen. No horn sounded, bringing the sorrowful news that Merewala was dead. One of Yrling's archers had killed the horn blower still up upon the rampart, and his brazen horn had tumbled to the clay after his fist loosened about it.

The invaders were everywhere now. All that was left was to search out and find any of Merewala's men who might be hidden, concealing themselves for a chance to make a sudden, desperate strike. The war-band ranged about the work yards, entering every shed and outbuilding, weapon-first, seeking resisters, finding only cowering serving folk within. A group of them forced the door of the great hall itself, to be met by women shrieking in both rage and in fear. The knowledge, sure and growing, that they had triumphed spread throughout the invading party, their war whoops changing in tone to those of victorious cries of glee.

The confusion of combat was replaced by the frenzy of rampaging conquest. Yrling had no horn to marshal his men, no way to summon them save his whistle, and in the tumult of the work yards even the shrillness of that signal did not carry far. He had left Merewala's body, and with Sidroc headed down the broad court between stable and hall. The bodies of the dead and dying were scattered upon the pounded clay they trod. They strode along the stone base of the hall to its end. Before they turned the corner they heard the wailing of women, rising above the noise of whinnying horses, squawking geese, and the glad yells of Danes.

They found the source of lamentation before them. Three women knelt about the body of a fourth. One of the women, her shoulders shaking, had her face buried in her hands. A second was in the act of tearing at her hair as she howled. The third and oldest woman was unpinning her shawl and laying it upon the narrow form they had gathered about. The quick look Yrling and Sidroc gave what she covered showed the dashed body of a young woman.

The mourners were arrested in their grief enough to recoil at the sight of them, yet they did not leave the side of the dead woman.

"Who is this," Yrling asked, in the tongue of Angle-land.

The eldest woman turned her face to the men who stood over them, swords drawn. If she felt surprise at being questioned in her own tongue, it was dulled by the grief on her tear-streaked face.

Her answer bore her anger and sorrow in equal measure. "Merewala's daughter, Wendreda, who you have despoiled, and so killed. She threw herself from the roof to escape more of your men!"

The lined face now turned upward to the gable peak of the hall of Four Stones, far above.

The eyes of uncle and nephew followed hers. A window on a slightly higher level of the hall gave out on the roof; she must have climbed out from there.

Both men looked down at the body the old woman kept one hand on. Long hair of light brown, unbound by any head wrap, spilled about the shoulders. Her eyes of blue-green hue were open, and staring, and the pale lips too were parted. Blood had run from one side of the face, near the temple. She had no more than twenty years, perhaps less.

"This is his daughter," Yrling repeated, eyes fastened on the corpse.

"That she is, or was; Heaven has her now. When the horn gave warning she wrenched off her jewels to save them. Would she had saved herself!"

He had told his men he would wed Merewala's daughter, and warned they should not touch her. With no silver or gold about her to mark her as the daughter of the hall, she looked as any maid of the place.

Merewala's death was needful; his daughter's, a loss. Yrling had counted on wedding her, to bind the folk of hall and village to their new lord. The two men stood there, wordless, over the weeping women, eyes locked on the dead girl's face. As they stood, a new and urgent cry arose above the activity swirling about them.

Fire had broken out. The gladsome yells of the victors were now cries of alarm, and action. The serving folk of the place, whether they had been shrieking or mute with terror, joined in this chorus of dread. Yrling and Sidroc ran back along the stone base of the great hall of Four Stones, and into a billow of grey and acrid smoke issuing from the door. The hall itself was burning.

It could not be known whether a serving man or woman within had purposely flung burning coals from the fire-pit to destroy the prize the Danes had won. A cresset or other small oil lamp may have been upset as folk ran from the warriors who had penetrated the stronghold.

But the hall went from smouldering warmth to devouring flames in seeming moments, the dry timber uprights catching as licking yellow flames travelled up to the thick thatching of the roof.

Warriors shed their shields and weapons, cast off their ring-tunics. Sidroc, Jari, and Asberg were amongst them. Toki, who was still horsed and had been riding through the work yards between animal pens and outbuildings, jumped down to join them. There was a drawing-well in the forecourt of the hall, and Yrling himself stood at the well mouth. One bucket had not been fully drawn up from its dark depths before another was dropped. It was to little avail.

At first men could, by taking deep draughts of air, run inside the hall to fling the contents of their buckets at the flames creeping up the timber uprights. But once the thatching caught, the smoke drove all away, coughing and hacking, back into the forecourt between hall and stable.

The stone walls would not burn, and the floor too was of stone pavers, but the lofty roof began falling in flaming clumps within the hall. Wisps of burning thatch drifted down amongst those gathered outside. With the Sun fully risen, the wind picked up, blowing clouds of smoke that smarted eyes and nose.

The nearest building was the great stable, roofed over with lead sheets. These could melt if the stable itself burnt, but would not catch flame. As precaution the horses still within were led, neighing and stamping their hooves in fear, to the adjoining paddock. The risk of other of the many small buildings catching fire, of the palisade wall itself burning, was real, and efforts turned from attempting to douse the hall blaze to wetting down those structures nearest. A timber building of no great size, and set slightly away from the hall, caught flakes of burning ash in its thatch and fairly burst into flame. Too late they saw the roof was marked with a cross of wood at its peak; it must have been a Christian temple, and perchance housed silver treasure. It burnt to the very base of its timbers, despite the water flung on it by those circling its base. All this was done amongst the grisly remains of the earlier fighting. Danes ran with buckets, dodging the bodies of their dead brethren, and the many bodies more of the vanquished.

The hall of Four Stones was in two parts, with a fire-break of stone between them. The larger portion burned, the long and thick timbers of its roof crashing down upon the stone floor, the thatch blackening and shriveling as the heat devoured it. When the flames damped down, the lesser, second part of the hall remained, soot-besmirched but sound.

Yrling's men had been joined by some of the serving folk in fighting the fire, an odd coupling, but one rooted in the love the folk bore for their home. And if all were destroyed, famine and death would surely come to those who lived. Merewala's folk knew this, and suffered singe and smoke to preserve what they could.

When no danger remained, the invaders stumbled about the forecourt, the heat of the blackened timbers making this cold day warm. They were ready to drop from exhaustion. Their bodies were sweat-stained, with faces grimed, and arms and legs aching from exertion. They were famished, and their throats as dry as the charred and collapsed roof of the great hall they had won. Some of them limped from sprains, or sported bloody linen from hurts they had taken. Yet, almost to a man, they now headed to the thegns they had downed to begin the taking of battle-gain.

Sidroc spotted his uncle, and went to him. Jari and Asberg had fought nearby nearly the whole battle, and were close. Despite Jari's growing abilities as a Tyr-handed fighter, Sidroc had still concern for him, and was heartened to see Jari already bending over the body of one of Merewala's body-guards. Asberg was sitting on a mounting block by the stable wall, leaning against it as he rested his sore head. Save for Asberg none of the four had suffered hurt, and Toki, they had seen, was hale as well.

Sidroc walked with Yrling to the opened stable doors, where Merewala had fallen. The body lay still upon its back, but both men, nearing it, stopped in their tracks. Both gave up soft oaths.

The old lord's body had been desecrated. The helmet was there, but the noble head which it had protected had been hacked away. Yrling's killing thrust had been at the throat; now another had completed the job with a skeg-gox. A bloodied stump of neck was all that sprouted from the ring-tunic, its gleam hazed by the darkness of blood.

Something else was gone as well. Strapped across the old lord's belly, over the shining links of his ring-tunic, had been a black sheath, from which hung his seax, its pommel ornamented in silver and gold. Sheath, blade and belt: all were gone.

A louder oath from Yrling was for all of it. He could scarcely believe one of his men would pilfer from his own battle-gain; he could without contest kill a man for doing so. But the way the daughter of the hall had been dealt with reminded him that many following him were renegades. He could place no trust in such men.

The hacking away of the man's head incensed him. The body was his trophy, and no other's. He was not sure he would not have served it thus himself, but the fact that one of his men had done so without his leave angered him the more.

They stood there, looking upon the fallen lord, as the rowdy singing of a drunken man filled their ears. From the direction of the kitchen yard came two Danes, staggering as they approached. Having discovered ale and drunk their fill, they paraded by, one holding a long pole on which sat a heavy burden: Merewala's head on the end of a pike.

JARL

THE first few days at Four Stones passed in a fog of action, and excess. Ridding the confines of the keep of the dead was the first task. The thegns were tied by the heels to lines strung from the saddles of the good horses found there, and dragged out through the great opening of the palisade gates. Yrling would have ordered the men of the village to bury them, but there were, oddly, few found.

Work gangs of Danes dug shallow graves out beyond the common pasture lands, and heaved the bodies in. Even Merewala's body suffered thus. Stripped of everything of value by the men who had killed them, some of the dead were dragged naked down the dull ribband of road. Merewala's head alone remained within the enclosing palisade. When the ashes had cooled enough a Dane stuck the pike bearing it into a chink between paving stones in the ruins of the hall. There it looked balefully down upon all which had been lost to the invaders.

Merewala had led three-and-forty warriors. All were dead, their bodies numbered by Yrling himself as the horses pulling them were driven by.

Their own dead amounted to two-and-twenty; nineteen of whom were killed outright and three who died within that first week of wounds taken. All were burnt, a great pyre fired outside and around the back of the keep. On a plain of rising land they had discovered an old and forsaken Place of Offering, a trench wherein bits of rusted metal still lay, choked by Winter-dried weeds. A beech tree, tall, majestic, boughs now empty yet spreading, led the eye there. Off to one side of the beech was the trench, overseen by a rotting but tall carving of a God. Parts of it had fallen away, but there was no mistaking from what remained that this was none other than Odin. The single eye of all-seeing All-Father betrayed this. Merewala had professed the faith of the Christians, but someone before him had followed the same Gods the Danes revered. Old Gye, who Yrling had sailed with on raids, had told him this; that before the men of Angle-land followed the cross, they had honoured the northern Gods. The Danes sent their newly dead to Asgard within Odin's gaze.

It was there too that All-Father received the ox due him. Yrling was not alone in making Offering. Every man of his company came forward with something to consign to the trench. The captured weapons of the vanquished thegns brought fresh and shining steel to lie next that eaten away by rust. Each man selected some item from his battle-gain to present to that God he most honoured. Blades of seaxes were snapped, sword blades bent, shields with their figured iron bosses smashed. The weapons of one's opponent were ever the most cherished winnings, signifying utter victory over a foe, but the warring Gods would have their due in such token.

Sidroc chose the long spear of the thegn he had tricked into killing his fellow with, calling out the name of Tyr as with a wood-axe he severed the shaft. The decaying carving of Odin was before him, there to witness his death-due, yet as he straightened up his eyes fell on the beech tree beyond, a thing thriving, vital, and alive as he. He found himself nodding to it, in recognition. That beech had witnessed much here, its girth telling it had mayhap watched from leafy boughs when the image of the God was first carved and painted.

When they were done the trench was heaped with shattered weaponry. This mass Offering was performed with the smoke from the bodies of many Danes still wafting from the smouldering funeral pyre.

Of the body of Wendreda, the old lord's daughter, and those of the dead folk of the hall, they never knew what happened, only that new mounds appeared in the small fenced-in area to one side of the village.

Yrling could not keep his men from ravaging through the crofts the first day or two, grabbing women. He put an end to it after that. They needed the village women to farm and care for livestock. Likewise, any women within the walls, those of the actual keep, he would not allow to be further abused; these were needed to serve them. Of the village men, there were but few left save the old or very young; some had been killed in the sham raid at the start, but some of his men carried the rumour they had fled.

Looking upon their efforts, it seemed a faultless attack, one executed with both speed and audacity. As a Winter encounter it gave added surprise. Danes sailed in fair weather, raided, then set sail again over the North

Sea to home as soon as they were satisfied, and with the weather still fair. Yrling's war-band, stranded as it was, was forced to try a different tack, one which had richly rewarded them. The fact that Bjarne had been killed by one of Merewala's body-guard was the greatest loss Yrling felt; he had been an able hand at managing food stores.

He could not grieve Wendreda's death; her rape angered him, but the fact that it had forced her to take her own life gave him pause as to her fitness as his wife. Such a woman lacked hardiness, he thought, or that native cunning many women possessed. A Jutland woman of any spirit would have pointed out to him her transgressors and insisted that he kill them. He would have, and all would be well.

At any rate there were women about the hall who would come to him willingly enough, and as the weeks went on some of the village women too became more pliant. These had need to be, as the village food stores were carried inside the palisade, the village animals slaughtered to feed Yrling and his troop. Four Stones had supported a war-chief and his forty men; even with his losses Yrling had more than sixty. The herds of sheep, cattle, and goats shrank with an abruptness which would have alarmed Bjarne, had he lived. The men feasted, each and every night. The hunger which had haunted their days was driven out, and more easily than the memory of Merewala's proud lordship here. His head above the ruins of his great hall kept him in mind, for the first few weeks at least. The grey floss of beard moved gently in the wind, bringing eerie life to the severed orb. The men moving below found they did not often look up at it.

Of the second, and far smaller building lost to flame, lumps of melted bronze and pocked fragments of silver metal told that here indeed treasure had been housed. Its loss occasioned more wailing from the women of the hall, and when human bones were found in the cooling rubble the Danes kicked at, speechless tears fell from the eyes of those women who dared watch. For the second time in his life Sidroc saw women lift hand to brow, drop fingertips down to breast, cross to touch each shoulder, and then join together; the gesture he recalled the thrall woman Berthe use. This sacred sign of the Christians would be one he witnessed whenever the folk of Four Stones felt special distress. The Danes cleared the ruins of the temple away to enlarge the entry to the paddock, and some of the women would so sign whenever they were forced to walk over the dusky ground that had held the lost building.

But at last the men had a roof under which to lie. The second, smaller portion of the hall of Four Stones became their home. It was of magnitude greater than Yrling or his nephews had ever stood in back in Dane-mark. A fire-pit the length of three men lay in the centre, edged round with large stones, blackened from years of heat and ash. The rest of the floor was of fitted pieces of red and charcoal-hued stone, set in a waving pattern that seemed to flow underfoot; a floor the likes of which none of them had ever seen.

The clay beneath it had been dug out to hold this portion of the hall, so that from the forecourt a few stone steps led down to it. Once within, a flight of wooden stairs hugged the wall to one side, leading up to a partial second floor. The rooms there under the roof were narrow, but the largest had shuttered windows giving out to the fore-court, and looked beyond the top of the palisade to the village. Little was stored in these rooms, but they might have value in the future. It was the body of the hall itself that would serve the men's daily needs.

Tables of old oak sitting on trestles of even greater age served for meals. The hall was well supplied with these tables, dark with age, their tops scarred with the action of knives, and yet in strength as sound as new wood. The supporting trestles looked even older, yet were as sturdy as young trees. These trestle bases sported carvings of twining animals and scrolling vines wherever these had not been worn away by the action of innumerable boots rubbing against them. Stout benches, long and short, provided seating. Food was carried to the Danes sitting at the tables by the serving folk, progressing along a dim and narrow passage near one end of the hall. It led out to the kitchen yard, from which their meals were from the start brought; the quantities needed were too great to admit of cooking at the fire-pit.

After the evening meal the tables were each night upended and stored against the stone block walls. Pallets of straw then covered the floor until dawn. All the men slept thus; only Yrling himself did not bed down in the body of the hall. His bed lay behind a door strapped over with iron, set into a wall of oak the thickness of a man's wrist. Behind this door was a small chamber, with a single window set high in the wall, which became the treasure room of Four Stones. The floor was of broad oak planks and not stone, warmer and more pleasant under foot, but still a solid base for all it housed. This room had already goods in it; chests of fine men's clothing, and other things secret to Yrling, for he alone looked inside some of the smaller boxes laid within.

It could not be known what goods had been lost when the main part of the hall burned, but in this newly-made treasure room Yrling had brought every pack from all the horses bearing his gains from the Abbey of Beardan, the fort of the coast-guard, and every war-band or farmstead they had triumphed over. The candle-holders of silver, lengths of cloth, gem-encrusted boards ripped from the stacks of thin animal skin, the odd and rare hand of silver, and all else was deposited here. Chests were carried in from store-houses in the work yards to hold the wealth of weaponry he had won, the swords and seaxes taken from the fallen. Another held spear-points, only awaiting new shafts.

Whole spears of varying lengths were set upright in the body of the hall itself, at the corners of the treasure room wall, where they were readily at hand. And the wall of the treasure room, at one end of the hall, was signally marked with a symbol of the victorious Danes. Upon its thick oaken boards Aki, so good at drawing, took a stick of charcoal and limned a vast raven, wings outstretched. The carrion-eating raven was a favoured symbol of warring men. Yrling had given himself to Odin, and Odin had two ravens. The dark eye of the bird Aki drew there was such that it seemed to look out over the men as they sat at table, or slept.

His men kept their own battle-gain as they would, in leathern packs into which each man had burnt his mark with iron poker. All had won treasure, and had more awarded to them by Yrling, so that some had two or three packs, filled with clothes, boots, seaxes and swords, scabbards and weapons belts, mantle pins of bronze, and handfuls of silver in coinage, jewellery, and hack-silver.

Cold weather deepened into Winter, and came on fully. Spared from damp and wet, and with ample food in their bellies, the men of Four Stones took full possession of their new home. The shattered rhythm of the keep was slowly, and imperfectly restored. Craftsmen and serving folk who had been killed in the taking of Four Stones left voids not easily filled. The men and women who remained were, in many cases, forced into other roles by necessity, and all, whether free or not, were now regarded by the conquerors as thralls – mere slaves.

Four Stones had been a rich and well-ordered hall; now, with no Lady to run it, its folk and produce suffered. The long-standing bonds between hall and village were severed; the village become a place of outright plunder for its grain, vegetables, and beasts, and before Yrling ordered it stopped, for its women too. Men seeking the touch of female flesh might bargain with the hungry village women for food, but mindful of Wendreda's Fate, he wanted no more rape.

Within the palisade enough of the cookery staff had been killed that others, as yet unskilled in the feeding of large numbers, were forced into the role. The brewers and bakers still lived, at work at their malting ovens and kneeling at their stone querns. They brought forth barley ale, and breads of oat and rye meal, all of good savour. Wheat was in the grain chests, so that bread of that fine tooth and flavour was also baked. But those doing such work muttered about the rapid depletion of the village stores, and the emptying of the keep's own grain houses.

The stronghold being won, certain Danes came forward to take the place of lost artisans. Men of Jutland and Laaland who were able took up the tools of hands which had been stilled in the attack. The fire at the smith's was re-lit, and the bright clang of hammer striking steel on an iron anvil rang forth through the work yard. Others turned tanners, scraping and soaking the hides of the cattle and goats they ate. From these, leather workers fashioned shoes, belts, and tunics. Of linen and wool the men had clothing enough from what they stripped from the bodies of all they had killed; but with no women of the hall spinning or weaving, the store of bed linens and towelling suffered.

It was a hall of men flush with conquest, unconcerned with the diverse and largely hidden needs of continued sustenance. Their shelter and bounty had been hard won, and they took time to relish it. At night gathered together at table they recounted their deeds, those skilled in such matters making Saga-tales of the small band who had sailed from Ribe and was now in possession of this rich keep. All deeds lived on in the skaldic art. The fire-pit blazed as the barley ale went round, men winking in the heat of fire, food, and brew. And oftentimes Toki, his yellow head bending near the painted yellow arms of his harp, would pluck out a song, his fine voice by turns plaintive and low, or loud and raucous. Men sung of were never forgotten after they themselves had become ash.

Yrling had gained more than thirty head of horses from Merewala's stable and paddocks, an unexpected and welcome boon. Many of the men he housed and fed had never sat astride a horse. Only the more prosperous of them, such as Une and Jari, had been raised with horses, and Yrling, with his deep attraction to their beauty, had bought his mare as a youth. Both Toki and Sidroc were good riders as a result. Now each man, however awkward at first, became a capable horseman under the training of those at ease astride the long-limbed steeds of this new land.

Their mounts were not only their means of swift travel and successful raiding, but also a source of treasure in themselves. A good horse, while not part of the war-kit proper, was prized by all warriors, a possession to aspire to. One need only to back a handsome animal to know this. The height and stature a horse gave its rider as it moved past those treading the ground was nearly as great a distinction as stood between a trained warrior with spear or sword and a peasant wielding a hay rake.

To house and feed this growing herd they scouted out a plain, lying to the northeast of the keep, hemmed round with thick forest growth, making of it a natural enclosure. With close to one hundred horses the need for fodder was great, and the animals could be brought into the keep yard in rotation. Merewala's red stallion became Yrling's favoured mount, and he gave Sidroc and Toki and his chief men all their pick in turn. A young bay stallion with streaming black mane and tail became Sidroc's, along with a few choice mares, so that he might increase his stock. Toki selected a showy cream-coloured horse, but kept on riding the grey stallion of the war-chief at Beardan, just as the dead man's gold-chased helmet now adorned Toki's head.

Snow fell that Winter. Hard frosts and sleet gave way to blowing flakes that whitened the ridges of the empty furrows of the village fields. The war-band did not ride out to raid; it had no need to. But before the advent of freezing weather, groups of men went out to hunt, augmenting the kitchen yard work tables with stags, and even twice, boar. The hunting in icy marshes and in hushed and dripping forests brought more food to their tables. And the hunt, with its rigours and dangers, served as sport as well. The first boar that was chased out of thick hazel undergrowth had up-curving tusks the length of a man's finger. Seven Danes surrounded it, spears foremost, and three of them struck the flanks of the beast with their spear points. Its grunting squeals did not long sound. One man, having made the first spear-thrust, was eager to approach the fallen boar. The hoary dark head had dropped to the frosted mosses, the small eye rolled up and dull. The Dane was crying out in triumph over the dead beast when the shoulders of the boar rolled. The snout came up, and the deadly tusks pitched forward, puncturing the man's belly. His own squeal was deeper and more final than the beast he had dropped.

Sidroc was one of the remaining six standing there. Toki and Asberg too were there, as was Gudmund, who had led them to Four Stones. They pulled the man back and away, to watch man and boar expel their last breaths at nearly the same moment.

That the hunter should fall victim to the hunted was irony not lost on the witnesses. The boar, headed for the belly of the one who had killed him, ripped that belly apart as its final act. Sidroc remembered, on one of his first raids, seeing a youth skewer one of his brethren with a toasting fork. The Dane had been knocked flat and senseless by a pot thrown by an old woman, and a boy of twelve years or so had delivered the death blow with a kitchen tool.

No man could know how he would meet his death, or if it would be ignoble or glorious. And rushing to claim what the Gods had not yet dealt out was fraught with peril.

Though Yrling did not ride forth to war that Winter, other Danes found their way to the gates of Four Stones. He they sought could afford to pick and choose those he would take in. More than a few times Danes were allowed no further than outside the closed gates. Uncle and nephews, Asberg, Jari, Gizur, and Gudmund would go out to them, look them over. Yrling favoured men well-equipped, the proof of their prowess on their backs, but did not turn away from any who were patently hungered; his own hunger on the move was still too close to do that. If the Danes were horsed and did not get off their mounts to address him, Yrling waved them on.

"If I were one, I would not get off my horse," Toki complained. There was danger of course in doing so, all saw that, but Toki was blind to the arrogance it showed.

Yrling was unmoved. "If a man will not meet me on the ground on which I stand, he can take his fear, and his pride, and seek another Jarl."

The Winter wore on, short days lengthening, the Sun setting ever further West in its low transit. The hard months on the move across Anglia and Lindisse were supplanted by the months of security and plenty at Four Stones. They built a longhouse, large enough to house twenty men, out in the shallow valley where they kept their excess horses, as a guard to that moveable treasure.

As the land began to green again, a feeling grew in Sidroc, of how good a place this was. Not just the keep with its tall palisade and many buildings, but the pastures, rolling meadowlands, deep forests, and coursing streams that marked the holding.

One day, riding his bay stallion from the valley of horses back to the hall, he considered what surrounded him. All his eye took in, he had helped win. It struck him of a sudden, his role in this wealth. It heightened his thoughts, made him ponder his own Fate, and means of working that Fate to his own best ends.

The stallion under him was young, strong, and highly spirited, well-matched for its rider. He felt aware of the beast's great power, of the animal's hot blood pumping from the mighty heart, of its urgings for speed and food and for calling mares to mount. The control and calm in which they moved now, down this pounded road, allowed him to embrace this union, and granted a deeper knowing too of his own distinct separateness. He felt his own blood as it coursed through his veins, fuelling the strength in his limbs, giving power to shield arm and sword arm, and speed to his long legs. It was blood and more than blood, this life-force, pulsing to and from that flaring centre of his being, the urgings of his loins. The animal's strength heightened the sense of his own man's strength, his keen and deep potential. Every impulse that had formed and created him brought him to this awareness of craving, and near-mastery. It was a taste that led him to desire more.

The sharp cry of nesting chaffinches flitting overhead awoke him to the landscape he moved through. Looking out above the spilling black mane of his horse he thought, This place is now my home; a better place than Ful's farm, than even my father's farm.

This was followed by a second thought, close upon the first: But there is a better. I will stay here until I gain enough treasure to set out for myself, to claim that better place. When I have silver enough, I will leave, take what I have won. Men too. Some of these men will follow me, want to throw in with me; Jari, I know, and Asberg, and others as well . . .

He had not thought of leaving his uncle before, but now realised that he would. He would not be ready to do so for a while, he knew, but the thought of leaving, of striking out on his own, his own men at his back, struck a deep and thrilling chord within him.

The road leading to Four Stones had begun to dry in the warming Sun of early Spring. Less mud meant easier travel, and down that ribband of drying clay came a group of horsemen. A moment's study by the lookouts on the parapets told that these were Danes, not Saxon thegns.

There were two score of them, formidably equipped in full war-kit, each man with helmet and ring-shirt, a sword at every side, a spear in each right hand. Only the richest of war-chiefs could so afford to arm his men thus, and the lookouts on the ramparts of Four Stones knew those approaching must be only a small fragment of a much larger force. The lookouts made quick count of the number, then whistled over the work yards, calling attention to all warriors of Four Stones. In a few moments Yrling and his chief men had climbed the ladders to the parapet, and themselves gazed upon their visitors.

They came at a walk, collected, their horses showing no sign of hard usage. Attackers would come at a canter.

The village these riders passed through had fallen silent, all doors suddenly shut, all children plucked from where they had been sitting just moments before as their haggard and thin mothers worked over wash tub or scraped a few seeds into the ground. What terrors these women felt as they closed themselves within, no man riding nor watching could fully ken.

Yrling, up on the parapet flanked by his nephews, had as well Gizur at his side, his marksman's arrow nocked in his long bow. They all stood the straighter as the troop reined up a few horse lengths before the closed gates.

The visitors had resolved into ranks of four. Now one of the horsemen in the first rank touched his mount's flank. The horse, a roan stallion with tossing head, moved up a little.

Of all the men in that war-troop, his rider was perhaps the least impressive. Being mounted on the stallion did not mask his relative lack of stature. He was a man of less than average height. This made him the more interesting to those who gazed down on him.

He wore a brown mantle, trimmed with some dark and plush fur along border and hem, making rich show where that fur rested against his horse's white-flecked rump. The rider's legs were clad in bright blue leggings, and the reddish-brown hue of the short boots on his feet gave strong contrast. The steel helmet on his head was highly polished, and had cheek-pieces extending down almost to the jaw-line. Between this, the eye-surrounds, and the strip of steel that served as nose-guard, little of the man's face could be seen.

The rider lifted his head to those looking at him.

"You that are Yrling, show yourself." The voice uttering these words was steady, and full of command.

Upon the palisade Yrling moved his head.

"You stand before him," he answered.

The visitor spent a moment looking through the eye-holes of his helmet at Yrling. Then he spoke.

"I am Guthrum."

There was no man on the rampart that did not feel startle, even if few betrayed it. The Dane who was the greatest of their war-lords here in Angle-land stood before them. Guthrum was renowned for his courage and ability, and even more for his canny and careful approach to his opponents. He had, as well, true kingship flowing in his blood, being a nephew to slain King Horik of Dane-mark. If ever a man might one day be called King here in Angle-land, it would be Guthrum. Now he was at their gates.

Yrling was nothing if not decisive, and his first act was to show this to his guest.

"Welcome in," he called down. He turned his head a moment to order, "Open the gates."

Yrling and his nephews were down from the ramparts by the time Guthrum and the first rank of his warriors rode in. Yrling waited by the broad oak door of his hall as they all came inside, filling the forecourt. Sidroc and Toki, at their uncle's side, had been joined by Jari and Asberg, an impressive line to meet the great Guthrum's gaze. Notwithstanding his greeting, Yrling had taken the precaution to have Gizur stay above on the palisade. If Yrling's welcome was to be met by treachery, the bow-man would avenge him.

Every warrior of Four Stones was also now ringing the area between hall and stable. The paddock was just beyond, and Yrling gestured that his men help lead the visitors' horses to the troughs there.

Now off his horse, Guthrum stood by the beast's handsome head. Yrling took the few strides to meet him. Yrling was not overly-tall himself, but was a full hand-span taller than the famed warrior he greeted. Yrling pointed to one of his men, signalling that he take the reins of the roan stallion, and lead him to the stable where he would be more fully cared for.

Then with a nod he gestured his nephews forward.

"Sidroc, my brother's son," he told Guthrum. "Toki, my sister's son."

Guthrum pulled off his helmet before them. More than a few flecks of grey streaked his light brown hair, and the short and curled beard hair was also showing grey at the chin. His eyes of blue-green scanned the person of the tall Dane, took in the long scar that marred the left cheek, then flicked up to Sidroc's flint blue eyes. At this point Sidroc had been so looked at by many fighting men. Guthrum's gaze set him apart. He seemed not to be gauging Sidroc's worth as a fighter, his own odds of besting him, or any such common inner inquiry. The look was something deeper, and yet perhaps simpler, some basic sorting into types, a Já or Nej about him.

Guthrum repeated his scrutiny with Toki, who shifted slightly under that steely gaze. A movement of Toki's lower lip told of his discomfiture as those cool eyes assessed him.

Asberg, looking on and realizing the next step was to offer refreshment in the hall, beat a discreet path to the kitchen yard. All there knew that visitors had ridden in, but they must be marshalled to provide food and drink.

Yrling at this point was holding open the door leading the few steps down into the hall. Though Spring, it would be cold within, and he trusted that some of the thralls would have sense to poke up the fire to shed more warmth for his guest. None had, but he jerked his thumb at the fire and sent two men at work mending a broken bench scurrying to tend to it.

A loud, scattered, and disorganized period followed, but at its end Yrling was sitting at the long table at which he and his chief men always sat. Guthrum was at his right, Sidroc next to Guthrum, and Toki at his uncle's left side. Guthrum's chief men then sat interspersed with Yrling's at other places along the length of the ancient oaken board. This table sat just before the treasure room wall, that wall on which Aki had drawn the raven with its outspread wings, so the great bird overlooked all.

The rest of the warriors divided themselves at the remaining tables so that to Yrling's left sat his men, and to Guthrum's right, his own. These two groups looked the other over, the men of Yrling not failing to note the superior war-kit sported by Guthrum's troop. Indeed, they felt themselves at disadvantage, for their own armaments were stowed, and they had only the brawn of their persons and worth of their knives to display in return. Those fine helmets owned by the visitors now sat upon the scarred and time-worn planks of the table-tops, and most of Guthrum's men had placed them so they balanced forward on the nose-guard, the empty eye protectors seeming to regard those who studied them across the fire-pit.

Ale came, the quality of which Yrling could have no qualms over. The cups that ale was poured into were mostly of thick-walled pottery. Only at the high table were they of bronze, many of which were well-made and highly embossed. Before his guest was seated Yrling had gone into the treasure room and withdrawn from a pair of locked and nested chests the large footed cup of etched metal he had taken from the stone table at the temple of Beardan. This cup was not only wrought of silver but the foot and rim were gold. It was this he placed before Guthrum, a cup that he himself had never yet drunk from. His guest's eyes rested on it a moment, and the strong hand closed around that stem when the cup was filled. That wrist bore a bracelet of gold, two thick rods of it twisted round each other, a fortune encircling his lifting hand.

Yrling could be reckless, but it was a calculated recklessness. Watching Guthrum's cold eyes fall on the precious cup moved him to speak.

"This cup is my gift to you."

It was a gift fit for a king, and Guthrum, having defiled many temples of the Christians here, knew it was also fit for a God; the markings on it told him so. He had a second horse with him, one nearly as good as his first; he would as token leave it as answer to his host's rich offering.

He nodded in thanks.

Bread of fine crumb, well-leavened, came with the good ale, but there was as yet little milk from which butter could be drawn, and of course, no cheese. Bread and ale were served out by men and women of the hall who in their hesitant and clumsy movements could not hide their fear of the warriors surrounding them.

Once thirst had been slaked Guthrum looked over the hall, then back at his host. Yrling had pulled benches so that Guthrum sat on the end of one, and he himself on another. Their talk so far had been of the most general sort, but now his guest went deeper.

"You have no wife," Guthrum noticed aloud.

Yrling's wife would have stood with him to greet the visitors, and welcomed them in. A wife would have assured the prompt delivery of food and drink, and even now, behind her smile of attention to the conversation about her, be planning the evening meal for so many additional men. No such capable help-mate had stood by Yrling's side. Indeed, there had been few women at all seen, and seemingly all of a thrall's estate.

There was nothing for Yrling to say save the truth.

"The daughter of Merewala – she died in the taking of the hall."

Guthrum gave a nod. The fingers of his hand lay gently curled about the graceful foot of the precious cup before him. Something about the way he held and drank from this cup told all watching that here was a man used to drinking from silver and gold. He lifted the cup and took another draught of the good ale within.

"Win one, if you do not wish to starve," the older man advised.

It was the last thing Yrling expected to hear, but he saw the wisdom in it. None of his men had shown the ability the dead Bjarne had possessed at managing stores, and no real chain of command had emerged amongst the surviving hall and kitchen folk; the haphazard and faulty service of those moving about the hall was proof of that, as were the diminishing supplies in grain houses, root cellars, and store rooms. If not for the alert Asberg, sitting at the end of the table, even this welcome-ale would have been delayed.

Sidroc and Toki were of course privy to these words, though both remained silent. For his response Yrling slowly nodded, and in a way that made clear Guthrum had been heard.

"Your taking of Four Stones was not expected," Guthrum said now.

Yrling had practice in maintaining a neutral demeanour, which aided him here. Again, it was almost an observation made by the war-lord. In tone it was far from an accusation, but the thought could not help flash into the minds of Yrling and his nephews that Guthrum himself had had designs on so great a prize as Yrling had won.

The new lord of Four Stones decided silence was the best response. There was no need to justify his desire for a hall to the man who had conquered so many throughout Anglia, in Northumbria, and even here in Lindisse.

Guthrum went on, nothing deterred by his host's silence.

"Tell me of Merewala's death," he said now. It was more command than invitation, though Guthrum's hazel eyes were full of inquiry.

Yrling rapidly gauged what the Jarl could have heard of the falling of the old lord. Guthrum was known for his ability to learn what others could not, and to use that news to serve his ends. He was forming his response when Toki, at his elbow, piped up.

"The old goat's knees were knocking. He never had a chance once Yrling squared off with him."

This, from Toki, who had not been there; had been still upon his horse, ranging through the work yards and the faltering ranks of thegns attempting to rally to their lord's defence.

Guthrum did not fail to register how Yrling's hand had jumped slightly on the table at this claim, nor how his lips parted as if in protest. Yrling's chin turned down, and his back turned the more against his nephew, as if to check his words.

Yrling's silence was no longer serving him. He must speak.

"We squared off, as my nephew says," he began, to put the best face on Toki's brashness. He inclined his head to Sidroc. "My other nephew was there, backing me; and Jari and Asberg were spearmen, fending off those who would break into our match." Yrling raised his hand and pointed out the men he named, sitting at the high table with him. He knew that Merewala had been famed as a warrior in Lindisse; how much greater might Guthrum's estimation of the dead man be. Every word Yrling spoke now mattered, and he would not disparage the dead.

"It was evenly matched; Merewala's body-guard was kept active by my spearmen, so he and I could fight without hindrance."

Guthrum sat listening with the same look of inquiry. Yrling had seen enough to know a becoming restraint in his telling would serve him better than any bluster from Toki or any other witness.

For this was the problem: Yrling had not killed Merewala. None knew this save those who had been at their sides in that fatal battle. And of those who had been Merewala's thegns, all had fallen. This left Yrling's closest men with the knowledge. A few had died later in the battle, but Sidroc, Jari, and Asberg all lived. They had seen Yrling get in a strike at the old lord's forearm, seen the seam of blood begin to run through his ring-shirt. But actual killing blow there had been none. They had watched Merewala's enraged face pale to ashen hue, seen the hand that clenched the sword rise to chest and throat. He had been felled by his own failing heart, the end of many a man of his years.

Guthrum was waiting.

"We used our swords," Yrling went on, realizing he had not as yet implied this. "I drew first blood, a swipe at his sword-arm."

Guthrum uttered a low "Ah . . . ", in response. Those drawing first blood ever had the advantage.

"My last blow was to his throat," Yrling ended, also the truth.

It seemed to be enough, for Guthrum's next question moved past the moment of death.

"And the head on the pike? Or is that a tale?"

"The head served as trophy," Yrling answered, a simple stating of fact.

Guthrum allowed himself a grin.

Yrling was straining to think how Guthrum could have heard of that, when his guest spoke again.

"I have heard you called Jarl."

It was more than slippery ground Yrling found himself on at these words; it was real ice.

Jarls were named by kings, or by common acclaim when they had garnered so many men and so much treasure that they rose far above petty war-chiefs. Guthrum's words now suggested a kind of usurper sat next him. All at this high table were now attentive; Asberg at one end, Jari at the other, Gizur there as well, with all other seats filled by Guthrum's picked body-guard.

"You are the great Jarl of the Danes here in Angle-land," Yrling responded, a simple demurring. Yet the fact was it was his own skill and daring that had wrenched this keep from one who had held it many years; one he had heard tell, whose own father had built it. He could not be modest about this; it was truth as well.

Sidroc, watching both men's faces, felt more could be said, but easier so by one not Yrling.

"Jarl Guthrum," he offered, so that the older man turned to him. "The men call him Jarl as I call him Uncle. Yrling sold all he owned to build his ship and sail from Ribe. We were one-and-twenty setting sail, half a year ago. Look now at what he commands."

Sidroc had lifted the bronze cup in his hand to the hall, packed with his uncle's men.

Guthrum took this in, his eyes sweeping from Sidroc out to the throngs of both war camps. He turned back to Yrling.

"I see what you have done. What you will do is what concerns me."

None listening could have expected Guthrum's next words.

"Pledge yourself to me, blood to gold." He lifted his right hand now, and with his left pulled off the bracelet of twisted gold he wore. "Your blood will bind you to my side, when I have need. And to my treasure, as reward."

Yrling was already rising to his feet. He pulled at the knife at his belt. "I will pledge," he answered, his words as solemn as the vow he undertook.

His rising, and that of Guthrum, made the noise of the whole hall drop away. Men holding cups looked to see all at the high table standing. They too stood.

Guthrum lifted the ring of gold in the air. "Pure gold demands the purest of drinks," he told all. He looked to Yrling. "Wet this with your blood, as token of your pledge to me."

He laid the gold bracelet on the table. Yrling had lifted his knife, and extended the fourth finger of his left hand, that which runs to the heart.

"Single-eyed Odin," he called. "You who see all, witness my pledge to the great Guthrum. Bind us with blood, and with gold."

A jab with the tip of his long knife freed the blood coursing in the pledge-finger. Yrling dropped bead after bead of red upon the bright gold, the sacred number of nine drops in all.

Gold, man, the ancient oak of the table with its hallowed wood, all were joined in those nine moments as Yrling squeezed his drops of living blood on the pledge-ring.

Guthrum picked up the bracelet, held the blood-smeared thing before all. Then he slipped it back over his wrist. He turned to Yrling and said what no other Dane in Angle-land could say with authority.

"Yrling of Four Stones. I name you Jarl."

Thus proclaimed, Yrling's men gave up a hooting cheer, calling out both name and title of he who had won them Four Stones. Guthrum's warriors, spurred by his lifting the golden bracelet before them, and by this new war-lord of evident prowess pledging, added their voices, so that the hall rang with glad cries, and shrill whistles of acclaim.

Something else had occurred as well, as powerful as it was subtle. By naming Yrling Jarl, Guthrum had assumed the role of over-Jarl, even King. No man was fitter for it, for none had treasure and warriors as did Guthrum. And Yrling had his part in granting Guthrum be seen as such, and before so many.

More ale was brought, not a little being spilled by the scurrying serving folk as they laboured to fill each cup extended to them. A draught was drunk by all, as they stood. When at last the warriors resumed their benches Guthrum looked back to Sidroc.

The eyes did not sweep across his face this time, but sought Sidroc's own. Yet the older man again surprised.

"There are no better men than mine," he told Sidroc, with a tilt of his bearded chin to where his body-guard filled out the table. Sidroc had regarded them well, noting one who was as big as Jari, another whose wiry frame suggested agile speed, seeing in every face the watchful alertness backed by skill at arms that must distinguish every man of them.

"If you think yourself their equal," Guthrum went on, "come and try your hand."

This might have been a summons, if not for the slight movement of Guthrum's eyes, one near to a twinkle. It was invitation and challenge both, Sidroc knew; also an honour.

He could leave Four Stones now, Sidroc realised, ride off with Guthrum and his men, taking his treasure with him, to seek more treasure under the greatest of all Danes on this huge island. As a temptation it was enticing, almost beyond resisting.

But something stopped him, in action and thought both. With some unnamed but deep certainty he knew his leaving must be of his own making, and not at the invitation of any other, regardless of their fame. He took one moment to sense his fylgja, see if she had word for him. She did, and he spoke it aloud, to Guthrum.

"My arm will be yours, when the time comes," he promised.

Guthrum paused but a moment, and nodded his head.

"That time will come," he agreed.

Both men were aware of two sets of eyes upon them, those of Yrling and Toki.

Guthrum looked past Yrling to the yellow-haired Toki.

"You too will be welcome, second nephew of Yrling," Guthrum said, but the way the war-lord named him second did not sit well with Toki.

But Guthrum was looking now to Yrling, a bright bead of blood firming up on his finger tip.

"And you, Jarl Yrling," Guthrum ended with a laugh. "Get yourself a wife, if you wish to keep your hall."

A BRIDE FOR A JARL

SPRING ripened to Summer. Yrling, who had once called himself Jarl as a hope and a goal, was now known as such through a growing body of Danes in Lindisse. That it had been the great Guthrum who had named him thus brought an ever-swelling stream of men to the gates of Four Stones, seeking to join its war-band.

There was an ebb and flow to the men who surrounded Yrling there. The worst he would drive away after they had shown themselves to be idlers, pilferers, trouble-makers, or worse. The best too he would lose, when they had acquired silver enough. These were warriors whose arms he valued, men who had won much, and who he had further rewarded with choice prizes from the greater spoils that were his at every strike. One morning such men might awake, saddle their horses, and be gone. They would take not only the treasure they had won, but oftentimes other men too, those who resolved to strike out with them, gather others about them, become a war-band of their own.

At times Yrling and his troop might meet up with men from either camp. Such were greeted without regard as to their leaving. War ever made strange bed fellows, and none could know if those who had been looked at askance might one day become firm allies in need.

Four Stones had now enough warriors that Yrling need only take some on each raid. Indeed, his necessity to protect what he had won meant that a standing force was always left to guard the keep. Often he fronted the raiding party, but as his confidence grew in his nephews he would stay behind himself, particularly if he had heard through fast-riding messengers from Guthrum or other Danes friendly to him that rival troops might be nearing.

Throughout Spring and early Summer the warriors of Four Stones conducted a number of raids, ranging ever farther, striking swiftly and retreating just as fast on their good horses. There was little to deter them, for this part of Lindisse was not a place of known strongholds. Four Stones under the dead Merewala had been the greatest of them, but the fertile land meant many farmsteads of prospering farmers, yielding cattle, sheep, goats, pigs, fowl, and bushels of grain. It was in fact foodstuffs Four Stones had greatest need of. The women of the village had barely been able to sow enough seed and plant enough vegetables to sustain themselves. Nothing more could be taken from them. Scavenged nuts became their only meat, that and the scrawny fowl who could no longer lay. A hall of ever-hungry men made demands which could only be satisfied through continual plunder of producing farms.

Their targets were not only aimed at filling their bellies; the men had ample time to practise their fighting skills against both Saxon warriors and competing Danes. More than once Yrling's men had cause to draw swords and wield spears against their Danish brethren, either troops that challenged their passing along a road, or which they met at a target of farmstead or keep, and who refused to share the plunder with them.

Fair weather brought calmer water. With it Danish dragon boats crossed the North Sea just as the lost Dauðadagr had last Summer. Coastal farms and keeps had been stripped to the bone, oftentimes torched and abandoned. Yrling had sought and found a fortress well inland, but succeeding waves of his raiding brethren were forced to strike ever deeper into the heart of the countryside, sailing their shallow-draught ships up rivers and streams, and, as he had been forced to do, stealing horses. No place was beyond their reach.

Fleeing to relative safety after a strike was the harder problem. Here the men of Four Stones were favoured. The fortress and its imposing palisade, its free-flowing water course and wells, its many structures for housing men and beasts made it a daunting objective for siege attempts. They never rode out without extra horses, not only as pack animals for supply and to carry off booty, but to give each man a mount should any of their beasts founder. They might steal through the greenwood, leading their horses through heavy growth, to approach undetected a chosen settlement. Once the folk had been killed or driven off, the place was ransacked with prompt efficiency. The horses were loaded, and the men back in the saddles of their mounts. The ride back to Four Stones would be done at speed, on open roads. That they could retreat thus, in almost brazen disregard of pursuit, was further proof of the defenceless state of Lindisse.

But such raiding could not be sustained. Parties must be sent farther and farther afield. And Yrling was forced to be mindful of the state of the keep. He must seek a wife, a woman to take control of hall, kitchen yard, and food stores.

To the East of Four Stones was a Saxon fortress. Its land holdings were extensive, and riders from Four Stones had struck at outlying hamlets, yet never at the village proper. Word came to Yrling about this fortress, Georna-ham by name. He was surprised to learn it was lord-less. It was instead run by a woman, Eldrida by name. She was the widow of the dead lord, ruling in her own right, one who collected rich rents in foodstuffs and goods from her holdings, and armed and kept a troop of warriors, headed by a trusted captain. She was a widow nearing fifty years, and the mother of a sole surviving child, a daughter.

Yrling resolved that in this daughter he might find a suitable mistress for his hall. And a rich neighbour like Geornaham as an ally, or at the least not an enemy, was a desirable end in itself. Beyond this, if the maid was the sole heir of the hall, mayhap it all would fall to her at her mother's death.

Guthrum had many halls but no fixed abode; Yrling could not easily send riders after him asking advice. Yet he had urged Yrling to wed. He would deal with the Lady of Geornaham, and her captain if need be, alone.

His first act was to send two riders with his message. The first rider would travel to the very gates of Georna-ham's walls. The second would stay in safety beyond the village, awaiting the return of the first, which, if he did not appear, would be answer enough. The message was of the simplest: Jarl Yrling, Lord of Four Stones, wished to visit, seeking union of the two halls through wedlock. It was no less direct than this.

He would not hazard sending either Sidroc or Toki to deliver it, despite the fact that they spoke the tongue of Angle-land with some ease. Yet those he did send returned late in the day of the morning they had ridden out, and with favourable answer. Yrling might approach, and terms be discussed. The day after next was offered.

He gave some thought as to his coming foray. His messengers had returned unmolested, and the man who had been admitted to the hall to speak with its lady had been treated with respect. A troop of thirty men at his back would impress, while leaving the greater body of his force to protect Four Stones.

He called his nephews into the treasure room next morning. He had had a stronger, heavier box-lock made for the door, and three keys that fitted it. He kept all three himself, but today for the first time took one from the ring where they were kept.

"Sidroc, you ride with me." Toki's mouth was already opening in protest; his uncle's next words shut it.

"Toki. You lead in my absence." Yrling extended the key to him.

The grin breaking on Toki's mouth stilled at his uncle's further words. "If you enter this room without need, for anything less than want of more arms at threat of attack I will hear of it. And you will regret it."

Sidroc thought he knew why he was to ride with his uncle. Yrling took note when he had spoken to Guthrum in support of his uncle's claim as Jarl. He might need him now, in his dealings for the woman he wished to wed. There was distinction in this, and pleasure in being chosen for the ride, and in the newness of discovery. It would after all be the first time they had entered a hall as guests and not as raiders. But being left, as his cousin was, in command of Four Stones, its men and treasure, was no small thing, even if it be for but a day. The slight pang he felt at this was one more reminder that each pleasure, and every gain, had its cost.

Some little time that day was taken to prepare. Yrling, Sidroc, and the remaining twenty nine would ride on the morrow. Yrling chose with care. Those backing him as he reined up at Geornaham must be quiet, orderly, yet make good show of strength and arms. All were to wear their best clothing, ride their most eye-catching horse. And those he left behind must be fully able to defend the keep should any danger threaten in the single day he was gone.

If Une lived, he would command when Yrling rode away. As it was, leaving the steady and bear-like Jari with Toki seemed the best tack. Gudmund too would remain; he who had led them to Four Stones was ever linked to it. But his faithful archer Gizur he wanted at his own side, and Sidroc asked that Asberg, who had proven the soundness of his thinking, be brought as well.

When they set out just after dawn Yrling was attired in the best tunic and leggings he had found in the chests of Four Stones. The tunic of linen was a rich madder red, worn over leggings of a deep and ruddy brown. Hem and cuffs of the tunic were adorned with a narrow band of tablet-woven trim in dark blue and red, the fineness of the yarn and tightness of the weave giving a lustre to the wool it had been fashioned from. New, low boots of brown leather were on his feet, their toggles cubes of polished animal bone, not unlike gaming dice. The leather straps wrapping his lower legs were of similar leather, uncreased yet supple.

About his neck he wore, as he did each day, the large silver hammer of Thor he had taken from the body of Yellow-sail's captain. He rarely touched it without thinking of that day of conquest, when he had of a sudden two ships instead of one. Touching it he thought too how quickly Fate could turn and withdraw what it had seemingly bestowed.

On his sword-hand wrist he had a broad cuff of silver, the handwork of some unknown people, Rus perhaps, more handsome in his eyes in the sheer weight of precious metal than for its simple design.

Sidroc too had taken pains in dressing. He had in his packs several tunics, of both wool and linen, dyed the deep woad blue he most favoured. Leggings of mid-brown set this off, and if he could have seen himself as others did, made his long legs seem the longer. His dark brown hair fell beyond his shoulders, and he plaited it in two plaits, secured with a short leathern thong at the ends. Of the scar on his face he could do nothing. He might grow a beard to hide some of it, yet did not. He had acquired a bone-handled razor from the sacked abbey and used it each week, and did so now, with soft lye soap to ease its passage over cheeks and chin.

He had no jewellery he especially favoured, though he had won much of it. But he often placed the silver chain he had stripped from his first warrior kill around his neck, and chose that.

At his hip was the sword he had taken from the thegn who had killed Une. It was still the best he had found, as befit the master swordsman the thegn had been. This at his side, and his favourite knife, would be enough. They would wear no ring-tunics on their backs, nor helmets on their heads. Yrling controlled those lands to the near borders of Geornaham, and while Yrling wished to impress by his men and arms, he was come to court, not fight. That this courting would be carried out largely in terms of what goods the maid would bring with her did not dull the need for him to show some effort in his wooing, for he knew the women here were proud.

Thirty-one horses had been carefully brushed, the leather of their bridles oiled, saddles wiped free of dust and grime. Sidroc had done this for his uncle's red stallion, as well as for his bay. Yrling had many mounts he could have chosen from, including one given him by Guthrum, but this horse which had been Merewala's was that which he would appear upon.

The troop moved easily and well in a morning of growing warmth, one blue-skied and with a gentle breeze ruffling the fully opened leaves. Setting off at an easy canter they must ride through their own village, and the women and old men at work in their crofts looked up gape-mouthed at them. Once past the common pastures and into open land they slowed, having no need to push. They kept to the main road, passing those tracks which led to the small hamlets they had already frequented. The Sun had not yet reached its highest point in the sky as they neared Geornaham.

They were met first by a mounted escort, four thegns, fully armed, awaiting them at the side of the road. These did little more than nod, and take up their position leading them. Trees hemming the road gave out to an open vista of meadowlands, and beyond this the pastures and then waving grain fields of the village fronting the keep.

A number of the crofts of the village of Four Stones had been destroyed in the taking of the keep, and left in ruins. This village of Geornaham was smaller than what remained. But the low-roofed houses, many of them round, were solidly built of stiff wattle and daub, and well-thatched for dryness within. The numbers of goats, milking ewes, and lowing cows told butter and cheese must be found in abundance. The folk about, men, women, and children at work in rows of beans or around animal pens, stopped in what they were doing to look at them. Sidroc, in the first rank behind the leading thegns, noted their expressions. It was not the dull fear they had this morning seen the village women of Four Stones wear, but a curious interest. The fact that this large body of Danes was led by their own Lady's thegns lent calmness to their watching eyes.

The palisade enclosing the keep was well-made, not so tall as that of Four Stones, but encircled perhaps greater area. Its doubled gates were opened; they had seen that from afar, and now they rode in. Stablemen came forward, ready to take their horses, and they quitted them. Of the many structures before them the great hall stood out, not only for being larger than any other, but for the three who stood before it, awaiting their approach.

They were greeted by Eldrida, the Lady of Geornaham, a wan and angular woman who held herself as straight as an iron rod. She wore few adornments, but even Sidroc could tell the linen of her light-hued gown was spun of thread of unusual fineness, and the coloured threadwork embellishing throat and hem had been stitched by a needle-woman of skill. Next her were two men. One, who the eyes of Sidroc and Yrling went to first, was a warrior, a man in full war-kit, ring-tunic as well, and with his steel helmet under his arm. He had a curled beard of light brown, and loose but thick yellow hair, paling now to grey, resting almost to his shoulders. The breadth of chest and brawn of the arm cocked to hold his helmet spoke much about the muscled thews beneath those linked rings of steel. The pale blue eyes looking back at Sidroc and Yrling wore the appraising gaze of an expert warrior gauging another fighter's worth.

As it turned out, it was the second man who would be far more vital to their dealings. He wore a long gown of almost black wool. About his neck was a thin knotted cord from which hung a cross of silver. A holy man of the Christians, they saw. He might have forty years or more, was thin-faced, and regarded the visitors with piercing eyes beneath arched and questioning eyebrows.

They were led in, all of them, to a hall not much larger than that where Yrling supped and slept each day, but of markedly greater order. A line of serving folk were already coming forward, bearing basins and towels of linen. The Danes would have been left standing dumbly before them if the lady's captain had not set down his helmet on a table, dipped his hands in the proffered basin, and dried them with the linen. Thus prompted, every man of Four Stones found himself doing the same, rinsing away the dust of the road and the grime from the reins they had so lately held.

The high table was easy to pick out, with a ewer of silver upon it, and a few cups as well of silver. Yrling and Sidroc were led to it by the mistress of the hall, while his other men took their seats at the tables set about either side of the fire-pit, in this warm weather banked low. Once at the table, Eldrida took up the ewer in her bony hand, and poured out a brown strand of foaming ale into each cup, passing one first to Yrling, next to the man she called her priest, then to the captain of her thegns and Sidroc, and finally for herself. Four Stones boasted no cups of silver, and as Sidroc wrapped his fingers about the one she handed him he thought the very thinness of its walls might enhance the flavour of the ale swirling inside. Serving folk moved between the other tables, filling up bronze cups for all of Yrling's men.

After the first draught was taken, they began. It was all done in so few words; few enough that both Danes were surprised. The daughter of the hall was a maid, never wed. Her dowry was large, both in lands and silver. But as a maid she must wed and leave her home, which the lady wished to give as endowment to a church in her home shire further West. Thus the girl would come to Yrling with a chest of gold, equivalent to ten years' rents.

The bride-price requested was the protection of Four Stones over Geornaham and all its holdings. That was all.

This speech was delivered by the Lady of Geornaham herself, in a tone low, almost rasping. Her priest, who she called Osberht, at times added a word or two; her warrior captain kept wary silence.

Eldrida, having delivered her terms, let the men surrounding her absorb them. She had been Lady of Geornaham for three-and-thirty years, and widowed for the last seven. Her two sons had died in childhood, as had two other daughters, the one only being left to her. The girl tended to piety, but lacked, her mother gauged, the firmness of purpose to commit herself to a life of prayer. It was in fact Eldrida who wished to consecrate herself as a nun. She had run her course, served lord and hall, borne children and grieved them. She had tired of the trials of the world before the Danish invaders had begun ravaging her properties, trampling her fields, carrying off her grain and her folk.

Merewala had been ally, and might have been more if he had lived. He had been widowed for years and with her own daughter of age a strengthening of that friendship might have been achieved through their wedding. Now, with her powerful neighbour dead, his keep taken by these Danes, she was hard pressed to see another, better solution to the quandary. No king or near-by lord was left in Lindisse to aid Geornaham. A union now might prevent complete capitulation later.

She had broached all this with both priest and captain, knew they were against it. She was not without intelligence, and a forcefulness of her own in the face of such opposition. Her captain's charge was defence, her priest's, to pray. One was pledged to protect her body, the other, her soul. Both had served her long, and for years before her husband had died. They had carried forth their duties to him and his family and his keep in unbroken chain when she assumed her lonely role as widow and head of this holding. She was weary of being hedged about by these men, trapped in the narrow confines of the needs of her hall and folk. A life of contemplation, of oration, of gentle service to women who like her had fled the world, now called her with a voice insistent and supernal.

She let her eyes, always discreet in their seeking, lift under lowered lids to the man sitting opposite her. This was the man who had overcome Merewala, who walked his grounds, ruled his people. Here was the new order of the land, before her, and the safest haven for her girl.

She regarded Yrling, allowing herself a full assessment. His person was not displeasing; a well-knit, even powerful body, the hair of mid-brown combed and trimmed; eyes of animal-like sharpness beneath the strong brow line. The jaw was equally firm. Only the nose gave discord. It sat slightly askew on the face. She wondered with fleeting thought if it had been well-formed, and been at one point broken.

Taking them both in, she was glad it was the elder she could present to her daughter. The younger one was almost ugly, the scar on his face drawing all eyes to it. And his height might frighten her girl. At least for such a tall man he was not ungainly; he moved with assurance. She had watched them both carefully as they neared, at first uncertain who was the suitor.

A movement of her priest's hand upon the table stopped her musing. With her eyes she bid Osberht speak.

"You will of course receive the Holy Sacrament of Baptism," he told Yrling. The priest had the palms of both hands flat upon the table, his upper body leaning slightly towards the man he addressed. "You will take one wife, your union blessed in the eyes of the Church, and cleave to her only, until one of you dies."

Yrling knew that the women of Angle-land expected to be the sole wife of their husbands. This did not trouble him. With a large holding such as Four Stones and much treasure, it made things simpler. His heirs would be limited to those children his wife bore him, and those natural children he chose to single out from any born him of serving woman.

"One wife," he agreed, not masking the slight irritation he felt at being so schooled. He spoke their tongue with a distinct and lilting cadence that marked the speech of the Danes.

But there was one condition he would not agree to.

"My Gods are my Gods," he asserted. The way he lifted his chin at these words and looked back at the priest suggested the matter was closed.

"There is one God, one Truth, one Light, one Way," replied the priest. He had assumed the patient tone of one dealing with a child.

"Odin," answered Yrling.

The priest suppressed his splutter, but Sidroc could catch the slight smile breaking at the corner of the captain's thin lips. He too, did not like this priest.

Sidroc glanced at his uncle, a look of inquiry, to which Yrling gave a nod of assent.

"The coming Lady will make sacrifice as she wishes," he began, unsure of the rituals of Christians.

"The sacraments are sacrifices, you are correct," answered the priest. "And I will travel with her to Four Stones to ensure they are observed."

Neither Dane relished this thought, but it was far from an onerous demand. This priest might hold great sway here at Geornaham, but would hold none at Four Stones.

Yrling nodded. "Then you will come and help my wife in her offerings," he agreed.

Osberht turned to the Lady Eldrida. A small movement of her hands as they rested upon the table top conveyed her acquiescence. Osberht had to squelch what would have sounded an angry exhalation of breath in response. He had wished for no less than the opportunity to usher this heathen and his followers along the path to conversion, and to do it prior to the wedding. The union as this Dane's reward for being sprinkled and blessed was true inducement. To allow him to wed her beforehand deprived all of them of the most compelling reason he should submit to baptism.

But the Lady of Geornaham had never counted on this Dane's conversion as a condition of wedlock. She had heard about the attack on Four Stones within a day of Merewala's death; knew as well that his daughter had perished. Geornaham had been prepared for attack of its own. Instead they had been left largely in peace. She had considered the possibility, which had arisen as a reality two days ago, of the new Lord of Four Stones suing for the hand of her daughter. The priest Osberht could do as he liked once at Four Stones, as long as he protected the interests of her daughter, and the children born to her. The union would be blessed by the Church, the coming children raised in it. That was what mattered.

Eldrida made this clear in her next words.

"In addition to Osberht, my daughter will come with such serving folk as she wishes to bring with her," she said.

As simply as that, the issue of Gods was set aside by this woman. The two Danes watching her were aware she had overruled her holy man, and likely the wishes of her champion thegn, in doing so. They had more than a small amount of admiration for her.

She waved her hand at a young serving maid, who had been standing all this time not far off, just visible in the shadows near an alcove.

"Bring Eadburh to me," she asked.

The girl was brought, as richly dressed as any husband might hope for. She wore a gown of yellow linen, the light hue of which did not hide the necklace of small gold beads about her throat, for between each bead was a red carnelian the size of a pea. Her head was wrapped in a veil of white cloth of delicate thinness, so light as to flutter in her wake. The hair coming down beneath that head wrap was a pale and ashy brown, falling completely straight just past her shoulders.

In person she was as thin as her mother, but far shorter. The face was that of a serious child, though they had been told she had seen fully eighteen years. Her unease, even fear, showed on her brow, though she tried to compress her lips into a smile. Eyes, nose, and mouth were not ill-shaped, yet nothing led to beauty. She had the comeliness of youth and little more.

"Eadburh," her mother was saying, "this is Yrling, Lord of Four Stones. Jarl," she added, recalling that this is how he had named himself.

A week later Yrling returned to Geornaham to fetch his bride. Sidroc was left this time in command of Four Stones, and Toki was there to witness the joining of hands between his uncle and his betrothed. It was more than a hand-fast. The priest uttered words, made signs in the air, dropped to his knees and rose, even placed a piece of bread in the bride's mouth. Yrling took the maid's hand and the priest made more signs over them.

There was a bride-ale, a modest one by the standards of the Danes, and then, on the same day Yrling and Toki had set out, they rode back to Four Stones.

Eadburh sat in a waggon pulled by two oxen, her priest beside her, a drover walking at the beasts' heads. She brought as well three serving women, all not much older than she, and goods in the form of two looms, a chest of clothing, a barrel of bronze table ware, a round salver of silver, bed linens, towelling, and feather-stuffed cushions. The real dowry was in the leathern saddle bag strapped to the far-side of Yrling's red stallion. A small wooden casket with a domed lid, filled with gold, was tied there.

The Lady of Geornaham had brought this out to Yrling a week earlier, after her daughter had been dismissed. It was perhaps the fairest thing to do, for the beauty of so much glittering gold would throw the comeliest maid into shadow. Latching his eyes on the coins, necklaces, rings, and ornaments within the casket made a plain wife easy to accept.

To carry back this treasure Yrling had brought sixty men with him, all fully armed. Baggage trains were readily ambushed, though he had taken care that none outside his own walls knew the day of his setting out. It meant leaving Sidroc with only thirty-odd to ensure the keep. But should anyone try their hand against Four Stones in his brief absence, he felt Sidroc best up to the challenge. As it was both foray out and back were uneventful, save that Yrling rode back a far richer man, and married.

There was a real bride-ale at Four Stones. Enough was drunk so that Eadburh ran up the creaking stair near the entry to the small rooms above, her serving women in tow. Osberht the priest retreated to the passage between hall and kitchen yard after one Dane jestingly lifted his gown to see if he wore leggings beneath. Toki played his harp and sang; and when enough ale had been passed, many other men raised their voices in song as well. Jari took on all who neared in arm-wrestling; even three-fingered his right arm bore such force he rarely lost. Gaming pieces, never far from any Dane, were brought out, the men moving from table to table as their luck-spirits demanded. And there was dice, with heavy wagers placed and not a few punches thrown. When Yrling went to retrieve his bride he found her in tears. He led her to the treasure room. He had hoped she would show more spunk than the first woman he had wished to wed, Merewala's daughter. Instead she cringed every time he touched her. He had lain with a number of women, both in Jutland and here in Angle-land, and never taken so little pleasure in a woman's body.

And her presence did not moderate the depletion of Four Stones' stores. Eadburh's mother had run a large keep, overseen a village, collected rents, and armed a fighting force. Eadburh seemed unable to muster even the cooking staff. She was cowed by the laundresses, fearful of walking in the village, evinced alarm at horses, and had no skill at brewing. She was ever in the company of her frightened serving maids, looking as though she might erupt into tears, or clinging to Osberht the priest, as he chanted over her.

Sitting next to Yrling at table, she seemed bewildered, if not lost. She could not glance at Sidroc without wincing, and Toki, to her horror, soon took to a sniggering and secret wooing of her. At first Yrling had allowed Osberht to sit at the high table with her, but seeing how much of her time was spent in prayer with him he banished the priest to take his meals in the kitchen yard. There he was better treated than in the hall, for the folk were believers; but his earthly pride was hurt.

At night, in the treasure room with Yrling, Eadburh spent interminable time mumbling her prayers. At times he would let his eyes slide to the iron-bound chest that held the domed wooden casket filled with gold. This was the only good he could find in her.

She was dead by Winter. There was no visible malady, only a wasting away. Her mother Eldrida had left Georna-ham to go as a nun, and the place itself left in the keeping of a steward. The convent which housed her mother was a three days' ride away. To Eadburh it might as well have been across the sea. The Winter was a wet one, with much frost and damp. The fever she took was just enough to carry her off.

CHAPTER THE TWENTY-SIXTH

HEAT, AND LOSS

The Year 870

YRLING and his men had the Gods' favour to have ridden inland and learnt of Four Stones when they did. The keep of Merewala could not have long withstood the predation of their rapacious brethren. Between Guthrum and other war-chiefs of fame, Lindisse was now almost entirely controlled by the Danes. They, and other smaller war-lords, Yrling amongst them, had carved up this wet but fertile shire and made it their own.

To Four Stones' immediate North was an ancient hall known as Turcesig, which Guthrum had captured. It was now heavily garrisoned by him, though he was rarely there. It was buttress and protection to Yrling but further hemmed him in. With so much now taken by the Danes, all were forced to raid farther afield. This held particularly true for Four Stones, a fortress with a growing number of men, a village that produced far less than it had in its prime, and with a hall unmanaged by any mistress.

There were rich holdings in the West, but Mercia and Wessex were the most well-protected Kingdoms of the

Saxons. Strikes for silver and supplies against these targets must be carried out with lightning speed. Booty was carried to a series of temporary, ever-changing camps, before the final dash, hauling it within Four Stones' massive gates. The months Yrling and his core group of men had lived, ship-less and without shelter, served them well here. Even the youngest of them hardened into seasoned campaigners, veterans of many skirmishes, used to rough living, cold food, and hard and fast riding.

After the loss of Dauðadagr and Yellow-sail, horses had been the means of Yrling's success. Horses remained the great treasure of Four Stones. Yrling took care in the bloodstock he had stolen and won, breeding up the best of the stallions to their equal amongst the mares, gelding the less promising colts so they put on flesh and became good mounts and pack animals, trading off fillies he had no use for. He had a string of horses he favoured as his own mounts, stallions and mares both, though every animal he had not bestowed personally on his men was in fact his.

Yrling's frustration with the village did not abate. Some of the women of the hall had taken up with his men, and he had his pick of any as bed-mate, though he respected the claims of those men who had singled out women to be theirs. But the village, almost all of women, refused to yield. He knew some of the women there would lie with his men in exchange for small amounts of food, even a single loaf of bread. But none would hand-fast with them. It seemed a perverse kind of pride that kept them from this union, one beyond any of the warriors' ken.

Out raiding they were sometimes followed by desperate Saxon women, begging, willing to trade themselves for whatever food they could spare. Such would appear at dusk, as they were setting camp, stepping from behind trees in groups to show themselves, their children left at a distance behind. These were women from nearby hamlets and trevs whose farms and substance had been earlier destroyed, either by Yrling's band or some other raiders. Now they hid themselves near road sides by water, likely places for men to stop for the night. Only desperation could have driven them to such peril, and in fact some hollow-eyed women looked half-mad, or cackled like witches as they snatched at whatever they were offered to eat. Then they would vanish into the trees with those who had fed them. Others clutched the food, took it in haste to their waiting young, then walked back with slower step to pay their due to the man who had passed them a wooden bowl of cold boiled grain.

Most of the men would avail themselves of the women who offered in this way. To couple with a village woman meant seeing her there tilling her row of turnips day after day, of facing some other man's wanting of her and the fight that would follow. And too, once she was gotten with child there was that to be reckoned with. The women would lie with the men but not wed them, and the babes since born were jealously guarded by their mothers.

These camp followers asked the same as the village women, food for their empty bellies, but none of the men need ever see them again. Appetites for women were heightened while riding out. These women had need of food and offered themselves, and the warriors found themselves walking towards them, waiting for them to near. Sidroc was one.

The women did not speak to him; some almost would not look at him. He knew he was ugly, and knew they submitted out of hunger and not desire. It was an exchange, almost silent in approach, acceptance, completion. He felt no shame in the potent urgings of his own body, yet knew these women acted in shame. He could not lessen that shame but might, he felt, not deepen it, in his manner to them during their moments together.

Later, bedded down on his hide ground cloth, his saddle at his head, a few fleeting thoughts streaked through his mind before sleep came. Often it was an image of a woman, her face beyond viewing, but the sense of her loveliness real, and calling. She did not issue from within, as the sense of his fylgja did. This was from without, coming towards him.

He would wed one day; he wanted a woman to share life and treasure with. It would not always be like this. Tonight a half-Moon, luminous and yellow, was rising over his head, and he stared at it. Its glow carried the old woman Åfrid to his mind, eyes twinkling in her wrinkled face, telling him of the bright woman coming to him, telling him he would want Freyja's favour.

He could no more picture the bright woman than he could the Goddess, though he tried. The woman he had just lain with was too near in memory. Nothing about her or the other camp followers – famished and unwashed, their gowns soiled, hair tangled – spoke of Asgard. He tried to envision the hall he hoped to possess. He could capture one sensation, that of sitting at a table, sitting next his wife, sitting so closely that their thighs touched.

He squeezed his eyes shut, to hold it.

The men around him were tossing and grunting, pulling at wool blankets, grumbling at the hardness of the ground. The fire had burnt to cinders. Before first light they would be up and on their way, to danger, food, and treasure. But before he fell into sleep he determined, I will Offer to you, Freyja.

It was early Summer when it began. They had ridden back from a raid to the West, at which they had struck at the village fronting a small but fortified keep. When the gates to the keep did not open to release enraged thegns, they counted themselves lucky and pilfered all they could carry from the supporting crofts. They had thundered in, scattering terrified folk who snatched at bawling children, pulling them from the path of the raiders.

On the way back they spied a baggage train ahead, progressing slowly along the same stone-paved road they had just travelled on; it must have turned on from some smaller track. It was a simple task to divide, have half of them wait as the others lightened their load, handing down newly-won foodstuffs, then gallop ahead to confront the few guards who served as escort. These were swiftly overcome, leaving cowering drovers and serving men quaking as they waited. Yrling made decision: take all of it back to Four Stones. Danes fairly owned the roads from here to his part of Lindisse, and so many draught oxen, waggons, and the dead guards' horses all had value.

But by the time they got back to Four Stones one drover was unable to walk, and was carted in amongst the goods his oxen hauled. None at Four Stones knew they had pulled in contagion.

The drover was the first to die. It was not the same quick but hot fever that carried off Eadburh, or the one that snatched children to their graves after swelling their tongues and making red their cheeks. This fever started slowly, with hot brows and chilled hands, then in days became aches throughout the body. A rash then sprouted on the torso, spreading across arms and legs, stopping short at the face. This rash broadened into open and running sores. The smell of rotting flesh oozed from the fluid that seeped from the lesions. By then the suffering men could stand no light, clawed at their eyes, acted out of their heads. For some a profound sleep came, giving rest; the rest of death.

Not all the men grew sick. Of those who did, some had aching bones, and a mild rash that burnt, but did not suppurate and weep. They could take drink, must lie abed as they had no force of strength in their bodies, but grew well. The other third were swept off to their deaths by this spotted fever.

As the fever spread, men who were well found themselves looking at each other. The question in their minds did not cross their lips: who would sicken next? One night, early on, Sidroc sat in the kitchen yard, lifting his ale cup to his mouth, and paused to look out at those near him. Tables, trestles and all had been brought out for them to eat, the hall being given over to the sick. Above their heads an orange and angry Moon was rising. He saw the same question in the eyes of his uncle, his cousin, and every other man who sat there with them at Yrling's table.

Yrling and Sidroc were amongst those who did not sicken. Asberg and Jari were also spared, though Asberg felt fevered for a few days. Toki was taken ill, and long enough after the first men had died so that he could see what might be his Fate. Sidroc watched his cousin pale, saw how he resisted showing any signs of illness, how his bluster became the greater in the face of so many lying stricken by this unseen hand.

Toki had a raw kind of courage, one that forced him to race, yelling taunts, into the thick of any contest of arms. There was no deeper well-spring he could tap, his courage flowed on the surface like a river. Sidroc knew this of his cousin, had known some part of it for many years. Toki had given himself to no God; he gave himself to no one. When, racked with chills he called out for his forsaken wife Ginnlaug, Sidroc knew it was the fever which made him call her.

He could not name what he felt for his cousin, but Sidroc did not want Toki to die. The blood-bond, tried as it had been through their boyhoods, was still that, a bond. Their parents were siblings. They had been born the same Spring, and after the loss of Sidroc's father, had been raised together. Toki's father Ful had birched both of them, and for shared deeds. And Toki had helped him bury Hlaupari, had helped drag the big hound to the stream bank, dig the hole into which he must consign his body . . .

Kneeling at the side of his pallet, Sidroc forced Toki to drink both ale and warm meat broth. He could take no food; none of the men so afflicted could stomach it, or some constriction of the throat prevented such swallowing. But all could see that those who could drink had a chance at life.

It was not only the warriors of Four Stones, and the men of the captured baggage train who fell ill. The fever spread throughout the hall and yards, but again keeping to proportion of those who never sickened, those who fell ill but mildly, and those who would die. The sharing out was capricious and cruel, as it ever was with contagion. To see able warriors who had survived many battles cut down by an unseen and unfightable foe was a bitter loss. And to lose any more of the hall's folk, all of which were needed for its functioning, gave greater concern to Yrling as to its continuance.

He had ever imagined himself master of a hall, and in these imaginings it was one flourishing with folk. Since the day of the taking of Four Stones little had flourished save the number of men he commanded, and horses he owned. His horses were untroubled, but his warriors had diminished in number, the keep itself and its village now depleted beyond quick reclamation.

The fever which had smote them burnt itself out. The Norns, those magical Jotuns who spin, draw out, and snip the thread of men's lives, had made their choices, and now moved on. Toki grew well again, and being as young and strong as he was, with more speed than many others. He rose from his pallet one morning as if abashed he had ever been ill. His cheek was still pale, and he had lost flesh. He moved at times those first few days as if giddy, but would not admit to any weakness. Nor, if he had memory of Sidroc kneeling at his side, holding his burning head to help him drink, did he mention it to his cousin.

The dead Danes had been burnt, singly or in groups, out by the Place of Offering; the folk of the hall buried where the mounds of Wendreda, Eadburh, and the other Christians who had died here lay. When Eadburh had died her priest Osberht had gone away, where the men of Four Stones did not know or care; but it meant the folk had no other holy man to lead them in their rituals, wave his hand over them, or exhort them as the priest had done.

At least the Summer harvests were good. The rye and barley and oats in the village were full-budded and milky, sweet early peas gave way to filling red beans, and huge cabbages swelled green and white as they unfurled leathery veined leaves to the sky. The baggage train had been loaded with sacks of grain, barrels holding brined haunches of pig, and two large barrels as well of smoked and dried eels. And the rueful fact remained that Four Stones had fewer mouths to feed. Eleven folk of the hall had died, and of Yrling's men, nearly thirty.

With fewer men but many horses Yrling began turning his attention to more than the snatching of foodstuffs from farmsteads, or skirmishes with thegns for their weapons and silver. Slaves had value, and good slaves – strong young men and comely young women – had great value. The light-eyed fair-haired youth of the Angles and Saxons garnered high prices at markets abroad. Yrling had no intention of taking any himself across the seas, but now knew of Danes who would be happy to pay him well for healthy young, male or female.

His surfeit of horses meant he could set out leading many rider-less mounts. A strike at a large farm or small village could garner ten or twelve slaves. Few if any of them could ride; these were all free crofters, and some were Saxon slaves, all without means to keep a horse. But a single woman could be carried on the saddle in front of one of his men, and the youths bound, by threats or leathern thongs, to the saddles of other horses. To Yrling's mind it was less wasteful than killing, though they had need at times to kill the kin of those they stole. Once secure they made for the Dane who would take them to the coast to sell them on. Sometimes this was a keep, at other times no more than a camp at a prominent crossing, by a tall cairn of stacked stones, or near a fording place of a rushing river.

Yrling was in his slaving as single minded as he had been in most of what he undertook. No woman could be kept by any of his men, for any amount of silver they might offer him; and no woman was to be abused. There were maids amongst the females they captured, and any who could be so presented brought more silver. And it was light work for his men. Given a choice of mounting a horse or death, nearly all captives chose the horse, though more than one woman wept bitterly, or thrashed and tried to bite or kick the man who held her on his saddle. The over-awed youths were altogether quieter, if they had not already fought back and been killed.

Their best slaving had been done in the West, in Mercia and Wessex. Both had strong kings, but both men were tasked with fending off assaults by Danes on multiple fronts. And the farmsteads and hamlets they targeted were at the borders of either kingdom, and sometimes far from the hall of the lord who collected rents in grain, wool, and beasts from those the men of Four Stones captured. They were rarely followed, and when they were had force of number enough to dump their living cargo under guard and ride back to engage the thegns who chased them. They had killed a number of pursuers this way, or laughed them to scorn as they watched the men sent after them turn the heads of their horses for safety.

That Winter a messenger appeared at Four Stones' gates, a Saxon. He and his fellow thegns, a party of five, mounted on tired and muddied horses, had been met by the guards posted as watch-men along the road leading to the fortress. They had been led to the palisade, and the chief of them admitted to deliver his message. Standing before Yrling, his nephews, and a few picked men he told them of his mission.

He was sent from a lord of Wessex, Ælfsige, reeve of Cirenceaster. This place was far removed, but Ælfsige's holdings were extensive, and that of his own father, still alive, also of large extent. Both men had lands in the easternmost parts of Wessex. It was Ælfsige, acting on behalf of these doubled holdings, who made offer. Yrling of Four Stones, called Jarl, had in numerous actions laid waste to their lands and people, destroying their substance and depriving them of their rightful folk. In exchange for a cessation of these acts and for future protection from same Ælfsige of Cirenceaster was prepared to present a sum of choice treasure. As further inducement to peace, and to bind the halls together, Ælfsige pledged the hand of his eldest daughter. This was a maid of seventeen years, and one, the messenger made somber haste to mention, renowned for her beauty.

The thegn delivering this proposal was of no less than thirty years, a solid, sober, and practised warrior by the look of his stance, quality of his weaponry, and the long scar he bore along the back of his sword hand. The voice was firm, the words unhalting but well considered. Not a few of the men he addressed had reason to respect the manner in which he conducted himself. He was a warrior standing alone in a hall stolen by Danes, offering an immense treasure and his lord's cherished daughter to the man who was ravaging the lands and folk he was sworn to protect.

"I will come," the Jarl of Four Stones said in answer, "and speak to your lord."

The following month Yrling rode West with a troop of thirty men. Since the offer from Ælfsige of Cirenceaster he had made no forays into Wessex, had harried no lands which might be those of the man he rode to meet. This cessation of hostilities would alone provide contrast to his past actions and serve as foretaste of the protection he would proffer in return for Ælfsige's promised goods.

An offer of protection to these remote lands was not in fact one he could make lightly. He could keep his own men from predation but assuring that his Danish brethren respected the accord he had struck with a Saxon lord might prove difficult.

He left Sidroc in command of Four Stones, taking Toki with him. He would be gone for many days and the charge to Sidroc was great. Roving bands of rival Danes could strike the same devastating blow to the keep Yrling had. The door from the kitchen yard had been the first thing Yrling had replaced, and newly crafted of oak and bound with iron strappings, was stronger than the palisade in which it stood. Yet weakness could be found in any defence, and Sidroc must safeguard both keep and all the hard-won booty it housed.

Toki as consolation had the pleasure of riding at his uncle's side as they set out, his grey stallion prancing eagerly beneath him, and the gilt helmet Toki proudly sported gleaming in the Winter light. There was no real reason for Toki to don it so early, save his desire for show. The other riders, Yrling included, stowed their helmets in their saddle bags while on Four Stones' land. Yet none, even Sidroc, could deny that Toki, with his ready grin, yellow hair spilling forth in two plaits from under the golden rim of the helmet plate, and great pale horse dancing under him as he worried the bit, drew eyes to him. Show was part of battle; not that part that mattered once weapons clashed, but a part that gave high and even reckless confidence to those about to take their chances with the spinners of Fate.

Yrling had left Jari and Asberg at the hall with Sidroc. No Dane pledged to another as did the Saxon thegns to their lords, but these two were known, without naming them as such, as Sidroc's men. Jari became so on the day of Une's death, and Asberg since the day of the taking of Four Stones.

In Yrling's absence, Sidroc sat to sup where his uncle always did. Each night Yrling sat at the high table flanked by his two nephews. The darkened oak of the massive slab had taken on new significance since Guthrum had sat there with him. Yrling had made a blood-vow here, drops of his own warm and living blood wetting gold, binding him to Guthrum. A drop or two had seeped into this ancient wood, like a table of sacrifice.

Now Sidroc sat there, in Yrling's place, with Asberg on his right and Jari on his left. Jari, now a Tyr-hand, ate with his left hand, and Sidroc had before jested he ever wanted him on his left, so his right elbow was not jarring him. It went deeper than a gibe between friends. In battle,

Jari's shield, now held in his right, gave added protection to any man standing there.

Asberg had proven from the day of the capture of Yellow-sail that he had a good head. He was slow to anger, a trait Sidroc had grown to value in a man. Asberg was neither tall nor broad, but as able a warrior as any. With a spear he had few equals. These two men he could count on sat at either side of him. Sitting at the centre of the long oak board, overlooking the massed tables of the hall, Sidroc felt the rightness of his place there. One day he would head such a hall, with such men to flank him.

His next thought went beyond this: Toki has thought the same. He has sat here, picturing himself a war-chief, even a jarl.

Já, he thought, of course he has. Toki shared with his uncle a certain recklessness of spirit. It would be easy for him to see himself as master of Four Stones.

That could not happen unless Yrling died. But Toki would not be alone in a contest to win it.

Yrling was gone for more than a week. Watch-men posted along the road now spotted the returning troop and galloped ahead to Four Stones, whistling and calling that Yrling was near.

They rode in, soiled with Winter mud, their horses' legs and chests spattered with it. The thralls of the stable hastened out to them as the troop filled the forecourt between stable and hall.

Sidroc went to Yrling's red stallion, holding the shaking head at the cheek-piece as his uncle swung down.

Tired and dirty as they were, a moment's look at the men told the excursion had been marked with success. No face showed that more than Yrling's, his grin broad and growing as he straightened himself before Sidroc.

Toki too was on the ground. He was always amongst the first to be horsed, and to quit his beast as well. He stood, a few of his followers about him, tossing his golden helmet in the air and catching it, his face gleeful and smug. Sidroc let his eyes shift to him. He stifled a laugh at his cousin's satisfaction in having made the journey, his boyish pretence of triumph, as if something had happened to gloat over.

Sidroc need not wait to ask his uncle of the outcome, he was speaking now, as they walked towards the hall door.

"She is coming, next month," Yrling told him. "And bringing treasure in silver, and in gold. Other choice things, too."

"And did you see the maid? She who is to be your wife?"

Yrling paused. "Nej. Her father did not bring her so far; she was back at his chief hall at Cirenceaster."

If his uncle was disappointed in this, he did not betray it.

"But he showed me a plate of pure gold, said she matched it in loveliness, and said she would bring it with her."

A plate of pure gold. Yrling's first wife had brought a small casket of coinage, jewellery, and ornaments of gold. Here was another, seemingly richer maid whose wealth was such she could even dine from the precious stuff.

"Do you know her name?"

Yrling gathered his thoughts before speaking the strange word. "She is Ælf-wyn. It means Elf-Joy. He told me."

"With such a name she might bear magic," Sidroc answered.

"Her silver and her gold will be enough for me," laughed his uncle.

ÆLFWYN OF CIRENCEASTER

The Year 871

YRLING had agreed to a Peace with Ælfsige of Cirenceaster. As with any vow, he had been willing to swear in blood as to its terms. Instead, surrounded by Ælfsige, Ælfsige's old father, and a few other cheerless and fully armed warriors he followed the ways of Angle-land. There was as well a Christian holy man there, priest or monk Yrling could not tell. He was presented with a scraped and stiffened lamb skin, covered over with swirling marks flowing from the hand of the holy man. He must make his mark on it as pledge to uphold the terms of the Peace, which were read to him twice by the gowned man. He chose the rune Ansur ᚨ, that rune of Odin, of knowledge, discourse, and of tests or trials. He took the goose feather in his fist, dipped the sharpened point of it in the pot of dark liquid as he had seen, and scrawled it where the man pointed.

Ælfsige did the same. Yrling noted that Ælfsige did not himself make the marks on the skin, nor did he seem to know their meaning. He had dictated the terms earlier to the holy man, that was clear, but listened just as carefully as Yrling did when they were read to make certain they were as he wanted. He screwed up his eyes at the black markings on the skin, just as Yrling had, when he looked at it.

Yrling had made this Peace, and now wished to tell Guthrum of it. Guthrum travelled far and wide over his holdings, and finding him was not easy, even with sending Four Stones' best riders. At last Yrling heard that Guthrum was near, in fact, just to his northerly borders, at his hall at Turcesig. He picked out a choice mare from his herd to take to him; Guthrum too had an eye for good horse-flesh, and had openly admired Yrling's animals in the past.

Ælfwyn of Cirenceaster would be on her way by now, taking an easterly route across Wessex to the borders of Lindisse, where Yrling would meet her. But seeing Guthrum took precedence. There was much to discuss with him, or rather much that Yrling hoped to learn. Guthrum was wily, and like all Danish war-lords told little of his own plans to his under-jarls. But with so much of the North and East of this great island now under Danish rule, it could not be long before the two remaining Kingdoms of the Saxons, Mercia and Wessex, also fell to Danish steel. A vast action was ahead, war on a scale that even Guthrum had not seen, and Guthrum would need all his jarls to fight it. And his neighbour to the South now had a particular interest to forward in return. Yrling, in making this pact with Ælfsige in Wessex had not laid claim to his lands; rather had pledged a stop to his harrying of them.

But when Wessex was overrun he wanted Guthrum on his side in his claim to his father-in-law's holdings.

It was Toki Yrling sent to meet his bride. Toki and a small troop of good men would serve as escort and carry bride and treasure back to Four Stones. Yrling would ride to Guthrum at Turcesig, leaving Four Stones to Sidroc's command.

Before he left Yrling gave both nephews a key to the treasure room. Toki and the rest of the escort needed two days to prepare kit and horses, and possession of one of the keys would keep him from sulking while he was still at Four Stones.

Yrling, travelling on his own lands to those owned by Guthrum, took a score of men with him. He did not need that many, but a fitting level of show was required. He was not certain of his return; he might remain at Turcesig for some days. Guthrum liked to hunt, and joining any man whose favour you sought in a chosen pursuit was good policy. Both cousins watched him ride off, their arms raised in salute. Yrling rode the stallion Guthrum had given him, a well-muscled sorrel, and led the black mare he had chosen as gift for his host. With a martin-trimmed mantle over his shoulders, and riding and leading such horses, he made striking display.

Toki would leave on the morrow. Sidroc was out in the kitchen yard with him, watching Toki and his men ready the food packs, when he thought of something.

"He sends her no gift." Indeed, their uncle had not set aside anything for Toki to carry with him as a welcoming-present.

"Gift?" Toki answered, looking up from where he stuffed a leathern pack with a small iron cauldron. They were sitting at one of the many work tables, the three who would ride with him doing the same. "She is the one bringing treasure."

"Já," Sidroc allowed. "But she is to be his wife. A lady of her like will expect, and needs, a gift."

Toki rolled his eyes, but his cousin was already standing, fingering the key to the treasure room. Both knew they were only to enter in the company of the other. Sidroc decided this was such a time. They quitted the kitchen yard.

The hall was nearly empty, some thralls hauling in more wood for the fire-pit, a few distracted-looking women scrubbing the table tops, now leaning upright against the walls, with wadded handfuls of straw. The box lock of black iron on the treasure room door yielded smoothly to Sidroc's key deep inside it. They shut the door behind them.

A ring of keys to every locked chest was hung just inside the door, and Sidroc took it up. Chests, barrels, and lidded wooden boxes were shoved helter-skelter about the room, piled upon one another. All the excess weaponry Yrling had won was stowed here, spears, swords, the angle-bladed knives the Saxons favoured, even ring-shirts and helmets. Here too was kept the choicest of other plunder, cups of silver and gold, jewellery of the same precious metals, tunics and mantles adorned with thread-work, baskets of furs from northern climes. Against one wall was Yrling's low bed, tumbled with bed clothes as he had left it. The disorder of all was great. The single window high on the wall gave good light, though, and Sidroc turned to one of the smallest chests, placed upon one of huge girth which was strapped with iron bands.

Within the smaller chest lay a fine casket of carved walrus ivory; his uncle had showed it to him. He had never seen into the contents of that casket, carved round with figures of men fighting and a curious scene of a couple with a babe in a kind of stable, with three men kneeling before them. The delicacy of the whole made him think that if anything lay within, it would be fit for a lady. He jiggled the bronze key in the box lock of the chest. There indeed sat the small casket, and he lifted it out. It had a tiny lock, but it had been broken. He opened the domed lid.

They both caught their breath. A tangle of red gold lay there, of flattened linked discs of that prized metal. Each of the golden discs was set with a single gemstone, in shades of red, blue, or yellow. He pulled it out. It was a necklace, and with it, two matching bracelets of equal beauty.

"This he must give himself," Sidroc murmured.

There was something else in the casket, in a tiny pouch of red leather. He pulled at the drawstring, and emptied the contents into his hand. A huge and flawless pearl, one shaped almost like the egg of a songbird, lay there. It had been drilled so that it was held between small caps of gold, fitted to a chain of the same precious stuff. He looked to his cousin.

"This," he told him. It had magnificence, yet being a pearl had also a chaste modesty fitted to a bride.

His cousin gave a whistle in response. "The giving of it is on your head," he reminded, but tucked the red pouch in his belt all the same.

With both Yrling and Toki away the hall took on a different tenor. It was not laxity amongst the men; Sidroc kept them to their work of repairing bridles and horse-hardware, the forging of spear-points and shaping of spear shafts, and every man took care in the cleaning of his weapons and honing of his blades. A few had claimed plots out by the longhouse in the valley where they grazed their horses, in expectation of someday wedding and building a house; and these spent time opening the cold and waiting soil to sow Winter wheat. But at night when all not posted at the longhouse gathered under Four Stones' timber roof to sup, a current of expectation flowed throughout the hall. Yrling would soon wed again, and the treasure his bride carried to him was rumoured to be vast. They would have their share in it, and there would be a feast at the hand-fast, a feast with much ale.

As the days passed, awaiting Toki's return, Sidroc more than once overheard men speak about the coming bride, and the fact that none would be surprised if the maid of Cirenceaster arrived at Four Stones a maid no longer. Toki had been sent to fetch her, and no man had Toki's luck with women. Why should she not invite him into her waggon on the way here? All he need do was smile and she might falter. If he sang, she was certain to fall. When one pointed out Toki's yellow harp, left behind and hanging on the wall, the other sniggered. Harp or no, if Toki wanted a woman, he was sure to get her.

When, on a chill and wet day, fog rising from the dark ground, the look-outs on the palisade ramparts began to whistle, all the men massed in the forecourt. Many climbed the ladders to the ramparts to see for themselves. There at a distance was Toki, his grey horse easy to pick out, his golden helmet on his head, spurring his mount, leaving those he led far behind. In his wake there were two ox-drawn waggons, and beside Toki and his men, three others mounted on horseback. These were thegns, riding in position at front and back of the waggons, and the treasure they bore.

With Guthrum now controlling Turcesig and Yrling Geornaham all near approaches to Four Stones were protected. The gates, for the sake of ease of passage from hall to village, were left open during the day. With Yrling gone, they were kept closed. Sidroc now ordered them opened.

He stood in the yawning gateway watching them approach. The waggon beds were enclosed by tall hoops, and covered over with tarpaulins of some kind, oiled linen or tanned hides; from the distance it was hard to know. But he could see figures on the waggon board of the first waggon.

The women of the village were come out of their huts, and were standing on the roadside which split their settlement. They stood there in the damp mist, their children at their sides, their babes tied on their hips or in their arms, to watch. As the waggons reached them, a cry, faint but unmistakable, rose from the village women, not of welcome, but of lament.

Sidroc moved back to the hall doorway as the riders neared. Toki came first, at a charging gallop. One of his men had nearly caught him in the race to be first through the gates. The oxen, like all draught beasts of their ilk, could not be hurried in their shafts. A drover walked at the head of the lead pair. Tied to the back of one of the waggons was a shaggy white pony of no great worth, small enough to have been missed at first viewing.

One of Toki's men who had raced through the gates now peeled back to confront the slow-riding thegns fronting the waggons. The thegns were held back, kept outside the gates, when the waggons, led by the single drover, rolled in. Sidroc signalled they stop, just before the burnt walls of the old main hall.

Toki was before him now. The broad breast of his stallion heaved from the gallop, yet the animal stood shaking his head and jingling his bridle hardware as if ready for more. Toki jumped down and came to Sidroc, pulling off the gilt helmet, grinning like a cat.

"Two beauties," said Toki, with a nod of his chin towards the first waggon. Two women sat there on the board, both young, and the head of a third, older woman, peered out from behind, over their shoulders. "At home Yrling would wed both."

Sidroc looked past his cousin to take in the bride of Yrling. The eyes of both young women looked back at him, before dropping and shifting away. One glance told him they were of exceptional comeliness, and while both fair, different each from each. He could not look longer; Toki, having delivered his charges, was already gone, cooling his horse at a walk in the paddock. Sidroc commanded Four Stones and must deal with waggons, oxen, pony, the thegns waiting outside, and the men of Four Stones, who stood staring at the new arrivals. None could look at the big waggons without gauging the riches held within; this thought had, when he spotted them, also crossed his own mind.

He ordered the drover unhitch both teams, and take them to the cattle pen, and told his brothers to return to their work about the yards. Then he stood a moment, uncertain of his next step.

"Sir," called one of the women. "Please to take my Lady and me to your Lord."

He moved to them. They sat side by side, so close their bodies touched. One was pale like the Moon, the other in her colouring, fiery like the dawn Sun. The one who had spoken was the fiery one.

They were both so young; he had heard Yrling say the Lady Ælfwyn had seventeen years, but neither looked it. Everything about them seemed fresh, even startling to his eyes. The brightness of their gowns, one in blue, the other in green; the fall of their hair upon their mantles; their head wraps of clean white linen. He had not seen women as well dressed since the meeting with Eldrida and Eadburh, but these maids, even sitting rigidly upon the waggon board, had a liveliness and vigour neither of those two possessed.

The fiery one, in a green gown and a squirrel-trimmed mantle, was looking at him, eyes full on his face, awaiting his answer. She did not flinch, looking on him.

"He is not here, but returns tonight, or tomorrow, or when he will," he told them.

He watched her turn to the other, the pale one. She would be Yrling's wife; the fiery one had called her, my lady.

He watched Ælfwyn's eyes roll up, the slightest bit, as if in cloaked anger. But whether aware of his scrutiny or from her own training, she composed herself, only pressing her lips together in response to this news. The fiery one's lips parted, as if she would speak again, but she did not, only looked back at him.

It gave him time to study her. She had hair in abundance, buckles of it, of a distinct and striking hue, a chestnut gold. She was even younger than her lady, he was sure of this, ten and four years, or a year more, perhaps, her face bore the trace of no more years than that. The roundness of her cheek, smoothness of her skin, wideness of her deep green eyes, all was that of a maid not far removed from childhood. The jawline though was decided, even firm, with the slightest of clefts in her chin. A few light freckles dotted her nose, a nose strong for a young face, but pleasing still. The lips beneath that nose were full and deeply bowed, the lips of a woman and not a girl.

He took a step closer, both to rouse himself, and in response to the proudly raised chin of Ælfwyn, her eyes lifting from the charred timbers of the old hall to the dullness of the grey sky.

He jumped up on the step of the waggon board, so that the maids stood, suddenly and unsteadily. He took Ælfwyn by the waist with both hands and swung her to the ground, then did the same with the bright-haired one. Their waists were slender and firm under his large hands. They both stiffened at his grasp, a touch he never could have allowed himself any other way.

Standing before them he could see them better, compare their beauty. Ælfwyn was much the taller, and more slender as well. Her hair was that palest of yellow shades, almost a shimmering and silvery gold. All about her was narrow, save her eyes, large and blue. Her nose was straight, rather long and thin, her chin pointed. Her skin was pale, unmarred by any blemish, almost luminous. Again, he thought of the Moon. A noble-woman's face, he knew, a face formed by generations of wealth and high taste and choice in who to wed.

The other – but now the third woman was struggling to get down from the waggon, and he turned with his hand to help her. A serving woman, older and stolid, clucking her tongue and glaring at him. Then Toki came over, with no little swagger in his step. They spoke a few words about who should guard the waggons until Yrling arrived, but Toki's eye was all the time roving over the maids he had delivered. They were proud, all three women, the maids biting their lips as if to hold back anger; the plump serving woman snorting out her dismay.

Sidroc remembered the man who claimed that Toki would have bedded the coming bride on the road, and had to hold back from laughing at the notion. These maids were young, but high-born, and sure of their value. He could not think either would throw themselves away like that.

He led the three women into the hall, saw how they stopped as they walked down into the body of it. He could not allow them into the treasure room, but until Yrling came back, the narrow room at the top of the stairs would serve.

After he had left them the serving woman came puffing after him; he was with Toki in the stable. She asked that the drover sleep outside the door of their upper chamber that night, and after his nod, thrust a silver coin in his hand before hustling away.

Toki began to laugh, and Sidroc could not keep from grinning.

"Any man bedding either will have to get through her to do it," Toki said, and Sidroc forced a laugh of his own.

The two maids from Wessex did not appear that night in the hall. Sidroc understood why, in Yrling's absence, they would choose not to show themselves before so many strange men. He saw their serving woman several times, moving through the passage to the kitchen yard, carrying a pail of steaming water, clumping down the creaking stairs with emptied food plates. It made him wonder about the second maid, the fiery one, the one who had spoken to him. She of the bright hair.

She could not be kin to Ælfwyn; Ælfsige would not send so marriageable a maid out of the range of his dealings. She was far from a serving maid; there was a boldness about her suggesting she herself had serving folk at her command. And the Lady Ælfwyn seemed to depend on her, was likely to confide in her, trust her judgement, young as she was. They were both estimable maids, and not only for their faces. Carted into a hall yard of gaping warriors, the intended husband absent, they reacted not in fear, but quiet, indignant anger. They showed their spirit in this, and he could but admire them for it. One thought of the shrinking and timorous Eadburh reminded him of how different they might have been.

He was at the table thinking these things, the clamour of the hall surrounding him. Men, having eaten, were sprawling on their benches, calling out for more ale from the serving folk. The men who carried it to them risked cuffing and tripping, and the women, pottery jugs in hand, were subject to having their bottoms grabbed, or being pulled into a drunken man's lap.

With Toki back Sidroc did not quite take Yrling's seat on the bench; he left a space there that he and his cousin flanked, awaiting their uncle's return. Toki, having been denied any ale on the journey to meet Yrling's bride, was taking full advantage of the flow of it now. He and the men who rode with him were recounting in loud and raucous voices the ride out and back. It was only a matter of time before Toki would fetch his harp and begin the making of a Saga-tale about it. Until then not a few of the men's large bronze cups were being knocked over by unsteady hands, spilling their contents onto the straw lying in low lumpen heaps upon the floor.

The plate at the high table had steadily improved since the first months after Yrling's victory over the keep. None could know what had been lost in the burning of the main hall, but when the Danes took their first meal at Four Stones, they ate from wooden plates, crockery bowls, and a few salvers of bronze. This was the serving ware they had carried with them on their horses, and those things scavenged from the kitchen yard. But now, after such success in raiding, Sidroc and Toki drank from cups of silver rimmed in gold, and Yrling, when he was there, from a cup of gold gemmed round with green and blue stones. It was far smaller than that which he had taken from the temple table at Beardan and given to Guthrum, yet gold it was.

Sidroc, fingering the gold-rimmed silver cup from which he drank, gave thought to how quickly his hand had grown used to the touch of his costly cup, how natural it seemed that his lip should rest on gold as he drank his ale. He had not owned it long enough for it to become commonplace, yet though it still gave pleasure to the eye, hand, and lips, it was not the thrill he had felt when first he had lifted it. All treasures were not thus, he felt; some continued to gain in value with use. Good horses were one such source of growing pleasure; anything alive, responsive, and subject to change stayed fresh. The cup in his hand asked nothing of him. His fine bay stallion asked much. Women too, he thought; women demand much. This brought his musings round to the two maids, lately arrived, who had already made deep impress on his thoughts.

In the morning Sidroc looked to the departure of Ælfsige's thegns, who had camped outside the gates. If Yrling was there he may have had message for them; as it was they must be sent off with only the knowledge that they had accomplished the task of bringing Yrling his bride. He had had the kitchen yard fill their food bags, and they were ready to mount. Toki wandered over, staring at the thegns as they stood, just outside the opened gates, checking girth straps and tightening their packs upon their saddle rings. The waggons still sat where they had been left, their tarpaulins tightly laced, their treasure undisturbed. Only those necessaries the women had asked for had been removed, hauled up the creaking stairs to their rooms. The eyes of one of the thegns were fixed on the waggons as he looked over his horse's saddle to where they stood, under the guard of two of Four Stones' men. Regret was in those eyes; any looking at the man could read it. Toki waited until the man's eyes shifted to his own hard and triumphant stare.

Toki began to move off, back to the hall. It was then that Ælfwyn and the bright-haired one appeared, their serving woman behind them. They had slipped wooden clogs on their feet against the mud of the yard, but even so walked with purpose towards the thegns and their horses. Toki had paused, and now trailed in their wake. Ælfwyn had something in her hands, a shallow but broad box of some kind. She extended it to the eldest of the thegns. Sidroc had to challenge her at this, learn what the box contained.

It angered her, but she passed it to him, telling him it was naught but a message to her parents. He untied the leathern thong that held the two halves closed. Inside one half was a layer of hardened yellow beeswax, with not a little, his nose told him, of sheep tallow mixed in. Marks were scraped into this layer, as with a knife point. They were not runes; he could read none of it. They were the markings of the folk of Angle-land; he had seen such before. He showed it to his cousin, who grimaced as well. He re-wrapped the thong about the halves, tied it in a knot, and handed it to her.

It was the Lady Ælfwyn's turn to show triumph, and the bright-haired one also. It lasted a moment only, then they went back to their leave-taking of the thegns. Toki went off, for good this time. What caught Sidroc's ear was the bright-haired one, telling the eldest thegn she swore to love Ælfwyn as a sister.

So she was not kin. He stood a moment longer watching, then the thegns pulled themselves up on their horses. He turned away then, knowing the two maids stood with their serving woman, watching those who had brought them from afar move off, likely forever.

There were things he must do about the hall, yet he did not move towards it. Ælfwyn and the bright-haired one were also slow to return. He saw Ælfwyn hesitate, speak to her friend, and then set off along the stone wall of the hall. The serving woman was at their heels, her shawl held tightly about her plump person. The steps of the three slowed the more as they reached the charred remains of the old hall. They stood looking over the fallen timbers. A few areas of stone floor were visible through the clotted debris, and the outline of the fire-pit could be discerned. He could tell by the closeness of their heads that they spoke of what they saw.

The day of the hall's burning, of the taking of Four Stones, was almost as vivid in Sidroc's mind as if it had happened last month. He saw himself running at Yrling's side through the kitchen yard, felt again the impact of the butchery knife on the shield with which he had protected Asberg, saw the phantoms of the men he had fought and killed, the shades of those brethren who had fallen. Today the mist in the air, and the wet of the burnt wood even conveyed a whiff of fire, a stale and cold smell of what had been a raging conflagration.

The eyes of the three newcomers had lifted to the pike upon which Merewala's head had been impaled. Its barbed tip was innocent of its burden now, but was upright, wedged between two paving stones.

He found himself coming up behind them as they stood there, looking upon this.

"They have not even cleared away this rubble," Ælfwyn told her friend. It was wonder, and complaint both.

He answered her.

"It is kept as a trophy."

They turned to him, unable to conceal their startle at his nearness. He went on, in the kind of boastful carelessness of tone he disdained in his cousin. "For many months the head of Merewala, the Lord of Four Stones, was stuck on that pike, until the ravens had their fill, and the skull crumbled under their pecking. Thus did he learn of our skill at war."

Ælfwyn stood her ground, and looked back at the pike. "He rests in honour still," she claimed. The pointed chin rose again before she turned her blue eyes back to him. She was not cowed; far from it, and was not afraid to let him see it.

He wished to know more of these two, and so would tell them something of himself. "You are a spirited one, Lady," he told Ælfwyn, "and are made of good stuff, for you stand up well to the nephew of Yrling."

Both looked to him, their lips parted in surprise. It was Yrling's bride who spoke. "You are his nephew?"

He smiled at her, both at her surprise, and at the pleasure he felt speaking alone with two such beauties. "Yes, I, and also Toki; but he is not my brother."

The Saxon words felt strange in his mouth, though he used that tongue to speak to the folk of the hall, to order them to some task. This was so different.

He now could ask that which he most wanted to know. He shifted his eyes to the bright-haired one, before looking back to Ælfwyn. "This Lady is not your sister, but your cousin?"

"No," Ælfwyn said. "The Lady is my friend."

Her tone was resolute, suggesting he could not understand the depths of such a bond between women. The bright-haired one stood the straighter at hearing Ælfwyn name her thus, and the shoulders of the two maids touched as they stood before him. They looked at him with something nearing defiance, had it not been softened by the strong and certain affection between them. These two would act as one, he felt.

"She is a good friend, then, to come so far with you," he noted.

It felt a feeble, even foolish comment, after what he had just witnessed between them. But it would allow another question. He looked at the bright-haired one. "You are then also from Wessex."

She would have to speak to him now, look at him, and speak. She had been the one to hazard doing so when they arrived, and he wanted to hear her do so, again.

"No, I have not come so far as my Lady," she said, "for I am come from Mercia, by the river Dee." Her voice in tone was slightly lower than that of Ælfwyn, and she spoke slowly, as if to make sure he understood.

He was smiling at her, saying anything to keep her speaking to him. "I would like to see that place. I hear there is great wealth there."

Her answer was much the quicker, almost a snap at him. It was not anger but alarm; she had tossed her head, and her nostrils had flared like that of a mare.

"Then you have heard a lie, for our lands are poor and marshy, and for many years we have fought the Welsh so that no store of grain remains from year to year."

He must ask now, and did.

"Who are you?"

The green eyes blinked at him, the curve of her shoulders lifting under the mantle that cloaked them.

"I am Ceridwen, daughter of Cerd, and my dead father was an ealdorman."

He did not know the title, a lord or war-chief of this place, he knew, to have such offspring as she. Her name came out in a rush of hard sounds, bright and demanding, washing over him.

He knew he laughed. Her youth, her tenderness, her beauty and fierceness forced him to laugh, and to say the next, which he meant in admiration.

"You are a true shield-maiden. I will be careful of you."

Her cheek coloured under his gaze, and her lower lip trembled an instant, whether in anger or in shame he could not tell.

He forced his eyes back to Yrling's wife. There was something he wished to learn from her parting from her father's thegns. He asked her what man here at Four Stones had written the message in wax for her. He thought only Christian holy men could do so, and one with that skill might be useful.

It was the lady's turn to smile. "Then I cannot help you," she answered, "for I know of no such man."

It was not the answer he wanted, and he told her so, not hiding the sternness he felt at her jest.

But the bright one, the shield-maiden, took a step towards him, a step shielding Yrling's wife from his stare.

"My Lady speaks the truth," she said. "She knows of no such man. I am the scribe that wrote the letter."

He wanted to laugh, but in astonishment. "You? I do not believe it."

Her answer was as swift and firm as had been her earlier declaring of her name and father.

"Then you do not believe the truth. I was raised by the Black Monks, and they gave me this art."

He could not help his smile. "I believe you, shield-maiden," he told her. He let his eyes linger a moment longer before addressing Ælfwyn.

"You do indeed bring rich treasure to Yrling."

He heard the serving woman make one of her sputtering clucks at this, but kept his eyes on the new Lady of Four Stones.

She returned his gaze with a mild and questioning look of her own, but there was quiet firmness in her next words to him.

"She is not treasure, nor is the cream coloured pony, for it is hers outright. Will you see that this is known, nephew of Yrling?"

He had to smile. This one, with her gentle demand, her fearlessness in speaking, would be a worthy help-mate to his uncle.

"Yes, I will see that it is known." He now looked to the shield-maiden at her side, seeming both proud and abashed to be spoken of in this way. He thought of the shaggy pony who had been led in with the waggons; it was hers. Had she ridden it from Mercia?

He could not help the next, and said it almost as he turned away from them both. He spoke now as much of himself as he did of the bright-haired one.

"But I would rather see her on a stallion of Yrling's."

TREASURE

SIDROC wanted to ride out, go saddle his bay and be off. He would turn the thick arched neck of his horse down the village road and canter to the valley of horses; or range farther out, keep to a westerly track, and with long, loping, and forgetful strides, retrace a part of the path the maids had taken. But he was in command of Four Stones and could not.

He could not leave; he could not enter the treasure room. The body of the hall with its matted and soiled straw upon the floor, and the thralls laboring to bring in more wood for the fire-pit offered no respite. The work and kitchen yards teemed with men, and more thralls. There was no place to be alone.

He went to the stable. On either side of the broad doors were work benches, where bridles, saddles and harnesses might be waxed and repaired. The stable man skilled in the making of saddles had been killed in the capture of the fortress, but the lads who remained were able enough, and one, he had seen, was good with horses as well. This youth now came forward from the shadows of the box stalls, rake in hand, alert to any order Sidroc might give. The tall Dane did nothing but nod at him; he was not needed. The lad went back to his mucking.

Sidroc took his saddle from off the racks farther down the wall and laid it on one of the work benches. A chorus of mewling and rustling from the hay loft above his head told of new kittens up there; the stable cats were good ones and he rarely entered the place without finding the remains of rats and mice near the doorway.

He turned to his saddle. He owned three, and six horses. The bay stallion was broad-backed and still gaining flesh. Sidroc had seen a chafe on the beast's back after his last ride, caused by the ill-fitting saddle in his hands. Now with chisel he chipped away at the wooden underframe of the thing, to shape it.

As he worked he thought of the shield-maiden.

He should have laughed at himself for thinking of her as such. The shield-maidens descended over the fields of battle on their magic horses, plucking up downed warriors and carrying the valourous dead off to Asgard, to feast in the Halls of the Slain. Some men believed the shield-maidens did even more; that they might hover on their flying steeds above the contest, and choose with pointed throwing spear those men they most admired.

They were proud and fierce, and he thought they must also be beautiful.

This one, come with Yrling's wife – the white pony was hers. She rode, and somehow with her look she had chosen him, singled him out, as fell a touch as a spear point to the breast.

He shook his head. She knew nothing of this; felt nothing of it. His hand grasped the chisel and pared away at the saddle-frame, but his thoughts were not his own to guide.

He had not seen one like her.

He recalled her look when he had mentioned the wealth of Mercia, the flare of her nostrils at his suggestion he might raid there. She was indeed like a beautiful mare, one who had never been backed or bridled, wild and free.

He considered her person, the green eyes, the striking hair. It was not red, like that of Jari. It was more the ruddy gold of certain choice ornaments he had glimpsed in the treasure trove of Yrling. But she was not treasure of Yrling, he was quick to remind himself. In this land Yrling could take but one wife, and he had taken the Lady Ælfwyn.

He was already thinking of her like this, the wife of Yrling. The shield-maiden – he had not expected her. He had not even pictured the woman Yrling was to wed coming with any other women, but of course now he realised that like the first to come here she would have at least one serving woman with her, some trusted thrall or freedwoman to tend to her body and her dress. The big and blustering one was she; the older woman's possessiveness and care was clear in the sharpness of her look, and pitch of her voice. But the maid with the bright hair . . .

She had not Ælfwyn's stature, but her hips and breasts bore a generous curve that the older maid lacked. In her speech too she seemed older than her looks, or perhaps it was the boldness of her words, and the way she lifted her eyes to his. Those green eyes looked fearless, even if at times her lower lip trembled. Her gaze seemed to question him, even when her lips were silent.

She was not kin, and not serving woman to Ælfwyn; the lady had named her friend. She was not bound to come in Ælfwyn's train, yet had somehow chosen to do so. Her loyalty must run deep to follow her here. He knew from his own life that a child's loyalties could be stronger than those formed later. He thought too that such a bond bode well for the forging of an even deeper bond, with a mate.

Her name . . . he knew of few names of the women of these parts, but her name had an odd and alien sound to it. But then she was not of Wessex, but another land, Mercia.

He thought of the exchange he had just had, with both maids. He had been harsh with them, taken aback by their forthright boldness and their challenging of him. They had stood up to all of it. It was in their blood to do so; both came from noble stock, though the shield-maiden had told him her father was dead. Ælfwyn's father was not; he was rich and had drive enough to make a Peace with Yrling on his own terms, not waiting for his King, Æthelred of Wessex to act. His thoughts flickered to his uncle, who had sat with Ælfsige and made this Peace with him. Yrling would be glad indeed to see the beauty the reeve had sent him, a daughter as desirable as the golden plate Ælfsige had displayed.

Of a sudden Sidroc could not wait for his uncle to return. He did not know when that would be, tonight or the next day, surely. Whatever he and Guthrum had discussed, however far they may have ranged on a hunt for upland boar or deer, he must return soon.

The chisel had been still in his hands; he had been caught up in this thoughts. He looked down at his work, the small pile of light-hued shavings from the elm the saddle frame had been crafted from. He thought of his bay, and the fact that the shield-maiden could ride. He wanted to ride out with her.

Yrling arrived that night, and close enough to the evening meal that nearly all the men were already gathered within the hall. The watch-men posted along the road at a distance spotted him, and one rode ahead at speed to let the hall know he was come. The gates were opened, and Sidroc and Toki stood by the stable to greet him, oil-soaked torches in hand. Yrling rode in, twenty men clattering behind him. Dusk was deepening, but the yard, now full of the stamping of horses and laughter of men, was full of life. One of the pack horses bore a gutted boar slung over its back, proof of the success of the hunt, and of Guthrum's liberality in sharing its fruits with his guest.

Once off his horse, Yrling fell in with his nephews. They made for the hall and the meal awaiting them. Before the ruins of the larger hall were the two big waggons, high-hooped, the tarpaulins laced tight. Yrling slowed.

"They are come," Sidroc told his uncle, of the waggons. He extended the torch further out, so the glare would not blind them as they looked.

"They?" Yrling answered. "The daughter of Ælfsige of Cirenceaster, you mean."

"Já. And another maid."

For answer Yrling gave a grunt of acknowledgment; of course she would bring a serving maid with her.

Toki was quick to speak. "You will be sorry not to bed both," he told Yrling. "But the second will be my woman."

Toki said this last not looking at his uncle, but at his cousin. Sidroc would let no anger show on his face. Toki rarely missed a chance at mockery, aimed at anyone who might possess something which Toki himself could not attain. The only surprise Sidroc felt was his cousin's already knowing that he wanted the other maid.

Yrling's step had slowed as he looked at the waggons. It was far too dark to accept their contents now; a show must be made of it before all the men, and in good daylight. They moved forward, to where the hall door stood open for them. He had a word for Toki, though, as they reached the steps.

"You will touch nothing that is of my wife," he warned. "And you have a wife, better than you deserve, in Jutland. Next year or so, we can send for her. Other women too."

The men within were loud in their acclaim when Yrling walked in, and grew the louder when he had the boar carcass hauled before them. Yrling now saw what his two nephews and all others within had already seen. The old straw, which had been ankle-deep in many places, had been raked away from the floor by the thralls. Fresh straw, pale yellow and clean, had been strewn, with a generous margin left bare around the fire-pit. There they trod upon the hard but clean surface of the red-and-black stone floor, of which most men had but dim memory.

"Your wife, already at work," Sidroc told him, at which Yrling gave a nod of satisfaction.

Yrling took his place at the high table, his nephews at either side, and the food was brought. The ale as ever was good, the bread also, but the porridge of dried beans and lentils was much the same fare they had subsisted on throughout Winter. Soon Spring greens could be plucked to lighten it. And soon, Yrling hoped, this young wife of his would take hall and village in hand.

The ale went round long after the wooden plates and crockery bowls had been cleared. All knew the treasure sent by Ælfsige of Cirenceaster would be unloaded on the morrow, and that the hand-fast would be held, with a bride-ale to follow. There was eagerness for all these things. Their war-chief was returned, and they would enjoy pleasures soon to come. But some also suspected that Yrling's time at Turcesig with Guthrum had not been given over entirely to the chase. Yrling seemed in no haste to share news with those picked men who broke their bread at the high table with him. Asberg often sat next to Sidroc, and as the meal was coming to a close raised his eyebrows to him in question. There had been rumours enough of coming battle, would Yrling speak of it?

That the men were restless in their way deepened their curiosity. Winter, with its mud, wet, and snow was not a time of raiding. And so much had already been claimed. Yrling had held off from any attacks on the easternmost reaches of Wessex, as part of the Peace with the reeve of Cirenceaster. Lindisse and all of Anglia was won, or nearly so, as was Northumbria; the trading town of Jorvik had become a prized destination for Danes with silver to spend. The vast Kingdoms of Mercia and Wessex alone remained.

When at the end of the meal Yrling rose and nodded to his nephews, all eyes at his table followed them. Yrling turned to the thick oak planks that made up the dividing wall which marked the treasure room, that wall on which Aki had drawn the raven. In the dimness of the hall the bird could scarce be seen. The three stood at the treasure room door as Yrling slipped his key into the box lock. Toki had grabbed a torch, and carried it in with them, setting it in an iron holder nailed into the wall.

Once inside the cousins surrendered their keys to their uncle, who restrung them on the ring by the door hinges. The shadows of all three men were huge, flickering over the bare wood of the floor, dancing brokenly upon the chests and casks piled against the walls.

Yrling turned to them.

"Hingvar and Svein have struck deep into Wessex," is what he said.

It was perhaps the last thing either cousin expected to hear. Hingvar and Svein were brothers who had fought for Yrling. Their tenure at Four Stones was brief. They had joined up when Yrling began slaving in earnest, and after a few months had ridden off, their saddle bags burdened with silver from their share in the takings. Though good warriors Yrling had not been sorry to see them go. They were, despite being brothers, often at each other's throats, and had a talent for involving other men in their many quarrels.

"How many men have they?" asked Sidroc. They had ridden off alone; he had not forgotten that either they had invited no man to join them, or if they had, that none would take up with them.

"Three score and five," came Yrling's muted answer.

Five-and-sixty men. It seemed impossible they could have gathered so many warriors so quickly, and yet they had.

"How does Guthrum know?" posed Toki.

"Guthrum has as many outriders as I have men," his uncle shot back, only a slight stretching of the truth. "In two days, three at most, he knows all of importance in the borderlands."

The report of the brothers' success hung in the air. Yrling now had ninety warriors, and was looking for more, Sidroc knew. But he had a base, a good one, the fortress of Four Stones, and had been named Jarl by Guthrum, the greatest of all Jarls here. Hingvar and Svein had attracted three score and five men with none of that, just with their fame and the silver they could offer. And their plans to win more.

Both cousins were staring at Yrling, waiting for him to speak.

"Guthrum is certain they will aim for Æthelred."

Kill the King of Wessex. Sidroc lifted his eyes to the timbers far above his head. Thick as they were they were almost lost in darkness, the torch light by which he had been watching Yrling's face failing to extend much into the gloom.

Toki had given a snort. "When do we ride?" he asked. He was already grinning at the prospect.

"Svein will not be happy to see your face again," Sidroc answered. Toki and Svein had come to blows over a dice game, Svein claiming that Toki had cheated. Yrling had not stopped them as they traded punches, but had stood watching until Svein broke off. Later Svein complained, loudly and to all who would listen, that Toki was shielded from the justice of a thrashing he deserved.

"If we ride, it will be to join Hingvar and Svein, not to fight them," Yrling said.

Yrling did not often confide in his nephews, and both were listening with intent.

Sidroc would hazard a question. "Ride – with Guthrum?"

"The two brothers may soon rival Guthrum in power. That is all I can say."

Yrling's eyes, always sharp under his hooded brows, stared back at Sidroc.

Sidroc looked back at his uncle. Danes at war were fluid; grouping and splitting, re-forming under a new war-lord whose chances at plunder they deemed greater. Ties were loose and easily sundered. Any chief's war-band could swell or diminish on a single rumour. Even the most famed of Jarls here in Angle-land faced this. But Sidroc had more than once seen Guthrum, and had lived amongst Hingvar and Svein.

He studied his uncle's face a moment longer. Yrling had made a blood-oath to Guthrum, on the great bracelet of gold circling that war-chief's wrist. He must ask the next, to see how far his uncle's thoughts had resolved.

"How will Guthrum move?"

"He may not," came his uncle's answer. "He will watch from afar, gauge the brothers' chances, I think, then make decision."

Toki could not accept such caution. "And let Svein and Hingvar win Wessex?" He shook his head, his yellow hair brushing against his shoulders as he did. His next words were spoken to his uncle, as much challenge as call to action.

"Either with the brothers, or against them, I say we move now."

"At what cost?" Sidroc countered, turning to face Toki fully. "Even for Guthrum there is risk, to move so many men so far. Four Stones must be defended. It would take two-thirds of our men just to match Hingvar and Svein's forces; by the time we arrive they may have many more. And to meet two who can never be trusted, two who were always warring between themselves."

There was more at stake, in Sidroc's eyes. To make a move to either fight or join with the brothers could be easily read as betrayal by Guthrum. He need not add that Yrling was counting on Guthrum to aid him in any future claim in Wessex.

Sidroc had a final question, for Yrling.

"Why did Guthrum tell you this?"

A slow smile spread across his uncle's face. "That, I have been trying to decide. But all I know is that I am one who he also watches."

Yrling gave a shake of his head now. "More ale," he declared, turning for the door. The noise of the hall had not abated in their absence. "Ale, and then let me go up and see what Ælfsige of Cirenceaster sent me."

The meeting did not go well. Yrling held his ale as well as any man, and better than most, but the long ride, the news he bore, the lateness of the hour all conspired to give his first encounter with the Lady Ælfwyn an edge unwarranted by her youth, beauty, and worth. Toki had nearly beaten the door down, that door to her narrow chamber lying at the end of the wooden stair, and all three females within could hide neither their fright nor their ire at this intrusion. They stood defenceless yet united in the harsh glare of the torch, their fingers digging into the woollen mantles they clutched about them. Any man being so roused would have drawn his weapon in response; these women had naught but their pride and their anger to bolster their fear.

Once again the bright-haired one had moved to shield her friend, tried, without speaking, to show her displeasure at the affront they had committed in almost forcing their way inside. Sidroc in turn had attempted to smooth their exit, prodding both Yrling and Toki to leave them be for the night. It was an act which had earned him a look from the shield-maiden, a look that seemed to hold some thankfulness to him in it. The men had but one torch with them, but dark as the room was behind the women, Sidroc could not help see the narrow beds from which they had arisen. Could not help see, and wonder which was that she had lain in . . .

The three came down next morning, into the hall when Sidroc, Yrling, and Toki were at table. They came in a kind of procession, one at a time, and with measured step. It was in every way the opposite of the night before, when Yrling and his nephews had burst into their room. They came now as they wished to present themselves, and Sidroc, sitting there, fixed his eyes on them as they appeared. The shield-maiden came first, in a gown of a shade that was a deeper echo of her own hair. About her waist, and pulled snugly enough to show off the roundness of her hips, was a long sash, covered over with needle-work in many shades, of birds flying and strutting. She wore no gemstones, but the thread-work alone told of leisure enough to stitch such things. The chestnut gold hair was wealth in itself, barely contained or controlled by her head wrap of white. Her eyes flicked past Toki to him, he felt, before fixing on Yrling.

Just behind her was Ælfwyn of Cirenceaster, arrayed as she had been when she sat so stiffly on the waggon board, in a gown of deep blue, and a mantle of brilliant red over her narrow shoulders. But this morning she had placed a multitude of jewellery on gown, wrists, and fingers, including at the neckline a round brooch set with garnets. Sidroc had never looked on a queen, and even the glimpses he had seen of the richest war-lords' wives in Dane-mark did not prepare him for this splendor of colour and precious metal. Resting on her breast was the choicest prize of all, for she had placed the great pearl about her neck, that which Sidroc had chosen for her from the store of Yrling's treasure.

Sidroc had not had time to tell Yrling of this, and his uncle's surprise at seeing the pearl was great. Ælfwyn had stopped and made a bow, and the pearl, hanging down freely from her slender throat on its gold chain, was as bright as a small Moon.

Yrling rose and came around the table to her. "The pearl – how did you get it?"

The lady looked almost as puzzled as Yrling. "Why, I wear it as your gift. Toki delivered it to me on the road here."

She looked now at Toki, who with a smirk glanced at Sidroc. Yrling chanced to look at Sidroc, and was made to understand.

Yrling carried it well. "I had forgot," he told her. "It was many days ago that I sent Toki with that charge." He had cause to grin, not only for the resourcefulness of his nephews, but for his bride's evident pleasure in the pearl, wearing it for him like this. The grin softened to a smile as he looked at her. "My gift is worn well."

The slightest movement of the shield-maiden's hands made Sidroc turn his eyes from Yrling to her. She looked at him for but a moment, enough for him to see she knew the truth behind the gift. It was Sidroc who had sent it, on behalf of a neglectful uncle.

But now Yrling was leading Ælfwyn to the table. Toki was just at Sidroc's side, and made a movement first towards the bright-haired maid.

"She sits by me," Sidroc told his cousin. His voice was low, and he spoke in Norse, but his look was enough to quell Toki's forward movement. Yet Toki gave a short laugh as he answered.

"But she will lie with me."

Sidroc heard this, low as it was, but gave no sign of doing so. Yrling had placed his bride to his left, and Sidroc took his place by her, the shield-maiden next to him, on his left. A glittering array of cups sat there. The gemmed cup of gold from which Yrling drank was before him, as were two new cups, neither of which Sidroc had seen before this morning. He watched his uncle pick up a second golden cup, one set with rounded chunks of rock crystal and cabochons of jet, and set it before Ælfwyn. Another cup was new, and Yrling passed it to Sidroc, that he might place it before the maid at his side. It was a small cup wrought of silver, and like his own, had a rim of gold.

Their serving woman went out through the kitchen passageway. She had been much in the kitchen yard since her arrival. The food that came was of unusual savour, far better than the meal last night, and the men knew it was likely her doing, rousing the kitchen folk to as yet unknown labours. And too, the waggons surely carried provender to help make this first meal a fine one. The roast fowl would have come from the hen houses in the kitchen yard, but the salt it had been sprinkled with was white and pure, with no trace of sour earthiness. There were as well bowls of dried and honeyed pears, apples, and cherries. Honey had not been tasted by the men at Four Stones in months; a crock of it must have been brought in the waggons.

This sweetness added to the meal, and to Sidroc was somehow played upon by the sweet odour rising from the young women flanking him. Even the poorest woman could pluck herbs and flowers and roll them in her hands, crushing the stems and blossoms to release their perfume. But such fragrance was as fleeting as the broken flowers themselves. Rich women used scented oils to anoint skin and hair. Merchants had stalls from which they sold tiny vials of them. Up at the trading town of Jorvik he had seen the minute flagons, and seen too how well dressed were those Danes who traded in them. These two noblewomen would have such oils, and their hair and clothing carried a wafting and spicy sweetness, fresh and heady both. All about them, gowns, and person, and hair, seemed so. There was a washing shed out near the kitchen yard, with basins and a low wooden tub, where the men could wash hands, face, and feet every day. Despite these ablutions Sidroc was more than aware of his own strong scent, one of sweat, horses, and leather. It was a contrast as great as that between his own hand, large, calloused, dark hair growing on the back of it, and the graceful, pale, and slender hands of the two Saxon maids curling about the body of their gold and silver cups.

Yrling spoke to his nephews during this meal, spoke in Norse. Sidroc, seated between the two maids, would have liked to have spoken to them, had them lean forward slightly on the bench and face each other with the smiles he knew they must often share as they spoke together. But Yrling was speaking of the movement of horses, telling Toki and him of those of his own he wanted rested in the forest-hemmed valley, and which he wanted brought back to the stable paddock within the keep confines. It was foaling time as well, and he wanted all dams nearing their time brought to the stable, or to the mares' paddock for safety. Wolves roamed the forest, bold enough in their packs to spring from the trees and run down a newly dropped foal.

Then, with an abruptness that made his bride blink, Yrling set down his cup. "We go now to the waggons," he announced, speaking in the tongue of Angle-land to Ælfwyn, "and I will accept the tribute that you bring."

He looked to his nephews, telling them to go now and ready the waggons. They rose, Sidroc with regret. He walked past the fire-pit, Toki ahead of him, knowing that his uncle sat there alone with his bride and her friend. There was something he wanted to say to them, not meant for his ears.

When they came out all the men at Four Stones were waiting. Those working at forge or smoothing wood came from their sheds, with tongs or adze in hand, summoned by the whistles of Sidroc and Toki. Others who had been rolling barrels across the forecourt, or carrying armfuls of wooden staves stopped, so they might see. Even the lookouts upon the ramparts turned to gaze down. The cousins had unlaced the tarpaulins, pulling them open so tantalizing glimpses of chests and barrels could be seen.

Yrling jumped up on the waggon board of the lead waggon, and held his arms up.

"I promised a hall, and have won it for you," he told the men in Norse. "I promised riches, and have won them, and shared them out with open hand."

These first words were met with cheers and whoops, the men beating their flat palms upon their thighs to applaud their Jarl.

"You promised women, too," called one in the back of the circle. It was only half in jest, for another man quickly added, "Win us some like those before us," and gestured to the two maids standing there by the wheel.

Yrling laughed, but Ælfwyn, though she tried to smile, understood the import if not the words.

Yrling grinned down at her, and pointed at her himself. "Ælfwyn is my wife, she who has brought all this across Kingdoms. This is what her father, Ælfsige of Cirenceaster sends as his tribute to me."

She heard her name, it was clear by the shift of her eyes, and her father's name as well, but what Yrling said of her she could not know. He turned to the contents of the waggon then, drawing forth things within, holding them up for the men to admire. A massive bronze pot, surely of Frankish make, was pulled forward, one embossed all over with wreathing animals and vines. Other, smaller pots, also of bronze, showing the same skill in their working. A bowl, a shallow dish, a large round salver, all of silver, and all so bright that one saw one's reflection within. A small casket of bronze, enviable in itself, bearing nothing less than pieces of gold, thinly beaten but of diameter greater than a hen's egg. Three bracelets of the same precious stuff, one sized for a man. Lengths of cloth of purple, which few men had ever before seen, and which Yrling held in his outstretched hands so that the rare colour dazzled their eyes. All this and more he pulled before them, laughing at the richness of his spoils as he did so.

Sidroc and Toki, standing at either side of the waggon, had full view of all the treasure as it was unpacked and displayed. The quality of all was almost dizzying. The ground of the yard was muddy, and the past many days had been wet and grey. Sun shone upon them this morning, yellow beams highlighting the deep green of bronze, the shine of silver, the gleam of gold. All was heightened by the sunlight, the laughter of the men, their surprise and awe at each new discovery they were shown. The two maids who had travelled amongst this treasure raised the pitch of expectation and pleasure another notch. Their youth and comeliness was fully met by these rich goods.

Sidroc watched the display of tribute as intently as any of them. He was aware, slowly at first and then fully, that this was a woman's treasure, things chosen with care not only for their costliness but for their beauty, or their value in everyday life. No weapon chest was there; no seax or sword with dancing, pattern-welded steel, no helmet of fanciful design. Mayhap Ælfsige could not countenance the sending of arms; not when he had lost so much to Yrling and other warriors. Ælfwyn's mother may have made up the treasure-list, filling it with such things as would meet her lord and husband's requirement as to worthiness. One glance at her daughter told him of the most precious item she had parted with.

Ælfwyn stood there at the waggon wheel, watching her new lord display what she had brought, listening to the crowing cheers rising from the men in response. Sidroc could not read her face; the lips were tightly pressed, bowed slightly upward as if in effort of a smile.

But the eyes of rich and clear blue were bright, as if tears glistened there.

The shield-maiden at her side stood so close to her, shoulders again touching, that it was only after a moment's study he saw that they had clasped hands. There at the level of their skirts, their fingers intertwined, half hidden in the fabric of their gowns. He thought again what he had thought before, that these two would act as one.

It filled him with a sudden burst of happiness, almost exaltation. The one would wed Yrling. The other, him.

TWO CALLS

"NOW we will wed," Yrling told Ælfwyn of Cirenceaster shortly after the waggons were unloaded.

They stood in the treasure room with Sidroc and the bright-haired one. It was the first look at the room for the two maids, and both, though modest in their movements, had been with their eyes travelling over the number of chests and casks already there, and the many more chests, casks, and baskets now added to the store from their waggons. One waggon had held things which had already been carried up to the narrow room in which they had been sleeping; several chests, and weaving looms. But this was the first time they had entered that room in which Ælfwyn would sleep with Yrling. The low bed was one of the last things their eyes had dropped to when Yrling had spoken.

"I will not wed today," said that lady. The flatness of her tone and quickness of her words made all three look to her.

Yrling's jaw tightened, but it was Sidroc who spoke. He kept his voice low, but he gazed at her fully. "You are come here to be wed," he reminded her.

"I cannot wed without a holy man." She had swallowed before she said this, a swallowing down of her fear, he saw.

It was again Sidroc who answered her. "There are none of your priests here, nor for many miles. It cannot be done."

He watched her lift her chin, look back at him. Her voice was just above a whisper. It held no defiance, yet was definite in its certainty. "Then I cannot wed," she told him.

There was no answer to this. The gaze of the bright-haired one went from Ælfwyn to Yrling. All of them could see the anger clouding Yrling's face, but it was she who spoke.

She took a small step, not to his uncle, but to Sidroc. Her eyes fastened on his own, which had been narrowed at his uncle's bride. Her movement towards him claimed his whole attention.

"Sir," she asked him. "There must be a monk or brother nearby. Please to find him so that my Lady's wedding may be a happy one."

A movement of her lower lip betrayed her fear, one she mastered enough to speak to him. Yet the wide green eyes did not falter as they held him in their gaze. Indeed, her eyes were fixed on him.

It was both plea, and challenge, directed at him. Yrling was watching him as well, watching to see how he would meet this unwonted demand. The lady had refused to wed; the shield-maiden had posed a solution, one which he could pursue or refuse.

But Yrling made decision. His uncle was speaking now, staring at him and giving him his orders. "Look for such a man. If he can be found before tomorrow noon, let him be present."

He looked to Ælfwyn. "If not, she will wed without him."

She did not move at his words. But the bright-haired one, having won this consent, bowed her head. "Thank you, my Lord, thank you, Sir," she told them both.

That night Ælfwyn and the shield-maiden again sat on either side of Sidroc. Each were both garbed in the rich dress of the morning, Ælfwyn with the great pearl lying on her breast, hanging from its slender chain of gold. As the two maids entered all eyes shifted to them, and as they passed leering smiles broke across the faces of the men they left in their wake. Sidroc felt an unreasoning umbrage towards his brothers, one as irksome as it was unmerited. The shield-maiden was unwed, and fair game.

Jari was one of the few at the head table who looked without lust. He was saving up silver for the coming of a maid he was pledged to back in Jutland, and had already begun building a house for her out by the valley of horses. Guthrum had ships at his command and had told the men of Four Stones he would ferry waiting wives and sweethearts to Lindisse when the time came. As far as Sidroc knew every other man considered himself a suitable mate for the bright-haired one. Even Asberg had mentioned her to him. Asberg, who was a good warrior, had Yrling's favour, and bore no scar upon his face.

When she slid in on the bench next Sidroc she kept her eyes on Ælfwyn, who was in fact looking at Yrling.

His uncle was taking in the loveliness of his bride with no attempt to mask his pleasure.

Sidroc made comment on this, leaning nearer the shield-maiden's head to speak to her.

"Your Lady is very beautiful; it is more than my uncle expected."

This made her turn to him, turn and even smile. He was aware of his own smile, aware too of the thoughtful way she looked at him now.

"Then your uncle will be good to her," she said.

He let his eyes lift a moment to where Ælfwyn sat, her head inclined to Yrling as he spoke to her. He looked back to the shield-maiden's uplifted face. "She will have all she wants, if she be good in return."

"She is very good, I can tell you that," she answered.

He had to laugh, a guard against his own feelings. Her innocence and earnestness, the lusting eyes of the men as they followed her, the way Yrling studied the maid of Cirenceaster who was soon to warm his bed; it all caused a churning frustration which found outlet in his countering words.

"I think she will be," he said, unable to curb his sneering tone.

She smarted at his answer. The sting of affront, low pitched but discernable, was in her next words to him.

"You gave Toki the pearl, did you not?" she challenged.

He let out a quieting breath. "Yes, I did," he told her. "Yrling would never think of such a thing."

She was as swift with her reply as she had been in seeing the thing. "Then it was given falsely."

"No, it was not," he defended, "for she would have had it sooner or later, by Yrling's hand. And it did much good, to come on the road as a welcome gift."

She got hot at this, the flare of her nostrils proving it, though she kept her voice low. "A gift given falsely never does good."

Again he laughed. "Did you not all remark over it when you saw it? Did you not squeal with delight? Did you not talk of the richness of it, or the generosity of Yrling?"

She had dropped her eyes under his words, as if in admission. His frustration now was aimed at himself, speaking to her so. He raised his eyes to the darkness of the roof timbers. No answers were there, but he ran his hand through his hair as he calmed his thoughts.

"Things cannot always be as we would have them, shield-maiden," he said, speaking more of himself at this moment than he could admit. "Your Lady knows this, I know this, and one day Yrling will know this."

She blinked at him, listening well to his words, taking them in. When Yrling reached out his hand and closed it around the pearl hanging around her Lady's neck, she looked away.

The next day Sidroc found a Christian holy man, though he had to ride nearly to Geornaham to do so. He took two horses and headed there, wagering that in her devoutness Eldrida, the past Lady of that holding, had succoured such men on her lands. There were surely none left at Four Stones. The temple had been burnt in the taking, and the priest Eldrida had sent with her daughter was as much in the hall's past as was the maid herself.

A tall stone cross stood at the meeting of two roads on the way, and Fate favoured Sidroc by placing a bony and balding man at its foot. He was on his knees at the base of the monument, his fingers clasping the deeply incised scrolls there, a design which ran its way up the length of the worn stone. He was garbed in the gown, brown in hue, that marked him as a holy man. He paid no mind to Sidroc's approach, and only when he called him out did the man rise and turn to face him, slowly, and with a look that suggested he was ready to die. Sidroc told him he was needed, then urged him up on the second horse. There the monk sat wobbling, and, no longer in fear of his life, began chattering away at his escort, who barely grunted at his prattling.

They were half-way back when a rider appeared, coming overland across a meadow fronting a forest. It was a warrior, fully armed, and having emerged from the woodland, now able to canter his mount. The monk gave a shriek. Sidroc had spear and shield, his sword too buckled on his hip, but riding as he was on friendly lands was free of ring-shirt or helmet. The first thing he did was place his fingers in his mouth and give the three-tone whistle which was Yrling's sign.

The rider reined, slowing enough to enable him to return a whistle: Turcesig. This man was from Guthrum, one of his outriders no doubt, returning.

The monk was none the steadier for Sidroc turning his horse's head to the newcomer. He spluttered and gasped, and jiggled his legs as they wrapped his mount's barrel. If Sidroc had not been also holding the reins of the second horse, it may have bolted.

Sidroc knew this outrider, had seen him both at Four Stones and at Turcesig.

"Do you ride now to Yrling?" the man asked. His eyes flicked a moment to the monk, whose horse was trying to turn in circles under the man's restless heels. Sidroc shortened the lead rein and pulled the horse closer.

"Já. Ælfsige of Cirenceaster sent his daughter; he will wed her today." Sidroc gave a slight nod in the direction of the worried monk.

"Guthrum will tell him to enjoy the wedding feast," answered the rider. "Hingvar and Svein are at war in Wessex."

Sidroc asked the same question he had asked his uncle about these two.

"How many men have they?"

"Upwards of one hundred, in two camps, one for each of the brothers."

Fifty men each. Such war-bands could act in concert and trap a force of even greater size between them, inflicting great damage in the panic that ensued.

Sidroc looked up at the sky, one pale blue, a tracery of clouds skimming it in narrow waves. Spring would soon be here. And Hingvar and Svein were already at war, in Wessex.

"Does Æthelred live?"

"They have not caught him yet," came the answer. "But they have had victory in three battles against his armies."

The King of Wessex still lived; he had eluded the brothers so far. Æthelred had craft, or luck, or both, though his forces had been hard hit. But Kingship was strong in Æthelred's blood. Two brothers had ruled before him, ruled and died doing so. And their father had been the great warrior-king Æthelwulf. Æthelred had seemingly bottomless store of silver, as had his brothers and father before him, silver to train and arm his thegns, and silver to buy off the Danes who posed too great a threat to him. The Saxons, when they could not win peace through arms, would buy it. What was this, but what Ælfsige had done, with the Peace he had made with Yrling.

The horses Sidroc had brought were two mares, both fast, both needing work. He would stretch their legs now; carry this news to Four Stones before any other rider did.

He nodded to Guthrum's man. "I ride now to bring Yrling your message."

He looked to the monk, fidgeting away.

"Get off. You must walk to Four Stones; the mare will break your neck if I leave you alone. Be there at noon or I come back and sling you over the saddle like the baggage you are."

The man slipped off the horse as unsteadily as he had sat upon it. Sidroc and the outrider raised their hands to each other, then each spurred their horses to their respective halls.

Sidroc passed the winded mares into the keeping of the stable boy. Yrling was easy to find; he had been leaving the stable as Sidroc rode in. They moved together to the paddock where the boy was cooling the mares, walking them, now saddle-less, in large circles.

"A monk is on his way, will be here shortly," Sidroc told his uncle, knowing that this would not explain the haste in which he had arrived, mares nearly lathered, and he himself slightly out of breath. He then repeated what Guthrum's man had told him.

"Toki will urge you to ride," he finished.

Yrling had listened to the report with eyes lowered, taking it in. Now he looked across the paddock to where the mares moved, tails swishing, the youth walking between them, leading them by their reins.

"Já," he agreed. "Toki is always hasty. Haste can mean being first to the table, or finding that the table is still bare."

He turned to look at Sidroc, and was pointed in his question. "And what do you urge?"

Sidroc was ready with his answer. He had been thinking of the path ahead the entire ride back.

"You have Guthrum's favour. I urge that you keep it."

He paused a moment before going on. "Whatever happens in the rest of Wessex, you will need help at Cirenceaster."

Yrling would not deny this.

"Já. Such a holding will be handed to no one, even one who has such claim on it as me." He thought a moment. "Ælfsige has no son. My wife is the eldest of other daughters. In law, she, or her mother, will have claim to it, should Ælfsige die."

Unspoken was the shared knowledge that if Wessex fell, its laws could crumble too. And a rival Dane who captured Cirenceaster would care little about the rule of law of the people he had overthrown. Only a more powerful Dane could force him to surrender Cirenceaster to the prior claim-holders.

"All the more reason to stay Guthrum's man," his nephew was telling him. He built now on what Yrling had told him of his meeting with the Jarl. "He knows of your marriage, listened well when you asked him to defend any future Wessex claim."

"A claim that may mean nothing if Hingvar and Svein grow much stronger," Yrling said. "To stay here and know they are after Æthelred himself . . . " He shook his head as his voice trailed off. "And Guthrum gave no pledge to me," he reminded.

They had been standing side by side at the paddock fence, their eyes on the circling horses, only rarely tilting their heads to glance at the other. They both turned, began to move off. The hall door was opening, and Sidroc saw first the shield-maiden and then Ælfwyn step out.

But Sidroc was not done yet, and would not be deterred. If Yrling must take wrong action, he wanted it to be for a right end.

"If you must go, go as Guthrum's man. Go on his behalf, as well as your own. See the brothers, then judge who to join."

"You have made up your mind," Yrling observed.

"Because I see clearly," came Sidroc's retort. "I would rather have Guthrum at my back, than face him shield first."

"He turned your head with his offer to you, that you come to him," Yrling responded. He spoke here of Guthrum sizing Sidroc up at their first meeting, and of the Jarl inviting him to join his body-guard of picked men. Yrling gave a short laugh before going on. "Toki was never so put out."

Toki would not last one week in such duty, and both men knew it.

"Já. I would serve as his body-guard," Sidroc answered, of this honour. "Would not you? Guthrum will be King of the Danes here soon." Yrling raised his eyebrows at this, but Sidroc's face showed that he fully believed it.

Sidroc felt a flame of anger arise in him, that his uncle could be blind to Guthrum's full worth. "I believe Guthrum will be King. But you are my uncle. You, when not much more than a boy yourself, took me from a place where I was not wanted. My loyalty is to you."

Yrling turned now to his nephew.

"Then you will back me, whoever I fight," he said.

"I will back you," Sidroc vowed.

They had rarely spoken like this, and the finality of Sidroc's answer sealed their tie.

The two maids were looking at them. Sidroc remembered his mission as he neared.

"I have found a holy man," he told them. "He will be here at noon."

The man finally arrived, and at Yrling's urging, mumbled some words over Ælfwyn, waving his hand above her in the Christian blessing. The bride-ale that followed was a riotous feast. It was late in the evening when the hall was broken down, table tops taken from the trestles, and the treasure room door finally closed behind Yrling and his bride.

Lying there on his pallet in the body of the hall Sidroc found his eyes wide open. The hall was shrouded in darkness, every torch rubbed out, the fire in the pit banked down. Most of the men about him were already asleep, too drunk for restlessness or even snoring. Off to one side, only a little more than an arm length's distance away from where he lay, stood the oak of the treasure room wall, behind which Sidroc knew Yrling was embracing Ælfsige's daughter.

Sidroc kept his eyes straight up. Above the stairs near the hall door he pictured the narrow room where the shield-maiden lay. Deprived of her friend, she would be alone with the serving woman.

He had been late to the hall. Before the food had come he had seen Toki speaking to her, and seen her answer. She turned from him abruptly, to where he himself was approaching the table. She rose and looked at Sidroc and invited him to go to Ælfwyn and Yrling, and wish them joy. He extended his hand, and she had taken it.

"Toki will be angry that you prefer my hand to his," he told her, as they moved off.

"You do not fear his anger," she returned, showing all her high spirit. "And for Toki any woman's hand would do as well."

During the course of the feast she had again sat next him. She was wearing the green gown she had worn the day they arrived, the verdant hue of which was an echo of her eyes. The fire had been heaped high, and besides the torches jutting from the walls there were oil cressets set on the tables. So much flame gave her chestnut gold hair an added gleam, bringing out the ruddy tints in it, making golden her skin. When she had picked up the silver ale cup in her hand and brought its gilded rim to her lips he could not force his eyes away. And she seemed happy, hopeful for her friend and nearly at ease amongst the revelry. When Toki sang she watched, but Sidroc saw, despite the sweetness of his cousin's song, the hardness in her eyes. When Aki got up and began tossing and catching three rings of brass, then wooden sticks, and then three bronze cups, she laughed with all the others at his skill. He had not heard such laughter from her.

They spoke together as well, more than they had at other meals. From their first words together she had listened with care, perhaps because his accents were not her own. This night his words and manner to her seemed less wrong to him, more true to how he wanted to sound. It might be just how her beauty affected him. With the women he had lain with, there had been no courting. The pretty whore in Ribe had not needed courting, only silver. The others he had known carnally back in Jutland had been due to drink, or here in Angle-land, desperation. Now she was come, a creature high-born, of another and unknown country. And he already fully expected her to be his.

In the morning the door to the treasure opened early. Yrling came out in the dimness, called his closest men to him, and set out on horseback to the valley of horses. There was no need for such a ride, Sidroc felt, other than his uncle's need to clear his head after both feast and hand-fast night. The ribbing and grins Yrling was the target of he shook off with a knowing grin of his own. But Sidroc was glad for the early air, the strength of his horse beneath him, the view of the Sun first paling, then staining the sky orange and yellow as it lifted above the dark trees.

When they returned and gathered to break their fast Ælfwyn and the shield-maiden came down from their upstairs chamber. Both were smiling. The new Lady of Four Stones went to her husband's side, and her friend came to him. Toki shot a look at him, one Sidroc refused to acknowledge. But his first words to the shield-maiden were of it.

"You make Toki jealous. He thinks you should sit one meal with me and one with him."

It made her pause. He had meant it lightly, but her answer was solemn in its questioning. "Yesterday when I said you did not fear Toki's anger you laughed. Was I wrong in saying this?"

"I do not fear Toki, though many men do," he told her.

The next she said with the same seriousness. "No, you do not fear him, for you are a better man than he."

It was his turn to pause. "You think I am a better man than Toki?"

Her words were decided, almost warm. "Yes, I do, for you try to shame us less in your words and looks, and so you act more honourably to both my Lady and to Yrling." After a moment she went on. "And it is clear that Yrling listens well to your words."

He was smiling at her; he could not help but do so. She smiled back, and so spurred, went on.

"And I think you are also a better warrior than Toki, for the scar you bear must be from a great battle."

His chin dropped so suddenly that she gave a little gasp. He raised his head and looked at her, aware in a way that he had not been for some time of the deep rive marring his left cheek from eye to chin.

"The scar I bear is from Toki, and he gave it to me when we were but boys."

She struggled for answer. "Perhaps he was jealous of you even then," she offered.

He gave a snort. "I think not," he said.

Her hand was about the cup she drank from, and now she took a sip, her eyes looking into its silvery depths. She was abashed, uncertain; he knew this.

He kept looking at her, considering her words. She saw the scar, but saw more than that.

"It is good that you think I am the better warrior, for I am," he told her. It was said without boast.

She turned to him, a smile once again playing about her lips.

He must name her again, make of his name for her the gift he meant it to be.

"You are a true shield-maiden. You do not turn from a scar on a man's face."

She met his eyes, and more than fully. A child's gravity was in her answer, that, and a woman's resolve.

"My father was an ealdorman, and his brother ealdorman after him. He taught me that a scar is the badge of honour of the warrior, and this I believe."

She did not stop looking at him. He saw her, and saw behind her, to her sire and kin. He could not but praise them, in his admiration of she who had spoken thus.

"I think I am glad we did not face your father and his brother in battle," he told her, "for they were of better stuff than what we have found here."

THE BEECH

SIDROC was, next morning, at the forge fire of the weapon-smith. He had wanted two throwing-spear points hammered up; the wooden shafts he had smoothed himself were in his hand. He was now ending his jesting talk with the Dane into whose keeping he passed them. The smith had a name, but all called him by Weland, after the weapon-smith of the Gods. Sidroc still wore his smile when he turned from the heat of the forge to see the shield-maiden enter the forecourt from the hall door. She was clad in her gown of russet brown, and walked towards the kitchen yard, intent on some errand.

It would have been quicker, more direct to go through the passage-way inside the hall; he knew this. Had she avoided the dim passage because some one of his brothers loitered there, one who she must walk past? None would try to touch her, he knew that; but what they might mutter, the way they might leer would be enough to make her choose to leave hall and men and walk out under the open sky.

She moved with purpose, head up, the wooden clogs protecting the thin and fine leather of her shoes no impediment. At times she lifted the hem of her gown with her hands, to avoid soiling the wool where mud might be thrown up by her footfall. About her waist she once again had tied her sash, the one with the thread-work of flying birds stitched into it. Today he saw she had something else tied there. A seax, the angle-bladed knife of the Saxons, hung there, encased in a brown leathern sheath, tied at her waist. He had not seen it before. It was large, too large for a woman to wear, though women often bore knives for everyday tasks they must meet. It must be her dead kinsman's, the noble uncle she had spoken of last night, or even her father's. And she wore it now, felt need to wear it, here as she walked alone through the yards busy with his brethren.

She had armed herself. Well, the shield-maidens carried spears. Now this young one of their ilk passed him, not seeming to see where he stood and watched. The gown was just snug enough about her breasts to express the roundness beneath; the sash at waist wrapped firmly enough so that hips and rump bloomed beneath that slender middle.

His eyes were fastened on her as she moved away. He stood watching, yet part of him moved with her, was there by her side, no longer his but hers.

It was a sensation never felt before, one of many welling up within his breast, and filling his brain.

It felt a kind of weakness. Weakness and fear had once been paired in his mind; through battle he had seen they need not be. He had felt fear before each battle, grappled with it, understood it well. Fear could walk, and strongly, with courage, be propelled along and transformed by courage. Fear was no enemy; he had harnessed it many times, used it to make him more alert, to heighten his senses, make him cherish his own life the more so he fought the better.

Weakness was utterly different. It could freeze a man, blind him to his options, bind him to a Fate he could not work. It was this he felt, but a curious weakness that despite its peril did not lead him to fear.

Watching her move away, he knew it fully. It was the deep and striking knowledge, painful in the chest to admit, that he had already given something to this one, something already in her keeping, which he could never reclaim.

She had vanished round the corner of one of the many store houses. He swung his head away, needing a broader view, a deeper aspect for his eyes.

He thought of where he would sleep when he had wed her. The hall at night was given over to a barracks of men, lying on straw-woven pallets which at dawn were collected and stacked in the alcoves running along the walls. Jari was clearing a plot of land out by the longhouse guarding the valley of horses, in readiness for when the maid he had left behind could be brought over. Jari was building a house for her too, of timber, helped along by a few men there doing the same. But Sidroc was in direct service to Yrling; he must be near him day and night. And the shield-maiden was the same; she in her way was in service to the Lady of Four Stones, who would want and need her near. His thoughts flickered upwards to the rooms at the top of the wooden steps. The larger of them had already been made their weaving and spinning room, and the other two rooms could scarce hold a bed for the maid, let alone one as tall as he.

But the yards themselves held space. The precincts of Four Stones behind the enclosing palisade were large. He could build a small house here, he saw. The animal pens and fowl houses sat to one side of the kitchen yard. To the other, where his eyes now rested, was a plot with a few fruit trees and berry vines. Grasses grew there, and the yard cows wandered in its untended herbage. A house there would place them outside the noise and bustle of both hall and yard, yet be close at hand to Yrling and his wife.

He saw in his mind's eye the house he would build, upright timber, gable-roofed, generous door, a fire-pit large enough for real warmth in Winter's snow. And he saw himself entering through the door with her, for the first time . . .

He shifted his eyes from the scraggly apple tress to the pale blue sky. His hand lifted to his hair and he ran his fingers through it, combing his thoughts, clearing them. He must tell Yrling, and soon, that he wanted this one. All the men looked at the shield-maiden, and she could not long remain unwed. Others in his uncle's favour might ask, even Asberg. It was the pressure of primacy he was aware of now, crowding his breast. Yrling must know.

He could not speak to his uncle until late in the day. He had seen the treasure room door close upon him and his new wife in mid-day; Yrling was taking full measure of the beauty of his bride. Toki had seen them too, and for his cousin's sake had thrown back his head in a stifled hoot of laughter.

It was late afternoon when Sidroc found his uncle. He was back at Weland's stall, collecting the newly mated spears, when Yrling passed, coming from the mare's paddock. He fell in with Sidroc, admiring the new spear-points, which his weapon-smith had embellished with an incised pattern chiseled into the hard metal at throat and socket.

A quantity of spears were always kept at the ready in holders in the hall, but each man had also his favourites, especially of the shorter, lighter throwing spears. Yrling and his nephews kept theirs within the treasure room, and they walked together so Sidroc might place these two new shafts there.

Yrling had closed the treasure-room door behind them; it was ever kept thus. The single window set high in the wall let in strong light; a sharp yellowy oblong striking the wood floor boards, making the slow moving motes of dust dance on its path.

Sidroc had not been inside since the bride-ale. His eyes were drawn to his uncle's low bed. It was transformed. Feather-cushions sat piled in abundance at its head, and over its breadth lay a throw of squared wolf-pelts, sewn together. The thickness of the fur, in shades of grey, black, and cream, gave strong contrast to the many hard surfaces of the room, and beckoned the eye.

"I am expecting news," Yrling said. "A rider."

Bed, cushions, and wolf skins were pushed out of Sidroc's mind. Four Stones had sent out its own rider to seek news of Hingvar and Svein.

"What I hear will tell me what I must do," his uncle went on.

"But you will ride, either way," Sidroc posed.

For answer Yrling gave a nod.

Sidroc did not expect to hear more, not now. And the rider had yet to appear, to sway his uncle's decision, whether to aid or oppose the two brothers.

His nephew's eyes returned to the bed.

"It is soon to leave your wife," he said.

"Já," Yrling allowed. "Riding away – " he did not finish, only gave a shake of his head. "But the return," he grinned, and himself looked to the fur-caped bed.

"I have no child," Yrling went on, "not that I know of. With my wife I hope to have many. Sons and daughters both."

Sidroc gave his own nod. Sons were needed to fight, daughters to wed and forge alliances with. Any offspring from the Jarl of Four Stones and the daughter of Ælfwyn of Cirenceaster would be both valued, and valuable.

Sidroc's next words were no idle praise. "If your sons take after you in arms, and your daughters after their mother in beauty, all Lindisse could be yours."

Yrling gave a short laugh, but with it an affirming nod. "Right now securing Cirenceaster is what concerns me. But if more of Lindisse comes my way . . . "

The pause that followed was broken by Sidroc. They were still standing not far from where he had propped up his new spears. There was a small table and two short benches in the room, but neither made for them. Like much of importance, what Sidroc wished to say was best said on his feet.

"I have had need to speak to you," he began. "It is, in its way, about your wife."

He had Yrling's full attention at this.

"The lady she has brought with her – I want her for my own."

He read the surprise in his uncle's face.

"She has, I think, nothing," is what Yrling said. They could hardly count the pony in her list of material assets; and his nephew had plenty of good horses.

Sidroc shook his head.

"She has all I want. I have silver enough, and soon I will have gold. But it is only she I want, as my wife."

Yrling looked at his nephew, and considered his declaration. He nodded. "Then I will tell Ælfwyn that the maid must wed you."

Sidroc was swift in his answer. "Nej."

He did not want her by force. He searched his mind to find something in Yrling's past to compare this to.

"Your chestnut mare, which you were so proud of back in Jutland. You bought her young, half-broken. You gentled her yourself, for you saw her value. You saw her spirit, and her beauty, did not want to crush either."

He let this stir his uncle's memory, and settle in his mind.

"It is the same way with me, and this maid. She – she is like a shield-maiden. She has a fierceness about her, which I do not wish to harm."

Yrling could do nothing but assent. "Then she is yours," he agreed. "No other will claim her." He began to grin. "Whether she will take the bit willingly is up to you."

Sidroc left both treasure room and hall. He stood a moment in the forecourt between hall and stable, saw his bay stallion there in the paddock. In the mare's paddock was another of his horses, a young bay mare, never bred, in every way a match to the stallion. Looking at her he recalled his vow, unkept, to Freyja, to make Offering to this Goddess.

Out on the road he had lain with a hungry woman of Lindisse and afterwards gazed at the night sky. An image of the woman he would want as his own came to him, of that Bright One he had been told of by Åfrid when he was still a boy. He had vowed that night to honour Freyja, to make Offering to her, so that she would bring that woman to his side. He had not. Now, despite his neglected vow, she was here.

It was coming dusk. He walked through work yards and kitchen yard, and out through that door through which he had stormed in one cold dawn, sword drawn, to take this place. The path, well-travelled through the Winter-dried growth, was there, leading to the Place of Offering.

He went there, to a place of death, a trench filled with broken weapons and the tattered carcasses of sacrificed animals. But one thing alive was there, at the edge, its boughs spreading under the dimming sky, tight buds ready to unfurl fresh leaves. It was the beech tree. As he looked it seemed to reach for him.

He was back at dawn, having taken a lump of amber and a small silver mantle-pin from his store of treasure. He would burn them together, offer their beauty in service to the Goddess. Freyja was Goddess of love and lust, and in claiming her share of fallen warriors to bring to her jewelled hall in Asgard she too was Goddess of war. There would be war ahead of him, he knew.

He turned his back on the trench with its scent of death, and its rotting statue of Odin. He went to the beech, so womanly a tree, its buds full of promise, like she who he desired. He had oil-sprinkled charcoal with him, and the striker he always carried. He knelt at the grasping roots of the great tree, and stacked stones to cup his flame. The charcoal sparked, a red ripple of fire sliding across its surface. The amber smoked, the silver softened. The two began to meld and mingle, the tree-gold of amber, and the circle of precious silver, falling inward on each other at the fire's touch, running together until they were one.

Here ends Sidroc the Dane. Here begins Book
One of The Circle of Ceridwen Saga.

THE WHEEL OF THE YEAR

Candlemas – 2 February

St Gregory's Day – 12 March

St Cuthbert's Day – The Spring Equinox, about 21 March

St Elgiva's Day – 18 May

High Summer or Mid-Summer Day – 24 June

Sts Peter and Paul – 29 June

Hlafmesse (Lammas) – 1 August

St Mary's Day – 15 August

St Matthews' Day – The Fall Equinox,
about 21 September

All Saints – 1 November

The month of Blót – November; the time of Offering

Martinmas (St Martin's) – 11 November

Yuletide – 25 December to Twelfthnight – 6 January

Winter's Nights – the Norse end of the year rituals,
ruled by women, marked by feasting and ceremony

ANGLO-SAXON PLACE NAMES,

WITH MODERN EQUIVALENTS

Æscesdun = Ashdown

Æthelinga = Athelney

Apulder = Appledore

Basingas = Basing

Beardan = Bardney

Bryeg = Bridgenorth

Caeginesham = Keynsham

Cippenham = Chippenham

Cirenceaster = Cirencester

Defenas = Devon

Englafeld = Englefield

Ethandun = Edington

Exanceaster = Exeter

Fearnhamme = Farnham

Geornaham = Irnham

Glastunburh = Glastonbury

Hamtunscir = Hampshire

Hreopedun = Repton

Jorvik (Danish name for Eoforwic) = York

Legaceaster = Chester

Limenemutha = Lymington in Hampshire

Lindisse = Lindsey

Lundenwic = London

Meredune = Marton

Middeltun = Milton

Readingas = Reading

Sceaftesburh = Shaftesbury

Snotingaham = Nottingham

Sumorsaet = Somerset

Swanawic = Swanage

Turcesig = Torksey

Wedmor = Wedmore

Witanceaster (where the Witan, the King's advisors, met) = Winchester

Frankland = France

Haithabu = Hedeby

Norse Place Names:

Aros = Aarhus, Denmark

Laaland = the island of Lolland, Denmark

Land of the Svear = Sweden

GLOSSARY OF TERMS

alvar: a stretch of barren (yet often beautiful) limestone landscape, supporting rock-loving lichens and mosses.

Anskar: (also, Ansgar) Saint Anskar began as a Frankish monk, born in Amiens. He was sent to Denmark as a missionary, and had success in converting King Erik of Jutland. He was permitted to build a church and to preach in Ribe in 854, but his adherents lapsed into heathenism following his departure, and death in Bremen.

Asgard: Heavenly realm of the Gods.

brewster: the female form of brewer (and, interestingly enough, the female form of baker is baxter . . . so many common names are rooted in professions and trades . . .).

browis: a cereal-based stew, often made with fowl or pork.

chaff: the husks of grain after being separated from the usable kernel.

cooper: a maker of casks and barrels.

(to) coppice: the act of sawing a healthy tree down, and allowing a ring of straight, round shoots to spring from the trunk; these were much desired as spear shafts and strong flexible poles.

cresset: stone, bronze, or iron lamp fitted with a wick that burnt oil.

dísir: female household spirits, celebrated at Winter's Nights feasts.

ealdorman: a nobleman with jurisdiction over given lands; the rank was generally appointed by the King and not necessarily inherited from generation to generation. The modern derivative *alderman* in no way conveys the esteem and power of the Anglo-Saxon term.

fulltrúi: the Norse deity patron that one felt called to dedicate oneself to.

fylgja: a Norse guardian spirit, always female, unique to each family.

Gandr: Norse magical spell-work. Norse culture was steeped in the belief of sorcery and spell-work. Galdr was another form, and was performative magic, in which the spell was sung. The use of magical charms and amulets, love potions, and curses was widespread. Women were typically the practitioners of magic, and the Goddess Freyja was revered for her magical prowess. Odin too practiced magic, unusual for any male figure. Seidr was the deepest, most dangerous form of magic, taught by Freyja to Odin.

hackle: the splitting and combing of fibres of flax or hemp with opposing brush-like tools.

hamingja: the Norse "luck-spirit" which each person is born with.

hamr: in Norse belief, a person's outer appearance and form as it appears to human eyes.

hugr: in Norse belief, the essential nature of a person, hosted by the hamr, or outer shell. The hugr could be that of a wild and ferocious beast; an "ulfshugr" was a man with the essence of a wolf.

Jutland: the large peninsula of Denmark, joined to modern day Germany at its southern-most point. The western coast of Jutland is on the North Sea, across which lies Great Britain.

kith and kine: kin – family members – and cattle.

knorr: also knarr. A merchant ship.

lur: a horn of bronze or wood, with a long curving neck, used to summon folk, marshal forces, and call cattle, in the Viking age.

medlar: a bushy tree, part of the rose family, which gives small, brown, and delicious fruit, eaten raw or cooked down into jams or sauces. Medlars were valued as they gave their fruit in Winter, when anything fresh was scarce. The fruit needs to rest, or "blet", so that it begins to ferment to reach its full flavour, thus it is a good keeper.

Midgard: the "Middle Earth" of men.

morgen-gyfu: literally, "morning-gift"; a gift given by a husband to his new wife the first morning they awake together.

quern: hand tool for grinding grain into flour. The domed top stone (the "handstone") often of sandstone or limestone, sits atop the quern stone, with the kernels of grain in between. The top stone is turned by a wooden dowel inserted in a hole atop the dome. This made grinding grain possible for almost all households.

rauk: the striking sea – and wind-formed limestone towers on the coast of Gotland.

seax: the angle-bladed dagger which gave its name to the Saxons; all freemen carried one.

scop: ("shope") a poet, saga-teller, or bard, responsible not only for entertainment but seen as a collective cultural historian. A talented scop would be greatly valued by his lord and receive land, gold and silver jewellery, costly clothing and other riches as his reward.

shingle beach: a pebbly, rather than sandy, beach.

skald: a Norse poet and singer of Saga tales, comparable to an Anglo-Saxon scop (see above).

skep: a bee hive formed of coils of plaited straw, built up into a conical shape.

skeggox: steel battle-axe favoured by the Danes.

skirrets: a sweet root vegetable similar to carrots, but cream-coloured, and having several fingers on each plant.

skogkatt: "forest cat"; the ancestor of the modern Norwegian Forest Cat, known for its large size, climbing ability, and thick and water-shedding coat.

skogsrå: "Lady of the Forest"; a womanly wood spirit who protected woodland animals, and yet guided hunters she favoured.

Skuld: the eldest of the three Norns, and she who snips the Thread of Life, signalling death. Her very name means "debt". The Thread of Life is pulled out to length by her daughter Verdandi, and spun by her granddaughter Urd.

spotted fever: typhus.

strakes: overlapping wooden planks, running horizontally, making up a ship's hull.

symbel: a ceremonial high occasion for the Angle-Saxons, marked by the giving of gifts, making of oaths, swearing of fidelity, and (of course) drinking ale.

tæfl or Cyningtæfl ("King's table"): a board game of strategy.

thegn: ("thane") a freeborn warrior-retainer of a lord; thegns were housed, fed and armed in exchange for complete fidelity to their sworn lord. Booty won in battle by a thegn was generally offered to their lord, and in return the lord was expected to bestow handsome gifts of arms, horses, arm-rings, and so on to his best champions.

thrummy: from the noun "thrum", meaning the rough, uneven ends of the warp strings left behind on the loom when the fabric is cut free. "Thrummy hair" would then be tousled, uncombed, or uneven.

trev: a settlement of a few huts, smaller than a village.

Tyr: the God of war, law, and justice. He voluntarily forfeited his sword-hand to allow the Gods to deceive, and bind, the gigantic wolf Fenrir.

Tyr-hand: in this Saga, any left-handed person, named so in honour of Tyr's sacrifice.

wadmal: the Norse name for the coarse and durable woven woollen fabric that was a chief export in the Viking age.

verjuice: "green juice"; an acidic juice from unripe grapes or crabapples, much used as we would vinegar.

völva: a female seer in the Norse religion, accorded much respect for her ability to predict the future. Völvas employed magical chanting and singing, the eating of herbs and potions, and the use of a scepter-like wand in their trances. (See Gandr for more on Norse magic).

woad: a free-growing herbaceous perennial plant, its leaves used for its astringent, antiseptic, and blood-staunching properties, and to produce the colour blue for fabric dying.

wither: the highest point at the top of the shoulder of a horse or deer, marked by a projecting knob.

withy: a willow or willow wand; withy-man: a figure woven from such wands.

wool-wax: (also wool-oil, wool-fat) All earlier names for lanolin. Lanolin was extracted from sheep's wool by boiling washed wool in water. When the pan was left to cool, a milky white grease would be floating on top – the sheep's waterproofing. The globules were further refined by squeezing them through linen cloths. Lanolin was invaluable as a simple remedy for chapped and roughened skin. Blended with powdered or crushed herbs, it served as a medicinal salve.

ACKNOWLEDGEMENTS

Sidroc the Dane was blessed in enjoying exceptionally dedicated, loyal, and happily secretive First Readers. Your enthusiasm at hearing Sidroc's story made working with you a pleasure, and a privilege.

My sincere thanks are due to: Janelle Bond, Judy Boxer, Rachael Lynne Eichelbaum, Janine Eitniear, Angela Elder, Paula Franklin, Karen Lynn Jorgensen, Kim Komaromy, Elaine Eakin MacDonald, Anna Morrison Markowitz, Diane T. Miller, Misi, Melinda Moorehouse, Jennifer L Morris, Kay Lynn Odle-Moore, Mary Ann Quirk, Ellen Rudd, Debra V. Saavedra, Suzanne Dixon Sheppard, Domino Isolde Truitt, and Sally K. Vollenweider.

A dear reader, Cheryl Snider, was called to Heaven before she could read the completed manuscript. I hope she is smiling down upon it nonetheless.

FREE CIRCLE OF CERIDWEN COOKERY BOOK(LET)

You've read the books – now enjoy the food! Your free Circle of Ceridwen Cookery Book(let) is waiting for you at octavia.net.

Ten easy, delicious, and authentic recipes from the Saga, including Barley Browis, Roast Fowl, Baked Apples, Oat Griddle Cakes, Lavender – scented Pudding, and of course – Honey Cakes. Charmingly illustrated with medieval woodcuts and packed with fascinating facts about Anglo-Saxon and Viking cookery. Free when you join the Circle, my mailing list. Be the first to know of new novels, have the opportunity to become a First Reader, and more. Get your Cookery Book(let) now and get cooking!

ABOUT THE AUTHOR

Octavia Randolph has long been fascinated with the development, dominance, and decline of the Anglo-Saxon peoples. The path of her research has included disciplines as varied as the study of Anglo-Saxon and Norse runes, and learning to spin with a drop spindle. Her interests have led to extensive on-site research in England, Denmark, Sweden, and Gotland. In addition to the Circle Saga, she is the author of the novella *The Tale of Melkorka*, taken from the Icelandic Sagas; the novella *Ride*, a retelling of the story of Lady Godiva, first published in Narrative Magazine; and *Light, Descending*, a biographical novel about the great John Ruskin. She has been awarded Artistic Fellowships at the Ingmar Bergman Estate on Fårö, Sweden; MacDowell Colony; Ledig House International; and Byrdcliffe.

She answers all fan mail and loves to stay in touch with her readers. Join her mailing list and read more on Anglo-Saxon and Viking life at www.octavia.net. Follow her on Facebook at Octavia Randolph Writer, and for exclusive access and content join the spirited members of The Circle of Ceridwen Saga Discussion and Idea Group on Facebook.

Made in the USA
Columbia, SC
07 November 2024